SOJOURN

AN ANTHOLOGY OF SPECULATIVE FICTION

Edited by

Laura K. Anderson

and

Ryan J. McDaniel

First edition: January 2014

ISBN-10: 0991487710
ISBN-13: 978-0-9914877-1-4

Cover design by Keith Curtis. http://kacurtis.com

TABLE OF CONTENTS

This anthology is dedicated to:

Dan Repperger, who made Fear the Boot happen,

The hosts of the Fear the Boot podcast, who are as obsessed as the rest of us, and

The Booters, who laugh and cry with each other.

FOREWORD

I picked up my first roleplaying game in 1988. It was a copy of *Star Trek*, as produced by the once-defunct and now-resurrected FASA Corporation. I had liked the idea of roleplaying games (aka RPGs) for years, constantly tantalized by the colorful artwork and imaginative scenes in the catalogs I'd collected. But roleplaying wasn't an easy hobby to start in the 1980s. Society was caught up in the second decade of moral panic over these games, imagining their players to be dangerously delusional at best, agents of a Satanic agenda at worst. Certainly not the right pursuit for a church-going boy like me. But one Christmas my parents got me that boxed set, and I've stuck with the hobby ever since, adding one game after another to my collection, contributing articles to fan magazines, and even writing a few games.

As time moved on, the moral panic seemed to fade away, replaced by a somewhat less insidious view of roleplayers as socially maladjusted twerps, sitting in costume in their parents' basement, arguing over the most ridiculous things. The image was equally incorrect, but at least these caricatures had no demonic masters.

Then in 2005, I was first introduced to the technology of podcasting. The idea was simple enough: create audio recordings, post them on the internet, and let interested parties grab them at their convenience. It had little cost and a worldwide audience, so the topic didn't have to appeal to any specific number of people in a local market. By early 2006 I was toying with a show idea of my own, and in May of the same year, I launched *Fear the Boot*, a podcast dedicated to the hobby of roleplaying games. In the time since, I've been fortunate to work with exceptional hosts, an incredibly supportive community, and professionals who were once nothing more than credits in the front of my game books.

What you're holding in your hands is an anthology of prose, not a book about—or even specifically for—roleplaying games. So what relevance does my very brief biography have to do with these short stories?

The misunderstanding of roleplayers seems to come from a misunderstanding of roleplaying games. While it's impossible to know for sure, I'm willing to bet the oldest pastime of the human race is telling stories. It's how we communicated warnings about nearby predators, braggadocio regarding our accomplishments, the tales of heroes to aspire to and villains to revile, anecdotes that illustrate the importance of moral codes and warnings against laxity in character. And though thousands of years have passed, our thirst for stories hasn't changed.

Roleplaying games are nothing more than an exercise in telling stories, though instead of hushing the audience, you invite their participation. You no longer need to yell, "Don't open that door!" to the protagonist on TV, since you can instead just decide the hero will take a wiser path. These interactions can be simple or complex, and rules often guide how they occur. But anyone that's played roleplaying games has spent a great deal of time trying to unravel how a particular person in a particular situation would think and act, teasing those truths into a cogent story.

As our podcast's community grew, it was only natural to find a significant number of people that were interested in moving beyond the relatively private storytelling of a roleplaying game, putting their ideas on paper to share with the world. And it was from that section of our community a writing guild formed. After securing the support of professional editors and published writers, we solicited submissions, and this collection emerged.

What you are about to read is not a collection of stories about games, but the work of people that have spent much of their lives perfecting an art that's as old as speech itself. The writers are a diverse group, and we exerted no pressure on them to homogenize their stories, so allow us to take you to the countless places the minds of our writers have already gone and are eager to show you as well.

—   Dan Repperger

INTRODUCTION

I'm always amazed when groups pull together to make something incredible happen. Fear the Boot is an online community like any other, because it's a group of people who have probably never met each other. But Fear the Boot is unlike any other online community because these strangers are time and time again able to come together and accomplish amazing things. I've only met a handful of Booters, though I've talked with dozens of them over Skype, and had lengthy chats on the forums. They're all amazing people, and even though we've never met, they've become close friends and new family.

Community is what made this anthology happen. Fear the Boot has touched the lives of so many people that when Ryan and Dan put out the call, many people answered. A lot of the authors are being published here for the first time, but that doesn't make their work any less brilliant than established authors' works. They're simply getting a rare opportunity to make something as a community, something that we can all be proud of.

I want to take a moment to thank James Lowder for his amazing advice and coaching. Without Jim's guidance we couldn't have created this anthology, and we would never have gotten it formatted correctly. Any errors are from Ryan and me, and are in spite of Jim's excellent guidance.

"Keepers of the Flame" by Robert J. Freund, Jr. is a story of a young boy who sets off to earn his name and become a man. Along the way he fights against cold and hunger, and meets one of the gods of his people, the Flamebearers.

Elizabeth Roper's story "Destiny" incorporates thieves and rogues of all sorts, and is about the young woman Tamsin's attempts to find the sacred Stone

vi

of Destiny. She is reunited with family, but she faces betrayal after betrayal and is never quite certain who to trust.

"Crossing the River" by Peter Martin is a different coming-of-age story, a tale of redemption and sacrifice. Kyran seeks to become a knight, but in order to do so he must swim the dangerous Kelst River.

"Forgotten Dreams" by Hans Cummings tells the story of the freed human Jahni, who lives in a universe where humans are slaves. Jahni is looking for Rana, who organizes the human resistance, but is Rana everything Jahni thinks she'll be?

"The Paper Shield" by James Lowder is about the *Chelston*, a ship run by the thunderous Professor Thaxton, and its research in the ocean. Thaxton has brought with him a crew of strange cultists, and it's uncertain what their purpose on board is. This tale is historical Lovecraftian horror at its best.

Thomas Childress' "Temps of the Dead" takes a more humorous turn and examines what might happen in a world where zombies and vampires (also known as Personnel Replacement Grade Undead) are hired as cheap labor. It doesn't sound like anything could go wrong with that, eh?

"My Father's Son" by Johann Luebbering follows the life of a gun and its place in an Irish family. This story takes a look at the spirit of the Irish as, in the future, they are once more rebelling against English rule over their land.

Wayne Cole's "Sick Day" is another light-hearted piece that dares to ask a serious question: are there aliens out there who are fanboys and fangirls of Earth culture? This is the type of encounter that James certainly wasn't expecting when his boss made him stay at home on account of illness, and along the way James learns that maybe he shouldn't take life so seriously.

"Blind Barthon" by Ryan J. McDaniel is written as an homage to the mythology and folklore of the Norse people, and follows the hero Barthon as he quests for the perfect wife. The gods try to push Barthon in the right direction until he finally meets the woman who is perfect for him.

"Top of the Heap" by Tom McNeil takes a look at a future Earth, one where humanity happily grafts machinery to its body and where Canada has hot, sunny beaches. Dale Medici meets up with Grant, an old friend he hasn't seen for a very long time. There are only five of them left—five of a group of twelve people who had their brains reconditioned and no longer age.

Matt Forbeck's story "The Bookrunner" envisions a future where books are dangerous tools, where words can become literal weapons. And when the government needs to investigate unauthorized sellers, one agent has to ask just how much these sellers know about weaponized ideas.

"Foresight" by Laura K. Anderson takes place in the near future, to a world where the drug Foresight has hit the streets. The drug supposedly lets people see the future. Marty is a reporter and meets Jack, a user who agrees to be interviewed about the drug. When Jack later appears and stops a robbery, Marty is left wondering: does Foresight actually work?

Chris Hussey's story "Unknowing Agents" posits a very important question: what if the games we play actually influence other lives in other universes? This tale of action and adventure follows a group of people as they play a tabletop RPG, but only one of them is aware that their decisions at the table are actually impacting a group of people in another universe.

"Sermon for the Third Sunday of Epiphany: A Report from the 68th Periodic Interspecies Theologians' Conference" by Shannon Dickson is an interesting take on what a galactic theological conference might look like. Alien physiology and history help to create unique religions, and this story seeks to find where Christian religion fits into a universe of varying beliefs.

"Surviving Sunset" by Dan Repperger follows the lives of Cassandra and her sister Penelope as their planet is attacked by the Sirini. The two girls find a small group of soldiers and agree to lead them to a safe place in exchange for protection. Cassandra's world has been wiped away and the life she once knew has been lost forever. Now there is only war and she must face her new reality head on.

I sincerely hope you enjoy reading these stories as much as I've enjoyed editing them.

—   Laura

Not enough good things can be said about the Fear the Boot community. That is because there is nothing bad to say about them. As a lot of online communities struggle to keep their head above the water of sexism, elitism, bigotry, and overall internet snobbery and depravity, the Fear the Boot community is mostly clean of those internet ills. The site goes above and beyond the call of duty in its countless charity events and the innumerable acts of generosity and compassion.

The community that began around a couple of dudes ranting about *Battletech*, riffing on *Rifts*, and raving about the antics of LARPers has grown into a force to be reckoned with. Over eight years the Fear the Boot community has a lot to be proud of and has breathed life into many good fruits (not even including the Fear the Fruit charity event). I hope that *Sojourn* becomes yet another branch of the Fear the Boot community from which more good fruit will come in the years to come.

—   Ryan

KEEPERS OF THE FLAME

Robert J. Freund, Jr.

Robert J. Freund, Jr., is a native New Yorker currently residing in Idaho with his lovely wife, two beautiful daughters, and a son who thinks he is already the king of the household. Whenever he manages to break free of paralyzing procrastination, Robert enjoys reading and writing science fiction and fantasy stories, doodling, and trying to instill a sense of wonder and imagination in his children. He hopes to one day earn a living off of the mental instability that the wider world calls creativity.

The boy kneels in the dirt, watching the small fire dance. Its smoke curls lazily to the hole at the top of the hide tent where it is swept away by the breeze. The silence is something he's not used to. He bends a twig in restless hands, but dares not break it, afraid the sound would be a thunderclap in the small space. Little sister is with the womenfolk, little brother in the great tent with the other children. For now, the boy has his mother to himself, and for the second time in his life she is quiet. He's weathered ten winters, encouraged by the strength of her voice, entertained by her stories. The only time he remembers her like this is when his father died.

"I am afraid," he says, finally, looking up to her.

"All little boys are afraid," she says, and she reaches forward to brush his hair from his cheek. Her touch evokes a childhood of memories, of tenderness and caring. "But you are nearly a man. You will not let fear guide your heart."

He closes his eyes. They've had this tent for as long as he can recall, and there are many spots where his mother's sure hands have patched it. It has

1

traveled with them over plains and mountains, through forests, into fertile valleys and back out again. He thinks he can still smell his father in it. It is a subtle scent, of woodlands and sweat and blood, and he takes as much strength from it as he does from the warmth of his mother.

"He would be proud," she says, like she can hear the boy's thoughts. He calls from memory the image of his father. Tall and muscled and brave.

"It is time, soon." Her voice is soft and almost breaks. The boy is old enough to know that even adults are not always certain, that they suffer doubts, too. Had his father been that way?

"Talk of him, before I go," he asks, the heat of the fire soaking into his skin. He will need to take as much of it as he can for later.

"Your father was named Bloodtusk. He earned his manhood by killing a longtooth with the tusk of a mammoth," she begins.

The words are familiar to him. She has, many times, told him of his father, who died when the boy was only five winters old. He is glad to have her voice filling the silence, glad to have a little more time before he must face the unknown.

They come not long after she has finished her story, solemn-faced tribesmen with white paint on their faces. The boy stands up, tilting his head back to look them in their eyes. His stomach feels like it is sinking to his feet, but he does not let them see his fear. Wordlessly, they lead him outside.

He does not look back at his mother.

*   *   *

"White for the bones of our dead," the chieftain says, smearing a handful of paint on his own face. His voice is rough, like the sound of antlers against wood. He is older than the boy can count; the boy's mother said that the chieftain has seen over thirty winters. The boy does not understand thirty, but it must be an eternity. The man is called Stonethroat for the wound that is now a jagged scar on his neck.

The chieftain raises his other hand, wiping paint on the boy's face. It is cold, despite the tent's heat. "Red, for the blood of our kin.

"Your father was Bloodtusk," says the chieftain, "who was killed by the white longtooth that stalks the winter night, The Bringer of Many Deaths, when she sought blood for her dead sister. She still hunts these woods. Do you fear her?"

The boy's instinct is to lie and tell the man he is not fearful. It is a test, and a man should be brave. But Stonethroat's gaze is heavy, and the boy can feel it penetrating his young heart, just as a fawn must feel the point of a thrown spear.

"Yes," he replies, and looks to the dirt.

The chieftain takes hold of the boy's chin with hard, strong fingers and raises the child's eyes.

"I am glad, boy. Nothing living is without fear but the Flamebearers, who stole fire from the sun to give to man."

The boy does not trust himself to speak, so he clenches his jaw, and hopes that the tears that threaten in his eyes do not spill.

For a long while, the chieftain stares, and the boy cannot look away. The solid fingers remain on his chin, allowing no movement. Tiny reflections of the fire dance in Stonethroat's black eyes, and the boy does not recognize the emotion in them. He doesn't know if there *is* emotion in them.

"Warm yourself by my fire, child," the chieftain finally says, releasing his hold on the boy. He rises and moves to the tent flap, pushing it aside. "Tonight we dance to celebrate your life, and feast to honor your death."

Then Stonethroat is gone, and once more the only sound the boy can hear is the hungry crackle of flames.

*   *   *

The boy stares at the fire, which reaches for the night sky with flickering fingers. He has seen many such blazes on many other nights when boys older than he were to earn their manhood. Never has he seen one so high, so bright. It bathes everything in orange light, burning in defiance of the darkness and the cold, warming the bodies of his tribesmen as they move around it to the frantic beating of drums.

His chest swells with pride, because he knows that this fire—this king of fires, taller than a mammoth, tall enough to set the entire sky ablaze—is for him.

The others leap and dance, men and women and boys and girls, stripped naked to show their spite for the early onset of winter. Since his earliest memories, he has danced with them, and has never been able to watch the hypnotic effect of it from outside.

The boy tears off another mouthful of meat, and he does not care about the juice dripping down his chin. He is warmed by flames and the presence of his people, warmed by food in his belly.

The music stops abruptly, and with it all motion. The boy's ears ring with the thunder of the drums, and his heart picks up its pace to echo them. He swallows the meat before it is fully chewed, and knows all eyes are on him now. There is one gaze that holds more weight than the rest, one that he is certain he can feel.

He stands, his legs heavy from having sat for too long, and turns to face the chieftain. Stonethroat is tall and broad-shouldered, with two warriors standing just behind him on either side. The people part, opening a path between the boy and the chief, and the child's lungs burn as he inhales. From this distance, the chieftain's eyes look like the black pits of a skull.

The boy is relieved when his feet obey his command and carry him along the path.

Up close, he can see that the white paint on the chieftain's face is flaking off at the cheeks, and drops of sweat have carried away more. He tilts his head back to look Stonethroat in the eyes.

Without speaking, the warriors step forward. One drapes heavy furs over the boy's shoulders, and their musk cuts through the smell of roasting meat and burning wood for a single breath. The other hands the boy a spear, and flecks of fire sparkle on the stone head.

"We drink to your life," Stonethroat says, and his voice is the crunch of iced snow underfoot. He drinks from a wooden bowl and then extends his arm to bring it to the boy's lips. The boy recognizes the sweetness of milk, though it has been long seasons since last he tasted it.

"We drink to your death." The chieftain sips from another bowl, and holds it to the boy as well. The boy does not know what it is, but the bitterness nearly makes him gag. He fights the grimace, the muscles of his jaw and neck tightening.

"Now you go. Return to us a man with a name, or not at all."

The boy stares into the dark circles around the chieftain's eyes for only a moment before he turns. Any longer would be to show his fear.

He follows the path left open by his people, and keeps his eyes fixed on the darkness beyond them. From the corner of his eye, he sees his mother, his brother, and his sister. He walks by them, and he does not look. He does not speak.

When he passes the last tent at the edge of their camp, he feels tears well in his eyes again. This time, he cannot fight them. He *will* return a man, strong enough to protect and provide. Or he will not return at all.

* * *

The night passes, and the sun stains the sky crimson and orange. The boy walks. He holds the furs closed with one hand, trying to ward off the chill that only deepens under the first light of day. Each time he exhales, a small cloud floats before him for a fleeting moment. This winter has come too early.

Around him, trees are still shedding leaves, which rustle in the breeze and sometimes spiral to the ground. Somewhere, birds chirp and sing. He has walked these woods before, but never alone.

There is no one with him. No conversation, no warmth.

"I am the son of Bloodtusk," he says aloud to fill the quiet.

The boy snaps his mouth shut. He does not like how small his voice sounds to his own ears. It is the voice of a child. Tightening his grip on the spear, he walks faster, and wonders what the white longtooth does during the day. Does she sleep while the sun shines? Are his father's bones still in her great gut?

The sun, the first flame, moves across the sky, in time vanishing behind dark clouds. The boy cannot worry himself over them. Just as all the other boys, he knows the laws that the Flamebearers spoke ages before. He knows what he must do.

Flakes of snow begin to fall. There are too few for them to find one another, and as the breeze picks up to blow his hair into his face, the boy knows what it must feel like to be a snowflake lost in fickle winds.

What is his mother doing now? Is she weeping for her son, or has she mourned him already like the others had?

Darkness creeps slowly across the sky above, deepening the shadows in the forest. From somewhere far off he hears the yowl of a longtooth, and it makes his blood cold in a way the wind could not.

The boy wants to feel the heat of his mother's arms. He wants to lay his head on her chest and cry, because he does not want to be alone. He does not want to be a man. If he turns around now, he thinks he can make it back to the tents, where he will find warmth and safety. If he is quiet enough, and sly enough, they may never notice he is back. Then they would not turn him away in shame.

While there is still daylight, the boy finds a large tree and piles wood near it. He places his back to the trunk and builds his fire, laying the spear over his lap and warming his hands as the flames blossom. He knows the laws: *walk towards the land where the sun sleeps, make a fire and hold vigil by night, eat nothing.* He knows, too, that he has no place amongst his tribe until he has proven himself.

For a long time, he watches the fire slowly consume the wood, and it makes him think of his own hunger. It is not so bad. He has been hungry before.

Without the tribe, the night brings new sounds. He hears the call of an owl and the death cry of the small animal that is its prey. He hears the trees moaning and sighing in the wind. And the braying of laughing hounds from afar.

The boy feeds another stick into the fire and grips the spear with both hands. He must not sleep. He must watch, and wait. To sleep out here is to invite death.

He is unaware of the passage of time; his eyes seek out the source of every sound, darting at what appears to be movement beyond the light of his fire. He thinks all he's seen are the shifting shadows cast by the firelight, but it does not comfort him. There are longtooth cats and laughing hounds, wolves and cave bears. He has been warned about them all, and has seen some of them himself. Worst of them are the beasts that walk like men.

When there is light in the sky again, he puts out the fire with fistfuls of dirt and resumes his walk. He cannot guess how far he is from his people. Only a day has passed, but it feels like he has walked a lifetime, and he worries that he will never find them again.

He stops to drink from a stream, the cold water making his stomach cramp painfully. With his weight on the spear, he waits for the discomfort to pass and forces himself onward.

The sounds of the woods are clearer today, and he can make them all out. The rustle of each leaf on its neighbor and every note of every song of every bird. The rush of the stream, the crunch of twigs beneath his feet. And the various animal calls, so many that he doesn't know, so many that he *should* know, so many that make his heart thunder in his chest. Despite the cold, his palms sweat on the wood of the spear.

After midday, he stops again, this time to study tracks left on soft ground. The hunters had shown him ones like this before, and said they belong to the laughing hounds. It looks like many passed this way.

Night approaches, and he makes his fire. The laughter comes under a fat yellow moon, and it is closer. It feels like his eyes might crumble to dust, and his stomach is twisted in knots, but he holds his vigil, waiting for either a Flamebearer or his death at the jaws of a predator made bold by hunger.

* * *

Snow falls heavily by midday, gathering in clumps on the forest floor. Shivering with cold, the boy staggers forward now because he knows that he will die if he stops. He does not want to keep going. He does not want his mother, or his people. All he longs for now is to close his eyes and sleep forever.

It is the memory of his father that makes him press on.

He finds the carcass of what he thinks was a deer at midday. Blood stains the ground all around it, and there are grooves left by teeth on the bones. Little flesh remains. The boy kneels, running his fingers over a paw print. It is the same as the ones he found the day before.

He stands, and his vision blurs. The entire world spins. He jabs the butt of the spear into the ground and grips it tightly. It is the only thing that keeps him on his feet. Staying as still as he can, he closes his eyes. Snowflakes fall on his skin only to melt away.

* * *

The boy is slow to make his fire. His hands tremble as he arranges the sticks. Wetting his cracking lips with his tongue, he struggles to ignite the wood.

The laughing hounds are braying happily, but the boy does not listen. He must light the fire, or he will fail.

Finally, just as his arms refuse to work anymore, smoke begins to curl from the wood. Getting on hands and knees, he blows on the embers, and they spark to life. He holds his hands up to it, but he cannot feel the warmth.

The boy tries to recall his mother's face, but sees only shadow. He tries to recall the feel of her fingers brushing the hair from his cheek, but there is only numbness.

At his back is a rock formation as tall as three men, sheltering him from the wind. He slides the spear into his lap and watches as the sun dies, leaving only the ring of light cast by the small fire. Shadows leap and twirl between gnarled boughs, and beyond is only darkness.

The hounds yip and howl and laugh.

Eyelids drooping, the boy leans back against the stone, easing tension from his tired muscles. The hounds smell his weakness tonight. They will come for him. He hopes he can kill one before they tear out his throat. Maybe that would be enough to make his father proud, and they could walk together in the land of the dead.

He struggles against sleep, clawing for the will to stay awake.

A branch snaps in the forest.

The boy jerks his head up. He scrambles to his feet and grasps the spear. Had he slept? His sight is blurred, and the night has deepened. Silence rules, making his heartbeat sound like a herd of bison fleeing a pack of wolves. It felt like he had closed his eyes for only a moment, but the fire is too low.

He removes a hand from the spear to feed more sticks into it hurriedly. The flecks in the stone spearhead shine like stars in the night sky.

"Lower your spear, boy," says a voice from beyond the firelight. He has never heard anything like it. It is like the sound of a far-off waterfall or the whisper of long grass in the wind. There is power in it, but there is frailty, too.

Tired and confused, the boy does not lower his weapon. There are many beasts in these woods, and some can walk and talk like men. He knows that the spearhead will likely snap off after the first blow, so he must aim true. He tries to steady his breathing, to slow his heart.

The figure emerges from the darkness, and the boy does not understand how he hadn't noticed it sooner. His fingers slacken on the spear, and the head dips to the ground. He knows what he is seeing. It is a Flamebearer.

It approaches in the shape of a man, but it is taller than any he's seen, with long, narrow limbs and a strange gait. Flames roil over its chest and arms. The face is nothing like a man's, covered in the shifting fire save for two dark holes where its eyes should be. Yet tongues of flame do not rise from it, and it makes no smoke. Its outline is cleanly defined. The boy wonders if it is a spirit made of fire, trapped in a vessel made to look like a human.

He falls to his knees, unable to stand any longer. This is why he's come. This is why he has endured the cold and the hunger alone. The Flamebearers are real, just as his people had said. And they are wondrous enough to make him want to avert his gaze.

"Your journey is nearly done," it says, and the boy can see no mouth move to form the words. "You seek a name. We will empower you to earn it."

Every member of his tribe who has become a man has gone through this, but none would ever speak of what they saw. It had always been the place of the elders to tell the children of the Keepers of the Flame. Before the boy stands one of the beings that has guided his people since their birth, one of the beings that has passed to them all of their beliefs and traditions, and given them the greatest of gifts. *Fire.*

"Nearby is a tribe of beasts that walk like men," the Flamebearer continues, and the flames are restless on its hide. "To prove you are a man, you must kill a creature that pretends to be one. Slay a beastman and bring me its heart and you will be named, according to the old ways."

The boy's eyes shift to the dark woods beyond, where the laughter of the hounds bounces between the trees.

"Do not concern yourself with them," the voice says. "Eat. Gain your strength."

It throws a fat hare down beside the boy, blood matting its fur. The carcass catches his attention immediately.

"When fire lights the sky again, you will hunt."

At the thought of fresh meat, the boy's mouth waters, but he does not allow himself to grab for the hare yet. He would only make a fool of himself and show disrespect to a god in his desperation.

"I will," he says, and looks up again. The Flamebearer is gone. He'd not heard it move, does not see sign of it, but why should he? They are not of the world of men. They are walking fire, and do not fear the bite of cold or the claws of a longtooth.

He skins the rabbit crudely, using the spear to tear flesh and fur, and eats while the meat is still sizzling. Not far off, he hears the whining cries of hounds in pain, and then there is only silence in the forest again. He sleeps until sunlight touches his face.

* * *

In the daylight, the boy resumes his walk with renewed strength and purpose. His journey is nearly over. He can almost feel the familiar warmth of his mother's arms, crushing him to her breast, the light path traced by her fingertips over his face. But he can no longer accept these gestures. He will be a man before the day's end, and a man does not suffer such from his mother. Only from the woman he takes to his tent.

Cut into the bark of a nearby tree is a circle with wavy lines around it. He touches the sap oozing from the symbol, and pulls his finger away sticky. Looking ahead, he sees another, and another even farther away. They are suns, the mark of the Keepers of the Flame. He follows them without second thought.

At midday, he finds the laughing hounds. Their thick hides are mottled with blood, and they swing lazily from where they are hung, entrails scraping the ground. He does not know of any creature that could kill an entire pack of hounds by itself, and is awed by the might of the Flamebearer. Remembering how hungry he had been, he thinks about the meat hung up to rot. The needless death, the wasted food.

Leaving the beasts behind, he continues to follow the marks that were left for him, taking handfuls of snow to melt in his mouth. And when he starts to see footprints that look like a man's, he slows his pace and watches his surroundings closely.

He first sees the camp through tangled brush that has refused to die despite the loss of most of its leaves, and crouches low to study it. From afar, it looks much like his own home. Large hide tents gathered together, with the smoke of fires billowing from most. He looks more closely, and realizes the differences. There is no wood used for the tents. Only bone.

Massive, sun-bleached bones are used as supports, tusks and skulls as adornment. He knows they have come from mammoths, and he wonders how many the beastmen had to kill to make their homes. His heart thumps in his chest, and he wonders if they are better hunters than he and his people.

The boy grips his spear, watching. Fear will not turn him away, not after he came this far. He sees some of the beastmen walking around between the tents, and they look no different from his people at first glance. But he sees the way they move, slightly hunched, and the broadness of their chests and shoulders.

The boy is smaller than their men, but he has been chosen by the Keepers of the Flame for this task. He will not fail them, will not fail his people. He thinks of his little brother, who will one day come out into the wilds to face his own test. He thinks of his mother, who has cared for him his entire life, and who deserves to have a man provide for her again. And he thinks of his little sister, who is so sweet and so pretty, who will have men fighting for her when she is of age.

There is shouting in the camp, and one of them turns and stalks away. The boy watches from his hiding place as the beastman passes, heading deeper into the woods. He can see its thick hair and beard, but does not get a glimpse of its face.

He knows it is larger than him, stronger, likely faster. But the boy knows what he must do. The Flamebearers stole fire from the sun by being clever, and he must be clever now, too.

Holding his breath, he waits until he can no longer hear the beastman's footsteps, and then he rises and creeps along the same path. He hopes that he is the only one who can hear his heartbeat. The spear is heavy, but it is reassuring. Once more, he takes strength from it.

As the boy moves, he thinks of the white longtooth that stalks the winter night. Tales say that she is nearly as large as a mammoth bull, that she can swallow a man in a single bite. The boy believes the tales, because nothing less could have killed his father. Like the great longtooth, the boy moves whisper-silent, placing his feet carefully. If he is swift and stealthy as a cat, but as cunning as a man, he will succeed.

The beastman's tracks seem to go on and on, and the sun moves ever closer to the place where it sleeps. The boy worries that he won't be able to catch up to his prey, even as he is glad that the bone village is farther behind with each step.

The sky is turning orange when the boy comes to the edge of a clearing, and he slows to a stop. He can see the beastman not far off, kneeling in the snow with its back to him. Its wide shoulders obscure the smaller, fur-wrapped figure before it. The creature is talking, but the boy cannot tell what words are being spoken by that deep, harsh voice.

He waits, and the beastman does not rise, does not look around.

The boy's hands are sweating again, and he twists his palms around the spear's wood. He has hunted before, but never anything like this.

Forcing himself to breathe deep and slow, the boy takes a single step into the clearing, setting his foot down into the snow carefully.

He takes a second step without making a sound, his entire body tense.

He takes a third step.

Ice crunches beneath his foot. His blood goes cold.

The beast that walks like a man rises and turns to look at the boy. The child is shocked at how similar its face is to those of his people. Its nose is broader, brow heavier. But the eyes that meet his are intelligent, and it holds a rock in one hand almost as big as the boy's head.

For a breathless moment, they stare at one another.

"You are a child," the beastman says.

The boy is shocked to hear the words of his people come from those lips. The beastman's voice is rough, but the words are spoken perfectly.

"Today I become a man," the boy replies. He can see the small figure just behind the beastman, looking between its legs. Is it one of the thing's babes?

"Your people have killed mine for long and long." The beastman frowns, his brows low, casting shadows over his eyes. "I make no war with you."

"The Keepers of the Flame spoke the words."

"They are no gods of mine," the beastman growls, drawing back his arm. "And you will not take her for them!"

The beastman's arm draws back. The boy shifts to the side, but he is not fast enough. The thrown rock hits his shoulder heavily, and he falls backwards with the impact. Pain skitters from where he was struck, running to every part of his body. Cold embraces him, snow working its way beneath his furs.

When the beastman darts forward, the boy knows his death is near. He acts instinctively, raising the head of the spear just as his foe leaps.

The boy feels the jolt as the spearhead scrapes bone and sinks into flesh. Then the beastman slams into him, and there is a dry snap.

The world is black, but the boy can still hear his heart thundering, his breath ragged and strained in his ears. There is a great weight pressing down on him, smothering him, and his arms are pinned. The beastman does not move. It smells of fur and blood and sweat, like the boy's tent.

He hears snow crunching beneath feet, and goes still. There are more, and he had been a fool. Searing tears stream down his cheeks. He hopes his father will know who he is in the land of the dead, even without a name, and that his deeds have been enough to make Bloodtusk call him a son.

Something grunts, and the weight is rolled off of him. The boy finds himself staring up at a sky shifting from red-orange to purple. Firm hands grasp his shoulders and haul him to his feet. The snapped spear shaft is still in his grip. He turns to his rescuer, and nearly falls down again.

It must be a Flamebearer, but it looks different now. Fire no longer swirls beneath its skin. It is silvery, like the scales of a fish, but its segmented hide looks more like that of an insect. He can see the sky reflected on it, and a dark shape that must be himself. It is like staring into the waters of a puddle, but the images are warped and twisted at strange angles.

"You have slain a warrior," says the leaves-in-the-wind voice that comes from within the darkness of the Flamebearer's face. "These beasts that walk like men accepted our gift of fire, long ago, but denied *us*. They choose to worship mammoths as life-givers. They are our enemies, and so they are yours."

It moves to the dead beastman, whose lifeless eyes stare unseeing into the darkening sky. The other part of the spear juts from the body's chest, wood splintered.

"You will be named Flintheart." It kneels to dab a finger in the dark blood pooling on the beastman's broad, unmoving chest, and uses it to make the sign of the sun on the boy's forehead. The blood is still warm.

The strange head turns, looking away from Flintheart. "There is another to kill."

The boy turns to follow the gaze, his limbs shaky and weak. He can see the fur-wrapped figure clearly for the first time; it is a young girl. She sits in the snow where the beastman had left her, staring at them with wide, dark eyes. She cannot be more than a five winters old, but she does not cry. She meets Flintheart's gaze, unwavering, and waits.

In her young features, he sees even more resemblance to his own people, to his own sister. He remembers the laughing hounds hanging in the woods.

"I cannot," he says.

The Flamebearer's head twists back to the boy, the dark eye-holes staring down at him.

"She is a babe," the boy says to fill the silence. To explain himself. He realizes that he has just defied a god, and his knees nearly give out.

"Very well," the Flamebearer says. It pulls a weapon from its hip with a strange scraping sound and walks towards the girl. "I will end her, and your tribe will know of your weakness. I will give you a new name to suit your cowardice."

The boy imagines his sister sitting there, cold and alone. Then he imagines himself there, staring at his father impaled on the teeth of the white longtooth that stalks the night.

His spear is broken, so he crouches and lifts the rock the beastman had thrown. No ice crunches beneath his foot when he moves this time.

There is a hollow *thunk* when he slams the rock into the back of the Flamebearer's head, and it echoes through the clearing. The being stumbles and falls to a knee. The boy hits it again, and again, and now he does not notice the hot tears on his face.

Its head-cover comes off, rolling away. The rock hits pale hair and flesh, splattering the boy's face with blood. The Keeper of the Flame falls onto its side. The boy sees its eyes, and its face. And he knows it is no god, because gods do not bleed.

It looks like a man, but its features are sharper, like stone chipped to shape an arrowhead. Flintheart shoves it onto its back with his foot, his lungs on fire.

Pale green eyes look up at him, and the boy cannot tell what emotion they hold.

"Backbiter," it rasps, blood trickling from its mouth.

The Flamebearer closes its eyes. The boy hesitates for three heartbeats.

He brings the rock down with both hands.

*   *   *

The others come from the woods, tall and lithe creatures that resemble humans. The boy is crouched over the body with the reflective hide, and his eyes dart wildly from one Keeper to another. There are seven more, at least, but none have the same sort of outer-skin as the first. They carry bows, and in the fading daylight he sees sadness in their eyes.

Flintheart looks up to the closest one. It is only a few steps away, regarding him with eyes the purple of summer flowers.

The boy picks up the Flamebearer's fallen weapon and stands between the girl and the others. There is blood on his face, mingling with the tears, but he is no longer afraid. He does not look away from the newcomer's strange, penetrating eyes.

"We must end the boy and the girl both," says one of the Keepers.

"No," says the purple-eyed Keeper in a voice so much like Stonethroat's that the boy's heart skips a beat. "He killed one that was already dead inside."

Four of the Keepers step forward. They crouch, not sparing the boy a glance, and take up the limp body of their companion.

"Our kind is not long for this world of ice," the leader says. "Perhaps it is time we let it be."

The purple-eyed one stands motionless, lingering, as they carry the body into the woods. Their feet make no sound in the snow.

One by one, the other beings drift away into the trees.

Adjusting his grip on the strange, flat weapon, Flintheart awaits the attack.

The only remaining Flamebearer kneels in the snow and picks up the fallen headpiece, turning it in its hands slowly. The mixed colors in the sky are mirrored on its strange, battered surface. It, too, is splattered with blood.

Wordlessly, the Keeper sets the object down in the snow again. Its gaze settles on the boy for another moment, and then it turns and walks away.

When it is gone, Flintheart's legs refuse to support him any longer. He falls to his knees, head sagging. He is a man now, he has earned a name, and he can taste the bitterness in his mouth. Generations of his people had obeyed the Keepers of the Flame without question. Why must he be the first to defy them?

A warm, gentle hand takes hold of his, and when he looks up he sees the little girl. She is crying, too. He wraps her in his arms and holds her until their tears are spent.

With the fire in the sky almost sunk beneath the horizon, the boy builds his own, the girl adding sticks to it. He settles the strange, cold weapon the Flamebearer had drawn over his lap. Between the two of them is the dented head-skin.

He knows the laws. By night they will build their fire and keep their vigil. And when the morning comes, they will walk towards the land where the sun awakens.

DESTINY

Elizabeth Roper

Elizabeth Roper is a computer geek by day and storyteller by night. The stories range from fantasy tales set in the mythical island of Barinth to bedtime stories for her two boys. Beth lives in Missouri with her true loves, husband Pat and sons Duncan and Connor. She has written numerous short stories and is hard at work on her first novel.

"If they were my sons, I'd knock their damn heads together," he slurred loudly, his waving hand sloshing what was left of the ale in his cup. His friends began shushing him and making half-drunken apologies to the other patrons. Tamsin leaned against the bar, observing the scene.

"Lower your voice," one of them hissed. "The king is...well, not himself these days."

"If the wrong person hears you talking ill of either of the princes, you'll be strung up or worse," the other one said. Tamsin rolled her eyes as she took another sip of her drink. *As if anyone gives a shit about what some drunks in Graycastle were saying about the royal family.*

"He's completely balmy, you mean. The princes are always fightin' over somethin'. I'm sick and tired of bein' in the crossfire. They're gonna tear this island apart if they don't knock it off." This comment started another flurry of frantic shushing.

The drunk would be easy. Almost too easy. He was already unsteady on his feet. A simple brush pass and his purse would be mine.

"The Council of Seven will keep us on the right course. Keep us out of a civil war between those grasping pups. My cousin is in the Duke's service, and he says not to worry," another said smugly.

The braggart would be more difficult. He probably knew to the copper how much coin he had. But an adjustment in my neckline would keep his attention. Men like him thought all women were panting for them. Easy to play into that fallacy long enough to relieve him of his gold.

"Would the two of you shut up? You'll have the guards down on us! They're family. They fight, but they hear us talking bad about one of them, and we'll get killed! That's what families do. Especially royal ones."

The cautious one. That was the real challenge. The purse at his belt was too lumpy for coin....a decoy purse full of rocks. Clever, clever. The real one was.....ah ha....in his boot. Well, he had to pay for drinks sometime...

The door opened and a crowd of fresh patrons came in with the damp spring breeze. A man flashed a subtle hand sign and Tamsin finished her drink. She brushed past the drunk and tossed a few coins on the bar. His purse was securely in her pocket. No challenge in that, but Rule Four said not to get caught up in the finesse if an easy play was available. Besides, there were bigger fish to fry tonight.

*   *   *

The little man stepped in the back room of the tavern and Tamsin glided in behind him, a smile on her lips. Shadows flickered across the sparsely furnished room. He looked at the austere surroundings and back to her. She pushed an auburn lock of hair behind her ear and motioned to the table and chairs. The door of the room shut with an audible click cutting off the noise in the tavern room.

Carefully, he sat down at the small table in the center of the room, and she settled herself on the other side waiting expectantly. She let him find his words in his own time. Clients didn't respond well to pressure. This wasn't technically a rule Lotte had taught her, but it was something Tamsin figured out on her own.

"My employer insists on the utmost secrecy," the small man said. Tamsin watched him shift uncomfortably in his rough wooden chair and smiled to herself. *This was going to cost him.*

He was out definitely out of his element. She looked him up and down from the top of his bald head to the soles of his carefully polished shoes. He was dressed in expensive clothes, but hopelessly out of fashion. He used a finely woven handkerchief to mop anxious sweat and toyed with it as he spoke. *His hands looked as if they had never held anything more dangerous than a quill*, she thought with a sneer. Attempting to calm his fears, she smiled serenely and said, "Naturally. I pride myself on discretion."

His eyes darted furtively around as he attempted to straighten his countenance. "Is it safe to talk here?"

Despite all his fussing, the man looked like a cat who jumped in a rain barrel, mewling and pathetic. She smiled reassuringly at him and tried not to grit her teeth. She'd have to hold his hand every step of the way. "I assure you that we are quite safe. I inspected the room myself," she said.

The man looked unconvinced, but began anyway. "A certain item has been stolen from my employer. He requires that it be returned as soon as possible."

Tamsin shrugged. That seemed easy enough. "What was taken?"

"It was a stone about this size." The man held up his hands indicating a stone with about six inch diameter. "It is gray in color."

Tamsin raised an eyebrow. "Quite a lot of fuss over a simple rock"

He gave her a hesitant chuckle. "It's far more than just a rock."

She had the urge the roll her eyes. *Everyone thought their trinket is unique.* "I need more to identify it."

"As I said it is small, small enough to hold in one hand. It also has some worn carvings on it of three lions. It will be heavily guarded, probably in a vault."

"When did it disappear?" she asked.

"It was taken two days ago. We have traced it as far as this city," the little man answered.

"Traced it how?" Tamsin narrowed her eyes.

"By magical means," he said.

She had to fight to keep her eyebrows at the same level. Practicing magic was not illegal or technically immoral, but it was highly distrusted and feared. Every nobleman who was anyone had his own private mage, and even the Temples consorted with them at times. Whoever this was, he was either a magic user or rich enough to hire a collection of tame wizards. Tamsin made a mental note to double her fee. "Why come to me then? Why doesn't your employer simply use magical means to retrieve it?" she mused aloud.

"That is, uh, complicated," the man evaded. His eyes darted away and he fidgeted in his seat.

A cold knot formed in Tamsin's stomach. This felt wrong. *I ought to show this guy out and walk away*, she thought. Rule Three: If the job smelled wrong, walk away. However, her money purse was looking too emaciated to ignore it. She pushed her doubts to the side and asked, "Was your employer able to trace who took the stone?"

"Alas, nothing positive. On a brighter note, there is one lead." The man shuffled through a sheaf of papers, and selected the slip he wanted. "We believe the stone is being held at this address."

Tamsin scanned the scrap of parchment, and registered an address in a fashionable part of the city.

"Seems straightforward enough," she said trying to convince herself. "Now we come to the fee."

"Ah, of course," he said. "Will five thousand cover it?"

It took all of Tamsin's training not to do a double take at the amount. She usually worked for one thousand, and had planned to ask for three thousand. This proved he was lying, but he was paying enough to make it truth. "Unfortunately, no. My fee for this kind of job is ten thousand," Tamsin said. *Let's see how deep his pockets are*, she thought. Rule Two: Always ask for more money.

The man's eyebrows furrowed in anger. It was obvious he was not used to being questioned. "But you said it was straightforward," he whined.

"I just seem to be thinking of complications," Tamsin said. "Complications mean money. You see, the longer we sit here and argue, the more complications I think of. I'm starting to lean towards fifteen thousand."

"Fine, ten thousand," the man huffed. "Half now and half when the stone is recovered. Until we meet again," he frowned at her like a petulant child. He hesitantly opened the door and rejoined the crowded tavern leaving Tamsin to contemplate what happened.

*   *   *

Tamsin returned to her room at the tavern after some perfunctory words to the others at the bar. As soon as the door had shut, she was out the window into the night and onto the rooftops, her direct highway to anywhere. Taking a meandering route, she found herself at the small room she kept for privacy.

After making sure she was completely alone, Tamsin descended from the roof into the outer hallway. Quickly, she opened the door and locked it behind her. The rough wood planks were slapped together to form a tiny room that wasn't entirely rickety. A small table, a chair and a bed covered with a clean, but threadbare blanket, completed the space.

Tamsin removed her dark cloak and hood. With relief, she took off the auburn wig that had become a continual part of her appearance and set it on its stand on the table. Sitting at a small, hazy mirror, she smoothed the mousy brown hair underneath. She removed the stage make-up that disguised her appearance. It felt good to scrub off the paint and feel the cool air on her bare skin.

Kicking her clothes into the corner, Tamsin pulled on a simple nightshirt. A blue and red swirl on her shoulder glowed beneath the white cotton. Pulling down the oversized neck, she looked over her shoulder at it in the mirror. The Assassin's Guild tattoo seemed to gleam with a light of its own. At times she could feel it burning under her clothes, an indelible mark of the change time had wrought in her. Blowing out the candle, she dismissed it from her thoughts, and left the mirror to its own devices.

She didn't know her client's name, or even the name of the servant he sent to speak with her. However, that in itself was not unusual. When running in these sorts of circles, if names were given they were probably aliases. Rule Five: Never use your own name or face.

Apparently though, this person was wealthy enough to have many servants and a magical council. *Why did he need her?*

Tamsin looked at the wig and cosmetics on the table. This disguise was getting old. She needed money to make a new start in a new town with a new persona. This job, as dangerous as it was, would give her enough money to leave and start over again somewhere else. *I will just have to be careful.*

* * *

It was midnight and the High District was shrouded in darkness. The only light was from the occasional glimmerings of the stars and a fingernail moon peeking through the clouds. Perfect. Tamsin was about to set her carefully honed plan in motion. She had spent a boring day blindfolded in her room to make sure her eyes would be accustomed to the dark. The blow gun was strapped to her thigh. Her hands were steady and her mind was clear. She was ready.

Moving from the protection of the tree branches, she slipped onto the ledge of the second story window. The window was locked, but it was easily picked.

Tamsin smiled to herself. Shimmying through the window frame, her crepe slippers sunk into the soft pile of silk carpets. The rich wood of the furniture gleamed dully in the faint moonlight giving off the distinct aura of expense. The silhouettes were all very simple and sleek, which meant they were purchased at an obscene price.

Once inside, she took care to move quietly through the hallway. The unmistakable scuffle of soft soles on wood floors made Tamsin freeze. She was not alone. Melding behind a door, she watched a shadow scurry through the hall. There was competition for the trinket.

Her training had left her ready for this. Rule Six: Be prepared. The blowgun was compact and deceptively simple. Loading the dart, she placed the small tube to her lips and waited. The shadow slipped forward with the ease of an expert until it was framed in the crack between the door and the jamb.

In a flash, the dart bore home through the protective clothing and a hiss escaped the shadow's lips. It would only be a few minutes before the poison began slowing the reflexes and clouding the mind. The shadow stumbled for one of the rooms. Tamsin moved to follow a thrill of pride singing in her veins. Pride turned to hubris as she forgot her training and stepped out of the doorway without checking anything. The tell-tale whistle of something heavy being swung through the air ended with a dull thud on her skull. Pain rocketed through her head and stopped her with a jolt. She was powerless to keep her knees from buckling and her body slumping to the floor as consciousness fled into the blackness.

* * *

Tamsin awoke with an aching head and an alarming feeling of disorientation. The world swam in and out of her vision and slipped through her fingers like minnows in the current. Staggering to her feet, she stumbled forward and pressed herself against a wall trying to remember what happened.

Her throat burned with unquenched thirst, but she couldn't stand straight enough to walk let alone find refreshment. She remembered the shadow and the poison. The shadow must have had friends, but why didn't he kill her?

It was more frightening to be left alive.

Coppery light crept in at the corners of the windows, marking it as either sunrise or sunset, she wasn't sure which. Gradually, the room stopped spinning and she made her tired eyes focus. What she saw was wrong; it had to be. Tamsin closed her lying eyes, and reopened them hoping for a new vision.

Gone was the beautifully furnished elegant home. It was replaced with a run-down hovel that looked like it been through a hurricane or an amazing party. Tamsin had been tossed on the rubbish bin like the rest of the trash littering the room.

She almost expected to find that she had lain unconscious for years spellbound. Groggily, she found her way out and on to the streets. No one gave her a second glance.

That was one of the closest shaves she had had in a long time. She was lucky to have gotten out of it alive, but she couldn't shake the strangeness of her escape. She should have been dead. Maybe she was, and was sent back to relive the rest of her life in some version of hell. Tamsin tried to push that out of her mind and figure how she was going to tell her client that she had failed. With any luck, she wouldn't have to.

* * *

"I don't understand why you left her alive," the man grumbled.

"I have my reasons," Karav snapped. *He's starting to question me a little too much.* He eyed his assistant critically. "Did you send messages to the capital, Gareth?"

Gareth nodded. "The couriers are on their way to Rilani. They will know we have the Stone by morning."

"Good. We've got what we came for. The quicker we get out this one horse town the better." Karav shuddered. He hated being away from Rilani. Even being in Graycastle for these few days felt like death to him. He needed to be in the mix of politics and power; he thrived on it. Now he had the key to it all, safely tucked away. Now he would make them all dance to his tune.

"I did have to tell them."

Gareth's declaration snapped him out his thoughts. Karav's eyes narrowed. "Tell them what?"

"About the girl. They said no loose ends."

"Of course. I would expect no less," Karav said jovially. "Come. The carriage is waiting."

Gareth looked relieved and followed Karav's outstretched arm beckoning him to the carriage. He never saw the blade as it slipped between his ribs.

Gareth had been an asset, but he had also been a fool. It was a waste, really. Fools are very useful. *Who was going to run my errands now?* Karav thought. He sighed in frustration. Gareth had betrayed him to the bosses, and worse yet he was stupid enough to tell him about it. *If you can't trust a fool with his own secrets, then he definitely cannot be trusted with yours.* Karav shook his head. Tamsin would never be foolish enough to betray him, let alone tell him about it. However, Tamsin's unexpected appearance had only proved the value of his quarry.

He had been warned that an agent would be sent, but he had never expected Tamsin. The Guild had trained her well. She would have to go back to Therril's men with a failure, and he knew the ambitious prince would accept nothing less than victory. They were going to kill her; it was a certainty now. He might have to do something about that too. It would be a shame if they killed his little sister. After all, she had just cost him one efficient errand boy.

*   *   *

The gloom was dark and deep, but Tamsin skillfully burrowed her way through it. The rooftops were her highway and the city walls her destination. Behind her, the city threw itself into the night, but she did not pay it any mind. The assignment had gone down in flames, and she had emerged from its ashes, the phoenix in flight.

Steps began to echo behind her and she picked up her pace. She had been careful, but not careful enough. She had forgotten Rule Seven: Never fuck with magic. Her former employer had obviously used his magical tracing mumbo jumbo to find her and now wanted to "discuss" her failure. She had no time for any remnants from her past life here. It was over and she was done with it.

Tamsin made a sharp right, darting anywhere as long as it was unexpected. The shadow behind her altered its course effortlessly to match hers. It was good then, this shadow. She darted again the opposite way, trying to catch it off guard. Heart pounding, she melted against the poorly mortared side of a chimney waiting to see if it took the bait.

The footsteps slowed and Tamsin could feel the hesitation in the set of its shoulders. In one fluid motion, the knife appeared in her hand and she slashed at its torso. A soft grunt confirmed her hit. Two quick feints and dodge kept her away from its blades.

Suddenly, Tamsin felt her knees give way and felt pricks of pain on her neck. The surprise on her face reflected in the shadow's expression as she slumped motionless to the slate roof below. Rule Eight: Never fall for your own tricks. *Damn.*

* * *

For the second time in twenty-four hours, Tamsin woke to the unknown. This was becoming an uncomfortable habit.

Keeping her eyes to slits, she attempted to inspect her surroundings. All was dark. Her hands had been hastily lashed behind her with knots any common dock worker would know.

Her fingers dug into the coarse fibers almost of their own accord. Working the knots through body memory alone, her mind was left to puzzle out what had happened.

The creak of a door and the soft padding of feet let her know she was not alone. Tamsin fell back on years of training and let her head loll on her shoulder in feigned unconsciousness.

She fought to keep the muscles in her neck lax and her expression passive as the figure bent over her. He was so close she could smell the garlic on his breath. Then she heard the distinctive *shink* of a knife being unsheathed.

Tamsin's legs began to move from sheer instinct and encircled the hapless victim and pulled. Flailing wildly, he lost his balance and tumbled into a perfect head butt.

His knife met the flesh of her arm as the last of the knots came free, and Tamsin sprung to her feet. The man attempted to defend himself, but a well-placed kick knocked the knife from his hands. He only had a few heartbeats left and it was buried in his chest.

The door creaked open and two figures were silhouetted in the doorway— a man and a woman. The man was older than her, but not by many years. There were the beginnings of lines around the mouth and his opaque brown eyes, but age had not left its mark yet. He pushed a lock of light brown hair off his broad forehead and smiled. He looked pleasant enough, but Tamsin bit back a curse. Some girls had older brothers who would tease them mercilessly then beat up any bullies who dared to take that privilege for themselves. Dreyden wasn't like that. He always watched Tamsin like an interesting bug he caught in the garden. He would apply different stimuli and take notes of her reactions with an unnerving detachment. She wondered how she would get out of today's experiment and what it would cost her.

The other figure, the woman, sent cold trickles of sweat down her neck. It was a face from the nightmare of the past, innocuous in its terror. Frizzy corn-colored hair fanned out around her rosy apple cheeks. Fleshy, square hands were primly folded atop a paunch that had probably recently developed. These all combined to make a picture of a jolly matron, someone's wife making a stop on market day. But Tamsin wasn't fooled into thinking she had mellowed. The watery blue eyes were still as cold under the smiling rosebud lips. Those plump fingers could still drive a knife into her back... and probably would, given a heartbeat of trust.

"Is this any way to greet your stepmother and brother?" Dreyden asked as he made a small hand sign.

Tamsin shifted onto the balls of her feet ready for an attack, but he only smiled as servants scurried forth to straighten the room. The unsightly body was taken away. The additional lamps and candles they brought revealed a small workroom with a desk and chairs. It was an austere little room with no pictures or personal items to expose any facts about its owner. The desk was immaculate and polished to a high sheen like the floors. It looked as if a particle of dust would have never dared to enter.

The woman flicked her eyes to the body then the single set bindings on the floor. Sighing she noted the lack of restraints for the legs and made a clucking noise with her teeth. She sounded for the world like the lady of the house observing the work of a careless servant. "How disappointing," she murmured in her breathy voice.

"You always expected too much of your protégés, Lotte," Tamsin said.

The strange booming laugh that was always out of place with her little voice pulsed in rhythm with the churning in Tamsin's stomach. "I warned him you were my best student."

When the room adequately tidied, the man took his seat behind the desk and motioned for the others to sit as well. Lotte and Tamsin stayed locked in some sort of battle in the middle of the floor.

"We need to talk, Tamsin," he said.

"I don't have anything to say to you. What could you have that's so important to tell me, Dreyden," she said never taking her eyes from Lotte.

"I think you'll be interested in what I have to say. Sheath your weapon and sit down."

"We are letting you keep it as a token of trust," Lotte said with her thin bladed smile.

Tamsin barked a short laugh. "Trust? Rule Nine: Trust no one. Ever."

"I taught you well," she said, taking a place at Dreyden's shoulder.

"Apparently not well enough." Dreyden said crisply. "Therril's assassin almost caught up with you."

Tamsin looked at him as if he had begun speaking in tongues. *"Prince Therril?"* A servant approached her with what looked to be a bandage for her wound, but she impatiently waved him away. "Did it slip your mind that I quit the Guild? I don't do politics anymore."

"You remember the rules. No one quits the Guild," Lotte said, locking eyes with Tamsin. It was the final lesson she had taken great pains to impress on her student. Rule One: You don't leave the Guild. It leaves you. The scar in Tamsin's chest began to tingle in remembered pain. She had created a matching one snaking down Lotte's side. Her knife was about to jump out of her hand to carve a new one, but Dryeden interrupted, "Politics didn't quit you it seems. A prince needs something stolen and he goes straight to you."

"What are you talking about? Wait—I don't care. Can I leave now?" Tamsin spat. Her know-it-all brother still knew how to push many of her buttons. But at least it wasn't Karav. He knew exactly what buttons to push to get what he wanted.

"I know all about your activities here in Graycastle," Dreyden said. He folded his hands on the desk with a placid expression that made Tamsin furious. "I know Therril isn't happy when he doesn't get what he wants, and that puts you in danger. You'd be a body in the sewer if Lotte hadn't been there."

Tamsin's eyes shifted to the older woman and appraised her carefully. Lotte had done her utmost to make her a body in the sewer two years ago. The only thing that could have stayed her hand this time was she was spending Dreyden's coin now and he must need her for something. No one could accuse her dear brother of sentimentality. She put down a shudder. Dreyden's tasks were never easy or fun.

"I also know that I can make this all go away. Now quit bleeding all over my floor and listen to reason," he said wearily. At his word, the servant approached her again with bandages. Tamsin sighed. She knew Dreyden well enough to know when she was beaten.

She gathered the shreds of her cool, and sat down across from him, and leaned forward waiting. Dreyden's price would be high, but he always followed through on a deal. It was a matter of pride to him. "Go on…"

"Have you ever heard of the *Lia Fáil*?"

Tamsin shifted in her seat uneasily at the randomness of his question. Dreyden was never random. Every move was planned far in advance like a game of draughts. She dreaded the course this deal was taking. "Everyone in the Seven Kingdoms knows about the Stone of Destiny," she said impatiently. "Just get to the deal, Dreyden."

A slow smile spread over Dreyden's face. "I want you to get it for me."

Tamsin could do nothing, but stare at him open mouthed. It had finally happened. Dreyden had lost his mind officially. "You're joking," she finally said.

"It's just another trinket. You deal with them all the time," he said.

"Really? Anything else, dear brother? Crown jewels? Head of the Queen Mother?" Tamsin sputtered at him. "Do you know what that thing does?"

Dreyden smiled tolerantly. "Enlighten me?"

She frowned at him furiously. "It calls down the wrath of the Holy Pair on anyone who holds it and isn't the rightful King of Barinth. I don't do magic. Rule Seven. Sorry."

He chuckled at her. "It's just a rock, Tamsin. Its only power is that others believe it's powerful."

He was probably right, but she'd never let him know that. "Still it has to do something or else you wouldn't want it. "

"True, but you let me worry about that."

She snorted. "And I don't need to worry my pretty little head about it?" She saw a smile play around Lotte's lips, but she ignored it. "That's easy for you say."

"All I want you to do is meet an agent who has it for sale. It's a simple exchange."

Tamsin let out an explosive sigh. "Fine. Just tell me where."

"We are heading to Rilani. Be ready in the morning." He rang a small bell. "Helms will take you to your room."

Tamsin nodded and followed, knowing she would get no sleep that night.

*   *   *

Rilani's open-air market place was the wonder of the city. Merchants from all over the Seven Kingdoms and beyond flocked there to show their wares. The smells of exotic spices drifted on the breeze that made the colorful sides of the tents sway. Shouts of customers bartering furiously in search of an elusive bargain rang out over the underlying hum of the huge mass of humanity gathered into too small a place.

Tamsin wandered among the stalls and wondered for the twentieth time why she was doing this for Dreyden. He was crazy to think this would work. The *Lia Fáil*. She wondered what he wanted with it. He never wasted his time on anything, and she suspected this was no different. Dreyden was just letting her waste her time though. This agent was late. She was heading for the exit, when she heard a voice from the depth of her childhood behind her.

"Looking for a bargain? Perhaps I can interest you in something."

Tamsin had spent a lifetime developing enough control to guard her reactions. Even so, it took all of it to keep from whirling around. She had been a child the last time she heard that voice, and ghosts of memory swirled around her. Dreyden was the scientist, Karav was the street magician. He would appear from nowhere and the world would seem brighter, the air crisper somehow. With his practiced nonchalance, he made the world sing with his laugh. Then when she came to depend on the lift, he disappeared in a puff of smoke. She was always left with empty pockets and hurt feelings.

Turning slowly, she said, "Karav. Well.... It's quite the little family reunion."

Some things never changed. His fair hair was still never out of place, and he was dressed in the latest fashions. She still had to look up to meet his eyes, and when she did his even white teeth were bared in a smile.

"It's good to see you, Tam."

"Is it?"

A frown creased his perfect brow. "Of course. It's been too long," he said, sincerity dripping from every word. He was completely oblivious that she might be upset with him. Typical.

"You never came for me," she whispered. Tamsin choked back the tears that shook her voice and threatened to make her feel more a fool than she already did. "You knew how it was for me. With that woman..." she pushed the words away with a wave of her hand, "...and Father pretending not to see. You promised you'd come back for me." Angry tears pricked into her eyes, and she turned her head, hoping he didn't notice.

Karav gently took her arm and deftly maneuvered her through the crowd to where they could talk easier. "I came as soon as I could, Tamsin," he said. "I couldn't take you until I had money, and by that time you were gone." His eyes pleaded with her to believe him and she felt herself softening despite her anger. "Our lovely stepmother said you ran away."

Tamsin snorted. "I only left because I had to. I waited for years, Rav. I couldn't stand it any longer. Do you know what she taught me to do? What I had to do to survive? I was only a child."

Karav stopped and put his hands on her shoulders and made her look at him. "I know. I can only imagine how it was for you, and for that I'm sorry, little sister."

Tamsin bit her lip in an uncharacteristically childish gesture. She wanted to believe him. She believed that Karav wouldn't hurt her intentionally, but he also knew how to say exactly what she wanted to hear. He squeezed her shoulder then offered her his arm.

"Now down to business. I hear you're trading in legendary items these days."

Tamsin fell into step with him and put her hand through his arm. It was an instinctive gesture from the old days. "I know you. This is just a ruse to get money out of Dreyden. Even you couldn't have gotten your hands on the Stone."

Karav laughed as they rode the wave of the crowd into a small coffee stall. The wayward shoppers were starting to gather for their afternoon mug of the rich local blend and a relaxing tobacco fix before dinner. Smoke from the hookahs and curling steam from the various pots formed a protective fog around them, seeming to hide them from the other customers. Tamsin let her eyes adjust to the darkness as Karav found a corner table for them.

"You underestimate me, Tam. I have it, and it was taken right out of Dreyden's hands. That makes it all the more sweet," he said pulling out her chair with a flourish.

A waiter put down a pot of fluted bronze and two matching cups on their table. Tamsin poured herself a cup and savored the scalding brew. "I don't believe you. Everyone knows it's in the vault at the Temple."

"Doesn't the Guild keep you up on politics these days? Our beloved king is crazy and the throne is up for grabs. The prince who can get himself crowned first wins. They need the Stone."

The tattoo burned on her neck and she resisted the urge to rub it. "I'm not in the Guild anymore," she said, her eyes dropping to the dregs of the coffee. Karav's eyebrows raised, but he said nothing as she continued. "That still doesn't explain why *you* have it."

"There was a theft attempt at the Temple, so it was moved to a safe house in Graycastle. It changed hands a couple of times, and I have it and am happy to sell it to the highest bidder."

Slowly things began to click. Graycastle. The "simple stone" she was sent to steal. Therril's assassins. It all fit into place. She had been sent to the safe house to steal the Stone and had been unsuccessful. No wonder they had sent men to kill her. She studied Karav across the table. Could he have been one of the shadows? No, she decided, he wouldn't dirty his hands with real work.

"So Dreyden is working for one of the princes?" she asked, toying with the cup.

Karav laughed. "You credit our brother with being too forward thinking. He's the master of the status quo."

"So what then? He wants it to put it on a shelf?"

"Use your head, Tam." He reached out and tapped her temple. "He's working for the Council of Seven. They *like* having an incoherent king. It lets them do what they want."

She brushed his hand away in annoyance. "I am using my head. I just wondered why Dreyden was so interested in getting a rock."

His amazed smile lit up his crafty face. "He told you it was a rock," he said almost to himself and castled his fingers in front of his face. "A rock," he repeated incredulously.

"Yes, a rock. Does this have a point?"

His eyes glittered in the candlelight as he leaned forward. "It's not just a rock."

"Come on. Those are just stories."

"I've held it in my hand. It's a conduit to something greater. Power itself."

Tamsin shifted in her seat uncomfortably. "Sounds like you don't want to sell it."

His white teeth flashed in a grin. "Oh, I'll let it go for a price, but money isn't the only thing I want. Influence is the coin of the realm now. That's something I can't get from Dreyden."

"Money can buy all kinds of influence, Rav. Dreyden will pay well. You know that."

"Aren't you the good little sister. Tell you what. Why don't you get what Dreyden will give me, and meet me tonight."

"Don't you even want to know what that figure is?"

"Nope."

Tamsin brought her eyebrows together. "That's not like you. What's your angle?"

"Me? An angle?" Karav's eyes widened in mock innocence.

"Don't try to play me, Rav. I know you too well for this bullshit."

He put up his hands in mock surrender. "Fine. The Stone is the power to bring change, and that change will stagnate in Dreyden's hands. I'm meeting another buyer tonight that can give me the price I want. You could come with me. We'll split the money and we can be partners. It will be like the old days."

Tamsin pushed her chair back from the table. "No, I won't betray Dreyden."

"Why, what has he ever done for you?"

"What have you ever done for me?" she countered. "You could be just selling me a stone from the path. I have no reason to trust you."

"A pledge of good faith," he said reaching into an inner pocket. He withdrew a fist sized gray stone. Time and many hands had worn it into a smooth oval. The only indentations were the faded carvings of three lions. He took her hand and folded her fingers around its cool contours. She glanced up at Karav, his eyes glimmering at her through the late afternoon shadows. She looked back at the rock in her hand. *It was just an ordinary garden stone*, she told herself.

But that wasn't all, somehow. It seemed to weigh more than its size, like the burdens of empire were contained within its gray walls. She looked from it back to Karav. His eyes bore into hers with an uncomfortable intensity, contaminating her with his obsession with the Stone. Her fingers tingled with a latent electric charge. It seemed to be buzzing with the hopes and dreams of all who had held it, and her own added to the mix. Voices in her head spun tantalizing fancies of what could be. She and her brother, together again, a family, just like they were always meant to be. It drove Dreyden's cold, hard cynicism to the periphery.

"You feel it don't you?" Karav said excitedly. "Would you put this back into the hands of man who thinks it's just a rock?"

Tamsin looked from the Stone to Karav again. She wanted so badly to believe he was right, needed to believe even.

"Where and when?" she heard her voice answering.

* * *

The stillness was punctuated with the steady drip of water seeping through old roofing tiles. A gurgle in the background was not the only reminder the warehouse was near the sewer. The faint stench of sewage mixed with mold and mildew to make a cocktail potent enough to make Tamsin's nose wrinkle.

Trying not to gag, she waited for Karav. *I spend my entire life waiting for Rav,* she thought. He was late as usual. She could only assume he was meeting with his other buyer. She wished he'd hurry up so they could get out of this dank hole.

Scuttling feet made Tamsin shrink instinctively back towards the wall slimy with mold. Something brushed her foot, and she prayed it was just a mouse and not a rat. The rat was not at her feet, but moving through the door in front of her.

It was obvious age and time had caught up with the figure as it moved stiffly across the floor. Her corn-colored hair glinted dully in the half light as she scanned the room. Lotte was the last person Tamsin expected or wanted to see.

Her mind began moving quickly. Dreyden must be on to the double cross, and he sent Lotte to deal with the mess. She had to warn Karav. Hugging the walls, she crept towards the door.

Thunk. A throwing knife embedded itself inches from her head. "I thought you remembered the rules. Rule Eight: Never fall for your own tricks. Especially ones I taught you," Lotte said.

Tamsin gave up her sneaking and stepped into the small circle of light from the grimy windows above.

"Never could fool you," she said.

"You always were my best pupil. If you had stayed, we could have done amazing things," Lotte said sadly, "but you always had that silly little conscience."

"And that silly little thing called free will. I'm not your game piece to control. Never will be. You should have just let me go."

"I never wanted to hurt you. You were like a daughter to me."

"But you did it. Love of me never stayed your knife, neither did love of Father. Now you serve Dreyden. Do you claim to love him like a child too, or is he just a means to an end?"

"Dreyden is Dreyden. You know that. Believe it or not, I was sorry to have to take those orders. Just as I am sorry now." At the end of the sentence, she pounced.

With that, the deadly dance was on, and her partner was one who had taught her every dangerous step. Tamsin was younger and quicker, but Lotte had the lethal patience of seasoned killer.

Tamsin feinted left then darted to the right with her knife, but Lotte twisted left and sucked in her belly leaving the knife with only empty air to cut. Tamsin stayed on the attack, and they met each other blow for blow, their blades silver blurs in the half light.

Lotte maddeningly stayed defensive, probing for a weakness. Without warning, her blade flashed and metal bit into Tamsin's shoulder and it tingled ominously. Her reactions began getting slower and the room began to spin. Lotte smiled as realization dawned on Tamsin. *Fucking Rule Eight.*

"Recognize it? It took me all night to stop that poison. I hoped I'd get to return the favor."

Tamsin had the antidote, but she had to get away from Lotte long enough to take it. Lotte was keeping her busy, running out the clock until the poison did the work for her. She'd better kill Lotte quickly or she'd be dead.

Tamsin slashed wildly, but Lotte knew all her tricks. Because it took all she had to keep out of reach of Lotte's blade, she was slow to make the connection. Lotte was in Graycastle. She was the other shadow. Her head swam at the implications.

"But that was Dreyden's safe house. Why?"

"Dreyden is a means to an end. I need the Stone for a client."

The art of the double-cross. Lotte was a master. "Which prince are you working for?" she maneuvered for a better position. "My guess is Revic. Therril already had me."

Lotte clicked her teeth in reprimand. "Some things are sacred, my dear. Surely you remember that."

Lotte's whirling blades were getting closer and Tamsin was getting slower. It was time to end this one way or another. In desperation, she let her knees give way and she sank to the ground. Lotte's wolf smile gleamed in the moonlight. She thought she had won. In the midst of Lotte's triumph, Tamsin kicked out and sent the older woman tumbling to the floor. In the scramble to regain their feet, Tamsin lunged at her and felt her knife connect and scrape bone. Blood spurted everywhere in a torrent of red. She could hear Lotte's thoughts as if she had spoken them. *I never taught you that.*

Dripping blood, Lotte attempted to limp away. Tamsin moved to pursue, but skidded on the stones made slippery with rain and blood. The older woman made it to the door, and Tamsin pursued with a curse. Before she could end it for good, shooting stars lit Tamsin's eyes as she slumped to the floor as the poison took hold. The last thing she saw was Lotte limping out the door.

* * *

Karav watched Lotte stagger out of the warehouse with a sinking feeling. One person should have walked away from the fight, and this was the wrong one.

He slipped into the warehouse and found Tamsin stretched on the floor. This was the worst case scenario. She was as clammy as the warehouse floor and as pale as moonlight. Froth foamed on her mouth and flowed down her cheeks.

"Hold on, Tam," he said searching her for the wound. He found one, but it wouldn't cause this. *Poison.* The crafty bitch.

"Rule Six, Tam. Were you prepared?" he asked her, searching her pockets. Karav grinned when he found the vial. "Good girl. You were always good at your lessons."

He popped the cap and tipped it into her mouth. Slowly, her breathing steadied and color began creeping back into her face.

"I'm glad you followed the rules," he said to Tamsin's silent form.

She moaned and her eyes fluttered then closed again.

Karav smiled and ran his hand gently down her cheek. "I'm glad she left before you were dead, little sister." He searched her pockets and smiled as he found the money purse. "Thanks to you and Dreyden for this."

Karav started to leave, but turned back. He took a couple of coins out of the bag and put them in her pocket. "Buy yourself a drink. You deserve it, Tam."

Leaving her sprawled form still on the floor, Karav crept back into the night.

* * *

Dredyen waited until Karav had gone into the warehouse before he had his men pull Lotte into the darkness. She went passed them in the alley without even checking the far corner. *Sloppy.*

When they brought her before him, she looked so relieved. *It was sad really.*

"Thank the Holy Pair it was your men, Dreyden. I need some assistance."

Dreyden inspected the deep wound she was trying to hold closed. "Yes. It looks as if she got you good. Interrupt your meeting with the buyer?"

"Of course not...I was getting the stone for you," she said, eyes wide with innocence.

He smiled ruefully. "Let us drop the pretense. You are double crossing me, and I know it."

"No...no..." she began.

"Stop," he said holding up a hand. "It was skillfully done. So well done, I could almost forgive you."

She looked at him hopefully and the only sound was her ragged breathing. He stepped closer to her, the smile still on his face. "But then you tried to kill my sister, and that just won't do."

Lotte never the saw the blade he buried in her chest. She slumped to the ground and Dreyden frowned at the blood staining his shirt. His retainer handed him another and he gratefully replaced the soiled one.

Dreyden could forgive her double cross, even admire it, but when she tried to kill Tamsin it was a bridge too far. No one hurt his family. No one. Lotte had had her rules. He had his. He was back in his carriage before Karav left. This was Dreyden's little secret.

*   *   *

Tamsin's hands were wet with blood, but she didn't know whose it was. Pulling herself off the floor of the warehouse had been a considerable feat. Gravity began dragging her back to the floor. Somehow she managed to keep upright.

Think, she had to think... she made a cursory check and the blood came from her. A wound on her arm, an empty vial next to her and the feeling she had drunk twenty-one shots of fire brandy. Poison...she should be dead. She sniffed the vial. This was the antidote. Tamsin didn't remember taking it, but she must have and it was a damn good thing.

Brokenly, she stumbled out of the warehouse into the nearby alleys and was met with another surprise. Body in the corner. She nudged it with her toe. Lotte. Well, Dreyden would be pissed. She shook her head again...no...Lotte betrayed them all. Playing her own game as usual. If there was a body in the corner, she needed to be gone.

Trying to maintain a pretense of normality, she mixed with the drunks heading to the dives in the inner district. It had stopped raining and the moon peeked at her between the buildings. It hadn't been out when she got here. How long had she lain on the floor? She couldn't be sure. Her throat burned and cracked like a desert. Water, she needed anything liquid.

It wasn't a bad idea. After the night she had, Tamsin felt she was entitled to a drink. Picking the first ramshackle building she saw, and pushed through the crowd to the bar. The mug she received was hot and surprisingly good. She wrapped her hands around it like it was last piece of warmth left in the world and tried to piece together what had happened.

It was coming back now. The money drop and the exchange, Lotte and the double cross. She and Lotte had fought; she remembered the poison. Then black.

There was only one body. Rav...Rav was there. Memories stumbled like crippled children. Rav was there, but he was not a second body on the floor. She searched her pockets and found only enough for the ale she was drinking. The money and the stone were gone...unless she had been so out of it she left it lying next to Lotte's carcass.

Slamming down a coin on the bar, she pushed her way back down the street like a salmon upstream. She was too late.

Two shadows bent over the body inspecting the carnage.

"It's not here."

"What?"

"It's not here. She didn't get it."

Tamsin didn't even hear the rest of their exchange. Rage passed through her and miraculously cleared the fog from her head. Fading back into the shadows, she left the two flunkies behind to ponder the missing stone. She had been reacting to events for too long. It was time she started making them happen.

*   *   *

Karav leaned back in his chair and took a long drag on his cigar. He lazily blew the smoke out in hazy rings and grinned. These outlander blends were expensive, but what did he care? He had hit the big time. It had started out a little dicey, but events had worked themselves out beautifully. He was getting paid for the same job twice, and well paid both times mind you. This beautiful suite at the most expensive tavern in Rilani was just the beginning. He had just begun to celebrate.

He couldn't have done it without Tamsin. He hoped wherever she was, she was having a nice relaxing drink as well.

He blew out another ring and set the cigar in the crystal ashtray next to his chair. After he brought Prince Revic the stone, his place was assured. He would be directing the island's politics for some time now. The Puppet Master of Rilani was here to stay. He leaned back in his chair and grinned again. He would have it all now—the power and the perks. And how he did love the perks. He smiled to himself thinking of the red-headed "perks" that were waiting for him later, and the blond ones after that.

The chair snapped back with a jerk and Karav felt cold steel against his throat.

* * *

Seeing Karav sitting and drinking while she lay dying on a warehouse floor, just simply pissed Tamsin off. He was so preoccupied with his cigars and his brandy, it was easy to slip in. Not to kill him immediately...well, that was another thing entirely.

"Word to the wise, brother dear. Don't piss off an assassin," she hissed.

Tamsin could see the wheels in Karav's brain began to spin with real fear. "Tamsin, you're alive. Thank the Holy Pair...."

"Save it."

"What are you talking..."

"It was you in Graycastle and it was you here. You hit me and dumped me. You should have just killed me."

"I couldn't kill you, Tam." It almost sounded sincere.

The edge of the dagger bit into his neck and he felt a trickle of blood. "Where is it, Rav?" she hissed.

He stammered trying to think of a way to get himself out of this. She could move with the knife much faster than he could and they both knew it.

"I don't know."

"Fine. Goodbye, Rav…"

The knife tightened on his throat and he spluttered, "No wait. I'll tell you."

"Make it good, my hands are impatient."

"We can share it, Tam, all of it. Revic is coming soon to get it and when he's king, he'll give us anything."

"I don't care."

"What's Dreyden to you? It's always been you and me, kid. You know that. Use your head, Tam. With your skills and my brains we can accomplish anything." He looked up at her hopefully and smiled. Tamsin put down a shudder. It was as if she was seeing him for the first time. He would drink in her skills, her youth, and her very soul until he had sucked her dry. He would leave her a desiccated shell, and somewhere inside her there was a worshipful little girl that would let him. The hand holding his head loosened and the knife slipped from his throat. Suddenly she felt so weary.

"No, Rav. It was always just you. I think I always knew that. Let's not pretend otherwise."

He went on smoothly as if he had never heard her, concentrating on the lack of pressure at his neck. "I knew you'd listen to reason, Tam. I knew…"

Tamsin gracefully flipped the knife and held it carefully by the blade. She brought the pommel of the dagger down on Karav's head with a dull thump. She felt it make contact with the back of his skull, and Karav slumped in his chair but his breath was even. He would live, but with the headache he'd have in the morning he may wish he was dead.

Maybe they were even, or maybe she still owed him. It didn't really matter. What did matter was that he could never fool her when concealing anything. She knew all his hiding places, and soon she would find the stone. The only thing he could keep hidden from her was his true motives, and she wasn't even sure she cared about those anymore.

* * *

The papers on the desk did not leave much cushion as the stone landed with a clang. Dreyden's eyes flew up with surprise.

"Here's your precious rock," Tamsin said. "Are we even now?" She stood glowering at him as flustered servants paraded in behind her mouthing excuses and trying to straighten the papers that went flying.

Dreyden waved them away and they reluctantly left throwing Tamsin scornful looks that she ignored.

"So you got it after all." He seemed as amused as if she had learned to turn a backflip for his entertainment.

"Just so you know. Lotte was a spy for Revic and she's dead. No need to thank me."

Dreyden just smiled at her in that maddening way of his. She sighed impatiently.

"Thanks for the concern. Now that you have the stone, I'll be going. I expect not to have any late night visitors from the dear prince."

"Oh, that's not the real stone," Dreyden said offhandedly putting his desk back in order.

"What?" The shock washed over her like icy water.

"I had the real stone all along."

Tamsin sank down in a chair. She had risked everything for a fake. She could barely believe it. "You'd better tell me the whole story."

Dreyden shrugged. "There was an attempt on the Stone. I put a fake in a safe house in Graycastle and laid a false trail. Then I waited to see who would go after it."

"So Rav was trying to bargain with the fake the whole time?"

"As usual, Rav didn't check his facts. Magic can be quite useful sometimes," he said with a smile. "But it worked out rather nicely. Both princes showed their hands, and I know who their agents are."

"So this was all an exercise in futility."

"It served its purpose. You being an agent to buy the fake back from Rav just added that extra amount of believability."

Tamsin shook her head. "And if Lotte had killed me?"

Dreyden shrugged. "I planned for that."

"Great. Glad I didn't inconvenience you." She sighed. Dreyden's callousness was unbelievable, but not surprising. She was just another expendable pawn on his game board, and she was so tired of games. "Our bargain is done," she said wearily.

"The bargain is done," he agreed. "I have enough on Therril to get him to call off his dogs."

"Excellent. Good bye, Dreyden," she said. She hoped she never laid eyes on him again.

"Don't you want this?" he asked tossing something to her.

She caught the rock out of instinct and looked at it strangely. "Souvenir?"

"Why not? You can tell everyone you have the Stone of Destiny." His laughter followed her out of the house and into the street.

* * *

The moon was on its downward spiral to the horizon when it highlighted a silhouette slinking across the roofs of the low district. She pushed on driven by a childish need to hide, and the last place of safety left was on the rooftops. Reaching the final place, she crouched in the corner made by the two chimneys and tried to breathe. The small gray rock passed from hand to hand and was wet with tears.

Tamsin had been stupid, so stupid. Dreyden had used her as a pawn in his great game, and she had walked right into it. As children, she could never beat him at any game of skill. She must have been a pathetically easy tool to manipulate.

Rav had played her like he always did.

He wound up the tune and she danced the predictable steps. It never failed and he knew it, knew that he could count on her dancing to his tune. She'd been practicing these moves since she was a little girl stealing cookies off the plates on the windowsills for a glimpse of his quick smile. Then when he was finished with her, he broke off the music and she slumped to the floor waiting for the next time he needed her to dance.

It was the simple truth, but it didn't make it hurt any less. It didn't make her any more able to resist when it began. It didn't make the loneliness ache any less when he cut the strings and discarded her. It throbbed like a toothache, ignored for days in the hopes it would simply go away.

She leaned her head against the cold brick of the wall. Two brothers and neither one of them cared whether she lived or died. It was funny if you thought about it. The irony burned bitter on her tongue. She could capture the wealth of kings, the riches of the island, but what she wanted was simple—a brother's love. A treasure that she would never be able to steal, no matter her stealth or skill. You can't take what never existed.

CROSSING THE RIVER

Peter Martin

Peter "Timespike" Martin is a bit of an "omni-geek." He builds computers, plays tabletop RPGs, and engages in PC gaming, blogging, fiction writing, and podcasting. He makes his home in a small Midwestern town (that has just a bit too much train traffic) with his lovely, creative, patient wife and absurdly affectionate cat. His thoughts on gaming, introversion, Christianity, technology, and the intersection of those things can be found at www.timespike.net or on episodes of the Saving The Game podcast (which he is a founding member of). This is his first published work of fiction.

A howling evening wind picked up fallen snow and whipped it past the two men walking quietly toward the Kelst River. One was not yet out of his twenties, but he walked with his shoulders bent and his head bowed as if he carried some ponderous, invisible burden. The other was older, his beard and hair long since turned silver, but his gait was the easy stride of a man with nothing left to prove or fear. Both were dressed in the garb of the Lantern Knight Order to which they belonged: a padded undergarment, chain armor, and a thick brown tunic and trousers. The older knight also wore a dark blue tabard with the order's simple lantern crest and a hooded, fur-lined cloak. Neither was wearing a weapon, but the older man carried an unlit lantern, a bundle which contained another tabard matching the one he wore and a newly-forged sword in its scabbard.

"What troubles you, Kyran?" the older knight inquired. "You walk as though the weight of the mountains presses upon you. The crossing is hard, but all who became Illumae have performed it."

Kyran, the younger knight, was quiet for a while before he spoke. "I'm not like the other Illumae, Arlin. My father wasn't a Lantern Knight. My fondest childhood dream wasn't to be the protector of lost travelers. I didn't grow up in this city, watching other knights haul poor lost souls in from the cold. I am *one* of those lost souls." He held up his left hand and pulled off his thick leather gauntlet, exposing a tattoo of a chain encircling a bundle of blackened tree branches. "This is called a Mark of Condemnation. The chain means that I'm an exile. The branches mean I confessed my crime. They don't mark people with these for stealing bread, Arlin."

Arlin reached over and took Kyran's wrist, drawing it closer so he could examine the tattoo. "Your self-awareness does you credit, Kyran, but which part of this indicates that within an hour of entering the city, you'd stop a potential murder? Because three of us saw you do that."

Kyran opened his mouth to speak, but made no sound.

"Do you think you're uniquely evil, Kyran? That your sin is somehow novel or noteworthy? That despite repeated assurances to the contrary, do you think that God has decided that you are the one He's going to make an example of?" He sighed. "Of course you do. Everyone does. No man or woman that has walked those twenty feet through the river has ever been convinced that they were worthy to do so. Why do you suppose that is?"

Kyran looked hopelessly at the older knight.

"Because every single one of them was right. Evil's borders wind through every soul, Kyran. None of us ever manage to stand on the side we wish to for our entire life. Cross the river, Kyran. You will emerge cleaner, and then I can give you these." He hefted the lantern and the bundle meaningfully. "This is where we part for now, Kyran. Go with God."

Kyran watched as the older knight turned quietly and walked away. It was about half a mile from where he stood to the bank of the river. The twilight had turned still, the wind from earlier had calmed, and he was far enough outside the city that he could not hear the familiar, comforting sounds of shops being closed.

He stood for a long while in the silence, alone, then turned back toward the Kelst and started walking.

As he drew closer, his thoughts became progressively more troubled. He had traveled far, both literally and figuratively, to stand here. But now the moment had come, and despite Arlin's words, he felt unprepared, unworthy, and very, very afraid. That fear slithered through his guts like a malicious serpent, knocking shameful memories and old guilt free of their resting places. As memories of blood and screams clawed their way to the front of his mind, he tried to keep his face passive, but he knew that some of his trembling had nothing to do with the cold. Yet the road had led here, and it could lead nowhere he wanted to go unless he continued forward.

As he approached the river, he mused that the twenty feet of rushing water he had to cross looked a lot larger than the equal distance of clean snow between him and the river bank. The Kelst was not wide here, but its steep banks made it almost eight feet deep in the middle, and the current surged past rapidly enough to pull even a strong swimmer under. The clear, clean water looked almost black in the failing light of evening, and even here on the bank, he was chilled and shivering. He couldn't remember the last time he'd been so cold. How could he possibly reach the other side in a full suit of chain? His training up until this point had included theology, medicine, languages, horsemanship, woodcraft, and swordplay. It had not included swimming, not that that would have helped him here. It had been years since he'd been in deep water, and that had been in the warm, safe waters of his boyhood home, far south of this frozen place.

As he took in the place where he was to cross, a note of despair rang in his mind. There was no way. There was no possible way that he could survive the crossing. The armor would drag him down, and if he didn't drown, he'd almost certainly freeze. His gaze fell upon the other knights gathered on the far bank. Arlin stood with Elsora and Tamaril, the two most recent inductees into the Illumae. The younger knights met his gaze from across the river with knowing looks. They had been here recently enough to remember, and they knew what he was feeling. Kyran could almost feel their eyes pulling him across the river. He couldn't back down now, not with them standing there.

Seeing before him his own mortality and regrets as much as the faces of his fellow knights, he took a step forward. Time seemed to slow as he trod slowly across the ten feet of pure, untouched snow between him and the river's edge. Almost as if to underscore the finality of what he was doing, a few snowflakes began to drift lazily down from the sky. Three steps to the river.

Two steps.

One final step of dry land. The water churned before him. He fixed his gaze on the lanterns on the far bank and took his first step into the frigid water. Raw, icy pain stabbed up his leg immediately. His vision blurred as his eyes watered and he gasped involuntarily.

Another step. His right foot howled the same dirge of protest his left had just moments before. He gritted his teeth and willed himself forward, his already-numbed feet uncertain on the rocky riverbed. This was his final punishment, it must be. Arlin's assurances must have been a ruse to lure him here. These noble and pure knights might have accepted him as an ordinary member, but he had been a fool to think he could become one of the Illumae. His soul was far too stained to stand among their hallowed ranks. There was no way they could be expected to accept a murderer.

The water tugged at his heavy, agonized legs, seeming all too eager to be his executioner. It was getting hard to move, so numbed was he from the cold.

The spray of the river was already creating an icy crust on the parts of him still above the water, and his armor felt heavier with every passing step. This was to be his final judgment, then. To perish before he could prove himself, to go before the Father of All black of soul and unclean of conscience, a failure, unfit for His presence. He would perish, and Hell awaited him. The fear that had been tearing at him gave way to crushing guilt. He deserved this, and could not deny it. He raised his numbed left hand to just below the surface and looked at the Mark of Condemnation that had been tattooed there before he had been sent away from his homeland. He looked back toward the lanterns, weeping openly now, and sucked in a last, desperate breath before he took the step that would put his head below the water's surface. The frigid air seared his lungs.

Feeling profoundly alone, he willed the feet he could no longer feel to take one more step, and the river closed over his head, and with it, crushing darkness. His cold-ravaged lungs burned fiercely, and the water pounded in his ears. His eyes reached for the surface, searched for the lights on the far shore. He strained toward the flickering light, which may as well have been miles away. He managed one more step before the current took him. His legs slid out from under him, and his armor pulled him down like the claws of the grave itself. His last conscious thought was a prayer for forgiveness, then the world went black.

* * *

Kyran awoke, only he wasn't on the bottom of the Kelst anymore. He was somewhere warm and still and quiet. He also wasn't wearing armor. His eyes still closed, he flexed his fingers, clenched a couple of muscles and found he could feel them and that there was no pain. He breathed deep and inhaled warm, clean air, scented lightly with what smelled like cinnamon and cedarwood. He felt comfortable. Safe. He opened his eyes. He stood on a grassy hill beneath a clear blue sky. A gentle breeze tousled his hair, and off in the distance, he could hear laughter and singing. He was calm, contented, at peace.

Suddenly a figure of pure light stood before him, impossibly bright. It was simultaneously the size of a man, and more massive than anything he could comprehend. Its brilliance tore everything else from his eyes. Its power washed his senses away. Its purity annihilated all else from his mind, and he could only gape in awe at the raw potency of it. He could not bear to look at it, but he could not stand to look away. Strangely, though, while he suddenly felt very small, he did not feel afraid.

And then it reached for him. Strong, loving, powerful, gentle arms wrapped around him in a tender, desperate embrace and pulled Kyran close, holding him, puissant and yet kind. His guilt, his pain, his fear washed away, and the words filled his senses, overwhelming all that was left in him. *My child! My precious, beloved child! How I love you! How dear you are to me!*

"But," Kyran started, "I have-"

I know what you have done, dear one. Your debt is paid. It was paid before you stepped into the river, before you sought the Lanterns, before you knew it existed. I love you. I have always loved you. I will always continue to love you. Do not fear. Do not ever fear. One day, you will return here. But today, I must send you back, for you have work yet undone. Carry My light to the lost. Let them know I love them, that I forgive them. All of it, all of them. It is all paid. Go.

*   *   *

Tell them.

Kyran coughed violently, heaving up frigid river water, and the cold came surging back. He trembled, lying on the bank of the river as the two young knights hurriedly set down their lanterns and rushed to his side. Strong, armored limbs lifted him to his feet, wrapped him in a heavy fur cloak and pulled him towards the roaring bonfire where the other knights stood. They left him there, shivering by its flames, his armor and clothes already drying from its powerful heat. No one spoke. They knew better. He had so many questions, but he no longer had any doubts. Arlin had been right; he would never again be ruled by fear. For Kyran Semnir, there was nothing left to be afraid of.

FORGOTTEN DREAMS

Hans Cummings

Hans "JediSoth" Cummings started writing fantasy when he was 17. That partial manuscript still exists, locked away in a safe place where no one will ever see it. Since then, he has been honing his craft. While writing has always been a part of his life, Hans has worn many hats in his life, from burger flipper, to retail drone, to corneal excision technician, and production coordinator for a small trade organization. He grew up in Indiana, Germany, and Virginia and earned a Bachelor of Arts degree in English from Indiana University in 2006. He is the author of The Foundation of Drak-Anor duology and the Zack Jackson series of middle grade/young adult science fiction novels.

"What in the Seven Galaxies is that thing?" Jahni could not believe her eyes. She brushed a lock of hair out of her eyes as she stared through the window into the pen. There, amongst the scrub brushes and rocks, was a creature as sensuous as it was terrible.

The creature had long, blonde hair, albeit matted and stringy, with a shapely body of pale skin, like one who had been out of the sun for too long. She squatted on one of the rocks, oblivious to her nudity, as clawed feet on backward-bending legs scratched at the ground. Her arms were long and spindly, ending in long spikes where hands would be. A small furry animal was impaled on one of the spikes, and she brought it up to her nose to sniff it. Jahni was surprised how kind and pretty the creature's face was until she snarled and opened her mouth to bite at her prey. Her tooth-filled maw tore into the animal with aplomb, blood running down her chin as she devoured it, flesh, bones, and fur.

"That is a Toridanus Banshee." Jahni's companion tapped on the glass. The banshee looked up and screeched, the sound muffled by the glass between them. She pushed off the rocks and leapt toward the glass. She could not reach, however, and fell short, tumbling to the ground and scampering back to her rock. She stared up at them, her face now a passive mask.

Jahni scratched her head. "Bestial one moment, then passive the next? She'd almost be pretty..."

"She's studying us. Trying to determine if there's a way to get to us."

Jahni stepped back from the window, backing up until she bumped into the rock wall behind her. Suppressing a shudder, she looked at her companion. Beryl was one of the Aelfar, the undisputed rulers of the Traxis Domain. He was still watching the banshee with his luminous purple eyes. The sharp features of his black-skinned face were framed by the long white tendrils which grew from his head and hung down his back. Beryl was short for an Aelfar and was one of the few who treated Jahni as equal, rather than vermin. Most Aelfar assumed Jahni was Beryl's slave, albeit one with an unusual amount of freedom since she was not on a leash. It was not an unreasonable assumption, despite Jahni's distaste for such assumptions, because humans in the Seven Galaxies were a slave race entirely dominated by the Traxis Domain. It was rare indeed to see an unleashed human in Aelfar space.

Beryl took Jahni on board as a passenger a few years ago and since then indulged her in her quest to find some cause, some purpose to her life as a freed human. She was never quite sure why the Aelfar captain took such an interest in her.

Beryl shook his head and looked at Jahni. The human stood with her back against the rock wall. "Does she disturb you?" He grinned, his lips peeling back to reveal sharp ivory teeth set within dark red gums.

"A bit. I don't care for the juxtaposition of innocence and savagery."

The Aelfar shrugged. "It is what they are. Some say humans are not far removed from that."

A cloud passed over Jahni's features. She hated how many of her kin were kept as slaves by the Aelfar. Most denizens of the Seven Galaxies viewed humans as ignorant savages, barely a step above animals, and treated them as such. It was this poor treatment of humans she witnessed that motivated her to find the freedom fighters she'd so often heard of in her travels throughout the Seven Galaxies.

"Come on, let's go." Beryl slapped Jahni's shoulder. She did not understand the point of menageries like this. They passed half a dozen more windows which looked down upon enclosures designed to mimic the natural environments of their inhabitants. From bollywugs and banshees, to Traxian battlecats and Varla zephyrs, it seemed the Aelfar caged just about any dangerous creature they encountered as they conquered their way across the Traxis Domain.

The final cage contained a display more vile than any Jahni could imagine. Scruffy, naked humans bickered and fought each other for the last scraps of meat from a battlecat that had been loosed in their pen for the amusement of the Aelfar who watched. Several humans lay dead, having fought the battlecat, and Jahni saw one of the humans tear into his dead comrades, eating his flesh. Jahni could stomach no more and turned away.

Beryl sighed. "Such a waste. They'd be much more useful doing just about anything other than fighting for scraps for the amusement of the aristocracy."

"Is this why you brought me here?" Jahni gestured to the pen. Her hand trembled with rage.

"Certainly not! I find this display as distasteful as you do. I didn't even know they kept humans in this menagerie. I just wanted to show you the banshee. They're terribly beautiful, don't you think? I was thinking of buying one for the ship." He led Jahni out of the menagerie into the gift shop designed to further lighten the purses of those seeking some remembrance of the caged creatures they had just seen. "As a mascot, you know. Perhaps for disciplinary purposes as well. I wonder if they're sapient?" Beryl scratched his chin as he examined a shiny, rust-colored cast sculpture of a banshee eating an Aelfar as she mated with it.

"I think it's a terrible idea." Jahni pushed past Beryl and worked her way out of the shop. She considered Beryl a friend, one of the few she had, but was amazed how thoughtless he could be. She found a bench outside the shop window and sat down to watch passers-by. Most of the people milling about were Aelfar, but Jahni could see several reptilian Silvarians, a handful of feathered Ciscips, a swarm of insectoid Ishixs, and even a bright red and yellow Zorrian pushing a cart and gesturing for people to partake of its wares with four of its limbs while walking on the other four.

She noticed a tall Aelfar watching her from across the plaza. Jahni could tell from her large breasts that she was a nurse. Aelfar were essentially hermaphroditic, but divided themselves into nurses, those who could nurse their young, and breeders, those who could not. Either could bear children, and with advances in technology nurses were no longer required by all families to rear the young, yet they still retained a large measure of popularity and influence from those who demanded nothing but the finest care for their families.

She wore a low-cut, silvery dress—a stark contrast against her jet-black skin. She toyed with a chain in her hands and yanked on it, pulling a bedraggled human into view. She said a few words to him, and the slave looked up at Jahni. The slave glanced back up at his master and then stared at the ground. The Aelfar nurse laughed, the sound cutting across the plaza like shards of glass, and then pulled a small device out of a pouch on her hip and spoke into it.

Seeing the slave and his Aelfar master made Jahni's skin crawl. She knew there were few free humans in the Traxis Domain, and none of them were welcome, particularly here in the city of Zor-Malus, its Grand Capital. Jahni rested her head in her hands and stared at the ground. The light from the twin suns of Gelfaar warmed her scalp, possibly the only pleasant thing about the Aelfar city.

It was the lack of that warmth that first alerted her to the Borandii's approach. She looked up to see the back-lit, hulking beast approaching her, his shadow looming over her and his hand on the pistol at his hip. This Borandii wore the uniform of the Zor-Malus Constabulary, and the pebble-textured green skin of his face was crisscrossed with numerous scars. Twin spiral horns arced backward from his temples, almost like a helmet covering his wiry, black hair. His thin black lips frowned as the Borandii regarded Jahni, and he tapped a claw on the human's shoulder.

"What's your designation?"

Sighing, Jahni shifted in her seat and place her hands on her thighs with slow, deliberate motions. "Jahni, free…"

With one smooth motion the Borandii drew his pistol and slapped Jahni across her face with it. Her jaw erupted in fire as the pistol's barrel cut into her flesh, sending her sprawling to the ground.

"Your DESIGNATION!"

Sitting up, pressing her palm against the bleeding cut, Jahni clenched her teeth. "My name is Jahni."

The Borandii fired his pistol. Blue electricity arced into Jahni, sending her body into spasms. She fought to keep her teeth clenched so she wouldn't bite through her tongue as her body convulsed. Her head smacked into the foot of the bench on which she'd been sitting, and just as she thought she might break her own back, the convulsions stopped.

"I will ask you one more time, filth: Your. Designation."

"8-7 Alpha 23. From Breeder Colony Thetis 4." Jahni had not spoken her designation since she became a freed woman. She hoped to never hear those words again.

"Where's your leash and master?"

Jahni gritted her teeth and pulled herself back onto the bench. "I am a freed human. My papers are in my pocket. If you'd permit me?"

The Borandii nodded. "Slowly."

Jahni reached down to the pocket on her thigh. She unsnapped it and pulled out a thick leather binder. She held her thumb over the biocrystal identifier until the cover popped open and then handed it to the Borandii.

He grunted and took the binder from Jahni. She pulled a handkerchief from her pocket and pressed it against her bloody cheek.

As the Borandii looked over Jahni's papers, a crowd of Aelfar gathered around, jeering at Jahni. Amidst catcalls and shouts for her to crawl back into her hole, the Borandii tossed the binder back to Jahni.

"Fine. So you're freed. Get back to the Warrens. We don't want your kind of scum up here."

"Well, what sort of scum do you prefer?" Beryl pushed his way through the crowd, grinning. "Come on, clear out, you lot! If you want to gawk at a human, go stare at one of the ones in the menagerie. It's feeding time!"

The crowd murmured their disappointment but dispersed as Beryl sat down next to Jahni. He handed her a purple stick candy.

"Can't leave you along for a minute, can I?"

Jahni shrugged and sucked on the candy. It tasted fruity and spicy. "I was minding my own business, just sitting here, when that Constable accosted me."

"Hey, are you sure you don't want to go with me? The Pleasure Pools of Persiphia are supposed to be spectacular this time of year. Males, females, and...others of all shapes, sizes, and species are there and are willing to bring you to a finish you've only experienced in your wildest dreams. Probably better than me, even." Beryl took the handkerchief from Jahni and dabbed at the wound on her cheek.

"I really wouldn't know."

Beryl shrugged. "Well, don't blame me for that." He often tried to coax Jahni into his bed but laughed off her constant refusals as though he didn't care one way or another if she accepted.

Jahni shrugged again. "It's tempting, but I have a purpose here. I just need to find her."

The only reason Jahni came to Zor-Malus was to find Rana, the leader of the underground freedom fighter movement. Over the past year she looked for her on half-a-dozen worlds in three of the Seven Galaxies, and her trail led Jahni here. Beryl was game for a while but informed Jahni before they arrived in Zor-Malus he was done carting her around on her personal errands.

"Who is this person you're looking for again?" Beryl reached into his pocket and produced a sanitizing wipe.

The wound on her cheek stung as Beryl cleaned it with the wipe. "I don't know much about her. Her name is Rana, and she's supposed to be ushering in a new era for humanity. An era in which we'll finally be able to come out of the shadows."

"Ah, one of those high-thinkers from Newhome, no doubt. Well, don't get your hopes up. The Eyes of Atriaxis will dim before Traxis Domain lets humans run around unfettered."

Jahni smiled and pulled Beryl's hand away from her cheek. "I know for a fact not all Aelfar look at us through such narrow eyes."

Beryl shrugged. "Common folk like me, perhaps. But to those in power? You're a wild animal just waiting for an opportunity to inflict your savagery upon a nurse and her suckling brood."

"I'm staying. I'm going to find Rana and do important things. Things will change."

Sighing, Beryl folded up Jahni's handkerchief and handed it back to her. "Very well. I think I've been more than generous, carting you around the Seven Galaxies, but I'm willing to let you continue to tag along, you know. You're all right for a human."

Jahni smiled. "You're all right for an Aelfar."

"I suppose this is where we part ways. Your female is not going to be up here, and I have no desire to head into the undercity." Beryl stood and held out his fist.

Jahni touched Beryl's fist with her own, bowing her head in the traditional Aelfar farewell. "Be safe out there. May you never find yourself in The Void without light."

"It'll never happen. The Pleasure Pools are on the other side of the universe, my friend! If you change your mind, you know where to find me. I'm not leaving for another day or so." Beryl walked away, a bounce in his step. Jahni's smile faded as she watched her friend walk away. She sighed and stood.

The longer I stay up here without him, the more trouble there will be.

* * *

Jahni ducked away from the crowds into an alley. Zor-Malus was a multi-layered city, and one needed to go deep if they wanted a place where freed humans were not immediately viewed with suspicion, even if they weren't actually welcomed anywhere.

The alley angled down from the main street. Nearby buildings blotted out light of the twin suns, casting deep shadows in which fungus flourished. Jahni knew the way to the Warrens. Zor-Malus would be like any other Aelfar city. All she needed to do was to keep going downward, and there at the bottom where all the shit flowed from the Aelfar, Silvarians, and other fine folk living above, would be the humans.

Below the sunlit plazas and gleaming glass residential towers was a world of industry and services. They were the businesses and machinery of Aelfar society that enabled those who lived in the light to enjoy their luxury. Jahni hurried past them, delving deeper. At the bottom, where the waste ended up and was reprocessed into useful goods, were the brothels, gambling dens, and other unrecognized and underappreciated cogs in the wheels of society. They were the places everyone knew existed but didn't think about, the places that people would tut-tut about at society parties and then go visit after a hard day's work, when the thought of going home to a loveless union of convenience was too difficult.

Before Jahni left Breeder Colony Thetis 4, the man who freed her told her this: "Seek out Rana. She moves around, but she's worth finding if you want to do anything as a free human. You need her. Find her."

Jahni had spent the last five years looking for Rana. She never questioned why she was set free instead of being sold. She was grateful for it and decided that questioning it might cause a reversal of fortune she couldn't live with. She knew when human females were sold rather than kept as labor or breeding stock, they were destined for an unpleasant life of sexual servitude, usually with people who had unusual tastes.

The last place she looked for Rana, The Spire, a spike-shaped arcology on Praxis in Yon's Eye, turned up only a crippled old Silvarian who claimed Rana had moved on to the heart of the Aelfar's dominion.

The only light in the Warrens was generated from the businesses; it was all artificial. Vents blew in stale air from somewhere outside, and Jahni wondered what would happen if the air handling system failed. She was surprised to see how many non-humans were in the Warrens, mostly Silvarians, but she spied a large number of species she had never before encountered. There were no Aelfar, though. She supposed it was too dark for them. They probably didn't want to risk something sticking to them, or in them, by coming down here.

Her sources indicated Rana liked quiet clubs. Jahni spent all her time en route researching clubs in Zor-Malus and narrowed down the list to one in particular. Nestled in a dark corner of the Warrens, Forgotten Dreams sat in between a body modification parlor and a noodle shop. A red- and blue-striped light hung outside the door of the club, advertising the sorts of services offered. Jahni wasn't familiar with the Aelfar's signage system but supposed she would find out what red and blue stripes meant soon enough.

The aromas wafting across the alley from the noodle shop set her stomach grumbling. She ordered a serving, tossing her credit chit onto the counter. The human serving her was a greasy little man with wide eyes and so few teeth Jahni imagined noodles were the only thing he could eat. He scanned her chit and pushed it back across the counter to her along with a bowl of noodles.

The steaming broth and noodles slithered down her throat as she gulped down her meal. Jahni watched the entrance to Forgotten Dreams as she ate, hoping against hope that Rana would walk out so she wouldn't have to go inside. Jahni laughed to herself at the thought; she didn't even know what Rana looked like.

Steeling her nerve, Jahni tossed her empty container into an overflowing bin and walked across the alley. The door to Forgotten Dreams had no opening mechanism, save a small string that led up and into an opening above the door. She tugged on it.

Jahni heard a bell ring from within the club. A small hatch she hadn't seen until it moved slid open on the door.

"Prrrr...yup, yup." A bug-eyed Noctax stared at her, its brown and yellow fur matted and tangled. "Whatoo want?"

"I'm looking for Rana." Jahni tried to look beyond the Noctax into the club. Red lights illuminated the interior, but the Noctax's bulbous body blocked her view.

"Yup, prrr...yup, yup. Back dere." The Noctax whipped its head back to gestured behind it. "Who ya?"

"Jahni. Sterling sent me." She hoped the reference was worth the money she paid back on Praxis.

"Sterling. Prr...yup, yup. Asshole. Rana say: let all Sterling send in. Prr...yup, yup."

The hatch slid closed, and the door opened with a click and creak. Jahni stepped through, and the Noctax shut it once she was through. It dangled from the ceiling by three of its arms while four more secured the door behind them. Another arm grabbed Jahni and pulled her close with a grip that felt like the powered clamps of an automaton. Its head weaved back and forth on a long, sinuous neck. The Noctax pushed its face close to Jahni's and kissed her, slobbering on her cheek, before it pushed her away.

"Prr...yup, yup. Tasty. You okay. Go see Rana. Cause trouble, be dinner."

Jahni shuddered and wiped her cheek, wincing as her hand dragged across her raw wound. She had never seen a Noctax up close before. Its eyes reminded her of searchlights, and she wondered how something that didn't look like it had teeth could eat her, not that she wanted to find out. She cocked her head and watched the Noctax for a moment, trying to figure out if it was male or female, then shook her head, and wiped her cheek again. It tingled where the Noctax left its slobber.

The entry hall led to a corridor bathed in red light. Doors lined both sides, and from the panting gasps and cries of ecstasy, Jahni guessed what sort of club Forgotten Dreams was. Jahni couldn't imagine why a freedom fighter would set up shop in a den of inequity. A Zorrian wearing red body paint beckoned her, waving two arms in her direction. She could tell she was female by the long dreadlocks which hung from her head; no Zorrian male was permitted to wear his hair in that fashion. *I suppose it could be a male dressed like a female, but I don't think Zorrian are into that.*

Jahni held up her hand and shook her head to indicate her lack of interest, but walked over to the Zorrian anyway.

"You sssay no, but come here anyway." The Zorrian's voice was a rasp, like a needle being dragged across wire. "What is your game, human?"

"I'm looking for Rana."

The Zorrian sucked in her breath, clicking her mandibles. "She visits, but not work here. You be disappointed." She ran her hand under Jahni's chin. The fine hairs on her digits made Jahni's skin crawl. "Me much better, look." She gestured into her room at a normal-looking bed. "Even have human bed. Comfortable. Stay the night."

Her eight eyes stared at Jahni in a way that suggested she would flutter her eyelashes at her if she had any. It unnerved her.

"Uh, no, thank you. I just need to talk to Rana."

She pointed down the hall. "Last room on left. Big room. Lounge."

Jahni nodded her thanks and trotted down the hall, avoiding eye contact with those who poked their heads into the hallway to view her. The last door on the left was closed, with stenciled lettering on it that read "Lounge." Jahni tried the handle, but the door was locked. Just as she reached up to knock, the door opened.

A grey-skinned, four-armed Kroze stood at the door staring at Jahni. The Kroze was bare-chested and covered with ritual scars that traced out tribal patterns on his skin. A large pistol hung in a holster on his hip.

"Got a token?"

Jahni looked up at the Kroze's beady silver eyes. "Um, Sterling sent me?"

"Asshole." The Kroze stepped to the side and opened the door wider so Jahni could enter. The lounge was bathed in red light. Soft music played from the speakers, the type most species found relaxing. Jahni thought she heard stringed instruments. A few dozen humans were lounging on circular cushioned sofas, enjoying quiet conversations. No one paid her any mind.

It was refreshing.

The Kroze closed the door behind Jahni and sat on a stool next to the door. He picked up a large-bore rifle and rubbed it with a cloth, staring at Jahni.

"I don't suppose you could tell me where to find Rana?"

The Kroze rolled his eyes and jerked his thumb toward the far corner of the room. "She's over there. The popular one."

Jahni looked in the direction indicated. She saw a woman laughing, sitting with her legs tucked under her. Her hair was cut short, and she wore cut-off pants and a sleeveless v-necked shirt. She looked like a pixie from the stories nursemaids told to children at the breeder colony. Surrounded by other people, she held her hands out while an emerald green aura surrounded them. Gears and wheels spun in the aura, coming together and flying apart in a dance as precise as it was memorizing. *She's a technomancer!* Jahni walked through the room, weaving around the cushions and people.

"Rana?"

She looked up at Jahni, a twinkle in her eye. "That's me." The gears and wheels floated down and settled on the table in front of her.

"Sterling sent me."

Rana laughed. "He's still sending people? That's precious." She gestured at the sofa.

Jahni sat down across from her. "It took me a few years to find you."

"That explains it. I'll have to get word to him that I have everyone I need, although…" She stretched and sat up. "What's your designation?"

Frowning, Jahni crossed her arms in front of her chest. "My name is Jahni."

"Good!" Rana laughed. "We have three Jahns already; we could use a Jahni. Freedonia Prime? Newhome?"

It was obvious Rana thought Jahni meant that she was from one of the few worlds humans claimed for their own. She shook her head. "Breeder Colony Thetis 4."

"I see, so you do have a designation. How many masters have you served?" The other people sitting near Rana turned away from them and became engrossed in private conversations of their own now that Rana was talking business with someone.

"None. I was freed instead of being sold."

Rana cocked her head. "Why?"

"Don't know. Don't care. I left as soon as I could." Jahni shrugged. "I figured if I asked too many questions, they might change their minds."

Nodding, Rana waved a server over from the bar. She whispered something in his ear and sent him away and then turned back to Jahni. "You should be fairly uncorrupted then. Good. I think we can find a place for you in our movement." She elbowed one of the men sitting next to her in the ribs. He grunted and turned away from his conversation to face Rana.

"Jer, does Morus still need help?"

The man nodded. "If his bellyaching is any indication, his need is greater now than ever." Jahni didn't like the look of him. His dark hair was unkempt, and his shaggy eyebrows grew together above deep-set eyes.

"Fine, fine. Send her down to Morus, then." Rana smiled at Jahni. "It's hard work, but would do a lot of good for our movement."

"What sort of work is it?"

Rana smile widened. "Morus can show you better than I can explain it. I assure you, no matter what you might think of it initially, it is vital to my…our purpose." She looked over to the Kroze guarding the door. "Take her down to Morus, please, Rokk?"

The Kroze grunted and slid off his stool. He opened the door and gestured for Jahni to accompany him. "Follow me, human."

Jahni hesitated. Rana returned her attention to the people around her, as though she expected Jahni to accompany the Kroze without question. A bead of cold sweat rolled down Jahni's back. She sighed and walked into the hallway with Rokk. The Kroze closed the door behind them and then stepped across the hall and opened the opposite door. Stairs led down into dank darkness.

"Down there?" Jahni sniffed the air. The stairwell was musty, and wafting up from the depth was a mixture of herbs and decay. She stepped into the stairwell and descended. The heels of her boots echoed on the bare concrete. The clomping of the Kroze following behind her sounded like one of the legendary stone beasts of Grax that caused the world to tremble with each fall of their mighty feet.

As they rounded the corner and continued down, Jahni heard the clanging of metal on metal. It reminded her of the clanging of pots and pans in a busy kitchen. She sniffed the air again.

"The kitchen? Rana is sending me to work in the kitchen?" Jahni was no longer sure she made a wise decision in joining Rana's movement.

"Nah. Morus can't cook." Rokk chuckled. "Sure can eat, though. You'll see. We're almost there."

The stairs led to a corridor not unlike the one on the upper level, though without the carpet and mood lighting. The walls and floor were bare concrete. A plain work light hung from the ceiling.

Rokk pointed past Jahni. "Third door there to your left."

Jahni looked ahead to the door he indicated. It was unmarked. She walked up to the door and opened it, looking back at the Kroze. He turned away from her and walked back upstairs. Jahni walked into the room.

The dimly-lit room stank of chemical preservatives. Steel shelves formed rows as far as Jahni could see, rows of boxes and crates. She could hear movement near the back of the room.

"Eh? Who's that?" A man's voice called out from the back of the room. Jahni could not see him but walked toward the sound.

"Rana said I should help you. I'm Jahni." She walked past a stack of empty crates and bags of fluffy packing material. A haggard, older man came into view as she rounded a corner. A scraggly salt-and-pepper beard did little to conceal the crags and lines of a face worn with age and hard work. His steel-grey eyes peered at Jahni as he stood over a crate, trying to hold down the lid while he sealed it with a handheld sealing gun.

"It's about time Rana sent someone to help me." He shoved the sealing gun at Jahni and pushed down on the crate's lid.

Jahni looked at the sealing gun. She was not sure how it worked, exactly, but before she could examine it further, Morus sighed and snatched it away from her.

"Fine, you push, I'll seal." He waited for Jahni to hold the lid shut and sealed it.

"What is it exactly I'm supposed to do here?" She hoped helping a cantankerous old man seal boxes and crates was not to be her ultimate contribution to the freedom effort.

Morus grunted and gestured to a pallet of small boxes. "You crate those up. Then you seal them." He pointed toward another pallet of boxes. "Then you crate those up and seal them. Someone will be by periodically to cart off the crates. Sometimes they'll bring more boxes."

"What do I do with those?" Jahni suspected she knew the answer.

"Crate 'em up. And seal them."

"What is all this stuff anyway?" So far, this was not the type of work Jahni envisioned herself doing when she set out to find Rana's freedom fighters.

"Medical supplies, I think." Morus grabbed a small box from a nearby shelf and walked away. "I'm going to eat something. Keep at it."

Medical supplies...of course, for freedom fighters all over the Seven Galaxies. Jahni stacked boxes in the next crate with renewed vigor. She worked through all the pallets Morus indicated, and when she was finished, he still had not returned.

Jahni looked around, hoping she missed a pallet. She didn't want to stray too far from her appointed task, as she didn't know where everything was or what she was supposed to do without Morus's direct instructions. Since there was little about being free that annoyed Jahni, other than being idle, she decided to go look for Morus.

The hallway outside the stock room was deserted. Jahni made sure the door was unlocked, then walked out to the left, away from the stairs that led up. She hoped one of the doors led to a break room or something similar where she would find Morus. The first two doors she came to were locked. One was unmarked, the other was marked "Generator."

Jahni stopped at the third door. Like the stock room in which she was working, it was unmarked. She tried the handle. With a click, the door swung open. The stench of old feces and stale urine hit Jahni like a cudgel to the face.

Suppressing a gag, she saw the cause. The walls were lined two-high with cages. Huddled within the cages were gaunt, naked Aelfar. Some were lying unmoving. Others were shivering, their eyes wide, darting from side to side. Some had no eyes, only raw, oozing depressions where their eyes once were. A grate covered the floor and Jahni could make out a sluice underneath the grating through which flowed the fluids draining from the cages.

There was a table in the center of the room. It looked like a surgical table. A series of conduits and tubing led from various ports in the floor and ceiling to the table, and there was a console at one end. She took a hesitant step into the room. The Aelfar nearest the door turned to look at her, and uttered a low, garbled wail; his tongue had been cut out.

"You shouldn't be in there, girly." Morus's voice called from the hallway.

"What is this place?" Jahni's voice was a desperate whisper. She wished she could unsee what she saw.

"Weapons research. Aelfar are tough. Rana wants to make sure she knows how best to kill them."

"Research?" Jahni turned to look at Morus. He was leaning against the door jamb, chewing, a sandwich in one hand. "It looks more like a torture chamber."

Morus shrugged. "Gotta break eggs. They're Aelfar. They've done worse to us. Come on. There's work needs doing."

Jahni shivered and suppressed a gag. "I need...where...where's the lavatory?"

"At the end of the hall. The door is clearly marked."

Following Morus out, Jahni lagged behind until the man went into the stockroom, and then she returned to the research lab. Shutting the door behind her, she shushed the wailing and moaning Aelfar. She knew what she had to do.

They don't deserve this. No one does. I have to set them free.

"Don't be afraid. I'm going to help you."

Jahni walked over to the console, examining the cage doors she passed on the way. The cages and their doors were all wired with electronics, no doubt to aid in monitoring. A touch of the screen woke up the console. It had an off-the-shelf Aelfar-designed user interface. *Apparently, Rana's people aren't above using Aelfar technology against the Aelfar.*

She scanned through the options in the interface, trying to ignore the implications of the titles of the experiments she was seeing. Pain Tolerance. Heat Tolerance. Toxin Resistance. Trauma Resistance. Surgical Solutions. She found one command tree labeled "Emergency" and drilled down into it. There were two options: Euthanize and Neurotoxin Release.

"Where's the command to unlock the doors?" Jahni frowned and backed up through the menus. She left the console and walked to the nearest cage. The latch and locking mechanism appeared to be internal. She grabbed the bars of the cage door and pulled as the Aelfar inside watched her with wide, cloudy green eyes.

The door did not budge.

The Aelfar's arm shot through the bars and grabbed Jahni. She gasped and looked at the Aelfar. She couldn't even tell if it was male, female, or a nurse, so extensive were its scabs and scars.

It opened its mouth and said something Jahni could almost understand. "Illll uzzzz."

"I'm going to help you. I'm going to get you out of here."

The Aelfar shook its head. "Ill uzz. Uny ay. Aain. Ohh ush aaiiin."

Jahni looked around the room at the caged Aelfar again. Some were gripping the bars, staring at her with clouded eyes. Some were oblivious to her presence. Some were alternately looking with feral eyes at her and at the other caged Aelfar.

She took the Aelfar's hand and tried to pry its grip loose. The skin on its hands and fingers sloughed off, revealing glistening, raw meat. The Aelfar recoiled, clutching its ruined hand and wailing. The other Aelfar rattled their cages and wailed.

This is a mercy. I wouldn't want to live after what they've been through. They've suffered enough. This is a mercy. She repeated the words in her head like a mantra. She knew the noise from the Aelfar would soon bring someone to investigate. She ran back to the console and started searching through the options again, finding her way back to the Emergency menu before she realized what she was doing.

She selected the option for "Euthanize." A prompt appeared, request confirmation by cage number. Jahni selected all of them. Another prompt flashed on the screen. "Please Confirm."

Her finger shook as she held it above the selection on the screen and she looked around the room once more. One of the few Aelfar who was not wailing met Jahni's eyes. She was chewing on her fingers, blood oozing from the wounds and dripping off her chin. Her yellow eyes were glassy, and she looked at Jahni as if she knew what the human was about to do.

Did she nod? Jahni could not be sure. Her finger hovered over the confirmation button, trembling. She shut her eyes, feeling tears run down her cheeks and pressed it. An electric buzz filled the air. Jahni felt the hair on her arms stand on end, and the Aelfar around her screeched in agony. The current coursing through their bodies threw them against their cages and dimmed the lights. The screeched stopped, and the air was filled with the stench of burnt flesh. With a loud "pop," the lights in the room went dark.

Jahni stumbled toward the door. She used the cages as a guide, yelping when she grabbed the still-smoldering hand of an Aelfar fused to the bars. Her heart was racing as she opened the door and looked out into the corridor. Jahni could hear angry shouts from upstairs, and the heavy footsteps of the Kroze. She tried not to panic as she ran toward the lavatory.

Flinging open the door, she slid around the corner into the lavatory just as a group of people led by the Kroze came downstairs. She closed the door and locked it behind her, leaning against it to catch her breath. Jahni knew she could not stay. There was no way for her to explain to these people that torturing the Aelfar was wrong. Jahni believed in freedom for all but not at the price Rana was asking her to pay.

Jahni could hear the commotion and shouting from the research lab and looked for an alternate means of exiting the lavatory. She risked a peek out into the hallway, cracking the door just enough for her to look around the corner. Hand-held lights flashed through the doorway of the lab, but the corridor was deserted. Across the hallway from the lavatory, the door was marked "Utility Access." She took a chance and hopped across the hallway. She gripped the handle of the door and against all hope tried it.

The door opened.

Jahni entered the dark room and closed the door behind her. She felt around the edges of the door for the light switch and flipped on the lights. Nothing happened. The only illumination came from a panel covering one of the walls of the closet-sized room. The panel appeared to be a communications switched board with wires leading to an electrical panel. Conduits from all sides entered the panel, like arteries and veins of a mechanical heart. In the corner on the floor was a grate. She walked over to it. It looked like it had a simple latching mechanism.

The grate opened into a small tube-like tunnel. The musty of smell of stale water and staler air permeated the draft blowing up through the tube. She lowered herself into it and closed the grate behind her. Jahni crawled forward, hoping the tube led somewhere safer.

The stench grew worse as she crawled in the darkness. She did not detect the precipitous edge until it was too late. Jahni tumbled down, through an odor-dampening field, and splashed into another tube. It was larger, but the rank fumes of death and decay told her that whatever sluiced out of the Research Lab passed through this tube. Light filtered into the tube from grates above her, spaced apart several feet. Jahni adjusted her position until she was reasonably certain she was not in the light.

She could hear voices above her. One sounded like Rana.

"This door was supposed to be locked. Who had access?"

A deeper voice replied. "Only you, Rana."

"That old fool said the new girl was in here."

"Yes."

"Deal with him. He should not have left her alone."

"It shall be done, Rana. What about the girl?"

"Find her. She's probably an agent of the Aelfar and ruined years of research, so don't bother bringing her back alive."

"It shall be done."

Jahni stifled a cry. The water seeped through her clothes. She shivered. Something touched her leg, and though she could tell it was just a bit of refuse floating in the water, she shuddered. Jahni forced herself to move forward.

Crawling through the drain worsened when Jahni realized that while she was in a storm drain, the building was old enough that most of the plumbing emptied into the same pipes. She spent several minutes trying to stay quiet while she retched.

Jahni continued forward. The sounds of the search for her echoed through the floor. She reached another junction and closed her eyes as she pulled herself over a precipice. Jahni tumbled down and landed in another pipe, banging her head. Bright light exploded in her vision, and she felt her speed increase. Joints in the pipe tore at her clothes and skin. She managed to get herself turned around as the current swept her along so she could see where she was going and saw a grate and light at the of the tube growing larger at an alarming rate.

She burst through the grate like a cannon shot, falling into a pool of fetid water. As she fell, she saw two Krozes working at the edge of the pool. They disappeared from sight as she flew past and bobbed below the surface.

Sputtering and coughing, Jahni flailed and kicked her legs in an effort to stay afloat. A hand grabbed her arm and hauled her out of the water. They were working on a platform near the pool into which the storm drain emptied. It looked to Jahni like she was in an even lower level of the warrens, based on the height of the buildings towering over them. She could see the sky far, far away and a small shack across the alley from the pool

"See, Bortz? I told you shit flows through those pipes."

The Kroze holding her shook her like a rag. "Nah, it's just a human." He laughed and tossed her to the ground.

Jahni coughed and retched, expelling the foul water from her lungs.

"You're not a runaway are you?" The one who grabbed her looked at her with his four beady eyes.

"Don't talk to it, Bortz. You'll never get it to leave."

Jahni coughed and shook her head. She forced an answer out in between heaves. "I'm...freed."

The Kroze squatted in front of her. Unlike Rokk, this one wore a utility jumpsuit, and Jahni could see no signs of ritual scarring. "What were you doing in that storm drain, then?"

"Escaping."

"Not good, Bortz. Not good. The Aelfar are going to think we're helping her. They'll kill us. Kill us. Chop us into food for the Noctax."

"Shut up, Lurcz. Go inside and get some towels."

Jahni pushed herself up and got to her feet. Her legs felt weak, and her sides hurt. The abrasions from her fresh wounds were on fire. The Kroze stood, but did not draw himself up to his full height. Jahni reached into her pocket and pulled out her papers. She showed them to Bortz.

"So you are freed. From whom were you escaping, then?"

"It doesn't matter." Jahni shook her head and gulped air.. "I need to get to the docks...34-AlphaGreen." She tried to catch her breath. "I have a friend there."

"AlphaGreen...fancy. All right. I'll help you, but you're not wearing those filthy rags in my car."

The other Kroze lumbered out of the nearby shack holding a stack of towels. Jahni took one. She stood there holding it while the Kroze stared at her.

Bortz rolled his eyes. "Like you got anything I want to look at. Fine. Lurcz, go inside and give her some privacy. I'll go get my car." Bortz lumbered off down the alley as Lurcz dropped the towels on the ground and returned to the shack. Jahni sighed and peeled off her clothes.

She dried herself off and wrapped a fresh towel around her body. She bundled up her clothes in another dry towel and made sure she had a good grip on her papers. Bortz's car rumbled around the corner. It was big and blocky, not unlike the Kroze himself. The door slid open, and the Kroze leaned out.

"Get in."

As Jahni stepped into the car, Lurcz ran out of the shack. He grabbed Jahni's arm just as she was about to close the door.

"Bortz! A bulletin just came over the InfoNet. It said this one's a runaway from Forgotten Dreams and Rana's paying cold, hard cash to get her back."

Jahni's heart sank. The wild look in Lurcz's eyes spoke to his intentions. Bortz reached across Jahni and pulled the other Kroze's fingers off her arm.

"If she's on the run from Rana, then I'm not inclined to take any money she's offering. You know when she's done with the Aelfar, she'll be coming after us next."

"But Bortz, with the money she's offering, we can get out of this shithole for good."

"Forget it, Lurcz. I'm not doing business with Rana. I'll be back in twenty. If you know what's good for you, you'll forget you saw this human and get back to work getting that pump working." Bortz nodded for Jahni to close the door. "And secure that grate!"

Bortz kicked the car into gear and engaged its thrusters. It rose into the air, the steep angle of the ascent pressing Jahni into her seat. The car was not made for human passengers, and she had to use her arms and legs to wedge herself in place as Bortz turned corners and avoided traffic.

"Do you think he'll turn me in?"

"Probably. I'll kick his ass when I get back, and we'll have a few beers later. It's just the way things are."

As Bortz drove her to the docks, Jahni closed her eyes and tried not to break down. She was so sure Rana had the answers she sought. She knew Aelfar did horrible things to people. She saw her own aunt raped and then butchered and fed to the fangbeasts of Ravus III for sport. Despite their crimes, Jahni could not...would not believe the path to freedom and acceptance lay in being as horrible to them as they were to humans.

There has to be a better way.

Lost in thought, Jahni failed to notice Bortz pulling up to dock 34-AlphaGreen. She started when her door popped open, and she gasped, grabbing onto Bortz's arm.

"Relax. We're here."

Jahni felt through her soaked clothes and found her credit chit. She placed it on the dash. "There's not much left, but it's all I have. I...I can't thank you enough."

Bortz waved one of his hands, and grabbed the credit chit. He handed it back to her. "Forget it. There are those of us who feel humans have a raw deal. Hell, Kroze are just as guilty of doing terrible things to you people as the Aelfar. Just because I don't fight against your oppressors doesn't mean I don't have sympathy for your plight. Just take my advice, yeah? Stay away from Aelfar cities, even if you think there are humans you can hook up with."

Jahni nodded and slid out of the car. Bortz closed the door and banked away from the dock, descending once again toward the Warrens and out of sight.

Beryl's ship was still docked. It was long and sleek and appeared to be carved from a large piece of dark crystal. Jahni knew its delicate, fragile looks were deceiving; the ship's hull was as hard as any in the Seven Galaxies. Its name was inscribed in gold lettering on the side but was written in an Aelfar script Jahni never learned to read. To her, it was always just Beryl's Ship. She walked up to it and pressed the call button. The docking hatch slid open, and Beryl's first mate, a dour Aelfar called Vala, scowled at Jahni.

"I thought we got rid of you. What do you want?"

"I need to talk to Beryl."

Vala looked up and down at Jahni's towel-covered body. The Aelfar often leered at Jahni, and the human felt the Aelfar's eyes evaluating her. "Dressed like that?" Vala chuckled and said something in High Aelfar Jahni thought translated to "whore." Still, she let Jahni pass.

Jahni walked onto the ship. Through the deckplates, she could feel the comforting vibrations of the engines. The heavy metallic clank of the door latching shut made her feel safe for the first time since before Beryl took her to the menagerie.

Vala pushed past her and entered a lift. She smiled as the door closed just as Jahni reached it. Jahni sighed and pressed the call button. As she waited for the lift, she adjusted her towel. The lift finally returned, and she stepped on to it. She knew Beryl would probably be on the bridge but decided to go by her old quarters first to see if there were any clothes she could put on.

Her old quarters were just as she left them. The only clothes she had, other than what she wore when she left were second-hand crew jumpsuits, but they were clean, dry, and fit well enough. She changed into them and left the towels and her wet clothes on the bed. The room was spartan, with no personal touches, but for the first time, it felt like home to Jahni. *I suppose nearly being killed and crawling through a sewer might have something to do with that.*

Jahni made her way to the bridge. Aelfar crewmembers she passed nodded in recognition, but more sneered than smiled at her. *Why should that change?*

Beryl was on the bridge. It was near the center of the ship, well-protected from external threats. He smiled when he saw her and spread his arms wide.

"Jahni! Vala told me you showed up asking for me in naught but a towel. What are these rags you're wearing? I'm disappointed!"

"I need a..."

The ship rocked as alarms blared. The lights on the bridge switched to red as all the screens switched to external view. Rana and her bodyguards were on the dock. Cerulean energy swirled around Rana, extending to envelope Beryl's ship.

He frowned and looked at Jahni. "Friends of yours?"

"They're trying to kill me, Beryl. They...they're not what I thought. They were doing things..." Her voice caught in her throat. "Experiments...horrible, terrible things to Aelfar they had in cages. I set them...I...ki..." She fought back a sob. "It was merciful. I had to do it."

Beryl shook his head. "So she's a technomancer. A rather arrogant one if she thinks she can do anything with this ship. Vala, engage the suppressors and prepare to depart."

Vala's head snapped around. "With respect, Captain, not all our crew are back from shore leave."

"But enough are, yes? Transmit a severance package to those left behind, and carry out my last orders. Clear?"

The contempt Vala felt for her Captain in that moment was palpable. She complied anyway. "Clear. Captain."

A flash of green light in the viewscreens was the only indication Jahni had that anything at all occurred. She saw Rana grab her head and stagger as Beryl's ship moved away from the dock.

"Five minutes to free space." Vala's voice was strained. Jahni did not envy Beryl the conversation he was going to have to have with her.

"Get yourself settled, Jahni." Beryl patted her shoulder. "I believe your old quarters are still vacant. We'll talk later."

Jahni nodded and left the bridge. She breathed deeply as she walked toward the observation deck, allowing the stress to melt away. She was safe for now.

She watched from the observation deck, a room near the top of the ship surrounded on all sides by crystalline glass as hard as the hull, as Beryl's ship navigated the various orbital traffic lanes and headed toward the ring of orange lights, sparkling in the distance, that was the WarpGate which would take them away from the Traxis Domain.

The ship drew closer, and the gate activated. Wisps of energy surrounded the ship and drew it in. The stars surrounding them rotated and stretched into their component colors, and the ship shot through the gate. Jahni sat back on a deck chair and watched. As the prismatic kaleidoscope wheeled around her, Jahni wept as the ship headed toward a new adventure, and away from her forgotten dreams.

THE PAPER SHIELD

James Lowder

James Lowder has worked extensively on both sides of the editorial blotter. As a writer his publications include the bestselling, widely translated dark fantasy novels Prince of Lies *and* Knight of the Black Rose; *short fiction for such anthologies as* Shadows Over Baker Street *and* The Repentant; *and comic book scripts for DC, Image, and Moonstone. As an editor he's directed novel lines or series for both large and small publishing houses, and has helmed more than twenty critically acclaimed anthologies, including* Curse of the Full Moon, Beyond the Wall, *and the* Books of Flesh *zombie trilogy. His work has been shortlisted for the International Horror Guild Award and the Stoker Award, and has received an ENnie Award and five Origins Awards.*

If the professor ever knew my name, he never used it. "You there," he'd bellow. "Careful with that crate! Its contents are worth more than the hides of this whole miserable crew!" Or sometimes he'd just bark something like "Move, you contemptible walking ballast!" when he was stomping from one end of the ship to the other and found me blocking his path. Now, I've long considered the sea my home, and even before that fateful mission with the professor I'd shipped out enough times to know how to keep clear of others on deck. Yet somehow I was always in his way. We all were. The *Chelston* was better than one hundred meters from bow to stern, a sizable enough freighter, but it felt like a river punt with him aboard. In truth, it's hard to imagine any place big enough for the likes of Charles Augustus Thaxton.

There was no way to avoid him. No corner of the ship was too dark, too distant for his rounds. Above deck he checked and rechecked the automatons and the modified heavy cranes he'd installed or quizzed the guards stationed around the other special equipment, which remained hidden from us beneath tarps for much of the voyage. Then he'd stomp off to harangue the glowbug about the wireless or the captain about the evasive maneuvers to be used in the event of a French airship attack. Below deck he seemed intent on inspecting every pump, valve, hatch, and seam. He even bulled into me once near the crew quarters. I turned a moment before impact to find him huffing toward me, green eyes piercing beneath the great bald dome of his head. He was too caught up in his thoughts to offer up an insult this time. He merely grunted through the mechanical speaking box clutching spiderlike to his throat before giving me a rough shove.

Startled, I dropped the magazine I'd been carrying, and old habit prompted me to try to retrieve it so it wouldn't be trodden upon. Apart from charts and logbooks, printed matter of any sort tends to be handled pretty roughly at sea; a page from *Sartor Resartus* will make a serviceable napkin or Bunco scorecard in a pinch. It takes considerable effort below deck to keep paper clean and dry, too, even for those inclined to bookishness, so anything brought aboard is usually seen as disposable. Me, though, I can't imagine going anywhere without something worthwhile to read—and doing all that I can to keep it safe. Respect for the word, printed or written, was something my father instilled in me. He was a schoolmaster, and in my reverence for knowledge, at least, I will always be a schoolmaster's son. Not even my awe of Thaxton could change that.

I wasn't nearly fast enough to grab the magazine. As I reached down he trod upon my hand, without malice but forcefully enough to send me back against the bulkhead. When I got my wits about me again I was relieved to see that he'd stepped over the journal. I picked it up gingerly with my bruised hand and gritted my teeth in anticipation of a harangue that would leave my ears aching as painfully as my purpling fingers. Instead, I found the professor glowering at me. More precisely, at the old number of *Scientific Alarums* resting on my lap.

The tiny gears and pistons of Professor Thaxton's speaking box clicked and whirred as it worked. He'd designed the marvel himself after a mission in Afghanistan went horribly wrong and a Russian scientist slit his throat. Some in the press claimed that Thaxton could have given himself the voice of an angel, but he'd chosen one that mixed the clack and rattle of a difference engine with the growls of a safari's worth of wild beasts because the resulting metallic snarl more accurately conveyed his intended tone.

"What's that trash you're holding?" he demanded in that awful voice. "Something for keeping down the fly population in the head?"

"N–No, sir," I said. "I was reading a piece in here on the possibility of aether-burning rockets and travel to the moon."

His expression wavered for a moment, teetering between annoyance and disappointed amusement. I'd seen that battle play out on many a master's face during my school days and even that of the occasional first mate during my time at sea. Fortunately, amusement won out this time, and Thaxton was smirking as he replied. "No doubt the editors of that dubious publication have concluded that the moon is a mirage—or a hoax, like they did with the clockwork detective I created to solve the Enigma of the Severed Head."

I should have let it go at that—smiled and gathered up my magazine and scurried off. Had we still been ashore, I might have done so. I've always been bolder once I've lost sight of land, though, and the chance to speak to the professor was too great an opportunity to let pass. "At least they share your disdain for Baglioni's theories on Atlantis," I offered, far too brightly.

"Those imbeciles deserve no plaudits for rejecting Baglioni's fantasies," Thaxton said. "There are foods so indigestible that even a starving rat would refuse them, but that's no reason to mistake the rodent for a gourmet." He gestured at the *Scientific Alarums*, dismissing it with the sweep of one grease-blotched hand. "Find something more substantial with which to better yourself, or at least something worthy to be trampled over. Even the flies deserve more substance from their doom than that rag offers."

Some element of that last pronouncement brought the professor up short and whatever part of his intellect I had momentarily distracted turned back to other, more weighty matters. As he stomped off deeper into the ship, he was muttering darkly to himself about things part of me wishes were still a mystery.

* * *

My assignment to the *Chelston* had been an unwelcome surprise. For a time after I got the orders, I wondered what I'd done to earn the Admiralty's scorn. The notification arrived on the heels of them rejecting me as automaton artificer on the *Terra Nova*. Instead of manning Scott's supply vessel for the First British Airship Antarctic Expedition, I would be stuck on a refitted lumber hauler bound for the Atlantic, under the command of a man notorious for loosing a revolutionary self-directed and, as it turned out, homicidal clockwork policeman on London back in '03—or staging a clever deception to that effect in order to cover for the misdeeds of a friend at Scotland Yard, if you believed his critics on Fleet Street and in the British learned societies. Excited as I was about the prospect of meeting Professor Thaxton, his mission promised to be rather less glamorous than the race to establish the first permanent airbase at the Pole. In fact, it sounded a bit absurd, as all his exploits were wont to do at the start.

A disagreement over the fate of Atlantis between the professor and a marine biologist by the name of Baglioni had set the whole thing in motion. Thaxton's plan was for a quartet of ships to trawl the waters northwest of Cape Juba, off the Continental Slope, using reinforced cranes and modified diving bells to bring up artifacts that he guaranteed would establish the truth about the fabled lost continent. Or at least disprove the theories put forth by Bory de Saint Vincent in 1803 and, most recently, Doctor Rupert Baglioni that cite volcanic eruptions as the cause for Atlantis's demise and identify the Canaries, Madeiras, and Azores as its remnants. It was the promise of those artifacts and their potential scientific and, of course, financial value that drew bids of support for the expedition from both public and private sources.

Our government seemed enthusiastic about the venture, which was a surprise given their skirmishes with the professor over the years. No one could accuse Thaxton of being disloyal to the Crown, but he did not always share the War Office's notion that all scientific research should have an obvious utilitarian, martial goal. His grail was truth, no matter its usefulness, no matter the consequences of its achievement, and he'd been quite vocal in the past about resources directed to the military that might have instead bolstered his operations. Most famously he'd told Lord Kitchener and the Committee of Imperial and Colonial Defense: "There was much Plato got wrong, but he was spot on when he identified ignorance as the root and stem of all evils, a blighted class which, of course, includes war. Conquer ignorance and you lot would be out of a job in a fortnight."

Still, when news of the proposed expedition hit the papers and the Royal Societies announced their support, the Admiralty was right there with a promise of several noted specialists—geologists, meteorologists, and the like—to assist the professor, as well as a score of nameless, less noteworthy sailors, such as myself, to man the lower decks. Thaxton took them up on the promise of engine room and automaton artificers, along with mechanical stokers for each of the four ships, but rejected the specialists on the grounds that he himself could provide whatever scientific expertise the mission required. If the Sea Lords took offense at that slight, they did not voice their anger, at least in public.

The press hounded both camps for a time, hoping to stir up the sort of ever-escalating row for which the professor was notorious, but no one rose to the bait. By the time we set sail, Fleet Street had turned its attention to the latest in a yearlong string of bombings and bloody assassinations across London. A few of the more radical journalists claimed that the chaos was the work of an apocalypse cult hurrying along the end of the world, but most of the papers pinned the terrorist activity on a boogeyman suited to their readers' tastes: French or Russian spies, any of a dozen homegrown anarchist groups, or immigrants of one race or another. The consensus held that the terror was meant to disrupt the start of the Festival of Empire. If that was the intent, the scheme failed. The opening at the Crystal Palace, scheduled for the night of our departure, went off without a hitch. There were fireworks over London as we set sail, but they were not for us.

I cannot speak to the mood aboard the other three freighters in our little group, but the *Chelston* was a grim place indeed. A decade waiting for a seemingly inevitable war with the French and the Russians—*sitzkreig*, as our allies in Berlin call it—had left most of the career sailors dispirited. At the outset of our expedition, a few of the engine room artificers tried to build up a camaraderie around increasingly rude jokes about the mermaids Thaxton was going to haul back for the London Zoo. There was no way such feeble efforts could compensate for the generally sour mood and the way in which the crew had been assembled. Sailors were arriving from all over the fleet right up until we cast off, so everyone was left to size up the men working around them even as they tried to get their bearings on the officers' expectations and the ship's routines. That's a certain course to mistrust, just as the secrecy shrouding large parts of the mission guaranteed a steady swirl of rumors. Logic proved even more useless than usual against this shipboard gossip because the professor's past exploits lent even the most fantastic yarns an air of credibility. In some cases, the truth proved stranger than the speculation.

Take the rumors about the phantom passengers. Such tales are common enough when a crew is patched together on a new vessel and the civilians on board aren't experienced enough to avoid getting lost below deck. Someone glances up from a duty to see an unfamiliar person wandering past, somewhere he shouldn't ever be, and they assume it's a stowaway. After a telling or two, it's a damned spirit prowling for revenge. The first week out, the *Chelston* was full of chatter about such things. I myself thought I'd seen some oddly dressed men creep onto the ship the night before we left, but let it go as a trick of the fog after the officer stationed on deck told me that no one had come aboard for an hour or more. Others said they'd heard eerie chanting rising from a part of the hold off limits to everyone save Thaxton. Fear of the professor's wrath prevented us from venturing down there to settle the matter.

It turned out that there really were a dozen men lurking in the *Chelston*'s hold: cultists, like the ones described in the radical papers. It was only when we'd sighted the African coast that the truth about them was revealed, at least a small part of it. Their leader was a smirking New Englander by the name of Marsh who dressed in the robes of an ancient Persian priest. I was on deck delivering a message from the chief artificer to one of the petty officers when Marsh led his people up from the hold. They took positions around the ship, praying in a language none of us recognized, as if to sanctify the work being done by the sailors and the automatons. The ministrations were not well received. The men—those not frightened by the sudden appearance of the rumored phantoms, anyway—made their unhappiness known with sharp elbows and sharper words whenever the chance arose.

It was then that Thaxton arrived, rushing down from the bridge. I expected him to grab the nearest cultist and pitch him overboard, but instead he roared at the sailors he passed, "Eyes to your work! Leave the priests to their business!"

Marsh soon fell into step with the professor. He walked not in his wake but at his side, an equal. Even the captain had not managed that feat in the days we'd been at sea. As they strode toward a hatchway, Marsh drew a thick, tattered book from the satchel slung at his hip and offered it to Thaxton, who waved it away. They were right in front of me then. The look on the professor's face was positively demonic. His eyes were wild, his teeth clenched in a mad grin.

Reeling with disbelief, I watched them disappear into the ship. I couldn't understand it. We were finally in position, readying the equipment for its first pass of the ocean floor. There could hardly have been a worse time to unleash this lot of mumbling mystics.

I wasn't the only one baffled by the professor's actions. In something of a haze I delivered the message from the chief artificer, then made my way down to grab a meal before I took on the afternoon watch over the automatic stokers. When I got to the galley, I found it humming with confusion and concern about the morning's events. I lingered in the passageway, wondering if I could stomach the uninformed speculation.

"I'm having second thoughts about going in there, too," said someone at my shoulder. The femininity of the voice was something of a surprise. The compulsory universal service laws hadn't been enacted yet, mind you, so distaff sailors were still a rarity in the fleet.

I turned to find myself facing the only woman aboard the *Chelston* and the only reporter who had ever gained Thaxton's trust. "I wouldn't let the cook hear you say such things, Miss Hayes, ma'am," I noted. "He might take it as a comment on his skills, whether you meant it as such or not. After that, you wouldn't want to eat anything he'd serve you for the rest of this trip."

She tried to muster a laugh at that, but the result was less than convincing. It seemed that the concerns plaguing me, or some variation thereof, had her by the throat, too. As I took in her worried look, I found myself staring at the scars on her face and the reflective circles of her goggles, the sure signs of a former aether addict. Awkwardly I forced myself to look away. She ignored my discomfort and invited me to join her in the galley. Soon enough we were sitting together at the end of one of the metal trestle tables.

Darcy Hayes was as far from my notion of a pressman as Thaxton was from my notion of a scholar. My uncle wrote for the *Cornish Post and Mining News*, but he was a tweedy sort, bright and conscientious and not terribly interested in anything adventurous or even out of the ordinary. Not at all like the ambitious London rumormongers you hear about, slinking around after indiscreet politicians and harrying crime victims, then rushing back to Fleet Street with their latest scoop. Not at all like Darcy Hayes. She was a stringer for one of the most aggressive of the radical papers, *Uncommon Sense*. I could see right away why Thaxton trusted her. There was a brashness about the woman, a cheerful insolence that let you know she disdained guile. Some former aether junkies hid their scars with makeup, but she left them alone, even the blackened tip of her nose. The ugly mark suggested that her use of the distilled element had been prodigious. Without the dark goggles she probably couldn't even see the mundane world anymore.

It was impossible not to catch fragments of the conversations going on around us. A few of the sailors hushed their voices to whispers in deference of Hayes, but many simply blurted out their opinions of the mission and Thaxton and, most pointedly, the strange priests.

"You're getting this as a proxy," I explained after the men nearest us left the table, grumbling and casting baleful looks back at Hayes. "They wouldn't dare speak so bluntly around the senior officers and they're frightened of the professor."

"Oh, this is nothing new. I've had respectable men, titled old codgers and the leaders of venerable societies, hurl insults my way that would make the saltiest seadog blush. Their anger's got little to do with me, though." She sighed and sipped her coffee. "They wouldn't know me from Eve, except for my association with Thaxton. But they aim their venom my way because they all understand that he'd brain them if they so much as looked at him cockeyed."

"I've read about those incidents."

"Don't believe everything printed in the newspapers," she said archly. "Anyway, if you're worried that I'm going to report your mates, don't be. I usually just let his critics have their say and let it go at that. No need to get him riled up about the buzzing of gnats. That's not to say your shipmates are gnats."

"When you're around Thaxton, it's hard not to feel like one. I ran into him below deck the other day." I held up my still-bruised hand. "The other marks are less visible."

"You should have seen me after my first meeting with him." That memory lightened Hayes's mood considerably, and she seemed to shake off whatever had been troubling her. "Look," she said, "I understand why everyone is so concerned. Those priests were a surprise to me, too. But they must have a purpose for the expedition, even if we can't see what it is just yet."

"Do you know who they are?"

"Members of a Yank religious cult that's been predicting the imminent end of the world since Fashoda set us on the brink of war with France. My editor at *Uncommon Sense* thinks they're linked to all the trouble the lapdog press has been pinning on free thinkers and immigrants. Their leader's a nasty piece of work. Involved in some weird doings on both sides of the Atlantic. I'm guessing that book he's lugging about contains some information Thaxton needs for the search."

It seemed reasonable enough on the surface, but if you plumbed the depths of the hypothesis at all, it sounded wrong. "You know the professor better than I do, but after all he's been quoted as saying about superstition, it seems to me that he'd just call the cultists dunderheads before snatching the book from their altar, if he thought it held some knowledge worth preserving. It's not like he's tolerant of ideas that contradict his. Look at the way he went after Doctor Baglioni for saying that volcanoes might have sunk Atlantis in his lecture on— what was it again: the morphology of the squid?"

"That's right." Hayes didn't give me the look of surprise I often get when I mention some obscure fact I've picked up from my reading, but I could tell she was recasting her opinion of me. "I can guess now why you know so much about the professor: You read the science press."

"The Baglioni lecture was written up in the news section of *Beyond Nature*, though other places picked up the story of Professor Thaxton bursting in from the wings and shouting him off the stage after the Atlantis comment. What I've never quite been able to figure out is how Baglioni ended up as the nemesis on the other side of this debate. The lecture was supposed to be his last before retirement. As far as I can tell, he'd never written about Atlantis before. He's a biologist."

"And a tough old mummy," Hayes added. "Not Thaxton's equal, of course. Then again, few are."

It was time for me to report back to the engine room. Hayes offered me her hand, transparent, aether-blighted fingernails and all, as we left the galley. "It's no good trying to second-guess Thaxton on any of this," she said, grinning. "It's not just that he's blazing new trails. He's blazing them across locales not found on any maps. We'll just have to see where we end up."

"What if those trails take us somewhere we don't want to go?"

Hayes's smile wavered just a little. "That's not really something to worry about," she said. "It's not like we can stop Thaxton from taking us all with him, once he's set his mind on a destination."

* * *

The diving bells the professor created for the expedition were remarkable things. They boasted echo-mapping systems decades ahead of the crude submerged sounding devices that were in use at the time around lighthouses, with hydrophones and noise filters that allowed them to send back clear reports of the seabed. Each bell also housed two guns capable of firing six belt-fed torpedoes apiece. The torpedoes were tipped with powerful magnets and attached to spools of heavy wire of a wholly original and incredibly strong alloy. Like the professor's infamous clockwork policeman prototype, the bells and torpedoes possessed a capability for self-direction and independence far beyond the most advanced mechanical constructs of the time.

The controversy surrounding the expedition's outcome has overshadowed the astonishing nature of these inventions, and some of his colleagues still deny Thaxton his due for their innovations. That's no surprise, really. All the bells used for the mission remain shattered and sunk at the bottom of the Atlantic. There were no spares, no back-ups. The professor has refused to release any information about them directly through the usual scientific publications, instead spreading the knowledge through a network of likeminded and similarly reckless truth-seekers. He's filed no patents, demanded no payments—though several braggarts falsely claiming credit for some facet of the inventions have found themselves battered and bullied into publicly acknowledging their deceptions.

It's a shame the original bells were lost. They were magnificent. I saw them up close, saw them in action. Once the mapping maneuvers started in earnest, many of us took shifts away from our regular stations to support the operations on deck. Apart from Thaxton's marvels, the search phase itself was tedious. For more than a week our group trawled in patterns dictated by the professor, who commanded all from the *Chelston*. He refused to supervise from the bridge. It was, he said, too removed from the actual work being done. He had the captain set up a station for him on the deck. In the final days before the discovery, he was a fixed point around which moved a scrum of men and equipment.

The doom-saying Americans lingered at the edges of this Thaxton-centric system. Their leader, on the other hand, tried to position himself close by the professor's side. Marsh was an inconsistent presence, sometimes forced away by sailors repositioning a bank of sensors, sometimes by the need speak quietly to one of his countrymen. When he managed to stay close, he created an uncomfortable juxtaposition. One moment the professor would call out sounding data for Hayes to enter into the meticulously maintained logs. The next, Marsh would crack open his moldy old book and croak out a prayer for his followers to ape back at him in ragged, broken chorus. Not even the most devout of the zealots could keep up with the professor, though. The Americans required sleep, where Thaxton, apparently, did not.

Ideal weather and a calm sea greeted us the day the search ended, all out of line with the unreal events that marked its close. We only knew that something unusual was going on when the ships were ordered to full stop and the wireless was relocated to the professor's command post. My duty station was close enough to Thaxton that I could hear his growled orders and the glowbug repeating them to the other vessels. Throughout the afternoon, messages flew back and forth, choreographing a series of complex maneuvers to position the bells. Once they were in place, they largely directed themselves in firing their torpedoes, which in turn swam routes to ensnare the object of our quest.

Hour after hour the work dragged on. The priests were hoarse from their chanting, the crew weary and tense before the maneuvers were complete and the torpedoes had each locked onto a bell with its powerful magnet. By the time Thaxton finally gave the order to raise the prize, the sun had sunk to the horizon. Its dying light washed the world in stunning reds and golds.

All except the thing we hauled up from the depths.

It emerged from the water between the four ships, pulled up by the groaning cranes and supported on a net of alloy wires strung between the diving bells. At first it appeared to be a gigantic column resting on its side. The more of the thing that rose above the waves, the more it became clear that it was not some remnant of a lost architectural wonder, but rather something organic. Not a whale. Not a giant squid or octopus. No, we had snared a single, gargantuan tentacle, and it reeked like all the charnel houses and killing floors in England flushed out at once. Its surface was the pale white of old death. No light from the sunset lingered upon it. Or perhaps the sunlight vanished into its blotchy bulk. Looking at it was like looking into nothing, the Void made manifest.

The initial cheers of triumph fell silent, and a dread settled over the ship as pernicious as the stink from our prize. The cultists dropped to their knees, screaming praise to the ancient thing from the sea. Some of my crewmates dropped to their knees as well, but their prayers were directed at younger gods and prophets.

"You shall be exalted for this, Professor," Marsh crowed. "Your name shall be legend among the faithful. You have proved the existence of the Dreaming One!"

Thaxton had been looking out at the ghastly white limb. Now he turned. The demonic grimace was gone. In its place was a snarl of utter disdain. "Yes, I've proved the thing you worship exists." He lunged at the American and clouted him in the ear. The priestly headpiece that Marsh wore tumbled to the deck. "I've wanted to strike that blow since I first heard of the schemes you and your idiot followers have undertaken in the name of that bloated corpse—the murders and the chaos you've sown. I've wanted to do worse since I first set eyes on you, you howling buffoon. You have no idea how much self-control it takes me to hold off bashing in your brain-deprived skull every second I'm near you."

Marsh pointed to the creature. "That is the doom of Atlantis. You have proved it to be so. Now it will be the doom of England and France and the rest of the corrupt Old World!"

"That thing has no power over England. England has science and reason. With those tools and my intellect I've pulled that beast up into the daylight. Look at it. The object of your worship is a thing of flesh and blood." Thaxton strode forward to loom over the cringing mystic, and through his speaking box he declared, "Since it is flesh and blood, it can be destroyed. Watch."

As the professor turned to give a command, Marsh scrambled away. He dropped to all fours, scuttled beneath one of the command post tables, and got to his feet on the other side, near where Miss Hayes was standing. There he held up the ancient tome from which he'd recited his prayers. "With this I have seen the things that dwell beyond the rational world," he said. "The feeble constructs of your science and reason cannot stand against their coming."

Marsh shoved the reporter aside and grabbed whatever logbooks and charts he could hold. Crushing them and his own book to his chest, he turned for the rail. Hayes was on his heels in an instant, a dirk in her hand, but it was I who tackled the priest—or rather, who knocked most of the books and papers from his grasp before he went over the side.

As for what happened next, the official reports claim that one of the cranes on the *Caria* gave way, so that the massive, lifeless object shifted awkwardly in the net. A crane on the *Chelston* followed suit. Then the explosives inside the bells and the torpedoes went off, as Thaxton had ordered, and it was all over. The unidentified salvage blew apart and sank back into the Atlantic.

I recall those moments differently. No sooner had Marsh gone overboard than the entire ship lurched heavily to starboard. The air was filled with the blare of klaxons warning of the impending explosion, but also the teeth-gritting whine of metal twisting and the roar of sudden waves pounding the hull. The deck tilted madly. I fell upon the logs and papers, and Marsh's old book, pressing them beneath me to stop them from sliding away. The angle of the deck was so great that, for a moment, I had a clear view of the weird prize in our net. Contrary to what the reports claimed, it did not simply lay there, lifeless. It flexed and pulled down with tremendous force. Only then did the cranes and cables give way, just before the explosives went off. Then something—some tool or piece of equipment from the commend center not properly secured—crashed into my skull.

I was gazing at the thing when unconsciousness took me. The whiteness of it drew me in, swallowed me and pulled me down with it to the bottom of the ocean. There I floated, aware of terrible shapes, aspects of an ancient being's form that emerged out of the surrounding darkness and then dissipated: a body like a bloated, scaly dragon; rudimentary wings; a pulpy head with a muzzle of tentacles that stretched along the floor of more than one ocean, a single strand of which Thaxton had pulled to the surface. I saw then that the beast lay sleeping among the submerged ruins of not just Atlantis, but all the great cities of mankind that ever were and ever would be. Its bed comprised their buildings and the bones of countless generations. My hands began to burn, and then my arms and my chest. I tried to hold back the shriek of pain, fearful that any sound would draw its attention, but I failed. The sound of my scream was the color of the beast. No sooner had the cry been uttered than the whiteness turned on me and took me into its smothering embrace.

They tell me that I was still screaming when they got me to the sickbay, where I was sedated and the books and papers finally pried from my grasp. The steward bandaged the scorched skin of my hands, arms, and chest. No cause was ever offered for the burns. They healed before we reached port, so the wounds rate no mention in the reports generated by the doctors on shore.

All four of our ships limped back to London, damaged though they were, with crews shaken as badly as if they'd endured a month-long battle. "Shell shocked" is the term the Army is using now to describe the boys returning from the trenches in Alsace and Sebastopol. The doctors used other words to describe what happened to me, mostly Greek or derived from the Greek. The scientific sound of them has provided more comfort and speeded my recovery more effectively than anything else the doctors prescribed.

On the day the *Chelston* made port and the expedition officially ended, Miss Hayes stopped by the sickbay to inform me that the surviving cultists were going to be set free. "Such are the professor's wishes," she noted with a shrug, then offered me a few words of advice on dealing with her fellow pressmen, who would be swarming over the story like, she said, "rats on a carcass." It was inevitable that the time she'd spent with the notoriously press-hating professor would sour her opinion of her fellows. Or perhaps she had witnessed this empty frenzy play out enough times with her own aether-warped eyes to recognize the game for what it is.

True to Miss Hayes's prediction, it was impossible to avoid reading about the professor in the expedition's aftermath. Claims of fraud, both intellectual and criminal, filled the papers day after day. The learned societies whose funds he had accepted declared that the entire misadventure was nothing short of a swindle, that he and Baglioni had staged the Atlantis debate to gain money and resources for a scientifically worthless monster hunt. The lack of hard evidence of the thing we dredged up and the confused accounts of the expedition's final day fed the fires of controversy, though they eventually died down, smothered, some say, by the government. Those looking for a reason to explain such an intervention, or for the support the Crown provided the expedition in the first place, might mark the notable decrease in the crimes attributed to the doomsayers in the months after our return.

Though I never again spoke with the professor, I did receive a communication from him toward the end of my convalescence, just before I shipped out again. My name was on the envelope, but in a different hand from the note inside. It was most likely that of Miss Hayes, who had been tasked with delivering the heavy package and this letter:

Sir,—

I am told by my associate, the bearer of this message, that I have you to thank for saving the logs and charts that the unconscionable cur Marsh attempted to take with him when he rid the world of his own pernicious presence. For that, I offer thanks, though I must also point out that you would have done a greater service to me and to the world if you had let him destroy his book of credulous gibberish instead of the few papers of mine to which he clung so obstinately as he went over the rail. Since Miss Hayes has also reminded me that you and I crossed paths aboard the ship, in an incident that I vaguely recall involved you taking a blow to stop me from treading upon a publication that is hardly worth even that low treatment, I cannot express surprise at your lack of discernment. Still, I recall you claiming an interest in knowledge, so by way of providing you with something more substantial with which to better yourself, I offer the enclosed. They are flawed, every last one of them, but they demonstrate thought. I hope it proves contagious and that by taking in what knowledge these volumes contain you will become a carrier. If ignorance and superstition can propagate in this fashion, so, too, can truth and reason.

—Charles Augustus Thaxton

As for the gift itself, it comprised well-read, dog-eared copies of *The Origin of the Species*, Hooke's *Micrographia*, Newton's *Philosophiae Naturalis Principia Mathematica*, Babbage's *Triumph of the Thinking Machine*, and a dozen more. Many have notes in the margins, in Thaxton's precise script, and a few have whole sections or entire chapters crossed out, with the word *rubbish* written across the pages. I value these books beyond measure.

Despite the challenges of keeping them safe from the grime and damp, I've carried one of the volumes with me each time I return to my home on the deep, on every ship I've manned since the *Chelston*. Some of my mates consider me a jinx because I served on the Thaxton Expedition—a venture as infamous as Scott's disastrous trek to the Antarctic—and they view the books as nothing less than tokens of ill luck. I've been told that rousing the thing, whatever it was, finally jolted the world into the war that now engulfs it from pole to frozen pole.

I see it differently. I have a mission, the one with which the professor charged me in that final letter. I am an agent of truth, a carrier of knowledge.

Like the cultists he let scatter back to their warrens to describe the rough treatment of their would-be god at the hands of one lone scientist, I spread the message: reason will triumph.

On most nights when we are gliding across the great shroud of the sea, my shipmates and me, I speak to them of the products of science that keep us safe from Russian submersibles and French airships. The echo-mapping system now outfitted throughout our navy would seem familiar to anyone who had seen the equipment aboard the *Chelston*, and the remarkable new alloy that has found such sudden and widespread use among the shipbuilders of Great Britain is particularly well suited for armoring hulls. But there are times when I am reminded that the enemies' weapons, too, are the product of science, and in those awful moments my mind conjures up an image of that thing beneath the Atlantic and its vast demesne, built upon the bones and works of innumerable dead priests and warriors—and scholars, too. On those nights I clutch the books the professor gave me a little more tightly and silently hope that they are, as he claimed, shields against chaos and not charts setting our course toward that unspeakable kingdom of ruin.

TEMPS OF THE DEAD

Thomas Childress

Thomas Childress, a reader of comics and an avid gamer, has too many ideas that he will get around to. When he isn't studying for his degree in Library Science he attempts to draw comics. His daughters, Allee and Emmy, think that he is the best artist in the world but his dog Rory isn't impressed. Once upon a time he travelled in a national drama company but currently lives in his home state of Indiana & when he grows up he wants to be Harlan Ellison. He can be reached at tbchildz@gmail.com.

"Let me get this straight... you feed them chicken brains?"

"Brains are vital to maintaining a healthy zombie," the rep said. For an older lady, she was cute. Sherry's green eyes peeked at him over her glasses, they had a dark leopard pattern on the frames that screamed of cougar. Bottled blonde hair and seductive, juicy curves that made it hard for Gary Martin to maintain objectivity.

"Healthy zombie?"

"Why do the undead, want living flesh, in particular brains?" she said. "Brain gray matter is what is needed to retard tissue degradation."

"Why chickens?"

"We used to use pig brains; did you know that pigs are smarter than dogs? The more developed a brain the better; that's why zombies crave human brains. The manager at the processing plant heard what we were doing and raised the price. So, instead of a pound of pig brain a day, we feed them five pounds of chicken brains a day."

Anticipating his next question, she continued. "Well-fed zombies are controllable. We use talismans to tell the zombies what to do and they do it. Our Personnel Replacement Grade Undead are an excellent, cost-effective ways to supplement any work pool. They are less maintenance than automation and easier to manage than pre-dead employees who require breaks, benefits and the daily drama."

"We package children's books with corrugate trays on the night shift," Gary said. "They're used as end caps or standalone displays, whatever. It's a manual process to fold it all, too complicated to use a machine. Our turnover rate is high and workers constantly call in or aren't any good. We spend more time retraining than working,"

"So how many can I put you down for?"

*   *   *

Colorama Publishing's building was in desperate need of therapy. The box truck was parked at the employee entrance, which sadly only had the Carcinogen Yellow color of cigarette butts on the ground (and piled like a topiary bush in the ashcan) to decorate it.

The driver climbed down. "Gary Martin?"

Gary nodded.

The driver handed him some duct tape held together by some clipboard. His jeans held onto his ass by the waist band of his visible Hanes. "Sign here and here," the kid said, "initial here, here and here."

He held up a bronze medallion hanging by a leather strap. "Your talisman, wear it. Show them what to do and they do it."

Gary reached for the talisman, the driver pulled it back just out of reach. "Remember. If you use this amulet and keep the zombies well-fed, they won't attack...usually...but they won't work. They stand around." The driver stared at him blankly, making a quick, low moan. "Keep the feeding schedule and use this." He handed the amulet over.

Gary slid the talisman around his neck; it was a heavy disc. Around the outer edge of it were carved symbols that looked terribly mysterious; hieroglyphs and Aztec type scratches.

The first zombie, wearing a moldy black suit, stepped onto the lift. The skin was stretched and cracking, flesh peeled away in onion layers. Shriveled lips formed a rictus grin, revealing gangrenous gums; one eye was rolled downward into the skull.

More zombies followed, a jaw dangling from one nerve ending on one, another with half of its skull carved away with mold-spotted-brain exposed, one with lower abdomen gone and upper torso supported by a rickety spinal column. The last had been a woman whose bodily fluids were soaking through her jogging suit, globs of pus oozing out of orifices.

"Take that one back," Gary said,

The driver shook his head. "Not without a good reason."

"She's leaking. I can't have that leaking pus all over the books."

* * *

Gary headed the macabre chorus line to the work area. He stopped, several times, waiting for the zombies to catch up. The warehouse itself was cavernous, as these things are, although this one was filled with a rather un-fun and mostly outdated track of conveyor belts and gravity rollers. The whole Tinker Toy-Mouse Trap mess was known as The Sorter and it made an awful *clackity-whizz-clap-thump* racket as it and the sound of it travelled around the warehouse.

Night shift employees stared as the baker's dozen shambled their way to the cavernous tray construction area. More than a few crossed themselves or muttered silent curses. Finally the lurch of zombies (that was the plural form, *lurch*) arrived. There were half a dozen of chest high tables, pallets of cardboard pieces sat next to each one.

The zombies continued walking. Gary fumbled the talisman up, "Stop."

They did and swayed in an unseen breeze of the queue. Gary sucked in a deep breath, unaware that he hadn't been breathing.

He stepped up to the table piled high with Christmas green tray parts. Gripping the talisman he said, "Okay. Watch me. This is how you put a tray together."

Gary felt like he was showing a primitive the magic of a lighter or something. He put the tray together, cracking the edges so they would be flexible and pre-folding tabs then fitting them into slots, another fold of the back to get the part that would be unfolded for the tray to stand in the store and the flat piece of thick, red cardboard became a small three tier shelf that books would face out from. Specific changes, cartoon or movie characters could be added later with a small insert that fit at the top. "Understand?" he said.

The zombies looked at him, blank and unreadable. "Right," Gary said.

* * *

"How much does a crew put together in an eight hour shift? On a really good night," Gary asked.

Susan rolled her eyes and flipped through the work orders and chased her computer's mouse around. She was a short beach ball of a woman. "Maybe two thousand on a really good night," she said.

"How many did we do tonight?"

She clicked the mouse again, "Almost three."

Gary whistled.

* * *

There was an incident that first week.

A zombie got in the way of another. While getting cardboard tabs to be made into insert shelves once folded, a zombie grabbed another zombie and folded it. Snapped bones, burst blood vessels and squeezed organs and fluids soon decorated the table like a Satanic Thanksgiving dinner.

On Friday, Gary called a staff meeting; forty people counting quality control, forklift drivers, order pickers and anyone else. His speech was rehearsed. "As you know we have had a few new faces around here lately—"

"Or lack of faces," Susan heckled.

Gary continued, "They're just temps. Like always, when it comes time to scale down our workforce we cut temps. We hire seasonally as we have need, when the need is gone you all still have jobs. You guys are what make all of this work; you guys are the real backbone to this company. I just want everyone to know that no one's job is at stake. This is just part of a cost effective way to get our work done. Now," he said, "Who has the feeding detail tonight? Make sure it's done a half hour before the shift ends."

* * *

"The zombies are better than our... what did you call them?"

"Pre-dead?" Sherry said.

"That's it. So the others you sent worked out too; we are way ahead of schedule."

"I'm glad to hear it Mr. Martin."

Gary nodded, a useless gesture to someone on the phone. "I need someone with higher brain functions. Do you have anyone that would be good at clerk duties? Like work order processing, spreadsheets and all that?"

"I have someone in mind," Sherry said.

* * *

The girl Sherry sent over was cute; she wore black with decorative buckles and studs. Her hair was long, her skin was pale. She said she was twenty seven; but she looked sixteen. Gary saw the quick flash of a tongue stud; he wondered what else she had pierced. "I can even run a shipping dock," she said.

Gary didn't say anything. He looked at her, and realized he was staring. She was *really* cute. "I'm sorry," he said, "I'm having a hard time focusing."

"It's okay, I'm used to it."

"Why'd they send you? I mean you aren't—"

"Dead? But I am. *Very* dead."

Gary's brows furrowed.

"It's why you find it hard to concentrate." She closed her eyes, bowed her head then looked back up at him with eyes that needed tears, "I'm a vampire."

She got up from her chair, crossed over to his desk. Gary stared at her, caught in the headlights. He flinched as her hand touched his, not from the cold of it, and it was cold, but from the sensation of her touch. It was the shock of contact carrying with it the faint buzz of attraction.

She placed his hand on her chest; his outer fingers so seductively close to her breasts. "Feel that?"

He gazed into her eyes; they were a turbulent blue, as the sky before a thunderstorm. "Huh?" he croaked.

"Do you feel that?" she said again. Her voice was the whisper of wind before the thunder. Gary swallowed audibly, "Huh?" he croaked again.

"My heart?"

Gary shook his head, not wanting to break the spell. "No heart beat?"

She smiled, now he saw the tips of enlarged canines between lips that were like two bloody strawberries. "I used to play that game, pretended to be a vampire."

He shook his head again.

She leaned in close to him. He caught the faint whiff of something; it was elusive, it was her. Seductive and innocent, beautiful and horrifying... vanilla and death?

"It's a game; we ran around pretending to be vampires. Except...I met a real one."

She leaned in closer; the only thing keeping her from pressing down on him was his hand over her non-beating heart. She said, every word a tempestuous kiss, "And... here... I... am."

Then she was back in her chair, like she had been sitting there the whole time. Gary still held his hand where she had been. "Any more questions?" she said.

His eyes fluttered and Gary coughed, "What's your name?"

"Tarot."

His voice cracked as he said, "You're hired."

* * *

They stood, Gary, Susan and Tarot, at the turnstile near the security office. In one hand Gary held Susan's time badge, and the other was offered in a handshake. They stood in the yellow and black stripped pedestrian lanes, where forklifts weren't supposed to drive. The electric trucks buzzed back and forth, coming to and from their prospective hives.

"There's no other way around it," Gary said.

Susan snorted, "How long until everyone is replaced?"

"It's not like that. It's across the board; a lot of positions are being eliminated."

"This isn't right," she said. "You can't do this. Trumping up bogus cost-effective downsizing crap three months after bringing in these...whatever you call them. I started as a temp," she said. "I wouldn't have got my job if I hadn't had the chance to come in and prove myself."

Gary considered her for a second.

He was stymied. A high pitched buzz teased his ears; a fork lift was approaching. He was about to capitulate; she wasn't going to budge. The buzz got louder.

"Really?" Tarot said and they both looked at her. Tarot smiled at Susan, displaying her teeth, more than happy to cast a little of her vampire aura which she usually favored keeping in check. It had the desired effect. Susan's eyes widened as the last thing she *saw* was Tarot and Susan panicked, she backed away from both of them and the last thing she ever *felt* were nine thousand pounds of electric forklift. Gary looked at Tarot sickened by what had just occurred and terrified by her wicked smile.

The security camera video recorded Gary talking to Susan, Tarot of course wasn't seen when Susan suddenly turned into the path of the forklift. Gary's reaction was easily taken as one of horror and shock.

After an extended period of time, perhaps forty-five minutes, Gary had made some sort of reconciliation with what had occurred. The hardest thing for Tarot about the whole thing was walking away from all that blood.

* * *

It was a gradual change with the workforce, the undead and pre-dead employee ratio was suddenly fifty-fifty, sixty-forty, seventy-thirty until someone bothered to notice then it became "overnight." Thousands were saved on benefits pay out alone; no one needed to send a zombie to the doctor for an analgesic cream?

And the employee ratio went to eighty-twenty.

"Impressive isn't it?" Gary said from behind Tarot, who sat at Susan's old desk. He motioned at the Monument Valley of twenty-two pallets of stacked red cardboard trays spread out on the warehouse floor.

"Yes, but—"

"But what?" Gary said.

"Anyone could do that if they didn't need breaks," she said.

"It's like replacing a person with a machine," Gary said. "But when a machine goes down it usually takes everything else down with it."

"Same with zombies," she said.

"You are one morbid chick."

Tarot stared at Gary's neck, the plump line of his carotid artery and she could *hear* the steady pulse of the blood flowing through it. She imagined taking a nice plump bite out of it, juicy as a ripe *Harry and David* pear, and caught herself. *Crap*, she thought, *when was the last time I ate?* "I like to think of myself as brutally realistic," she said.

"Morbid," Gary emphasized. "A machine is more expensive than a zombie. It has more moving parts; more can go wrong with it. A zombie can lose parts; eyes, ears, fingers and still function." He sniffed, sniffed again and said, "Turn on the Big Ass fan, the zombie stank is getting thick in here. And make sure the zombies get fed."

*   *   *

The following night the Friday rush started early. Work stations were cleaned, the pre-dead workers lined up at time clocks, *ready to go*. Gary normally didn't mind a little early Friday knock-off. He was the last one out before the security guard anyway.

Turning up the car radio, Van Hagar played as he drove out of the parking lot. At the exit he turned it up, work forgotten for the weekend.

*   *   *

Monday afternoon.

The parking was full in the dying orange sunlight.

The security guard was missing from the shack as Gary went in. The song of production sang out, rollers and conveyors were providing their *clackity-whizz-clap-thump* rhythm section but missing was the melody of the electric forklifts.

Gary passed the picking racks of opened book cartons into his office, not bothering to notice that they were void of first shift workers finishing up as second came in. It was when he sat down and looked out the window that he finally noticed that there weren't any people.

"Meeting," he said. The fact that there was no meeting scheduled did nothing to deter his reasoning.

After a half hour he looked around. Forklifts were still parked haphazardly, paperwork not filed, and boxes of books continued their circuit around the shipping The Sorter not getting sorted to their destinations.

He started to walk around to the different departments, Receiving, Processing, Returns; then thought better of it and got an orange electric scooter to make his rounds.

He was rounding the corner at full speed and there she was. Tarot.

He jumped on the brakes and braced for impact. The scooter stopped at Tarot's feet, the back end bucked.

She wore a Tinkerbelle t-shirt under a black coat and she accessorized in her usual *gothiness*. "This is so obvious it's a movie cliché, Tarot said. "If life were a horror movie you would be the one in the haunted house that had a copy of the *Necronomicon* in it being read back on a tape recorder by a serial killer."

"Huh?" Gary said.

She shook her head, "Never mind." She sat on the back seat of the scooter, "Shipping."

They drove and Tarot spoke, Gary missed most of what she said from the whine of the scooter's electric motor. "First shift... seven... morning... hungry...buffet..."

They rounded a corner and almost plowed into a wall of zombies. Shoulder to shoulder, they stood with backs to them. There were a lot more than normal it dawned on him where the additional zombies came from. "Oh my God," Gary said.

"God had nothing to do with this," Tarot said, "How did you not notice the blood? It was smeared all over. You really are thick."

Moaning started at the sound of Gary's voice, the cries of the zombies doing their zombie thing as they turned to face him.

"We're in trouble," Gary yelled.

"What do you mean we?" She could barely be heard over the zombie moan which was like out of tune cellos being played with hacksaws.

Tarot giggled and the vampire's laughter didn't echo. "That talisman isn't going to do you any good," she said as Gary fumbled for it.

The zombies, were crowded onto the shipping dock. Some pale as a fever patient, freshly dead. Some had been working on their overall state of decay for some days. Many were bloated, their stomachs writhing with verminous insect larvae.

"Stop," Gary said, holding the talisman up defensively. The zombies didn't. "Did they get fed?"

He glanced at Tarot who was looking to the ceiling and whistling in a cat-ate-the-canary.

He stuffed the talisman into a pocket and dashed over to some stacked pallets, found a loose two by four and swung at the flanking undead.

The swing was wild, a grand slam of *whistling* air. He swung again, it was a solid smack and a neck twisted ripping rotten flesh and cracking brittle cartilage. The zombie, head now hanging upside down from the tattered neck, continued coming.

Gary dashed through an opening. A zombie with skin like flaking paint grabbed his shoulder. Its grip as strong and silent as steel.

The zombie pulled him close. It moaned, with it came the stench of the grave.

Gary wedged the two by four into the mouth, levering it like a crowbar. The jaw tumbled to the floor, the zombie let go, looking down at the lost part.

Gary ran beneath the shipping conveyors. He bolted through a stagger of zombies and ran up the steps to the upper levels of the conveyors.

At the top Gary stopped, panting. Below, the zombies stopped their pursuit at the foot of the steps.

"They have a real problem with stairs," Tarot said. She was drifting casually in mid-air, floating off the side of the Sorter mezzanine. She landed easily, daintily.

She stepped towards him, he held up the club. They walked around each other, a Mexican stand-off of sorts.

"Why?" he said gasping.

She glowed like a demonic Marilyn Monroe in a Dali-directed *Some Like It Hot* and said, "I'm a vampire. *Duh.* I'm making the world better for my kind. I wasn't a victim... I *asked* for this. It's what I do, it's fun."

Tarot let her vampire's aura reach out to him.

Gary's club wavered slightly.

Her lips were pouty and her eyes were big and dreamy and bedroom-y. The club dipped to the floor.

She was close now, the club slack in Gary's hand.

Their lips brushed, quick and jolting. She leaned in, pressing herself against him. She was cold but her lips and eyes were hot. Gary closed his eyes as she kissed him.

Then it all came back like a slap in the face. Her body was clammy but he was hot, her eyes weren't fiery but blood red; he felt the daggers of her nails dig into his back.

His eyes jerked open; she no longer kissed him. Her head was back, jaw distended and fangs extended.

Gary brought the wooden club up as she bit down for his neck. Instead she bit into the wood, driving her teeth all the way in. He pushed her off; stumbling she tried to pull the two by four out from her mouth. Tarot chomped through the wood, splinters of it blew apart.

He landed on his belly on the metal grating, the zombies moaned below and... A wooden shard of the two by four, serrated like a carved stake, on the grate next to him.

Gary grabbed the stake, Tarot's eyes widened... then she snatched it from his hands and threw it away and it landed with a clattering *smack*.

Gary scrambled to his feet, looking around frantically. Then he tumbled, the talisman's leather thong dangling from his pocket caught on the conveyors and he was pulled over. Gary rode the length of the belt then slid down the gravity rollers to the dock floor. He skidded along the rollers that carried boxes down to shipping floor and slowed to a stop.

Moaning came to Gary as the lurch of zombies surrounded him.

Gary looked up, Tarot gazed down from the mezzanine waving a little wave. He raised a hand in supplication to his fallen angel. He saw her, framed with zombies then didn't as they leaned in. Each bite tore more than his flesh but felt as though it poisoned his soul, he screamed then those ended as his voice cracked and died. Then there was that cold touch of merciful death but not what he expected as Tarot grabbed his outstretched hand and pulled him free.

She drifted upward pulling him as she went, past the conveyors and the reach of the zombies. Gary bled from dozens of wounds, chunks of flesh had been ripped away, tatters of flayed skin hung from him.

"You... s–saved me," he croaked out.

Tarot smirked. "Did I?"

* * *

Colorama Publishing's building was getting its therapy. A paint crew was applying a liberal shade of sky blue. The box truck was parked at the employee entrance, which now had flowers of several colors trimming the employee entrance and a *real* topiary bush. The newest night supervisor, Tarot, waited outside in the waning dusk. The sunlight was very indirect, causing only minor discomfort for her.

The zombies shuffled in and more zombies followed until one was left on the lift. Its bodily fluids were soaking through its clothes, globs of pus oozed out of orifices.

"Take that one back," Tarot said.

The driver shook his head. "Not without a good reason."

"He's leaking," Tarot said. "I can't have Gary leaking pus all over the books."

MY FATHER'S SON

Johann Luebbering

Johann Luebbering has been a gamer, as well as a consumer of science fiction and fantasy since the age of five. His writing was first published in 2002 by Mystic Eye Games. A graduate of Columbia College with an unused degree in Business Management and Accounting, he works full time running a local computer repair center. An avid collector of discarded hobbies, his house is littered with everything from an Appalachian dulcimer and djembe to poi and woodworking tools, most of them covered in a healthy layer of dust. Johann currently lives in small town Missouri with his wife, three children, and ever increasing herd of household pets.

It hung over the kitchen fire, the barrel long and brown. I remember staring at it as a child, with the smells of potatoes, cabbage, and fresh baked bread hanging heavily in the air. The old oak of the stock was a deep brown, worn by centuries of handling. The steel of the barrel fascinated me, throwing back the light of the fire across the kitchen. I spent long hours in the kitchen, staring at it and wondering.

My mother always seemed to be cooking, or canning, or any of a thousand other tasks that life required. She would bustle past me, smiling down fondly at me as she went. One day, she was out of the kitchen on an errand of some sort.

I can't say that I remember what it was, or even if I knew exactly. I was only six or seven years old at the time. Left alone, staring up at the object of my obsession, I pulled a chair across the kitchen and used it to scramble up to the mantle. I pulled the gun down from its hanger and took it with me to the kitchen table.

My father kept it well cared for, always oiled and polished. I passed my hands gently over the surface in wonder, feeling the burnished steel of the barrel and polished oak of the stock slip beneath my fingers. The smell of the oil filled my head, and I could see the blue-grey of the old steel beneath the brown.

Then I was caught.

He burst into the room, rushing over to me, and cried, "What are you doing, lad? You shouldn't have taken it, boy."

I'm not sure what possessed me then. Normally, I would have been terrified of his anger, expecting the strap. Instead of apologizing or explaining, I instead stood from the table and picked up the gun. I placed it on my shoulder, as I'd seen soldiers do once when I saw a parade in a city and marched across the room to him, passing it forward to him in a child's imitation of "Present Arms."

Something in my serious manner set him off for certain sure. The fury faded from his eyes, replaced by mirth. He kept a straight face for a few seconds before bursting out in laughter. It was a rare thing to see my father laugh. We had few reasons for humor at that time.

"Well," he said, "I suppose I shouldn't be too shocked to find that you're a little rebel, eh boy? It's a thing that's in your blood. Just like that old Fenian gun." He mussed my hair a bit and took the gun from me. Strolling back across the kitchen to the table, he sat down and gestured me across from him. "Have yourself a seat, m'boy. Let me tell you about this old gun."

* * *

The gun, it turned out, was an 1853 Renfield. It was originally purchased by the Irish Brotherhood back in 1864 as part of the attempt to arm the rebellion against the English. My many-greats grandfather, John Murphy, took possession of it and used it during the Fenian uprising.

We all know how that turned out. Most of the rebellion was scattered before it began and the leaders were hanged. John Murphy was one of the few that tried to fight on. It didn't work out well for him, but he was able to return home to his family, although a bit more full of holes than when he left. He felt he was doing right by his family name, though, as *his* great-grandfather had marched in the rebellion of 1798.

John settled down after that and lived out his life on his farm, though I'm told he never quite walked right again. The gun stayed in the family, though, and made its way to his grandson, Peter. Peter Murphy, I hear, was a bit of a layabout and a ne'er-do-well, but when the time came, he took up his grandfather's gun to join the Easter Rebellion in 1918.

He didn't make out quite so well. One of his comrades, though, had heard the story of the rifle and brought it back to his brother, David. David was a good family man who hung the rifle over the mantle in remembrance of his brother, and the rifle continued its way through the family.

David's grandson, Mark, carried on the family tradition, so to speak. In the 1970s, he joined with the Irish Republican Army in their attempts to reunite Ireland again. As far as I know, he never used the old rifle, but he kept it on the wall, and told his sons the stories about it and the Murphy family history.

David was caught in 1978 and imprisoned in London. He died a month later, killed by another prisoner.

David's grandson, Joseph, eventually inherited it. When the Irish Unification came in 2024, he took part. Since firearms were illegal then, excepting antique family heirlooms, he took down the rifle yet again. He even made new molds for the rounds, seeing as how the originals had been lost. When we took back the north and made Ireland whole again, he came home a hero. I hear tell there was a welcome home feast in his home town in his honor.

Of course, it didn't last. Soon after that, The Famine struck. The whole bloody world was starving, and the charlatans in charge decided that unification was the best way to go. That, of course led to the Compromise. All the great powers of the world claimed what they felt was "theirs" and the entire bloody world became five massive empires. They thought that would help "alleviate the problems suffered by the poor."

Ireland was, without our bloody consent, put back under the control of the English, along with all the other old colonies. The rest of the world didn't fare much better of course, but at least most of them don't have to tolerate the insufferable pricks that we do.

The rifle passed down through the generations again, and ended in the hands of Joseph's grandson Mark. Mark Murphy was my father. He took up the rifle again.

It was back in 2067, you see. The Global Compromise had had enough time to settle firmly into place, and the gobshites in charge of the British Reorganization were beginning to get fat and lazy from the profits they were pulling in. The Canadians, Aussies, and Kiwis were treated pleasantly enough and had few enough complaints about the takeover, from what I've heard. In Ireland and India, though, the old blood was still a bit too fresh.

It was only a matter of time, I suppose, before the New Troubles would start. They were all young and foolish. Just a bunch of poor kids with grand ideas in their heads. My father was fifteen when he joined with the Sinn Féin. Apparently, it was an old political party that someone found in a history book and they took the name for themselves.

His group was only about twenty boys from Castlecomer, but they joined up with a few hundred from across Kilkenny. They mostly had antique hunting rifles they had pilfered from their fathers and grandfathers. They had no training. Oh, sure, most of them knew how to shoot a gun, but not one of them knew a damned thing about fighting a war.

What they did have was heads full of golden ideals and grand stupidity. They did a bit here and there against some of the English garrisons before anyone back in London really caught on. Then came the response.

The boys had decided to ambush another group of English troops out of Wicklow. They made their attack, mostly noise and bluster, before running back inland. They had made it about as far as Greenan when the drones hit them.

Back then, of course, they weren't quite a bad as they are now, but they were still bad enough. Each of them was about the size of a rugby ball, and silent as death. A few scores of them flew into the midst of the boys and, in seconds, had dropped their payload and vanished into the sky. The small explosive charges they left went off a few seconds later, blistering the entire area with plastic shrapnel.

Most of the boys were torn to pieces instantly. Those that weren't mostly died within minutes. Back then, the shrapnel that they used was an unstable polymer and within a minute or so of exposure to air, it would violently expand and vaporize. So even getting hit with a tiny piece of it would leave a fist sized hole in you. Of course, it had the added benefit of leaving no mess behind, except the corpses. Very ecologically conscious are the English.

My father was one of the lucky ones that day. He was partially behind cover, and only got a couple pieces in him. He showed me the scar on his arm that day. The flesh was sunken in beneath the puckered skin where the muscle had never fully regrown. It was something that stays in a young boy's mind.

He managed to stop the bleeding enough to stay alive, and slunk his way back home to Castlecomer. None of the other boys from there made it back.

That, of course, wasn't the end of things. Others took up the fight against the English, they were just a bit more subtle about it. Roadside bombs, Englishmen killed in dark alleys if they were foolish enough to go out alone. The English would respond to every incident with an arrest and hanging. No one believed for a moment that the people getting hanged were the guilty parties, but "innocent until proven Irish" has always been the motto of the English.

*   *   *

By the time I took down the gun in the kitchen that morning, the New Troubles had gone on for more than twenty years, and the English bastards were damned hard on us for it. Tax rates were up to around 80%, and there was less than 10% employment in the Bogside, and it was even worse down in Cork and Kerry.

Then there was also, of course, the draft. Now, the draft was very carefully written not to discriminate on nationality. By the letter of the rules, an Englishman was just as likely to be drafted as a good Irish boy. That's not quite how it worked in practice, though. Your odds of being drafted were based on a number of things, but one of them was gainful employment and another was level of education. Since hardly any Irishmen could find a job or afford an education, it tended to put us at the top of the list.

Sean, my older brother, was drafted when I was twelve. He had turned seventeen just two weeks before we got the notice. My poor mother was devastated. She locked herself into her bedroom for the rest of the day. We all tried to pretend that we couldn't hear her sobs.

All of us knew what the draft notice meant. In truth, it was a damned death sentence for Sean, and there wasn't a thing any of us could do about it. The Irish contingents always seemed to end up on the front lines in the most dangerous areas with the least training and the worst equipment. It's downright amazing how coincidences like that happen around the English. What a funny old world it is.

Of course, there wasn't a great deal of option, though. Draft dodging was punishable by death, and aiding a dodger was punishable by transportation, which is at least as bad. Naturally, the immediate families of draft dodgers were always found guilty of aiding and abetting, even if they hadn't seen the boy in years. Funny old world, like I said.

Da started taking Sean out at night, along with the old gun, teaching him to shoot. It's not like learning how to use an old musket was likely to do Sean much good, but I suppose it was all our father could offer him.

So it was that two weeks later, Sean left us. We stood at the kitchen door to watch him go. I remember the silent tears on my mother's face like it was yesterday. We stood on the step until the transport was out of sight. None of us spoke another word that night. We ate our meal in silence, and we went to our rooms in silence. It was there, awake in the darkness, that I heard the wailing cries of my mother. They went on for a long, long time there in the empty night.

*   *   *

It was about three months later that the men appeared at our door. Three of them stood there. Two were Indian fellows, young men with sorrowful eyes. In front of them was an officious English officer.

He looked at my mother as she opened the door. "Mrs. Adele Murphy?"

"That's me," she answered quietly. An army officer at your door was never a sign of good things to come.

"Mrs. Murphy," the officer said, his voice a combination of boredom and irritation. Apparently we were wasting the man's precious time. "It is my sad duty to inform you of the death of your son, Private Sean Murphy. The details are classified, but I am instructed to inform you that he was killed in action while on duty in the Falkland Islands. As he had not reached the mandatory six months of service, there will be no pension. Additionally, as his duty pay was insufficient to cover the expenses of his gear and funeral expenses, we have brought you the bill for the remainder." One of the Indian boys behind him stepped forward, presenting my mother with an envelope.

"You, *fucking bastard!*" my mother screamed and threw herself at the officer, swinging a hand at his face. The blow rocked his head to the side. The third young man had grabbed my mother's arm, restraining her. The officer turned slowly back to face her, a crimson handprint clear on his cheek. A predatory smile crept across his face.

"Adele Murphy, I hereby place you under arrest on the charge of assault on an officer of His Majesty's army." His smile turned to me. "What about you, boy? Would you care to join her?"

I was young, not stupid. When I didn't respond, he turned and led the way back to his Jeep, his men following behind, pulling my mother with them.

As soon as they were out of sight, I ran. I ran hard, and I ran fast. I had no idea what to do, and the only thing I could think of was that I had to find my father.

*　*　*

There was nothing he could do, but I stayed there with him until he could leave. We tried to visit mother, but were turned away. No visitors allowed. Of course.

There isn't much to say here. She struck an officer in front of witnesses. There's not much of a chance of defense for that.

There was a trial a week later. It lasted about five minutes. She was found guilty and sentenced to hanging. Then she shocked everyone there by asking for clemency, pleading her belly as cause. No one expected that; not even my father knew. The trial was adjourned to allow for a medical exam to be performed, and we went home.

That was the last time I saw my mother. We received a post several days later stating that her execution had been commuted and that she was sentenced instead to transportation, which had already been carried out.

I'm sure you're familiar with transportation, and it was about the same then as now. You're loaded on a ship and sent to New London, on the edge of the Sea of Tranquility. Once there, you're required to work for the British Lunar Administration, usually in the mines, until the price of your transport has been paid back. After that, you're free to go. Of course, the process generally takes about ten years. Even if you live that long, bone starts to permanently degenerate after three years, making it impossible to ever return to the Earth. Luckily, there's always jobs open with the BLA. Dangerous, low paying jobs, of course, but what do you expect?

* * *

My father was a broken man after that. He took to drinking hard. He built an illegal still in the shed, claiming that we could make some extra money selling the whiskey, but I don't think he ever sold a drop of it.

He didn't talk too much anymore, but he started taking me out with the gun, just like he had Sean. We had a bit more time together, and he taught me how to shoot, how to clean it and keep it working. He showed me the proper way to get sulfur from the water filters on our house. He showed me the potash filters he had set up with the manure piles in our garden to distill the potassium, and how to mix it all together with charcoal to make a simple black powder. He also showed me the mold he kept under his bed to make the balls for the musket.

Then, one day about two years later he never came home from work. I went out searching for him the next day and found that an English guard has been killed and robbed in Derry, and that my father had been arrested for it. As far as I knew, my father hadn't set foot inside Derry in years, but the truth rarely matters in cases like this. "Innocent until proven Irish."

He was allowed no visitors, and the trial was closed to observers.

I was allowed to attend the hanging, of course.

* * *

After that, I was on my own. At fourteen, with no real skills or trade, it can be a rough life. I ran my da's still for a while, and made enough money to scrape by. Apparently there's a closet market for Irish moonshine, particularly in England. Of course, I also had the sulfur and potash filters, and there's always a market for explosives these days, even simple ones.

I did alright by myself for about a few years between that and any odd jobs I could pick up. Then came the riots in Derry. By the time the army was done "quieting the situation" most of the countryside was burned to the ground, including my house. Apparently "quieting the situation" includes dropping firebombs on rural villages. Funny old world, isn't it?

I was able to save a few things from the fire. I got out some photos of my parents, and of Sean. And I took my father's gun, as well as all the powder and lead I could haul.

This time, the English had pushed us too far. Irishmen were taking up arms by the thousands, all across the countryside. Not knowing where else to go, I decided to head toward Castlecomer. I figured I might as well pick up the fight where my father left it off. The same fight that my family had fought for centuries. I knew there was a good chance that I would be the last of my line to take up the fight, but better that the Murphys go out with a bang than with a whimper, right?

I met up with more folk as I made my way south. I was actually even a bit amused when I found out they were calling themselves Sinn Féin. Some things never change, I suppose.

Of course, other things stay the same, as well. We fought our best, but it took less than a month for the army to track us down. The drones took care of things from there. Now, of course, the drones they use are far more humane, public opinion being as important to the government as it is.

Instead of explosive rounds, they release a highly charged plasma field. The charge from the field floods the nerves in your body, overloading them with pain signals until they shut down. It'll knock you out for a good four or five hours until your nervous system recovers. Feels about like being dropped in a vat of boiling oil, too. The English have never been too clear on the whole "humane" concept, I think.

So, the drones came, the pain started, I passed out, and I woke up here in my cell. Apparently, the courts are a bit backed up right now, what with all the criminals they've been catching. A guard told me last week that orders from up high are that no more than two hangings per day are to be held in each city. After all, they wouldn't want stories of mass executions spreading. That would be inhumane.

That's my story. It's how I've ended up sitting in this windowless English cell awaiting my fate. You're only in for stealing, so you should be out in a few years. Maybe you can tell my story to someone else.

It's bad enough to think about being dead, but dead I can handle. It's not like I had much left to live for anyway, right? My family is dead, and my family's musket is melted to slag. I hate, though, to think about being forgotten. If no one remembers who you were and why you died, what's the point? We have to be remembered, because the next generation has to keep up the fight. Otherwise, we'll never be free.

SICK DAY

Wayne Cole

Wayne Cole has been podcasting since 2009. He has released serialized fiction based on the post-apocalyptic setting "Skies of Glass", audio fiction based on his RPG character Richochett from the "Knights of Reignsborough" actual play podcast, and written articles on various topics for Fear the Boot and www.ideologyofmadness.com. He and his wife often work with various local animal charities and have two adopted dogs and two adopted cats. His pets frequently show up in his works of fiction in some form.

The tree branches swayed as the wind blew through them, causing the shadows on the ground to dance wildly. I could hear birds chirping, dogs barking, and a car alarm going off in the distance. In other words, it was a perfectly normal Thursday—with only one exception. I had never been sitting on my back porch in the middle of a workday before.

It wasn't that I didn't like being outside. Quite the contrary; I loved being outside. It was one of the few things I could do to relax. Long hours at work and a list of projects around the house just didn't leave time for it. I had plenty of vacation time saved up at work, but I never took much of it because returning to work after time off just meant a larger stack of work waiting. That thought led me to refresh my e-mail and see five new messages waiting. I sighed as I worked through them.

I had to be near death to take a sick day, and while I felt horrible that morning it was not my choice to take off. My boss was afraid that I would infect the whole office when I showed up the day before and couldn't go a half hour without a coughing spell so he had sent me home with strict instructions that I could not return until my fever broke or I could hold a conference call without needing my mute button to avoid coughing in people's ears. Instead I went to an Urgent Care and spent a half hour on a breathing treatment before being prescribed a round of pills and an inhaler. That didn't stop the e-mails and I spent most of that morning constantly checking in to see what was happening without me and if I could keep work from piling up.

I felt the cool breeze against my cheek and leaned back in my chair. It felt good. There was something about the fresh air that just made me feel better and helped fight off the coughing spells. I shut the laptop and set it on the table next to me. Tilting my head back, I closed my eyes and took in a deep breath. "Why can't everyday be like this?" I asked out loud and then immediately answered my own question after a small coughing spell. "Because I have a mortgage, car payments, bills, and all those other responsibilities that need money."

That thought process naturally led me back to my laptop, but as I reached for it a cold nose stuck itself in my palm. Chloe, my black boxer/lab mix, had decided that she had enough of my work for the day. She put herself directly between me and the laptop while proceeding to lick my hand. Her big eyes stared at me and she lowered her head. Her face just screamed for attention and as I rubbed her behind the ears my resolve melted away. "Come on girl, let's go for a walk."

Chloe had been around me all morning, being a good dog and not causing a fuss while I ignored her entirely. I wasn't sure if I was physically up for a walk to the park, but I would have gone to work that morning if my boss hadn't told me to stay home. If I was willing to push my health for work I should at least be willing to give my dog the same level of consideration. I grabbed my inhaler and tucked it into my pocket. A quick snap of the leash on her collar and we were ready to head out. I was hoping the walk would help alleviate some of the guilt I was starting to feel about ignoring her.

She was overly excited about the walk and I found myself struggling with her leash. While it was difficult to control her I had to admit that I was feeling pretty good about the walk myself. I tried to remember how long it had been since I had taken her out like this. If it was too long ago to remember then it was certainly too long, and I started feeling guilty again. The park was straight ahead and I realized that I had never taken her wandering through the woods like I had my old dog. Back then it had seemed like I had all the time in the world.

I led her into the woods and we walked together for almost five minutes. She darted around from tree to tree making sure that she sniffed absolutely everything. Suddenly, she snapped to attention and started barking wildly. She pulled tight against her leash and I found myself struggling to keep hold of her. I had seen her behave like this when there was a squirrel around, but never so strongly. The sheer force in her pulling caught me off guard and a coughing fit came upon me. I struggled with the leash, but lost my footing and fell to the ground hard. The leash slipped from my grasp and I looked up in horror as Chloe ran further into the woods.

I was hacking and choking for breath as I pulled myself up to my feet against a tree. "Chloe," I gasped between coughs. I remembered my inhaler and fumbled in my pocket for it. I was wheezing pretty heavily by the time I got the first spray in. I had been doing so well I had almost forgotten about the respiratory infection until it left me doubled over.

I tried to call her name a few more times as I stumbled after her. She was too far into the woods for me to see and I was getting very worried. Even though she had a collar and was microchipped I still had a feeling that I was never going to see my dog again. She was the one thing that I could depend on and she might be gone forever. I could never catch her. Hearing her bark in the distance was the only thing that kept me moving forward. I carelessly pushed through the woods and didn't see the root sticking out of the ground until it caught my foot.

The world spun as I tumbled down the hill. I could feel rocks digging into my side with each impact until finally I came to an abrupt stop against a tall oak tree. The back of my head smashed against the trunk and as it did I saw a bright blue flash of light. My vision blurred to black and I slumped into unconsciousness.

* * *

There was a licking sensation all over my face. I tried to remember what happened and why my head hurt so much. I struggled to open my eyes and the wet tongue didn't help me. I brought my hands up to push her away, but the skin was smooth instead of furry. My vision blurred back into focus and I let out a loud scream.

The creature before me looked kind of like a dog in size, tail, and head shape, but I had never seen a dog with six legs and antennae before. Its skin was black and white in a similar color pattern to Chloe's. As it bounced around and ran in a circle I realized it was just as energetic as her, too. A high pitched sound was coming from its mouth that would have been painful even if a headache wasn't forming. The closest I can describe the sound is a combination between a dog's whine and a bird's chirp. My instincts told me to run away, but the creature reminded me so much of Chloe I had a hard time thinking of it as dangerous.

I reached up slowly and petted the animal on the top of its head. There was a collar around its neck and when I saw the tag I was hopeful that I might figure out what it was. Instead of words there were strange symbols on the tag that were made up of a series of dots, lines, and triangles. I sighed. The tag not only didn't clear up the situation it made me even more confused. I remembered hearing once that you can't read in a dream, but I couldn't remember if that was true or just an urban legend.

For the first time since waking up I started to look at my surroundings. I was on the top of a hill now, not the bottom. There were still trees around me, but they were wrapped in vines and moss grew up the first seven or so feet of the trunk. Even the bark looked weird. It was more green than brown and was frayed at points. I started searching for landmarks, but nothing looked familiar.

"I'm not going to get any answers lying around here, am I girl?" I said as I struggled to my feet. The animal let out another sharp squeak. When I took my first step forward there was a crunching sound and I felt something give way under my right foot. I glanced down and there was a small metal disk on the ground. It was reflective silver and I could almost see myself in it.

I picked up the disk to take a closer look. There was a small rectangular box attached to the underside of the disk. It was cracked and I could see a wire being pinched by the crack. I reached down to push the wire back in and yelped in pain when I got a hard shock from it. Out of reflex I flung the disk away and it smacked hard against a tree trunk. There was a flicker of light around the disk and a rock appeared around it. The image faded in and out and I thought I could smell the distinctive scent of burning electronics. I hoped that I would remember all these details when I woke up, because this would be a dream I could entertain people with at parties for years.

There was a loud high pitched screech behind me and I spun to see what it was. There was a person standing there screaming at me. It looked so much like a human that I might have actually thought it was if not for the four arms and antennae. While I was pretty sure it wasn't human I could only guess by her soft facial features, long blonde hair, and shapely breasts pushing tightly against a sweatshirt that this was a female. Her skin was almost yellow and her facial features didn't quite match any nationality I was aware of. Her thin cheek bones helped to draw focus to a small slightly pointed chin.

When she saw my face she stopped yelling. She held all four hands up in a placating manner. I listened closely to the sounds she was making. They were starting to sound more familiar and she was speaking much slower. "Anata wa nihongo o hanasemasu ka?" That time they almost sounded like words. Finally she said, "Do you talk English?"

"Yes, I speak English," I replied excitedly and her face lit up in a smile that rivaled my own. It was then that I noticed the sweatshirt she was wearing was also in English. It was for *Galactic Peacekeepers*, my favorite, albeit slightly corny, science fiction TV show. I wondered where she had one custom made because a four sleeved version couldn't be official. *How strange dream logic is,* I thought, *that I would wonder more about the sleeves than the arms that were in them.*

"Good," she said speaking slowly and in an accent that sounded like a blend of Japanese, English, and the occasional mixed in clicking sound. . "Are you okay?"

My mind raced with questions and I had a hard time deciding which to ask first. "Yeah, I'm fine. Where am I? Who are you? What are you? What's that animal? How do you speak English?"

Her face wrinkled in what I can only guess is confusion. "Whoa, whoa, slow down please. I'm good with English, but it is not my first language. I think you asked a lot of questions. Can we start over?" She pointed to herself with her top right hand. "My name is Cera and you are on..." She paused and her antennae twitched as she thought. "There isn't an English word for our planet because Earth hasn't found it yet. You *are* from Earth, right?"

"Yes." I couldn't think of anything else to say.

"Oh goodie." She clapped both sets of hands together and did a little jumping motion like an excited child. She started to talk again in the first sounds that I could not understand and then stopped herself. "I could tell you the name of our planet in my language, but it would probably just sound like noise to you." She smiled at me. "I couldn't really make out any of your other questions so I'll ask one of my own. What's your name?"

"James." I was even more convinced now that I was dreaming, but she was kind of cute as far as strange dreams go, so I decided to play along. If I thought I was awake I probably would have had a breakdown by then. "I'm on another planet?" She nodded her head. "How did I get here then?"

She made a motion with her four arms that I think was shrugging her shoulders. "I don't know. I only figured you were from Earth because of how you look." She pointed to the rock that was fading in and out around the silver disk. "I'm here to look at that. The boss called and said they were getting power fluctuations and were losing signal. It's supposed to be my day off, but I figured since this is almost in my back yard I would just take Cricket for a walk." She reached down and petted the strange six legged creature for a few moments then walked over to the silver disk.

Kneeling down, she picked up the disk and flipped it over. She pulled a small black box with a cable hanging from it out of a pouch in her belt. The cable plugged into the square box on the bottom of the disk. There was a spark and she let out a gasp. Her black box lit up and I could see it had a screen with scrolling information on it. After a moment she looked up at me. "What did you do to this thing? I'm going to have to replace the whole unit."

I started to answer, but all the moving had gotten to me and my coughing fit returned. I struggled to get my inhaler and took two quick puffs. My arms wrapped around my stomach as I gasped for breath that finally did come. I wheezed and slumped to the ground against the tree.

When I looked up Cera was reaching one hand out towards me with a look of pity on her face. "That cough doesn't sound good. Maybe we should get you out of this cold." I took her hand and she helped me up. "I live real close and I need to grab a spare receiver to replace this thing anyway." When I didn't move, she said, "Look, I don't have all the answers for you, but I bet I can explain a lot. If you stay out here you are just going to get sicker or someone else will find you. Come back to my place, get warm, and we can figure out what to do next. Okay?"

I nodded and started following her through the woods. I was burning up and the walking didn't help. She moved fairly fast, but every time I found myself struggling to keep up she seemed to glance back and slow down for me. When I didn't think I could walk much further we came out of the woods at a large fenced-in back yard. The chain metal fence had a triangle design in it and I noticed that there were gates not just on either side of the house, but one here at the back as well.

The house itself was a pinkish color with flat outer walls made out of a smooth metallic material. Its shape was typical of a house on Earth except the roof was made out of a reflective metal and was curved like a dome instead of coming to a point. I could see other houses nearby and they all had a similar shape, though none of them were so brightly colored. The front yard was higher than the back so I could only assume we were going into the basement.

Cera held the gate open for me and I nearly tripped as Cricket shot past me into the yard. He ran in circles around Cera until she opened the back door and let him into the house. Looking up at me, she motioned towards the door so I stepped inside. I was instantly struck by a wall of heat. It was easily over 90 in the house and I froze in place, trying to adjust to the sudden shift in temperature. The sweat that had been beading up started pouring off of me.

Cera for her part hadn't noticed my reaction. After I stepped in she came in and walked around me. She had pulled off her sweatshirt to reveal a blue t-shirt with more symbols like what had been on Cricket's collar. "Cera," I gasped. "It's a little hot in here for me."

She looked back at me. "Really?" Her antennae twitched again and her head tilted slightly to the right. She smacked herself on the forehead with her top right hand. "Oh yeah, your climate is different than ours, isn't it?" She walked over to a closet and started sorting through a box on the floor. "I always forget about that because it's so close. I always forget to adjust the temperatures to match ours when I'm doing my translations, too. Ah, here it is." She came out of the closet with a device that looked similar to a tiny flashlight. She held it up to me and hit a button on the side. A blast of cold air hit me in the face and it was suddenly much easier to breathe. "Here you go. Just press this button here and you should be good."

She rushed over to a couch with very short arm rests and cleared off boxes, electronic tablets, and small items that I could have sworn were toys. "Have a seat. I need to get that new receiver programmed before we can talk, but you can watch some TV while you wait." She rushed paused at the bottom of a stairway and held up a small black cube. There was a flash kind of like a camera. "Wow, I can't believe I actually have someone from Earth in my house." The cube projected a picture of me sitting on her couch. "Perfect, shame I can't show it to anyone without spending the rest of my life in jail." Turning back she ran up the stairway.

I sat down on the couch and aimed the fan at my face. The room was still hot, but with the air directly on me I could finally start to adjust and relax a bit. Dream or not I could get used to a mini-fan this powerful. I looked around the room and took it all in. There were posters on two of the walls and I was surprised to see that I recognized one of them as another science fiction show I watched. Above the posters, just under the ceiling a shelf ran all the way around the room. It had some sort of train running around it. Finally I found what I assumed was the TV. It was a large flat black screen in front of me. There was a remote control sitting next to me so I grabbed it and pressed the round button on top.

The TV lit up and the first thing I saw was a TV show from Earth called *The Watchers*. I couldn't understand a word they were saying, but I knew the faces. I chuckled at the irony of this being the first show that came on. It was about aliens spying on humanity to determine if they were a threat. After a mishap with the volume buttons that nearly deafened me, I started to flip though channels and found there to be an even mix between their programming and ours. My biggest surprise was when I turned to a channel playing Earth pornography.

There was a gasp behind me and I turned to find Cera standing at the bottom of the stairs holding a box. Her face was turning an even brighter shade of yellow. She yelled out a string of her language that I could not understand and the TV turned to *Galactic Peacekeepers*. It was in English with the symbols I had come to realize were her language on the bottom of the screen. She spoke quickly and her words stumbled, but I understood her meaning. "The TV doesn't actually need a remote. It is voice activated. That was a gift from a friend of mine because I'm such an Earth junkie and all."

She moved over to a table and started opening up the box. I could see that inside it was another disk like the one I had broken in the woods. She pulled the tool out from her belt pouch and plugged it into the device. She was avoiding eye contact with me and not looking anywhere near the TV. I decided to try and break the tension. "So if I'm on another planet, where did you learn to speak English? How do you even know about Earth?"

She kept her eyes on her work, but her face seemed to return to its normal color. "This is a receiver. We discovered your planet about fifty years ago. We find your entertainment so interesting that we set these things up to capture your broadcasts and sent them back here."

"What kind of broadcasts?"

"Everything. Sports, music, movies, reality TV...pretty much anything you broadcast. I love science fiction, personally. Sometimes it's hilarious how much is wrong, sometimes it's fascinating what you actually got right, and it can even be used to predict what technology you will develop next. What's not to love?"

"So does everyone here speak English?"

"Oh no. Most people only get the dubbed channels. I'm a bit of a geek, though, and like to watch the broadcasts in their original form. I don't even like the subs because they are always wrong. Because of my job I can get my hands on the originals and translate them myself. I have a bit of a following."

"So how do the receivers work?"

"Well, we have a transmitter on your world and a receiver on ours. The transmitter captures all of your broadcasts and sends them back here through...Well I don't know the English word for it. I'll be honest. I just fix the things; I don't really understand all the science behind them. Even if I did I don't know if there are English words for it. Just trust me: it works. I've been doing this since I was a teenager." She hit a few more buttons on her screen and unplugged the cable. She came over and sat in a chair opposite me.

I tried to let it all sink in. Not only did aliens exist, but they were hooked on our mass media entertainment. I was more than a little conflicted about *that* being their introduction to humanity. I was really hoping that this was a dream because if it was real I could only imagine their opinions of Earth. "If you've been watching for that long why haven't you made contact?"

She laughed at me and despite all our differences it was a laugh just like a human's. "Please, didn't you hear me say we watch your TV? If we made contact you would either riot or try to kill us. You people just aren't ready for something like this." She looked at me and her face grew a little brighter yellow again. "Well, maybe some of you are, but as a whole you people just couldn't take it. Besides, you have far more interesting entertainment than we could ever hope to and there are people making a ton of money off of translating and rebroadcasting it. Our worlds aren't so different that money doesn't mean power here, too. People making money would do anything to keep making money. We're afraid that direct contact would contaminate your culture and spoil the entertainment."

"Okay, so you just watch us. That sounds really creepy by the way. That doesn't explain how I got here."

"I have no idea. I just hope you didn't break the transmitter on your side."

"Couldn't you just send another one? I could take it over when you send me back."

Her eyes opened wide and she let out a bit of a gasp. Her antennae twitched a lot and when she spoke she was energetic. "Sending something to Earth takes mountains of paperwork and approvals. It has to be done sometimes, but the oversight is huge. There's no way we could send you back like that without letting people know you were here and that's a bad idea. They're serious about not letting you people know about us so they might not let you go back at all. Besides, plenty of the wrong people would pay a fortune for the chance to directly examine a human."

For the first time since arriving on this strange planet I was worried. My shoulders slumped and the hand holding the fan slowly sang into my lap. "So I'm trapped here?" The realization that I would never see my friends, family, or dog again was sinking in. All of the problems with work that I had been worrying about just hours before seemed so small in comparison.

She glanced down. "You could always stay here with me. I could keep you safe right here in my basement and we could watch TV together and you could tell me stories about Earth, and..."

"I can't stay here. I have responsibilities back home and a missing dog to find. I still don't understand how I even got here. I just fell down a hill and when I woke up your dog was licking me. This has to have something to do with those disks."

"Yeah probably." Her face suddenly lit up with a huge smile. "If we can figure it out and keep it a secret maybe I can come to Earth. I'd love to see it first-hand. I'd have to come in disguise, of course, so your government agents don't try to cut me up like in *Visitor From Another Planet*. It'd be totally worth the risk to see a new movie in an actual movie theatre."

I could tell how excited the idea made her. "What about your life here though? You would risk your job trying just to see a movie. Think of all the trouble you could get in. It sounds like you could get into enough trouble just trying to help me."

"Yeah, but so what? Life isn't about a job, that's just what you do to pay for life. Life is an adventure! And what adventure could be greater than visiting another planet?" Being on another planet without a way home, I couldn't quite find her enthusiasm in it, but I also couldn't help smiling with her. "Besides, I wouldn't just lose my job, I'd probably go to jail. Just means I can't let us get caught."

I found myself wanting to know more about this woman with such a strangely infectious energy. "What would you do on Earth if you could come for a visit?"

She looked me in the eye and seemed to seriously think about the question. "Well I suppose I'd have to find some cute Earth man who owed me a favor to show me around. Dinner, movies, and shopping sound like the perfect night out to me. Just think of all the neat memorabilia I could get if I were actually on Earth."

"You don't think you would stand out a bit?"

"That's not a problem. I cosplay human characters all the time for conventions. I know all the tricks." She was smiling, but her face was turning a slightly darker shade of yellow again. "Um, that's enough about me. What about you? What do you do for fun back home?"

"Work doesn't really give me much time for fun. I like to read, but I don't have much time for it so I listen to audiobooks when I'm in the car. At least, I do when I'm not on a conference call. Other than that I mostly just watch TV. I can usually get a few things done while it's playing in the background."

She looked at me with her mouth slightly parted and I felt a little nervous under her gaze. "You have all those opportunities for fun and culture on your planet and you spend all your time working?"

"What I do is important, I…"

She cut me off with a raised voice."Important? We know of 123 planets with life on them. Do you think your job is any more important than any of the jobs that people on those planets do? Do you think it means anything here? On your own world in 100 years will anyone remember whatever it is that you did? Gah! That is the one frustrating thing about you Earthlings: you get so wrapped up in defining yourself by what you do that you forget who you are. You are James and that is what is important not what you do to pay your bills.

"How are you any better? You came out into the woods on your day off."

"Yeah, and you're damn lucky I did." She sighed. "Sorry if I came on too strong there. I love your culture and it just makes me sad to see someone missing out on it. You only live once and you get to live on Earth. Do you know how jealous that makes me? "

"Got to live there," I corrected her. "Do you have any ideas on how to get me home?"

"I still don't know how you got here. How about we go replace that receiver and take a look around where you came through?" She reached out a hand and I let her help me up to my feet. She put her top two hands on my shoulders. "I'm going to do everything I can to help you. We'll find a way to get you back home." Her words were comforting, but I saw doubt on her face. I decided it was best to just nod and let her lead me out the door.

We stepped outside and a nice cool breeze hit me in the face. It felt good after the hot house and I switched the fan off. I heard a shiver behind me and turned to see Cera with her arms wrapped around her chest. "I forgot how cold it was out here. Let me grab my sweater." She turned and ran back into the house.

I stared down at the fan and slipped it into my pocket before she came back out wearing a knit sweater. "Okay, let's go."

I followed Cera through the woods back to the hill where I had woken up. I had no idea how she found the hill because to me the forest all looked exactly the same. I couldn't find any real distinguishing landmarks. When she got to the top of the hill she sat the disk down and went to work on her tablet again. After a few moments a holographic rock appeared around the disk.

"We're in luck. I'm getting a signal from Earth. It looks good so far. I'm getting a nice strong signal from your side and it is acknowledging the sync commands from this side."

"So the receiver can transmit too?"

"Oh yeah, it has to be able to update the transmitter from time to time. Besides, when you rip a hole in space and time it doesn't exactly go one way." She seemed to think about what she said for a moment and then hit a few more buttons on her screen. She stood and walked around behind me. I turned to face her.

"Well, James it was a pleasure meeting you." She grabbed me by all four arms and pulled me into a deep kiss. Two of her arms slid around my back and two went over my shoulders. It was a bit awkward, but my arms slid between hers to return the embrace. Her tongue was softer than any human woman's that I had ever felt. I don't know if it was the best kiss I had ever had, but it certainly was in the top five. As suddenly as it had started the kiss was over and she shoved me with all four arms away from her and onto the ground.

I fell for what had to only be seconds, but felt like an eternity. I could see the smile on her face and two of her four arms rose up to wave goodbye to me. Then I felt the ground crash into my already sore head and the disc dig into my back. I saw that strange bright blue light again and then everything faded away.

* * *

I woke up to the sound of barking and a tongue licking my face. Chloe had climbed up on my chest and was doing everything she could to wake me up. The coughing fit that came from the extra pressure was expected, but I was not going to let her get away again. Reaching out, I wrapped my left hand around her leash and gripped as tightly as I could. Gasping for breath, I pushed her off and pulled myself into a sitting position against the tree. She fought to keep licking me.

I was back at the bottom of the hill leaning against the tree that I had hit my head against. I didn't have a watch on and I had left my phone at home so I had no idea what time it was, but judging by the sun I had been out for at least an hour. As I sat there petting my dog I began to wonder if the whole thing had happened at all. My head was screaming in pain and after touching the back of it with my hand I realized that I was bleeding. "Come on, Chloe, let's go home."

I realized that I didn't exactly know how to get home, since I had blindly chased her through the forest when she ran away. I never had the greatest sense of direction and the lack of any street signs didn't help. Thankfully the forest was fairly small so I knew if I wandered long enough I would find my way out. After a few minutes we found our way out onto the side of the interstate. I couldn't help but sigh, realizing we were on the far side of the park and had quite a long walk to get home. I took solace in the fact that at least I knew where I was now and how to get home from here.

Eventually I found myself at my own front door. By that point I had convinced myself that Cera and everything that had happened was just a drug-induced dream. My head was still throbbing to support my theory. I dug around in my pants pocket looking for my keys. Instead I pulled out the small flashlight-shaped fan. A smile crept across my face as I hit the button. Nothing happened. I glanced down at Chloe, who was sitting patiently waiting for the door to be open. "I guess I broke it when I fell down."

I grabbed my hidden key, duct taped to a branch on the bush by my front door. As soon as the door was open Chloe ran inside, almost tripping me, and went straight to her water bowl. I set the fan on top of the entertainment center and collapsed on the couch. I had been feeling better after sitting on Cera's couch for a while, but I was still sick and all the walking had really taken its toll. For at least an hour I lay there, having the occasional coughing spell, just thinking about the day's events and wondering if I had finally gone crazy. Eventually Chloe jumped up on the couch and curled up by my feet.

I looked up at the laptop lying by my head, where I had left it just before the walk. I had been gone for hours and I cringed at the thought of all the work e-mail that would be waiting for me. I reached up for it, but as I did the fan on the entertainment center caught my eye. I thought about Cera's care free attitude and everything she said to me. I imagined her smile and remembered her kiss before sending me home. I pulled my hand back from the laptop. "Work can wait until I feel better."

I turned on the TV and *Galactic Peacekeepers* came on. I knew that from that day on the show would always remind me of her. I found myself hoping that she would find a way to Earth someday and I swore that no matter what I was doing even if it was a work day I would drop everything to take her to a movie.

BLIND BARTHON

Ryan J. McDaniel

Ryan J. McDaniel is an aspiring author and is credited with starting what was then called "The Fear the Boot Anthology" back in March, 2013. Ryan, who is eighteen years old, is the youngest contributing author to Sojourn. This is his first publishing and editing credit. He is usually found playing PC strategy games, reading a history book, or nagging himself for not writing more. Ryan lives on his five-acre Illinois home with his family.

There was a boy named Barthon who was a child of Highspring River. He had reached his fourteenth winter and was ready to become a man. Barthon's mother came to him, lifted his arm and said: "Look, your arm is strong and the time is right. Pick up your spear and carry your shield, for you must become a man." Barthon was ecstatic; he picked up his spear, carried his shield, and ran outside. The Highspring-men joined together, shield to shield, shoulder to shoulder, and heart to heart, as they made ready for battle. With shield, axe, spear, and bow, the Highspring-men marched forth and raided the nearby thrall villages. Barthon did excellent battle. As his spirit soared in the shifting of feet and the dance of iron, Barthon reached the height of life and became a man. Barthon cleaved through his enemies just like his forefathers had in the age of old. But they had cut down frost trolls that wished to swallow the world in darkness, not hapless thralls. His elders were impressed, but they would never show it. To be a good warrior was to be expected. After the battle, the thrall girls were aligned, and the task of choosing three was always given to the boy-turned-man. Barthon chose without anxiety. Great congratulations were given to Barthon for his choice of thrall girls.

What usually occurs to boys-turned-men is that they choose a wife, or a thrall girl with good blood, and they would live in Highspring fathering sons and raising daughters. However, that would not be the case for Barthon. After Barthon left with the men to fight the thralls, Barthon's mother fell into a deep sleep.

In her dream she realized that she was standing upon ice. It stung her bare feet, but after the initial surge of pain she became used to the prickling feeling. Around her swirled mists and mystery, and her eyes could not pierce the veil. The voice of Odor, the god of battle and destiny, spoke to her and revealed the path that her son had to walk.

"Why?" was the only question that Barthon's mother could bear to ask.

"Your people have grown weak with bad blood," the god said. "Once, long ago they had the strength to fight off the frost trolls, the most terrible and vicious creations. Now they spend their time fighting thrall tribes. Strength must be imbued back into the blood of your people. Now go and tell your son his mission."

Barthon's mother awoke and the furs of her bed felt as cold as ice. She was not a heartless woman, though, and she did not steal the little joy that the boy had left. She let her son attend the feast that stretched into the night, allowing him to enjoy his last hours of normalcy. Pulling him aside, she told him his destiny: Barthon was denied the right to marry a local girl and forbidden from marrying any girl along the Highspring River or the land of Athalia. He had to journey forth, away from his home, and trust in the guidance of the gods to find his true wife.

He was annoyed at his mother's weirdness. Through laughter Barthon brushed off the idea. "No," Barthon's mother snapped. "You shall not taunt the will of the gods."

Now Barthon was angry. Here he was, a man who had just killed men twice his age, had chosen the best thrall girls, and was currently being celebrated by the elders. Now he had to put up with this! Barthon stormed off and went to Biemgar, and informed him of Mother's madness. Biemgar was a drunkard and tonight, as his boy became a man, he was laughing and drinking at a voracious rate. *Could there have been any better time for Biemgar to dismiss his wife?* Barthon thought. But upon hearing the story Biemgar sobered up and was serious. "And where did Mother say she heard this command?"

"From the gods, Father," Barthon said. A strange light came into his father's eyes.

"There shall be no disregard for the gods in Highspring! You will fulfill the wishes of your mother."

"Or else what?" Barthon asked clenching his fist.

"Or else you will be banished from Highspring and a high bounty will be placed for your death." Considering the issue over, Biemgar continued laughing and joking with his friends. Barthon was quiet and drifted to the shadows of the room.

*   *   *

As he prepared to step forth on his journey, his mother strode up and announced: "May luck travel with you, Barthon, and do not come back until you have chosen your true bride. If you return with the wrong bride then you will be sentenced to exile and a high bounty will be placed for your death."

Barthon left the Valley of Highspring and went west, and traveled through forests of pine and evergreen. Leaving the woods of Athalia he entered Normomdor. From the region's twisted coastline the Normons set forth into the insanity of the seas as they face down waves the height of mountains. With barely a moment's hesitation the Normons charge into the maw of a whirlpool or joyfully sail off the edge of the sky. Only to return months later speaking strange tongues, dressed in gaudy wealth, and holding dark-skinned wives by their sides. The Normons are married to the craziness of the sea, and grow sick if they cannot smell the salt in the air. To the ports Barthon searched. After a few days of searching, he found a fisherman's daughter and Barthon loved her. He was about to claim her when Galadra, goddess of war, in the form of a she-wolf confronted him. "Do you not see what is wrong, Blind Barthon?"

"Why she-wolf," Barthon said, "there is nothing wrong, she is perfect and I love her!"

"Blind Barthon, where is her fierceness? Her hands are soft and strangers to the handle of an axe. When raiders come, she will quail in fright and run, leaving your child defenseless. Your wife should be as I: a she-wolf at heart."

Luckless Barthon lowered his head and continued his search. Traveling south, following the Emna River, he entered the land of Astrogad. For every mile there seemed to be another tribe and each one more deadly and warlike than the next. The land was both poor and rich, the forests both full and empty. Astrogad was neither fully plentiful nor widely desolate. It contained both wealthy and poor tribes. And so the tribes were either powerful or subjugated. It was here that Barthon discovered the warrior's daughter. Her features might have been made of stone, but men were lured to her all the same. She was so cold, so rigid, so pure and noble that men wished for the glory of claiming her icy hand. Barthon loved her and was about to claim her when Fesia, goddess of love, came to him in the form of a doe. "Do you not see what is wrong, Blind Barthon?"

"Lovely doe," Barthon explained, "I followed the advice of the she-wolf and chose a woman as strong and fierce as the mountains. Why do you question my choice? She is perfect in every way and I love her."

"Blind Barthon, where is her love? Her eyes are stiff and her voice is of dying things. So fierce is she, that when your child cries, she might kill it, seeing it as a sign of weakness. Your wife should be as I: a loving doe."

Luckless Barthon lowered his head and continued his search. Barthon went south into the land of Thallonia. It was a fair country without deep forests, thick swamps, nor towering mountains. The land was fertile and there was enough for everyone, with plenty to spare. They were ruled by what they call a *king,* which was like a chief but weaker and wealthier. Laws and paper govern the land instead of strength and blood. Compared to Barthon's homeland it is a land of peace and comfort. There he met the farmer's daughter. Like last time, right before he claimed her, Galira, goddess of strength and earth, came to Barthon as a heifer. "Do you not see what is wrong, Blind Barthon?"

"What could it possibly be now," Barthon sneered at her, "creature of the plow?"

"Blind Barthon, she is beautiful, she is loving, and she will fight for your child. But she is missing something, you fool. She will not endure the hardship of the north or of the grueling days of her work. Your homeland will fall upon her, like it falls upon everyone, and she does not have the power to resist. She will become resentful of her work, will poison your house, and turn your son against you! Your wife should be as I: a strong heifer."

Tired Barthon lowered his head and continued his search. To the east Barthon traveled, and arrived at the wide grasslands of the Reach. Here the land was of spun gold bending to the caress of the wind and shining with the gleam of the sun. The people in the Reach were horse-masters and did not live in houses but rather traveled with their herds across the land. It is here that Barthon discovered the horsemaster's daughter. She was perfect: she-wolf, doe, and heifer, all in one. Barthon loved her intensely because he felt that his quest was over. As he opened his mouth to make his claim, Thruem, god of wisdom, appeared, disguised as an owl. The boy of fourteen was furious, yet again proven wrong by the gods.

He took his axe and attacked.

The owl was unimpressed. It flapped its wings and a piercing light blinded Barthon. He fell and thrashed in the tall grass. The foolish boy was powerless against the brilliance and purity of wisdom. Fear took him as he could not see the world. All was darkness. Struggling onto his knees Barthon begged for everything, and most of all forgiveness. Chuckling, the owl gladly relinquished him and gave him back his sight. He had seen this countless times before. "Do you not know what is wrong, Blind Barthon?"

"No, wise owl," Barthon said, relieved that his sight was returned to him. "I have learned much during my quest and nothing I know is wrong with the horse-master's daughter; she is perfect in every way and I love her."

"But you two are of the same age. And isn't it wise, Barthon, for young men to marry older women, and likewise for older men to marry younger women? For young men, such as you, are rash and thoughtless and require the maturity of a lady to cool your fires. While old men are rigid and need a budding flower to awaken their days."

"But wise god," Barthon said, "is it not also wise to marry a girl that is sure to be fertile? Isn't the familiar more safe to marry than the strange?"

"Where is your ambition, Barthon? Have you forgotten it underneath a rock? Is that the place where you left your wits as well? Gold is just beyond the horizon and here you settle for manure. Go beyond yourself and seek greatness and never look back. Marry the horsemaster's daughter if you wish, I shall not stop you. Your children will receive only what you have claimed. Barthon, you are a part of something much larger than yourself. You are a single strand in the great tapestry. I speak of wisdom, Barthon, that which you do not possess."

Tired Barthon was homesick and fed up with his journey. Desperate, he asked for the recommendation of the wise creature. The owl told him to head north into Harrowfell. The pine forest of Harrowfell was dark and grim, full of strange creatures and stranger men. The forests were said to never end and to extend to the very edge of the world. The ancient red trees were taller than the mountains and touched the heavens. The trees whisper with the breeze and hold its breath as night begins. The elk appear and vanish as quickly as an extinguished fire. Harrowfell was a place to find witches and blood mages, not a true bride.

Barthon found a cabin next to a stream. It was the home of a woodsman's widow. She had all the qualities that the gods had told him a wife should have. However, this time Barthon did not love her. She was a stranger to him. It was only his fear of the gods that made him claim the widow's hand. He returned home with her and Highspring rejoiced because he had chosen the true bride. Life continued on like nothing had happened. And for the time the woodsman's widow was still a stranger to Barthon. It was only a year later when it happened, when he heard the cry of his first son, when he saw his lineage in her arms, wrapped in furry skins. All at once, the veil fell from his eyes and his wife was no longer a stranger. Hope and love filled him up to the brim. She was all the animals and more. Her name was Edda, and she was an elf queen.

TOP OF THE HEAP

Tom McNeil

Tom "Clintmemo" McNeil lived in New England in the mid 1960's, he gained his love of science fiction from reading Asimov's Robot novels and watching reruns of Star Trek. Though he has long thought about writing, this is his first published work. In addition to Science Fiction (which he admits he reads far too little of), he enjoys fantasy, games of all kinds, tae kwon do and music. He is currently a software developer that lives in Louisville, Kentucky with his loving wife, brilliant daughter and three overzealous dogs.

The Palmy Pines is a beachfront cafe in the Thousand Island section of the Saint Lawrence river. The café emitted an aroma of garlic and butter that was carried down the beach by the gentle river breeze. People walking the beach often stopped to take in the smell. By late afternoon, they would be lined up to put in an order.

The café was constructed out of logs made from both the palm trees that were becoming more common in the area and the pine trees that were disappearing. The pine trees used to be everywhere in this part of the world, before the climate change of the 21st century turned most of Canada into a temperate zone and the Thousand Islands into a tropical paradise. Most of the United States was now a desert and everything along the equator had become an oven of raging storms. A growing population chasing after disappearing resources spawned a world-wide revolution. Billions died. The survivors fled towards to poles. It took a miracle of science to stop the runaway global warming but by then, the world had changed forever. Two hundred years passed and only a handful of people survived from that time. One of them was Dale Medici.

Dale Medici walked into Palmy Pines in the very late morning, not long before the daily lunch crowd. The bartender waved at him but none of the patrons noticed him. People often failed to notice Dale. Dressed in a tee-shirt, khaki shorts, and carrying a brown satchel over his shoulder, he was not too tall, had brown hair with a touch of grey, and was a little overweight. He was the type of person you would forget seeing once he passed by, if you even noticed him at all. Dale had spent a very long time learning to look unimportant.

The cafe was about half full. The sun had almost reached its highest point, its heat blocked by the high roof of the cafe. The three open sides let plenty of airflow through. The cafe was cooler and darker than the beach. Dale let his eyes adjust for a few seconds as he scanned the cafe. He was looking for an old friend.

Dale spied his friend at the bar, munching on a fish sandwich, a bottle of beer perched on the counter in front of him. Grant Summers looked like he was in his mid-fifties, but Dale knew better. He was shorter than Dale, with grey hair still containing hints of the red it used to be. His left arm was an obvious prosthetic composed of a metal alloy. It had an obvious hinge at the elbow and fingers that looked too thin and too flat. It was fully functional but several generations out of date. His right leg was also prosthetic—a much newer model, also functional but appearing so realistic that to the casual observer it just looked like a normal human leg, as fleshy and hairy as the one it was crossed with against the bar stool.

"So," Dale said, sitting himself on the barstool on Grant's right, "I hear this place has killer potato wedges." Grant looked at him, puzzled, and then his eyes grew wide in recognition. He swallowed hard.

"Dale?" Grant asked quietly.

"In the flesh," Dale responded.

"What in the world are you doing here?" Grant asked.

"Happy birthday, old man," Dale answered with a smile. Grant sat up, cocked his head to the side and then chuckled.

"Wow," Grant smiled. "It's been so long, I'd forgotten."

"They say memory is the second thing to go," Dale quipped.

"Oh?" Grant asked mockingly, "and what's the first?"

"I forget," Dale answered with a grin.

"You never get tired of that joke. Do you, Dale?" Grant asked.

"Some things just never get old," Dale answered.

"Well," Grant sighed, "we would know all about that, wouldn't we?" He paused, took another drink from his beer, then took a quick glance around the café. No one else was paying any attention to the two old friends.

"How long has it been?" Grant asked.

"About a hundred years," Dale answered quietly. "That restaurant in Reykjavik. You were eating a fish sandwich then, too, as I recall."

"Fish is brain food," Grant said. "Our brains are special. We have to keep them fit."

"Special doesn't begin to describe it," Dale whispered.

Grant stared at Dale for a moment then nervously took another look around the cafe. He picked up his beer bottle and took another long drink.

"We probably shouldn't hang around here too long," Grant said and then took a big bite of his sandwich. Dale's growling stomach reminded him that he hadn't eaten yet. He ordered something for himself to take with him and then paid for both meals, in cash, over Grant's objections.

* * *

The two men strolled down the beach. Dale munched on his order of potato wedges as they went. Both carried liters of water, which, like the wedges, were contained in biodegradable paper containers. The beach was not too crowded, despite the glorious weather. Children ran up and down the shoreline, squealing with delight as their parents "kept an eye on them" while tanning or hiding from the sun under the safety of an umbrella. The rolling surf added a calming, ambient background.

"I'm still not quite used to this weather," Grant said. "Didn't we used to make jokes about Canada being in perpetual winter?"

"That and all the bears," Dale answered, shaking his cup of potato wedges.

Grant sighed. "I miss bears." He took a few more steps and added, "The future didn't turn out the way we expected it to, did it?"

"Two hundred years and still no flying cars," Dale said.

"We did advance in some ways," Grant said, waving his artificial arm around in front of him.

"True," Grant admitted. He looked down into his cup, selecting his next morsel.

"It's too bad about all the knowledge that was lost in the war, though," Grant said.

"Some of it is probably better lost," Dale muttered.

"Well," Grant said after a few more steps. "I think I'll just hide out here and wait for whatever comes next."

"You picked the perfect place to hide out," Dale said, finishing another potato wedge.

"Did I?" Grant asked.

"Oh, yes," Dale answered, brightening up. "It's hard to hide video surveillance devices on a wide open beach and the constant sound of the waves interferes with anything trying to pick up audio. Large crowds of people come and go on a regular basis so it would be easy to slip away if you needed to. Plus, it's not obvious. When people think of the beach, they think of the ocean. They'd be looking in Maine or over in British Columbia, not on an island in the middle of the Saint Lawrence. Even if the People's Security Police did think to look for someone in this area, there are a lot of islands around here to search. It would be hard for the PSP not to tip you off to their presence."

"Huh," Grant said. "I never thought of any of that. I just came here because I like the beach."

Dale laughed. "I guess maybe it's better to be lucky than good," Dale said.

Dale looked at the others on the beach. Their bodies were mostly tan and sometimes nude. Several sported obvious prosthetic parts made of metal, plastic or some type of composite. A few others had prosthetics that were far less obvious to those with a lesser trained eye. There were also a handful of people with prosthetics so obviously artificial that they no longer looked human, "bugmen", as they were called. One bugman was running down the beach on his five long spidery legs, each a different shade of purple, at nearly the speed of a groundcar, snapping up garbage with four long tentacles, each a different shade of red, with a three-fingered hand on the end.

"I remember when they just got tattoos," Dale said out loud.

"Tattoos never bothered me much," Grant responded. "It was the piercings. I remember a girl in some music video that had a chain that ran from her nose to her ear. What was the point of that?"

"Now look at them," Dale said sadly. The bugman scrambled by them, snatching up an empty water bottle from the sand.

"You know," Grant said, "I always thought you would end up like that. You were the systems guy, after all. If anyone of us would have ended up as mostly machine, I figured it would be you."

"Not me," Dale answered. "I like working with them but I don't want to become one. I don't want to end up like Sanderson. He wound up a brain in a jar attached to a building."

"I wonder whatever happened to him," Grant mused.

"He died," Dale answered, chewing on another potato wedge. Grant stopped in his tracks.

"Really?" Grant asked. "How did it happen?"

Dale took a drink from his water before answering. "They said it was a power failure," he said, finally. "Some think it was self-induced. It happened about three years ago."

"You mean after two hundred years and all those upgrades he just decided to switch himself off?" Grant asked.

"Looks like it," Dale answered. "He wouldn't have been the first of us to commit suicide."

As they moved down the beach, a commotion erupted behind them. The two men stopped and turned around to see what happened. Apparently, the bugman that was cleaning the beach got too close to one of the nude bathers. He had set the tip of his stiff, composite, spidery leg down on top of, and consequently right through, the bather's organic, soft, fleshy calf. When Dale looked, the bugman was holding the bather upside down, their intersecting legs forming an 'X' in the air.

"God damn you!" the bather wailed, flailing his arms about. The bugman scrambled to remove the man with his tentacles, sliding him down and off the tip of the bugman's thin leg, apologizing as he went. It left a thin trail of blood along the bugman's leg.

"I'm so sorry, sir," he managed to say, setting him gently back in the sand.

"You're *sorry*?" the man screamed. "Is that all you can say? What the hell do I look like? Body trash? God damn, that hurts!" Already, the bather's internal medical nano-bots were working to repair the damage. There had been very little blood. In less than an hour, there would be no visible sign left. Dale and Grant turned and continued down the beach.

"You really need to have that arm replaced, Grant," Dale said seriously, looking over at his friend.

"Why?" Grant asked. "It still works well enough."

"Because it's a model J27," Dale answered. "It's almost as old as you look. In a few years, people will start to wonder. Artificial limbs aren't like classic cars. People don't drive old ones just for fun." Dale paused. "How did it happen, if I may ask?"

"Train accident in Sweden," Grant responded. He held up his artificial hand in front of his face and turned it over, glancing at both the palm and back, waving the metal fingers in the air.

"The snow bomber?" Dale asked.

"Yup." Grant sighed. "I'd been in hiding for a hundred and fifty years and I almost got killed by an eco-terrorist. Sometimes I forget that just because we won't die of old age doesn't mean we can't be killed."

"Believe me. It's never far from my thoughts," Dale said.

"Actually," Grant said, "I was thinking about that when I had this arm installed. It has a special hidden feature." He held the palm of the hand up for Dale to see, showing him the tiny whole below the wrist. Dale whistled.

"Nice," Dale said. "Particle projector?"

"Yup," Grant said. "But you're right, I need to have it replaced or modified. It is looking a bit like an antique."

"What about the leg?" Dale asked. Grant looked at him in surprise.

"You noticed that?" Grant asked. Dale nodded. "Bone cancer took that one about twenty years ago," Grant answered. "Very nasty business. By the time they found it, it was easier to just replace it."

"It's a Q45, isn't it?" Dale said admiringly. "Excellent craftsmanship."

"Yes," Grant chuckled, smacking his artificial leg with his real hand. "No hidden weapons here, though. What about you?"

"I'm all natural, 100 percent organic," Dale beamed.

"No way," Grant answered, grasping Dale by the elbow with his still natural right hand. Both men stopped in the sand.

"Oh, they're not all original parts," Dale conceded. "I've had all my organs replaced at least twice, plus both arms and legs. The left leg three times, in fact. I either had them all regrown or took something from an organ donor. I even had my skin reconditioned a couple of times."

"All organic?" Grant asked. "That must have been incredibly expensive."

"Oh, it was," Dale conceded as they continued walking. "There are probably only a few hundred people on the planet that can afford that many organic procedures. Since most of those people do it for religious reasons, I just tell the surgeons I don't allow artificial substances in my body. I'm sure some of them have suspected something over the years, but I pay them so they don't ask questions. Besides, I never use the same surgeon twice."

"What about medical repair bots?" Gant asked.

"Not a one," Dale bragged. "I figure if I made it through my childhood riding a bike without a helmet, I can make it a few centuries without doing anything too dangerous. I play things pretty safe these days." Grant shook his head in disbelief.

"Why bother staying organic?" Grant asked. "Look around. Artificial limbs are everywhere and it's not like you can hide a gun in a real arm."

"It has its advantages," Grant said mysteriously. "Also, I guess at least part of it was that I felt like I had been altered enough already."

The two men continued strolling down the beach, the surf on their left. Up ahead on their right, a small party of religious protesters stood, holding placards above their heads, the rotating messages printed to look like spray paint, switching every few seconds: "God Hates Upgrades," "Upgrades are the Devil's Tools," "Do Not Remake What God has Made." The protesters called out to people on the beach, advising them to repent. They were largely ignored.

"And then there are some things that never change," Dale said after they passed the protesters.

"There's always someone that thinks the end is near." Grant added. "Religion will never go away. It doesn't matter how many questions science answers, there will always be more."

"I thought you didn't believe in God," Dale said.

"I don't," Grant answered. "Not really, anyway. Though, sometimes I wonder if the climate disaster wasn't God's way of punishing us."

"God didn't cook the planet," Dale said. "People did. Remember? We were there when it happened."

"Oh, I know," Grant said, "but after two hundred years, maybe my perspective on things has changed." He stopped and looked back at the protesters. "They'd probably stone us if they knew who we were. I doubt the PSP would even stop them."

"Then let's make sure they don't find out," Dale said, moving on.

Grant looked wistfully out over the surf. Another bugman was out swimming in the river, he and his fins barely visible, obscured by the violence of his own wake, but towing three water-skiers. A bugman and bugwoman were flying above the beach on butterfly wings, occasionally fluttering together for a brief moment of affection. Grant looked up at them and smiled.

"I would like to try that sometime," Grant said.

"Which?" Dale said, grinning. "The flying or the romance?"

"Either," Grant chuckled. "Haven't you been married a few times?"

"More than a few," Dale conceded. "Seventeen, in fact, but I gave it up after Lucinda. She figured out who I was and blackmailed me. I faked my death to get away from her. She thought she got all my money, but it was really only a small part. I had dozens more aliases she was not aware of. Still, it would have been a lot cheaper to just kill her, and quite a bit more exciting." Grant stopped and looked sternly at Dale.

"I hope you're kidding about that," Grant said, his hands planted on his hips.

"Oh, I am completely serious," Dale said with an absolutely straight face. "It would have been *much* cheaper to kill her." Both men looked seriously at each other for a moment. Dale smiled and then Grant started chuckling.

"You had me going for a second," Grant said, still chuckling. "But you need to be careful about making jokes like that. I'd hate to think you were a murderer. Besides, even *talking* about murder can get you a visit from the PSP these days. That's a little more excitement than we need right now."

"You know," Dale said after a moment, "that's the problem with living too long. Everything gets boring."

"What do you mean?" Grant asked.

"Don't you ever feel like you've done everything before?" Dale asked. "I don't have to work. I have more money stashed away then I could ever spend. I never find entertainment satisfying. Sure, some aspects of technology have advanced a lot in the last two hundred years but all it has allowed us to do is experience the same simulated thrills in less time and with fewer consequences. I've done all the fun things I ever wanted to do ten times over. The only thrill I get any more is doing something that I can't repeat." Grant stopped, held his arms out to each side, looked around and took in a deep breath. He looked back at Grant.

"Well," Grant said, smiling. "I still like the beach." Both men chuckled.

"Come on," Grant said, still laughing. "Follow me. My place is just over here."

* * *

Grant lived in a small white house made from a simulated wood composite. It sat in a cul-de-sac facing the road, the back of it facing the beach. The front door was near the left side of the house. Across the front of the house grew a neat row of lilies, alternating yellow and purple. The grass was freshly cut and devoid of any weeds. Grant led Dale through the front door and into the kitchen, which was not as neatly kept as the front yard. The counter was covered in old papers and several dishes and glasses were piled up in the sink. Grant apologized for the mess, then went into the refrigerator, retrieved two bottles of beer, old fashioned glass bottles, and led the way out the back door.

The back of the house had a large deck that sat only a few steps above the beach. The water was less than thirty feet away. The shore of the mainland was at least a half a mile off. There were two deck chairs and a small table. Dale took his satchel off his shoulder and sat in one of the chairs. Grant took the other chair, opened both bottles, and handed one to Dale. They both looked out at the waves and listened to the surf for a moment. There were a few cargo ships gliding quietly over the water. Gulls flew by, squawking as they went. They could barely hear the playing children back towards the cafe. They saw no one on the beach in either direction.

"This side of the island has a private beach," Grant finally said. "Only the residents are allowed on it. The rest are old retirees so they don't swim much. I'm the youngest one out here."

"I doubt that," Dale corrected.

"Well," Grant added with a smile, "as far as they know."

"Then here's to the ignorance of your neighbors," Dale said tipping his bottle.

"May they remain forever blissful," Grant answered and they both took a long drink. "We may have lost some knowledge since the old days, but I'm glad we never forgot how to brew."

"Do you really think your neighbors would turn you in if they figured out who you were?" Dale asked.

"Probably," Grant answered, "but I'd rather not find out. Do you think anyone is still looking for us?"

"I evaded a PSP security detail two years ago in Seattle," Dale admitted. "I escaped by buying my way onto an underground shuttle to Perth at the last minute."

"How did you manage that?" Grant gasped.

"Cash," Dale replied. "I handed the crew a duffle bag full of hundred credit tokens. They were more than willing to escort me through all the security checkpoints and right into the train's command module. I sat on the control deck and watched the security detail rush across the platform to try and stop the shuttle. Now *that* was a thrill and not one I want to repeat." Dale smiled. "The crew actually let me drive the shuttle for a few minutes about halfway under the Pacific."

"What tipped off the PSP?" Grant asked. "I thought you wiped us out of the records when we went into hiding."

"I did," Dale said. "A new picture of me surfaced. It was found in a just-opened time capsule. One last posthumous parting gift from Lucinda. She wasn't totally convinced about my fake death. I was at a stadium when a facial recognition scanner picked me out."

"What in the hell were you doing at a stadium?" Grant asked.

"I really wanted to watch a baseball game," Dale confessed.

Grant laughed. "Didn't you say something before about being careful?" he asked.

"I only made it because I was careful," Grant objected. "I have contingency plans set up everywhere I go: escape routes, alternate identities, stores of cash." Dale counted off on his fingers. "It's a good thing all that talk about all-electronic currency never came to fruition. People always talked about the convenience of cash but the real reason it never went away is that they like to be able to buy things without other people tracing it. Sometimes they just want to remain anonymous. Sometimes they need to break the law."

"Well then here's to a couple of old lawbreakers," Grant said, raising his beer to toast.

"To us," Dale responded. The both took long drinks again then set the bottles on the table. Dale belched. "That," he added, "is damn good beer."

"Yes, it is." Grant said. "The glass bottles make all the difference. I'm out," he added, getting up. "I'll get a couple more." He conjured his own belch and walked into the kitchen. Dale could hear the glass bottles clinking as Grant began rummaging through the refrigerator.

"Hey, Dale," Grant called from inside the house. "I was just thinking. How did you find me, anyway?"

"Oh," Dale began. "The truth is. I never really lost you. I've been keeping tabs on all twelve of us since we went into hiding." Grant rushed back onto the deck with a bottle in each hand.

"You've been spying on us?" he asked.

"No," Grant said. "Nothing so dramatic. Just keeping track of where you were, or were most likely to be. Given that I had a starting point and that I knew all of you well, it wasn't really that difficult."

"So," Grant said. "You knew about the train in Sweden."

"Yes," Dale admitted. "I was just being polite. I was afraid you didn't want to talk about it. I'm sure it was traumatic."

"It was," Grant said, glancing at his artificial arm. He sat down again and handed Dale an open bottle. "I've been thinking," Grant said. "When we had our brains reconditioned, did the process change us, beyond the obvious, of course?"

"What do you mean?" Dale asked.

"Well," Grant said. "Look at Sanderson. I seem to remember him always trying to one-up everyone—always getting the fastest car, newest gadgets, the hottest girlfriend. Look what happened to him. He upgraded himself almost completely. And you? You were the systems guy but you were also the facilitator, keeping track of everything, keeping us all on task. And look at you now. You still keep tabs on all of us and you have all these aliases. Heck, I bet you have all their account numbers and passwords memorized."

"I do, actually" Dale confessed.

"Heck, look at me," Grant continued. "I was always the peacemaker, the long term thinker, the dreamer. And where am I? Sitting on the beach!"

"Interesting," Dale said, "but what do you think it means?"

"Maybe the process changed us," Grant said, "subtly. Maybe it made us, I don't know, *more* like us. Maybe it focused our personalities."

"Maybe we're all just in a rut," Dale countered.

"Ok," Grant laughed. "Maybe you're right. Maybe I am overthinking it." He drummed his fingers on his beer bottle. "By the way," he said finally. "How many of us are left?" Dale reached into his satchel, pulled out a small notebook and flipped to an earmarked page.

"Five," Dale responded. "That's really why I came to see you. I wanted you to know you were number one now."

"Number one?" Grant asked.

"The twelve of us were the first ones to have our brains reconditioned," Dale explained.

"Well," Grant interrupted. "We did invent the process. That's why we were together."

"Even if all the ones we processed later had not been executed by the revolutionaries," Grant continued, "you would still be the older than any of them." Grant slumped in his chair in thought.

"What about Marcus?" Grant asked. "He was 59 when we had the process. I was only 54."

"Marcus died last fall. Carol was older than you, too, but she died back in 2273. That makes you number one. Congratulations. You are the oldest living person on earth. How does it feel to be the king?" Grant looked down at the deck chair that was his throne and the house that was his castle.

"I look more like a hermit than a king," Grant said.

"Well, you are also a criminal, according to this society, anyway. You and me both," Dale responded.

"Then here's to us," Grant said, making another toast. "Here's to two ancient criminals, forever on the run. Let's hope we can avoid execution for a while longer." They both took a long drink. "By the way, how did it happen? What killed Marcus? The last I heard, he had locked himself up in a palace down in Antarctica, surrounded with so much electronic security no one could get anywhere near him. Surely he didn't kill himself."

"Spontaneous replacement failure," Grant explained. "Limbs, organs, circulatory nano-bots, they all failed at the same time. Without them, he died in less than a minute. He didn't have very many organic parts left."

"How could all of his parts have failed at the same time?" Grant asked. "Something must have caused it."

"Good old fashioned EMP," Dale said. "Someone set off a fair sized pulse right next to him—destroyed all the circuitry."

"Someone murdered him?" Grant gasped. "Why? Did they find out who did it?"

"They didn't even look," Dale said, "once they figured out who he was. Marcus was a criminal after all. They just confiscated his money, sold his belongings, and went on their merry way. As I recall, it wiped out about a third of their national debt. I'm sure they'd probably thank the murderer if they ever found out who it was."

"Such a waste," Grant said, shaking his head.

"Yes," Dale said, "we were. We could have done great things, had some of us not gotten power-hungry."

"That was a long time ago, Dale," said Grant, "and those people are all dead. And besides, it wasn't us. It was the ones we reconditioned."

"Yes," Dale responded, slamming his bottle onto the table. "The ones we reconditioned. The monsters we created. It would never have happened if not for us. Too bad for them the revolutionaries confiscated all of our records after we disappeared. I'm sure it made hunting them down much easier. The revolutionaries needed someone to blame and who better than the greedy unaging? They were going to live forever, so they wanted it all. It was their greed that cooked the planet. I'd say the blame was well placed! But they didn't get all the culprits, did they? They may have killed all the monsters, but their creators escaped!"

"We didn't know what was going to happen," Grant interjected. "We were scientists. We were trying to make people's lives better!"

"Organ replacement was all the rage when we started," Dale raved on. "After all, a heart is just a pump that circulates blood. Who cares what the poets said about it. A kidney is just a filter, the lungs are merely a system for exchanging gases. It's the same with all the organs and limbs—except the brain. Modify the person's brain and you change them forever. Replace the brain and you replace the person. 'Save the brain,' we said, That was all the mattered! If you could save the brain, you can live forever—for the right price. We succeeded all right, and we gave it to ourselves first. Oh, we told ourselves it was an experiment, but we knew better. Then we had to give the process to the world, except that it was so expensive only the richest and greediest people could afford it. All it did was make them richer and greedier. Maybe you were right. Maybe it did change them as well as us. It was their greed that nearly destroyed the planet." Dale was almost in tears. Grant looked at him his eyes wide open in shock.

"Dale," Grant finally said, "it was a long time ago. No one blames us anymore. People have moved on."

"People's memories may be short," Dale said, "but their history archives will outlive us all. We are wanted criminals. The People's Secret Police are looking for us still, even if they don't remember why. We won't live forever. Our days are numbered."

"Well, in that case," Grant said, clearly trying to calm Dale down. "I think I'm going to just enjoy sitting on this beach a while longer. After all this time, I've learned to enjoy the simple things." The two sat in silence for a moment.

"I'm sorry, Grant," Dale said finally. "Sometimes I get carried away."

"Don't worry about it," Grant said softly. He then used a voice of mock command. "As king, I command you to drink and be merry."

"Well," Dale said finally and more calmly, "you are the king and it is your birthday." Dale then sat up and smiled. "That's right. I almost forgot your birthday present." Dale began rummaging through his satchel. "Just what every king needs, a court jester." Dale pulled out a doll about half a meter tall. It wore a brightly colored jester's outfit, complete with curly slippers and a three-coned hat with bells on top. It came to life as soon as he set it on the table, dancing and juggling. It bounced about with a mischievous grin, its jingling bells cutting through the faint background sound of the waves rolling up on shore. Grant watched and laughed, clapping his hands as the jester executed a double back flip.

"That's great!" Grant laughed, forgetting about their argument. "Where did you find this?"

"I picked it up in Perth while I was down there. It's even programmable. I added my own routine. Watch," he said, reaching out and squeezing the bell that hung from one conical section of the jester's hat. "I'll show you the trick I added. First, he walks on his hands." The jester began to walk on his hands, just as Dale predicted. "Then, he springs back to his feet and juggles for a bit." The doll complied, tossing itself back onto his feet, then tossing his three balls into the air. It deftly juggled the balls for a few seconds. "Lastly, he jumps up into a triple front flip and lands on one knee with his arms outstretched."

The jester did each movement even as Dale said them, but as he landed on the table, there was a faint popping noise. The doll collapsed in a heap. Grant jerked back and his prosthetic arm fell with a thud onto the table. He looked at

Dale in horror, but the expression turned to pain as his face became wrinkled and flushed.

"And then," Dale said, "he ends his routine with a good old-fashioned EMP burst. Why? Because our time has passed. Not that it matters, but with you gone, I move up to number three. Someday, I'll be number one, then the only one. And when I'm the only one left, I'll make sure knowledge of the process we discovered dies with me. Then we will be no more. No one deserves to live forever."

Grant fell sideways onto the sand and went into convulsions. Blood was seeping out of his ears. He lasted less than a minute.

"Goodbye, Grant," Dale said to himself. He picked up the jester and tossed it into the river. It immediately began to dissolve. He pulled out his notebook, flipped it to the earmarked page and scratched out Grant's name. After looking at the next name on the list, Dale began walking back up the beach toward the ferry. It was time to go to Alaska.

THE BOOKRUNNER

Matt Forbeck

Matt Forbeck has been a full-time creator of award-winning games and fiction since 1989, designing games and toys and writing stories of all sorts. He has twenty-seven novels published to date, including the award-nominated Guild Wars: Ghosts of Ascalon *and the critically acclaimed* Amortals *and* Vegas Knights. *His latest work includes the* Magic: The Gathering *comic book, the MMOs* Marvel Heroes *and* Ghost Recon Online, *and his novel* The Con Job, *based on the TV show* Leverage, *as well as the* Dangerous Games *trilogy of thrillers set at Gen Con. For more about him and his work, visit* Forbeck.com.

I enter the shop, and I can smell the books already. After a glideboat ride through the fresh air of Manhattan's wider canals, the musty stench makes my nostrils itch. I wrinkle my nose and repress an urge to sneeze.

The store's owner—a young Caucasian woman with a long red ponytail— sits behind a glowing display counter to the left, and she glances up from an old copy of *LIFE* as I walk in. I don't need to call up the instant ID layer in my optical display to peg her as a Luddite. The cats-eye reading glasses perched on her nose mark do that for me.

I punch up the layer anyhow, and my NSA facial recognition software kicks in. The glowing text that hovers around her labels her as Adina Clark. She lives in a boat-up apartment in Chelsea with at least three other people, probably more either bunked in illegally or timesharing their beds. She homeschooled through Khan University, graduated three years ago, with honors.

Officially, she's unemployed because officially this building doesn't exist. It was scheduled for demolition a decade ago, but the city council doesn't have the stomach for it, so here the shop squats in a space that once housed a jazz club. It's stacked floor to ceiling with shelves and shelves of books: paperbacks, hardcovers, even deluxe leather-bound slipcases. Everything from coloring books to encyclopedias, all used and long past their expiration dates, their pages yellowing, even crumbling, sliding through their slow-motion decay into dust.

A crimson halo appears around Adina, and I blink at the alert. The system inside my eyelids scans my retina and IDs me as having proper access to the NSA's criminal database. Her long rap sheet scrolls out alongside her. Nothing violent, mostly information charges like possession of unlicensed materials. That's one of those so-called victimless crimes that no one cares much about, me included, but she's also been arrested for dealing and trafficking. So far, no prosecutor's been able to make those stick.

She puts down the magazine and wipes her hands on her jeans as she stands to greet me. They get plenty of older Asian-American men like me around here, I'm sure, but she appraises me like a first-edition Hemingway. Something about me—maybe my shaved head, or more likely my cheap suit— must scream "undercover cop."

"Can I help you, Officer?"

I fake a smile I'm sure does little to affect her opinion of me. "I didn't think a bookseller would have the optics to recognize me."

It's a dig at the fact that few people in her profession can afford retinal displays like the ones burning in the back of my eyes, but it glances off her emotional armor. She doesn't bother to return the smile. "I know the smell of bacon, but not your name. Can I see your badge?"

I fish my ID out of my jacket and flap it open on the glass-topped counter. A weathered copy of *No Country for Old Men* stares up at me past it.

"Agent Lao Wai of the National Security Agency?" She looks at me over the rims of her glasses to compare my face against the image on the card.

I nod to confirm her suspicions.

"You're a meme killer."

I stuff my badge back in my jacket. "We prefer to be called vaccinators."

She rolls her eyes at me just like my great-granddaughter does, and I repress the urge to smack her. I've had a lot of practice at that over the years.

"Aren't you trolling in the wrong threads?" she says. "Don't you have some sort of vicious clip of cuddling kittens you need to rub out?"

I make a point to peer around the store. "Dangerous information comes in all kinds of formats. Some of them might not look like as much trouble as *The Prepper's Bible* channel on the surface, but that just makes them more pernicious."

"Those guys were just loudmouth assholes exercising their First Amendment rights."

"And their Second."

"Once you went after them, sure. You could have just left them alone."

I grimace at her naiveté. "Rights come with responsibilities. Like not shooting at federal officers serving a warrant."

She crosses her arms. "Do you have a warrant?"

"Are you going to shoot me?"

She repeats herself, stopping between every word. "Do. You. Have. A. Warrant?"

I shrug. "Isn't this place open to the public?"

Without looking back, she points at a sign attached high on the bookshelf behind her. It reads, "We reserve the right to refuse service to anyone."

"It's all about rights with you, is it?"

"I think you have a responsibility to respect them."

I turn and stroll deeper into the store. "Actually, I have a sworn duty to uphold the law."

She slips from behind the counter and follows me as I browse the books on the shelves, inspecting them at random. Maybe they were placed in some kind of order at one point, but if so that plan's long been abandoned. They're loosely grouped in sections by genre or subject, but when I spot a *Dungeon Master's Guide* stuffed next to a set of Osprey books about the Hundred Years' War in the history section, I see they haven't applied much rigor to that criteria either.

"What do you have against books?" she asks as she trails behind me, watching me like a mother wolf anxious about her cubs.

I run a finger along one shelf. It comes back covered with dust. "Nothing. I learned how to read on books. Not the electronic kind. The ones you hold in your lap while you turn their pages."

I glance back to see her goggling at me. "Just how old are you?"

"Old enough to know better. But then, so are you."

She narrows her eyes at me. "You're a Methuselah. Indentured, right?"

I spread my arms wide in surrender. "Guilty. What gave me away?"

She snorts. "No one with an actual job can afford total organ replacements like that."

I gesture toward myself. "It's not the principle that gets you. It's the maintenance."

"So you signed away your life for your life."

"It beats dying."

"'I would rather die on my feet than live on my knees,'" she quotes.

"I'll send flowers to your funeral then."

Most people poke at me about my unnaturally extended life out of jealousy. They're both repulsed and intrigued at the same time. They don't enjoy the idea of having to work for a sponsor forever, but they appreciate the notion of a long, lingering death even less.

The trouble is that sponsors don't offer up deals like that unless they have absolute trust in you. The procedures are too damn expensive, and you can't just repossess upgraded organs. So if you want them, you have to earn an offer within the span of a single lifetime—and show unwavering loyalty along the way. Few people are up for it, and the top candidates compete for a small number of slots.

Most of them grow out of it. Age has a funny way of reworking your principles for you.

I pull one of the books off the shelf. A hardcover of *The Hitchhiker's Guide to the Galaxy*. I check it for a price but can't find one.

"How much does something like this run?"

"One dollar. Cash."

"Only a buck? That seems like a bargain. But who carries real money these days?"

"You'd be surprised."

I pat my pockets and grimace. "Guess I'm out of luck."

"You could bring in a book to trade."

I cock my head at her for teasing me like that. "I don't happen to own any. Not anymore."

She shrugged.

"You realize that selling books without a license is a federal offense."

"Of course."

"And do you have such a license?"

"You already know the answer to that."

I scan her face. "You don't seem too bothered."

"I don't sell books here."

I heft the *Hitchhiker's Guide* in my hand. "You just offered to sell me this."

She shakes her head. "You asked me how much it runs, and I told you. But we don't accept money of any kind here, virtual or otherwise."

I glance around at all the stacks of books, and it hits me. "You're running a library."

"We call it a book-lending cooperative. Libraries have to keep electronic copies of their records and make them available to the government. As I'm sure you know."

"Do you keep records of any kind?"

She shakes her head. "We operate on an honor system."

I can't help but laugh. "An honor system? For paper? Do you know how much these things are worth on the black market?"

She pushes out her chest, defiant. "And yet here they are. People see the value in our un-library, even if you don't."

"Call it whatever you like. We can let a judge figure it out."

I let the implied threat hang in the air as I wander deeper into the shop. She waits for a moment, thinks about it, and then tags along after me.

"Do you like your job?" she asks.

I consider the question. "Like is a strong word for something I've been at as long as I have. I respect it. It's a job worth doing."

"You make it sound like blocking the free exchange of ideas is something noble."

"I've saved a lot of lives."

"By keeping people from thinking."

"From thinking the wrong thoughts."

"And who gets to say what's wrong?"

"The NSA, also known as the employees chosen by the appointees of your duly elected representatives. And the Supreme Court. Don't tell me you're too young to remember Hollywood."

I look at her, and I know I'm right. She couldn't have been born when that happened. Still, no one grows up in this country without learning about it. Even revolutionary terrorists like the ones she hangs out with.

"Holly*weird*, you mean?"

"Let me guess." I point at the books all around us. "You 'read' about it."

She shudders with frustration, but she still recites the facts as she knows them. "April 11th. A screenplay supposedly from the hottest writer of the day is released to all the studios simultaneously. It contained weaponized memes, and everyone who read it became a frothing sociopath. They go on a killing spree that only ends after the feds shut down the entire internet and permanently cordon off the city." She swallows. "I suppose you're going to try to defend the bombing."

"A lot more people would have died."

"So you say. But does that make it all right for the U.S. government to murder thousands of its own citizens?"

"If it saves millions?"

"Bullshit. The government wanted to kill those people. They wanted to destroy Hollywood and cripple the internet, and they were all too happy to use whatever excuse they could find. Or construct."

I laugh, and she glares at me. "Oh." I wipe the wry look from my face. "You're serious. How can you be an educated person—a reader, no less—and believe that black flag nonsense?"

She counts off the reasons on her fingers, one at a time. "The government had the means, the motive, and the opportunity. And just look how well it's turned out for them. People are afraid to read."

"You're living in a different dimension than me. Where I work, the President made the only call she could to combat a nasty, hyper-infectious meme like that. You either cauterize the wound, or you let it fester until it kills the entire body."

She goggles at me. "You really think you can weaponize an idea."

"You don't? Just look at history. Watch how certain revelations sweep through it, both good and bad. Everything from dictators to religion to even science. The internet only made it worse. Now ideas can spread globally at the speed of electricity, with little in the way of friction to slow them down."

She opens her mouth to interrupt me, but I press on.

"In the old days, people just stumbled over the ideas, concocting and spreading them on their own. Once we figured out the science behind them, it was only a matter of time before someone turned it into a weapon."

"You've been working for the government too long if you buy all that."

I allow myself a vicious grin. "You want proof?"

She gives me a dubious nod.

"Ever see those notices about flashing lights they put on some videos or games? How they can induce seizures in some people?"

"In epileptics." She doesn't see how this connects.

"That's an accident, a strange circumstance that shows just how external stimuli can affect susceptible brains. But if you know what you're doing, you can do the same thing on purpose, and through the language centers of the brain instead."

She lets loose a troubled sigh. "I think you need to leave." She's knows that's not going to happen.

I say a word no language can spell. I modulate my tone and pronunciation in precise ways, and I tailor my efforts especially for her.

She hears the word, and she freezes. She doesn't realize it, because it's probably her first time, but I just induced a petit mal seizure in her.

She stares forward, her eyes wide open but blank, her mouth hanging open without a word on her tongue. I walk around and stand behind her, and I wait.

Half a minute later, she blinks and gasps. "Where did you go?"

I tap her on the shoulder as gently as I can. Despite that, she screams.

She whirls around and spies me standing there, giving her a little wave. She screams again.

"What? Did you just teleport?"

I shake my head. "It only seemed that way to you."

She backs away from me, her skin crawling in revulsion. "Don't ever do that again."

"I think I made my point."

She draws a ragged breath. "What do you want?"

"Out of life?" I know what she means, but I want to hear her say it.

"From me. Why are you here?"

"I'm here to close this place down. Unregulated offline information storehouses are just too dangerous."

Her face grows drawn and pale, as if she's been sick for weeks. "You let people read whatever they want to on the internet."

"Within well-monitored limits."

She fades another shade of white. "You admit you're controlling the content on the internet?"

"Me personally, no."

"But the NSA denies that. Always."

"Every time."

"And that never changes?"

"We get better at hiding it." I give her a sympathetic shake of my head. "What did you expect? We created the internet. We own it."

"It's open source. And global."

"Which means open to us too. We have bots that scour the entire web, aggregating data and hunting for dangerous memes. They locate and eliminate those threats better and faster than any team of humans."

"But they can't work outside of the internet." She looks like she might vomit. "That's why they still need people like you. And so you're here."

"I have a job to do. At the moment, you're it."

"Me?"

"And your shop."

She juts out her jaw. "But I'm not doing anything wrong."

"So you say. But offering unregulated and unmonitored access to books of any kind is a felony."

She tries to act unfazed but fails, her façade starting to crumble. "It's not my place. I just sit here and read."

"Ah, the lies we tell each other. And we just met."

She takes a step back, "I haven't done anything wrong."

"Maybe not wrong. But illegal? Yeah."

Since she's giving me my space, I decide to poke around a bit more. I work my way farther into the shop.

"You need to leave."

"If it's not your place, then you don't have the authority to kick me out."

I've caught her in a trap. To give me the boot, she needs to claim at least custodianship of the store, and if she does that, then I can charge her with that. Which I'm planning to do anyhow, even if she still seems to hold out some hope against that.

"Why don't you go find the owners?" I say with my smarmiest smile.

"You don't want me to do that." She says it like it's a threat.

"Oh, I really do."

She hesitates, and I keep moving. "What will they do with all the books?" she asks.

"The crime scene team will catalog them for the trial. The good ones in decent shape often go to a real library."

"One where you can keep track of the things people read."

"The rest get pulped."

"You can't do that! These books are classics. They aren't making ones like these anymore. Literally."

I turn the corner and stop dead in front of the shelf waiting for me there. It's filled from top to bottom with thick books of onionskin paper bound in crimson pleather stamped with gold foil.

Gideon's Bibles. Hundreds of them all jammed together and forming a wall.

I think about taking one out to examine it, but I fear the entire structure might avalanche down, burying me beneath a stack of moldering scripture.

"That's a lot of hotel rooms raided." I hated working that detail. Most hotels turned their books over voluntarily, but not all. I still check everyone I stay at, out of habit.

Adina stands behind me and gazes up at the books. "People need to read, right? They wind up someplace alone, nothing to do. A book offers them comfort. Enlightenment even."

I scoff at her words.

She slips past me and plucks a book from the shelf. I flinch, but the shelf remains upright. She opens the book and starts to flip through it.

"Have you ever read the Bible, Agent Wai?"

"It's the bestselling book of all time."

"But have you read it?"

I nod. "It's been a while."

"What's your favorite passage?"

I don't hesitate a second. "'Blessed are those who hunger and thirst for righteousness.'"

She purses her lips at me, impressed. "'For they shall be satisfied.'" She finds a page and hands me the book. "This is the bit I think says the most."

Someone had taped a piece of paper there inside the Bible, right between Matthew and Mark, and the words printed on it had been designed to find a spark of sympathy for Adina's cause and fan it into flames.

And damn me, it works.

I look down at the printed words, and before I can help it, I'm reading. The words flow into my head like water through a torpedoed dam, and I can't stop them. I try to shut my eyes, but it's too late.

The weaponized meme's already in my brain.

I fight it hard. My training kicks in automatically, probing the new ideas flooding my mind, hunting for some kind of exception.

I feel like the Grinch. My heart grows three sizes, bursting with books. Mentally, I jump up and down on the words that erupt from them—from every book I've ever read. I try to stomp them back, but they take me like a toddler in the tide.

I have a strained relationship with books. I love them, but I know how dangerous they can be. Despite the fact I work with them every day, they make me feel like a moth charging straight into the flame.

Somehow, I always manage to hold myself back. At least till now. The words in Adina's Bible strap a jetpack onto my back and rocket me straight into the heart of the sun.

As the meme cements its hold, the scent of Adina's free library stops making my nose itch. Now it smells like brewing beer, the scent of rising yeast leaving me heady.

The shelves no longer tower over me like traps. Now they surround me like the walls of my childhood home. Tight, cozy, safe.

Adina herself doesn't seem like a danger any longer. Or a perp I'm here to arrest. She's a curator, a fellow lover of books, a compatriot with a common cause.

When I'm done reading those damned words, I look up from the page, and she eyes me like a teacher who just got her worst student to answer the hardest question.

"You think you're the only one who understands the power of words?"

I shake my head, and my cheeks flush with shame. I want to knock her to the ground, cuff her, and call for a pickup, but the meme won't let me. The library needs to be protected, even from people like me, and that demand echoes in my mind so loud it drowns out everything else.

"This is exactly the kind of thing I'm supposed to be on guard against." I grind my teeth in frustration. "I let you lull me into a sense of superiority. It made me overconfident."

"And the pull of a powerful curiosity didn't help," she says.

"At least I come by that naturally."

I wonder how long she thinks those words will affect me. Could they be permanent? Will they fade from my memory after a while and set me free? Do I have long enough to find out?

I was exposed to words like this during my NSA training. On purpose. They wanted me to know how it felt to get memed, and learn what I could do about it.

The short answer? Not much.

I got over that test meme by staying up for more than forty-eight hours. Then I crashed hard and woke up to a brutal alarm after only a few hours' sleep. That kept my brain from sorting my short-term memories into long-term ones, and once I couldn't recall the words any more, they lost their hold on me.

I had a full NSA support team helping me out that time. I don't think Adina plans on allowing me that kind of aid.

I decide to be blunt about it.

"What's your plan now?"

She stares at me with lost eyes for a moment, then walks back to the front of the store. I follow in her wake. I don't have to. I want to, which makes it that much worse.

"Did you bring anyone with you?" she asks.

"I came alone."

"Does anyone else know you're here?"

I shake my head. "No."

She casts me a suspicious look over her shoulder. "But eventually they'll realize you're missing. What happens when they do?"

I shrug. "I'm supposed to report in at the end of the day, but I skip that often enough I doubt anyone will notice until tomorrow morning."

Her shoulders lower a couple inches. She's been holding the world on them, and now that she thinks it won't come crashing down on her, she can relax.

"By then, we should be long gone."

"Where are we going?" Meme-induced camaraderie with her aside, I can't help but be a little nervous. "You're just going to abandon all these books?"

"If we have to." She shows me a sad smile and then gazes at the shelves that surround us. "I'll put out the word, and people will converge on the place and scavenge what they can. If we move fast, we should be able to save most of them."

"And what about the new ones?"

She impales me with a surprised glare. "You know?"

"Shaking down free libraries is a little below my pay grade. They send me after serious smugglers—bookrunners like you."

She blows out a long sigh. "I should have guessed."

"Just be glad you stopped me." I put on a weak smile. It seems to make her feel better.

"More than you can imagine." She pushes her glasses higher on her nose and then leans in and speaks to me in a conspirator's whisper. "Would you like to see them?"

"They're here?"

She grins, her relief growing into giddiness. "Follow me."

She walks me back to the wall of Bibles. I stare up at them, wondering if she'll pull the shelf back on well-oiled hinges to expose a hidden printing press and bindery. It's hard to come by blank paper these days, especially in the quantities you need for making books, but the big bookrunners manage it.

It's like any other prohibition, I know. You can't fight basic economics. Back when the USA made booze illegal, the demand didn't stop either, and the price shot up. Rumrunners brought in liquor just like bookrunners bring in stories now, and they backed their play with bribes and guns.

It got damn bloody. This time around, though, it's about a lot more than money, so it promises to be even worse.

Adina reaches up and pulls a random Bible down. I half expect the shelf to swivel aside like something out of an old horror film. Instead, she opens the book to the title page and hands it to me. There, in crisp black ink, it reads:

Fahrenheit

451

Fahrenheit 451—

The temperature at which book paper catches fire and burns

Ray Bradbury

Introduction by Neil Gaiman

I haven't read this story since I was a kid, and I don't need the meme's help for the sight of it to make me smile. The fact that it's wrapped in a cover from a Gideon's Bible feels right. I raise it toward my face and inhale the smell of fresh print.

"New insides with an old outside?"

"The covers are the most expensive part of the book, and the Bibles are so thick we can often stick a few different stories inside them. We have them printed in Mexico." She swells with pride. "Immigrants bring them across the border for us, just a few a time, and they make their way north."

"And if they get caught?" The NSA's seen an influx of new books, and we've been trying to stop the flood of them for months. So far we've failed. Now I know why.

"How many Homeland Security officers worry about finding a few Bibles in an immigrant's pack?"

"None." For them to spot the problem here, they'd have to open up the books and read them. Bibles are so common that most people don't give them a second glance, especially ones that look like they were swiped from a hotel room or a dump. A diligent officer might flip through a few pages, but most DHS agents are skittish about actually reading the printed word. With what's storming around in my head, I understand why.

"So far," Adina says.

I offer to return the book to her, but she refuses to accept it. "Keep it," she says. "How long has it been since you've read a real book?"

"For fun?" I try to remember and fail. I end up chuckling at myself instead. "What's next?" I ask.

She freezes. "I'm leaving, of course, but I'm not sure what we should do with you."

"Is there someone you should ask?"

"I wish." She winces and smiles at the same time. "We're not nearly as well organized as the NSA."

"I don't know. Grouping into independent cells that can't give each other away? Sounds smart to me."

"Except when I need a fast answer for a dilemma like this. Do I send you back to work for the NSA as a mole? Do I just take you with me and run?"

"Or do you kill me?"

She blushes, and I know this is the question that's burning at her most.

"I don't know. It seems like we'd be missing out on a huge opportunity if we do, but I can't see how safe it is to keep you alive."

My guts run cold. I want to talk her out of this, but the meme weaving through my head forms a net I can barely see through. "Either way's not safe. But you probably already knew that."

"I don't want to kill you." The stress lines forming on her face show me she's not lying.

"Have you ever? Killed someone, I mean?"

She pales at the question, but she doesn't answer. She doesn't strike me as someone who would kill unless forced into it—but that hardly means she's innocent. Or incapable.

"Have you?"

"It's not easy. But sometimes it comes with the job."

She sets her jaw. I can see sometimes it comes with hers too.

I rub my chin. She's looking for a way out of this situation, and I need to help her find it. "Who else is in your cell?"

"What do you mean?"

"Well, you can't run this whole place by yourself. You must have some kind of help. Maybe they can help us get some perspective on this. How do you get a hold of them?"

She chews her bottom lip. "Betsy's due to take over from me in a few hours."

"Well, we can probably wait that long before we have to decide, right?"

"I don't know," she says. "Do you?"

"No one else from the NSA should disturb us until then. I think."

"What would make you sure?"

"A crystal ball. I'm about ninety percent certain we won't have any troubles." I let the unspoken "but" hang in the air like bait.

"But?"

"Just in case, are there any other ways out of here?"

She sizes me up one more time, then curls a finger at me and leads me farther into the shop. She takes me through a triple-locked back door that lets out onto a fire escape that looks out over a watery courtyard. Someone's bolted a floating dock to it, and I climb out onto it.

I point to a lone alley-canal off to the left. "So you take deliveries in through there?"

She joins me on the dock. The sun's setting somewhere else, and the hole of the sky we can see straight up blazes a fading purple-orange above us. "They come in under the dark of night. It's the only way."

I bob my head in an approving way. Then I lean over and look into the still waters. It smells awful back here, but that's like much of Manhattan these days. You can't chlorinate the canals.

Adina stands next to me and peers into the waters too, watching our dark reflections. I've been wrestling with the meme's restrictions and reconstructions in my head, and I think I spy at least a partial way out. I hate to do this, but I don't have much choice.

First I make sure she's listening. "Adina?"

"Yes?"

Then I say the seizure-inducing word.

I don't have much time, and I have to struggle against the weaponized meme's effects every instant. It compels me to support the bookrunner movement, but it's nebulous about her.

Sure, she's one of them—one of *us*, the meme's internal logic tells me— but I can separate the person from the group. Mentally cull her from the herd.

I kick her into the water, and I watch her sink to the bottom, her unprotected lungs filling with filthy water. Long seconds later, the seizure ends, and she starts to thrash about in the darkening pool. She reaches for the surface, but it's too far and too late.

I reel backward against the railing of the fire escape, and I struggle to catch my own breath too. I've stopped her maybe, but the meme still has its hooks in me good. It can't force me to grieve for her or regret what I've done, but I know I have to stay here and wait for Betsy to arrive to relieve Adina.

What may happen then, I can't say.

I go back into the free library, and I walk through it, trying to ignore the books, but failing. I reach the front counter, and I sit down in Adina's chair behind it.

I crack the Bible she gave me, and I turn to the first page of *Fahrenheit 451*. I begin to read.

The book opens with an epigraph from Juan Ramón Jiménez. It says, "If they give you ruled paper, write the other way."

I wonder if I can force myself to think the other way instead. But I keep reading.

I may never stop.

FORESIGHT

Laura K. Anderson

Laura K. "Jahaili" Anderson picked up her first science fiction book when she was in first grade and she's been in love with speculative fiction ever since. While she generally writes fantasy, she was influenced by Philip K. Dick to write "Foresight." This is her first published work, though she has written one novel that is in the editorial process and has begun outlining her second novel. In addition to writing and editing, Laura is finishing a Master of Arts degree in literature and creative writing, and intends to begin another Master's degree in special education teaching.

The news van rolled into the parking lot amid the shrieks of children and parents desperately trying to reign them in . Marty, in the passenger seat, was looking into the small flip mirror on the visor. Was that a spot on his teeth? Or a shadow? He frowned and leaned closer to the mirror just as Dan slammed on the brakes. Marty jerked against the seat, feeling the seatbelt jam into his ribs as it locked into place.

"What the hell was that about?" he demanded, glancing into the mirror again. At least the hair spray was holding.

"Some damn kid," Dan muttered.

"This is bullshit," Marty said. But he buttoned the top of his shirt as the Channel 5 news van pulled up to the curb. The news van bore the station's logo —"Channel 5 News. The Coverage You Expect. The Balance You Deserve."—

plastered on the side. Above the logo the faces of the evening anchors, Sandy Rhodes and Dana Atwater, beamed down at passers-by.

Dan climbed into the back of the van while Marty opened his door. Almost immediately the smells of the carnival—stale and burnt popcorn, fresh cotton candy, grease and oil from the rides, hot dogs and hamburgers—invaded his senses. Marty could hear the sounds of Joplin's "The Entertainer" playing too loud, begging the crowd to enter.

People had stopped to stare, or were milling about where they thought the crew might be shooting. "Hey, folks!" he called. The crowd glanced at him, then back at the van, as if they thought Sandy Rhodes and Dana Atwater were about to climb out. People always expected their faces when they saw the van. Marty continued, "I'm doing a piece on the carnival here. Want to give me an interview?"

A cute redhead with a kid tugging at her pockets held up her hand tentatively. "Yeah, come on over here." A few more women with children clinging to their hips joined in, taking their cue from the redhead. Hopefully he'd be able to get some good material from at least one of them.

While Dan began setting up the camera, Marty went over the questions he was going to ask. *Where are you from?* and *How often do you come to the carnival?* and *What brought you here today?* He practiced the questions in his head, making sure they sounded natural, sounded like he cared about the answers.

Maybe later I'll be able to interview some of the carnies, Marty thought, not sure whether he should grin or shudder at the idea.

"You about ready?" Dan asked, holding out the microphone.

"Not really," Marty replied, but took it anyway.

It was a short shoot, only about an hour to interview the women. They were packing up when Marty glanced at a man sitting on a bench nearby, staring at them. He had been there for a while, silently watching the crowds trickling in and out of the carnival, but now he was staring intently at Marty.

His eyes were clouded over, milky-white and hauntingly deep. "Dan," he hissed, grabbing his colleague. "Get the camera."

Dan looked up from the gear and scowled. "What, you find another interview you want to do?"

Marty nodded his head at the man on the bench. "Foresight, Dan. Nobody's gotten an interview with a Foresight user, let alone while they were actually *on* the drug."

Dan froze and stared at Marty. "You have got to be kidding me, Marty. You seriously want to go over and talk to a user *while he's high*?"

"Almost nobody knows anything about Foresight," Marty said, pulling out the mic. "This could be a really good opportunity for us."

"For you," Dan corrected. "I just hold the camera."

"If I get promoted because of this, I'll put in a good word for you," Marty promised. "This kind of thing is a career-changer."

Dan considered for a moment. "Fine. But you owe me lunch tomorrow."

"Deal. You have no idea how much this means-"

Dan reached for the camera. "You sure this guy is going to be willing to give you an interview?"

"Don't care," Marty said. "I want you to film the entire thing."

"Yeah, sure. That way if your doper kills you, I have it on film for evidence," Dan said, hefting the camera onto his shoulder.

Marty gripped the mic in his hand so tightly that his knuckles turned white and approached the man like one approaches a stray cat or dog. Small, slow steps, being careful to not look threatening. The man didn't move, however, just watched the two men approach. Or at least stared in their direction. He sat so still that Marty began to wonder if the man was blind, not high. Marty glanced back at Dan, who shrugged slightly and motioned Marty forward.

Marty cleared his throat loudly. The man didn't start or show any sign of surprise, so Marty inched forward. "Excuse me?" he asked. "Sir?"

"I can see you just fine," the man said. He tilted his head to the side as if he was studying Marty or listening to something that Marty couldn't hear. "You're an interesting man, now, aren't you?"

Marty glanced over at Dan nervously. "I suppose so, sir. I, uh, was wondering if you might be willing to give me an interview...?"

The man barked out a laugh. "An interview? What about?"

"Well...about Foresight." Marty shifted his feet nervously and glanced over at Dan again. "About what it's like. What you can see."

The man raised an eyebrow, then nodded.

"My name's Marty, and this is Dan, my camera guy."

"Jack," he said. He leaned back and stretched his arms above his head. "Not going to make me look like a crazy man, are you?" Marty couldn't help but smile wryly. "So what kinds of things are you going to ask me?" Jack said.

Marty glanced at Dan, who nodded just slightly, an indication that he was recording. "Isn't that something you should know?"

Jack laughed, a single guffaw. "Naw, man. That's not how it works. You don't get to see everything."

"No?" Marty frowned slightly. "I thought Foresight lets you see into the future."

"Sure," Jack said. "But you only get to see the important things."

Marty nodded. "Important things. Like what?"

Jack shrugged. "Like...how your man over there is gonna have a little girl." Dan and Marty exchanged surprised glances. Marty hadn't realized. He almost never asked about Dan's wife.

"We don't know the sex," Dan said hesitantly. "But yeah, Jessica's pregnant."

"That could have been a guess," Marty said. "Or maybe you've seen Dan and his wife around somewhere."

Jack nodded. "You doubt. It happens to everyone, until they actually try Foresight. Until they see something and then it comes true." He shrugged.

Marty glanced over at Dan, who looked visibly shaken, and decided to change the conversation a little bit. "So, how does it work?"

Jack grinned widely. "See, now, guys like you, always wanting to know how it works, why it works, piss me off. You can't just accept that it *does* work and let it be."

"So that means you don't know?" Marty asked.

Jack leaned forward a little bit, staring hard at Marty. "You ever had that feeling of déjà vu? Or like you think you know how something's going to turn out, even though you don't have any real good reason to think you know?"

"That's just the mind noticing things that you didn't consciously realize," Marty said. "Your subconscious picks up on way more little details than your conscious knows."

"Sure," Jack said. "That's what pop psychology says." Jack smiled, a stupid, wide grin. "So I got this theory that everybody can see the future. Except most of us never do much about it. Yeah, you get some of those mystics, the Buddhists and New Agers and Pagans, who try, but they never really do any good at it. So we all got this ability, but we don't use it, and I think that's cuz we just don't know how. Foresight just lets you figure it out for a little while."

Marty shrugged. "Okay, let's say I believe you. How could a drug unlock something like that?"

"Chemicals," Jack said. He sounded patient, almost patronizing, like he was explaining to a child. "Like pot calms you down, or meth gives you energy, or acid makes you hallucinate. It's how the chemicals in your brain are working. Foresight just makes some of them work different, I guess."

"What's it like, being on Foresight?" Marty asked, trying to force his voice to sound calm and conversational. He wanted to hit the doper for using that stupid patronizing tone.

"It's like…" Jack tilted his head, considering. "Like there are these strings attached to everybody, and you can see where they're gonna lead. And if you pluck at 'em with your brain, you can get pictures of what's gonna happen."

"Have you ever tried to change what you saw?" This came from Dan, to Marty's surprise.

"Oh sure," Jack said. "It's hard to do, but yeah, you can change it. So you can see some of the big things that are gonna happen, and you got this information now…*now* you can change it."

"So you could stop a murder, if you wanted?" Marty demanded.

Jack's smile grew sly, and Marty shifted uncomfortably. "Tell me something, Jack," he said. "Foresight *is* a drug, isn't it?"

Jack frowned slightly. "What do you mean?"

"It's a pill, yeah?" Jack nodded and Marty went on. "Most drugs are addictive. That's what makes them drugs. They make people feel good, that's why they take them originally, and then they get addicted. Does Foresight work that way?"

"Course it does," Jack said quietly. "Imagine being able to see the future. Do you know what that feels like? It's a rush. More than a rush. You've got complete power and control. But the drug, man…once you get that power, you don't ever want to give it up. *Ever.*"

* * *

The next morning was gloomy, low clouds hanging in the sky weighed down by rain. Walking into the bank, Dan just behind, Marty felt like the clouds were trying to reach down and suffocate him.

"You know this is probably the stupidest story I've ever covered?" he said.

"You know, Marty, you're in a really bad fucking mood today," Dan said. They entered the bank in silence, neither of them looking at the other.

The bank had been open for an hour, but there were still plenty of customers chatting with tellers. Marty could hear the sharp squawk from the four parrots near the tellers, and he grimaced. They were supposed to be part of the ambience of the building and a desperate attempt to keep old customers and bring in new ones, but he couldn't imagine banking with birds shitting right next to him.

"Damn birds," he said. "I fucking hate—oh, *hi!*" His voice became sugary-sweet as a well-dressed man approached. The other man, who must be the bank manager, wore a pastel purple button-down underneath a black sport coat, and both the coat and his tailored pants were well-ironed. "You must be Donald McGuinness, am I correct?" Marty held his hand out, and the other man shook it vigorously.

"I am!" Donald said, showing them his blindingly white teeth. "I'm so glad you're both here to cover our bank. This is really exciting for all our employees." He waved his arms behind him, and Marty glanced back. None of the employees were looking in their direction. "You'll want to set up where the birds are kept, right? So you can get them in the shot?"

"Do they make that noise the whole time?" Dan asked. "That might be a problem with the microphones." He hefted the camera onto his shoulder and began looking around to see where the lighting was good.

Donald looked a little downcast, but nodded. "Maybe we can bring one of the birds into the shot?"

"That's definitely something we can do," Marty said. He was amazed that he was still managing to sound reasonably polite, when inside he just wanted to start yelling about how idiotic this whole thing was. "The whole interview is about you and your employees and customers interacting with the birds, and how the birds are helping your business out. Getting some of the images with them will be great."

"You're going to interview some of our customers?" Donald asked. "We don't normally like bothering them, you know, just getting them in and out as fast as we can."

"It'll be a volunteer thing," Marty explained. "Only the folks who have the time and want to be interviewed will be bothered, and most folks like to have their minute of fame."

"Hey Marty," Dan interrupted. Marty turned to look at him, surprised by the tone of voice. Slightly hushed, almost awed or afraid. Dan was staring at a customer who had just walked in—a familiar looking man, with a tailored suit and well-combed sandy brown hair. It took Marty a minute to place him, and then he started in surprise. "His name was Jack, right?"

"Yeah," Marty said, frowning as he studied the man. "What's he doing here?"

"Looks like he's going to be opening up an account," Donald said as one of the managers hurried over to Jack. "Do you know him?"

"We met him yesterday," Marty said. "He's–"

The doors burst open, then slammed shut as two masked men hurried into the bank. "Everybody get down!" one of the men yelled. "Put your hands out in front of you where I can see 'em!"

Marty spun to Dan. "Get that camera rolling," he hissed. He remembered from the news last night—five banks in as many weeks. And here he was, in the middle of it, with his cameraman at the ready.

"If you think I'm going to be in the middle of a bank robbery and aim the camera at the robbers' faces, you've got another thing coming to you," Dan snapped back.

"I said, on the ground!" the masked man bellowed again. Dan immediately dropped to the ground, but Marty saw Dan get the camera going and set it on the ground—pointed in the same general direction as the robbers.

I'm going to regret this, Marty thought, but he held his hands out in front of him, showing that they were empty. "Hey, guys, no need for anyone to get hurt here."

The masked man swung his gun in Marty's direction. Marty felt weak, like he might collapse, but he took a deep breath.

And then he heard two simple shots and both of the robbers collapsed. Blood began to pool on the ground, trickling from their bodies slowly. Marty spotted the new gunman almost immediately. Jack stood confidently, a pistol gripped professionally in both of his hands, a slight smirk on his face.

Dan stood up, camera in hand, swinging it around to focus on Jack, who kept the pistol trained on the two men, writhing in agony on the floor. Jack walked up to them and kicked their weapons away from their bodies, then glanced over at the tellers. "Call the police, please?"

The woman was staring at him slack-jawed, but when he addressed her, she immediately reached down and pressed a button under the counter.

"My God," Donald said, his voice shaking. "You saved us. You–you really saved us. They could have shot us, and you saved us all."

"Son of a bitch," Marty swore softly, glaring at Jack.

"Man's a hero," Dan replied. "We're going to have to interview him, as soon as the cops get here and have done their thing." He kept the camera on Jack, who strolled around the bank, his eyes still on the bleeding robbers.

"How can we ever repay you?" Donald asked. He was on the verge of sobbing.

"For now," Jack said smoothly, "Just keep calm until the cops get here. We can figure anything else out once they've arrested these men."

"Son of a *bitch*," Marty said, his voice louder. He pointed a finger at Jack. "You *knew*."

Jack raised an eyebrow at him. "I don't know what you're talking about, man. I was just in the right place at the right time."

Sirens whirred in the distance, screeching closer, and Marty thought he was going to punch Jack before the cops could get there. The son of a bitch was on Foresight yesterday when they had been talking to him, and he must have gotten a glimpse of Marty's future, must have seen what a big day this could have turned out to be. And what, he had shown up here to steal the spotlight from Marty?

Flashing lights pulled into the parking lot, sirens blaring, but they were dull compared to the rage pounding in Marty's head. He had been this close to a chance at something bigger, something better, and Jack had stolen it.

Marty sat down on one of the plush chairs as the police began checking the robbers and calling for backup. One of the officers came over and offered Marty a cup of water. "You okay?" the cop asked. "I know these things can be kind of rough. We can take you down to the hospital to get you—"

"That man's a drug addict," Marty said, pointing at Jack.

The cop raised an eyebrow. "That's…quite an accusation."

"He takes Foresight. I know he does. I saw him on it yesterday. I interviewed him outside of a carnival, and he was on Foresight." Marty stood up and waved his arms in Jack's direction.

"If that's true," the officer said, "Shouldn't we regard him as a hero? I mean, he did stop a bank robbery, potentially saved several lives. That's a good thing, right?"

"Oh, sure," Marty said. "But I was gearing up to do all of that, and he just comes in and shoots 'em. What about me? Wasn't that supposed to be *my* moment of triumph? And he just comes in and steals it away from me like that?"

The cop glanced at something behind Marty. "Sure, pal. If the only thing you're concerned about in life is your moment, getting the spotlight on you, I can see why you're so pissed off. But it isn't about you. It's about the folks who were saved, the bad guys who were caught. Living as if they don't matter...there's something wrong with you there."

Marty sat back down, staring slack-jawed as the cop turned around and went back over to talk to the others. Dan sat down next to Marty. "Anything you want to talk about?"

"No," Marty said coldly. "No, I don't want to fucking talk about this. Today was a waste of my time."

"Fine. Jack said he won't do an interview with us. You want to head back to the station?"

"Just go without me. I'm going to head home." Marty glared at Jack. "I've got someone to talk to, first."

Dan rolled his eyes and sighed loudly. "Don't do anything stupid, Marty. Got it?"

"I just want to talk to him," Marty said. "No big deal. It's not like I'm going to punch a guy carrying a gun."

"Better not," Dan said. He held up the keys and jingled them in front of Marty's face. "Last chance."

Marty turned away from Dan and began watching Jack. The cops took down his statement, interviewed everybody there, then clapped Jack on the back and waved goodbye. Marty stood up and went over to Jack. "I want to talk to you."

"Sure," Jack said. "I'm not really surprised."

"Was that something else you saw?" Marty asked, lip curled as he scowled at Jack. They headed down the street, walking aimlessly.

"Nah, man. Just the robbery."

"So you *did* know what was going to happen today," Marty accused.

Jack nodded. "Sure did. Saw the robbery was going to happen, saw you becoming a great reporter."

"And you took that away from me," Marty said.

"It wasn't ever yours to begin with," Jack pointed out. "It was just something that *could* happen, that was *going* to happen, but you can't claim it belonged to you."

"If I put down money on a car and it's damaged before I can take it home…"

"This isn't a car, man. This is a *possibility*. You can't sit there and tell me the possibility belongs to you. That something that hasn't actually happened is yours."

"I was going to help those people," Marty snapped. "I was going to stop the bank robbers."

"Yeah," Jack said. "And become a big hero. Sorry, man. I gotta make a living somehow. Folks just throw money at heroes."

Marty grabbed Jack and shoved him into the wall of the building they were passing. "That should have been *my* money, you sonofabitch!" he roared. "My money, my job, my time! How can you do this kind of shit to everybody you meet?"

Jack dug into his pocket and pulled out a small plastic baggie. There were two tiny pills in there. "It's easy, man. Swallow pills. See the big things that are gonna happen. Be there when it does and take action. Folks will love you for it." He waggled the bag and grinned at Marty. "I'll give you one for free."

Marty froze and let go of Jack. "Are you joking?"

"No, man. First one's free. Go on, try it." Jack's grin was huge. "You can see what it's like, you can maybe find someone else and get your own moment of fame like I did. Make some cash at it, have everybody like you." Marty reached for the baggie, but Jack pulled it away. "Just the one, now. Got it?"

"Hand it over before I change my mind," Marty said, impatiently holding his hand out.

Jack reached into the bag and pulled out a pill. "Now you go ahead and take it, and come back to me when you're ready for your next one." He handed Marty a card along with the pill. "You'll be rich before you know it."

Marty popped the pill into his mouth, closed his eyes, and swallowed, ready for a little bit of fame and fortune.

Unknowing Agents

Chris Hussey

A marketing director for a local television station, Chris has earned several Emmy nominations and been honored with a National Edward R. Murrow Award for Best Documentary. He's also the marketing director and beloved cohost for Fear the Boot, a podcast you might have heard of while at a swank dinner party with the elite of the tabletop gaming industry. Chris wonders why he doesn't get invited to those parties. Chris has also authored and contributed to several projects for FASA, Alderac Entertainment Group, Catalyst Game Labs and others. His most recent co-authored work 'Games Most Wanted' can hopefully be found on your bookshelf. Originally from northern Minnesota, he now lives in Iowa with a wonderful woman who actually married him and then helped produce four wonderful offspring. Randomly pooping in places, the family dog roams the grounds.

Jeremy Latham settled himself into his customary and favorite place to sit at the table when on a mission. He wasn't alone. The others had also gathered and had taken their places as well. "Evening everyone. How the hell are ya?" Jeremy spoke happily to the rest of the team.

While his seat didn't allow his back to be directly against the wall, it was close enough to allow a full view of the room, along with the staircase leading up. It was his habit to sit this way, even before joining the agency. The last to join the team, it had taken some cajoling to secure the seat, but it was his now, without question.

With careful precision, he rested his briefcase on the table, ran both hands across the case's faux leather surface, feeling the details of the stitching under his fingers. Smooth and cool, the stitching and fake leather added weight to the lie that lay inside, under the false bottom of the case's interior. His hands moved down over the edges of the briefcase then toward the front where the metal clasps rested. He'd been warned sternly about security for the case, but Jeremy never saw the need. Creating a personality quirk of being overly protective of the case worked better than any combination lock. No one touched it out of respect or possibly fear over Jeremy's reaction. No, in this case deception was the order of the day, and that deception was the perfect security. The dials on the cases' locks were all set to zero. *An unbreakable combination,* Jeremy joked to himself.

The only team member who persisted was Kelly. Despite the relationship the two shared, Jeremy never let her look inside, and though she would ask from time to time, she never–pressed the issue. Kelly carried plenty of her own emotional baggage, which Jeremy always showed respect for, and was happy to see it returned.

His weekly hands-across-the-case ritual complete, Jeremy returned his attention to the rest of the team. His eyes ran first to Alex, old t-shirt far too small for her heavy frame. Curly, messy hair and an acne-scarred face bore a healthy smile for her friend. Physical qualities didn't matter for the team. Jeremy respected Alex's mind. The woman was one hell of an Operations Agent, even if she didn't know it. She'd saved their hides more times than Jeremy could count.

Jesse was the opposite of Alex, rail-thin and gangly almost to the point of sickness. Socially awkward outside of missions but all business when around the command table.

Across from Jesse, by design, was Kelly. Jeremy wanted to sit next to her, and she wanted the same, but they both wanted team cohesion more. If anyone else knew about their relationship, it might not only damage the team, but break it up. That wouldn't sit well with Command. In fact, Jeremy was already breaking protocol by dating her.

Ben was last. The Mission Administrator. Average build and a decent hairstyle, Ben liked to run the show, and he deserved to. Only Alex had served more time, and she was too much in love with the down and dirty work to move up to be an MA. Ben liked the Big Picture, and the rest of the team was happy to let him have it.

Although they were his friends, they couldn't know the truth. If the rest really knew what was going on, it would color their coming actions, and for some be too much for them to bear. This mission was too important. Jeremy needed everyone on their 'A' game, even if they didn't realize they needed to bring it.

Jeremy pulled the reference manuals, mission notes, and his field agent's profile out of his case. Then Jeremy's eyes settled on what was the worst part of the job in his mind. *You sons of bitches are what ruin everything.*

The nerds in R&D had all kinds of pet names for them: Fate Finders, Chaos Cannons. On and on. Known as 'Destiny Engines,' agency–R&D marveled at their simplicity. Jeremy hated them to the core. Unreliable, unstable, and the worst piece of equipment an agent could have. He'd seen too many good men, women, and others die because of these things. Each report for every fallen agent left a mark on his heart. If Jeremy thought about it too much, deep guilt settled in from all the years when he was like Alex, Jesse, Ben, and even Kelly: unknowing agents in real battle against evil.

"Jeremy, you ready?" Ben asked.

Jeremy looked over at Ben. He looked ready. His screen sat in front of him, mission notes just in front of it. As the MA, he needed to be the conduit to the dimension they'd be breaching so Jeremy and the others could link up with their field agents. Ben, for all his six foot seven, two hundred pound frame, was the most critical component of the mission, even if he absolutely no clue to what was really happening.

"I'm good, bud," Jeremy answered.

"Jess?" Ben looked across the table.

Jesse placed his Destiny Engine in front of him, gave a grim smile and nod.

Ben looked to both Kelly and Alex, who responded with their own affirmative thumbs up. Jeremy stole one last look toward Kelly, who returned the look with a wink. Jeremy let a small smile show on his lips.

Jeremy slid his right hand down toward his briefcase, which now rested close by his legs. He found the second brass stud that was positioned next to the lock release on the right side and gently touched it. A small tingle stung his thumb followed by an ever so slight vibration in the briefcase as the Gateway Device was activated. The conduit would open in seconds and they'd soon find themselves in a new dimension, but still perceiving this one. Jeremy looked at Alex. She gave a slight shiver, the sign that the Gateway Device was not only active, but working. Kelly also seemed to adjust herself in her chair in reaction to the device. Jesse didn't move. Jeremy never understood why men never had a reaction to the device, but now wasn't the time.

Ben spoke. "Take out your agent profiles. Kelly, get us started on sitrep while I bring the portal into focus. Here we go, people!"

Jeremy smiled. He needed to. Everyone else was smiling. This was his favorite part of job—the mission launch. He knew Ben wasn't really saying those exact words. In fact, he was saying something quite different, but Jeremy had been at this job for so long his mind adjusted the terms and verbiage to what he was hearing.

* * *

Max Deckard's knuckles were white as he tried to squeeze the controls of his modified Dorsedyne Class E freighter even tighter. The words of his flight instructor, uncle, and mentor as echoed in his head as he jerked the ship hard to port, as well as dip. *"A soft touch leads to the greatest control,"* he would say in admonishment. Deckard never listened or learned. "Sorry, Uuncle," he muttered. Deckard liked a tight grip. It made him feel more in control, and in the situation he currently found himself and in his crew in, he desperately needed some control.

His multi-armed co-pilot, a member of the Soriliath species, hissed her protest at the lurching of the ship in her native tongue. Deckard only picked up part of the curse and it wasn't a pleasant one. His grasp of Sorilese was minimal. The best Deckard could tell was that it had something to do with his father and a pack of Norgling hairless baboons. "Hey, no need to get personal, Vennseera," Deckard shot back.

"Personal?" the alien retorted. "I'm praying to Unnallay to save me from your abysmal flying."

"I really need to work on my Sorilese," Deckard mumbled as he switched his gaze from the cockpit viewport to his instrument panel. "My abysmal flying is the only thing keeping us alive at the moment. Maybe you need to shoot a prayer up to Unnlooloo to make sure we make it to the planet's surface."

"Unnallay," Vennseera corrected. "And do not disrespect my god. You humans, for all your talk of peace and inclusion, are always so quick to insult."

Deckard scoffed. "I'm not sure which humans you're thinking of, sweetheart. If you haven't noticed, those are Concordat fighters on our tail. The only thing they seem to want to include us in is an explosive fireball." Deckard patted the side panel of his ship. "But the *Dragonsfire* here isn't about to let that happen, are you?"

"Why you speak to a non-living object like it is one, I will never understand." Vennseera sounded annoyed.

"Oh, she's alive. Trust me." The captain of the *Dragonsfire* spoke with concern. "The Concordat shouldn't be this far out." Max keyed his comm. "The rest of you idiots in position yet? I need those guns online now!"

A burst of static hit Deckard's ears. "Relax! In position now. Gun's still in boot mode," the first voice answered. It was Ren'tregg, the Volorvian mercenary. Deckard was actually surprised that the big, hairy alien could fit into the combat seat of the lower aft gun.

Deckard was about to answer but was cut off by Daytri. "No, you can bypass that. Hold down the firing stud and key in five-three-four-six-alpha on the pad. That'll hot-boot your weapon. You'll be short on accuracy for a bit, but you can shoot."

Deckard cocked his head. *What?* "Daytri, have you been messing with my ship again?"

"Improving," was the alien's only reply.

"Whatever. Stop touching things!"

The Volorvian cut the conversation short. "I'm ready. Not my preferred way to fight, but I'm more than happy to send these Concordat bastards to your human hell."

Deckard smiled. "Roger that. Daytri, think you can shoot things as well as you 'improve' them?"

The joke went completely over the alien crewman's head as he returned an honest reply. "I'm not much of a gunner, sir."

Deckard let it go. He had plenty of other worries. "Do your best, just watch those energy levels." He returned his focus to keeping the ship out of the firing arcs of the Concordat fighter squadron pursuing them. Maneuvers and shields were keeping the *Dragonsfire* out of serious trouble, but that wouldn't last forever. Shields wear down, and unless Daytri and Ren'tregg could even the odds, they were outnumbered five to one.

The ship rocked under the impact from a Concordat fighter's particle blast. Deckard felt his hands tighten even harder on the control sticks. He cut to starboard, then pulled into a steep incline. He kept his vision focused straight ahead. "You got a prayer to your god to get out of tight spots?"

Vennseera chuckled. "Yes, but you wouldn't like what it entails. Maybe you should pray to your ship."

The *Dragonsfire* shuddered again under another blast, causing Deckard to curse. "They're too fast for us. They're going to cut off all our escape angles soon. Any ideas?"

Vennseera reached one of her rear appendages behind her, her fingers spreading over a multi-buttoned panel. "A Split-S, with no upright? That would place Ren'tregg's gun in a better firing arc. I'll release some countermeasures to cloud the others sensors."

Deckard nodded. "I like the way you think." He punched the comm channel for his gunners. "Hang on, guys. Ren, you're going to have a few pick shots."

Deckard wrenched the controls and goosed the ship's throttle. The *Dragonsfire* arced downward into its rotation. Once it completed the flip, Deckard nodded and Vennseera hit the keypad. There was a quick, high whine in the cockpit as the ship released its countermeasures. Used normally against incoming missiles, they would have no effect against the particle cannons of the fighters, but at close range, they'd cause temporary havoc with their targeting sensors.

A savage growl erupted over the comm system as Ren'tregg celebrated his hit. Deckard smiled as he continued evasive maneuvers on the *'fire*. "Keep it up, everyone. We may just get out of this yet!"

* * *

Jeremy looked around the table at the rest of the assembled group, save Ben. Jeremy had purposely adjusted his body to angle himself away from the

Mission Administrator. A symbolic gesture, but Jeremy always had suspicions. He wanted to hide his plans from Ben, even though there was no way Ben could know what the rest of them might be thinking.

Training had taught Jeremy that the Mission Admin was nothing more than a conduit, fed the illusion of control via the advanced tech and supernatural forces at work within the manuals and Destiny Engines used during missions. The MA provided the very necessary human element that allowed the agents to interact with the environment. It was very much akin to a human sacrifice, but without the death of the subject. In essence, a living gateway to the dimension. Jeremy found that hard, if not impossible, to believe. Ben *had* to have some form of control and influence over what was happening. At the very least as much control as the rest of the agents.

In his time serving as an MA, Jeremy never once felt out of control or overtly influenced by the events going on around him. Hell, he even remembered denying the results given to him by the Destiny Engines on several occasions.

"Destiny Engines aren't perfect, even if the tech guys say they are." Jeremy remembered the words from his trainer, Carlos. *"At least on the MA side. The mission is the mission and when it comes to those times that you think you are changing the outcome, all that really means is that the Engine failed, like a bad sensor read or a spell that failed to be cast."*

Regardless, Jeremy still didn't believe it, so keeping his back to Ben was a good way to play it safe, regardless. "So, why the hell are they there?"

"The Concordat?" Kelly looked back at him. "I have no clue."

"This is definitely out beyond their borders, an ancient Soriliath world to be exact, but not so far out that it would be unusual," Alex added quickly.

"But they wouldn't be going outside their borders to begin with." Jesse looked up from his notes toward Ben. "They've been having internal troubles, right? Wasn't there some sort of coup going on?"

Ben nodded. "There *was* but it was settled a while back. The wrong side, from your agents' perspective."

"Well, that enthusiasm is going to be tempered a bit if Ren'tregg gets another shot," Jesse retorted.

Jeremy smiled at the comment, then remembered an important detail. "If I remember right from the profile we saw on their new leader, he's obsessed with artifacts and tech from the ancient Soriliath Imperium."

"Well, now we know why they are here. Vennseera won't be happy." Kelly looked at Jeremy and smiled, pointing a finger gun at him. "Good catch...Captain."

Ben took control. "All right, back to work." He gestured toward the map in the center of the table that showed a spacecraft and several pursuers. "They still have a bit of an immediate problem to deal with first."

Jesse stood and grabbed his Destiny Engines. "I told you. Ren'tregg has this under control." He looked toward Ben in challenge. "Bring it!"

* * *

A satisfied grunt signaled the downing of another Concordat fighter. Deckard noted that Ren'tregg's marksmanship had been amazing this fight. *Just what we needed.* That left the fighters down to just two.

Deckard was getting ready to spin the *Dragonsfire* around once again when the Concordat ships broke off their pursuit. "What the-?" he muttered.

"They're breaking off." VenseeraVennseera uncoiled her third arm toward a bank of switches to assess some of the damage done to the ship.

Ren'tregg celebrated the retreat. The shout turned into song, a Volorvian victory hymn Deckard had heard more than once.

He switched off the comm.

"Do you want to pursue?" Vennseera

Deckard shook his head. "No. Those fighters are attached to a larger craft hiding somewhere. Take a note of their trajectory." Deckard looked toward the planet through the cockpit's viewport. The brown and green ball loomed large ahead of them. "If the Concordat is here, they're after the same thing we are. Those fighters were meant to delay us. We need to get to the surface and find it before they do. I want that item in the hands of your people, not the Concordat." Deckard turned the comm back on, and shot some feedback to quiet the still singing Volorvian warrior. "Hang tight, guys. We're going planetside."

"We're not going to pursue?" It was Daytri.

"Negative. The Concordat is not the job. The item is. We need to finish the job and get the hell out of here before the Concordat becomes our job."

Deckard keyed in the last of the security measures on the *Dragonsfire* as the crew exited the craft. He knew the Concordat was here somewhere, and if his hunch was right, Deckard was sure that Flemming was going to be among them. Hell, for all he knew, Flemming was behind all of this. It was the last thing he needed, but the first thing expected. *It only makes sense. This is a job Flemming and I would have taken back when we were partners. Back before it went bad.*

Deckard had landed the ship several kilometers away from the target site. The *Dragonsfire* would be hidden in the rocky valley he'd found. The electronic countermeasures on the *Dragonsfire* were robust enough to keep it hidden from all but the most sophisticated non-natural eyes.

The captain broke into a trot to catch up with his crew. Ren'tregg sat at the controls of the small, multi-wheeled land rover. It was an older model, barely running and free of any armor or weapon mounts. Deckard wasn't a rich ship captain, and often had to put most of the funds back into the *'fire*. He knew one day he'd end up regretting that.

Daytri urged his captain to hurry to the craft. Easily one of the more unusual alien races the human captain had seen, Daytri's race, the Toobeht'raef, spent most of their lives walking on all fours. They lacked a discernible head, replaced and instead by a general sloping of the shoulders upwards to a rounded top, where multiple eyes allowed for a full three hundred and sixty degrees of vision. The sloped structure housed the creature's massive brain assembly. It was this that Deckard admired the most. Daytri was one of the smartest beings he knew, and his expertise had saved the crew's ass (not to mention the ship itself) many times.

The alien continued to wave a hand and Ren'tregg started to pull away. "Come, Captain. Your chariot awaits."

Deckard heard Vennseera give a hiss-chuckle at the remark, and doubled his pace. He reached for an arm of the Soriliath and pulled himself on board. "Thanks for waiting," Deckard joked as he settled in.

Ren'tregg gunned the engine and the craft rumbled toward the horizon.

* * *

Jeremy's eyes moved back and forth across the massive collection of books on Ben's shelf. *So many worlds.* It was an impressive array, even larger than his own. *So many missions.* Jeremy knew he'd never have the time to go on them all.

"So many games, so little time, eh?" It was Kelly, the only other in the room. The group was taking a break. All but the two of them had either stepped outside for the important cellphone call to a loved one, a raid on the refrigerator, or in Ben's case, to make love to a cigarette or two.

Jeremy huffed in agreement, a canned response to questions like this, then realized that he had allowed himself to hear Kelly's actual words. *Games*, not *missions.* He turned.

"Always the case, isn't it?" He spoke as he moved toward Kelly and pulled her close.

"Hey, be careful. We don't want anyone catching us," Kelly said playfully as she returned his embrace.

Jeremy stole a quick kiss. "Good point."

Kelly cocked her head to one side, and looked concerned. "You okay tonight? You seem a bit distracted."

Jeremy misdirected by grabbing a book off the shelf while moving towards Ben's seat at the table. He was worried about the mission, but also felt like a bastard for having to hold such a secret from her. "Me? Yeah, I'm good. Work's just been a bit crazy and all. Lots going on." Jeremy used the book as a shield, thumbing through and looking down.

Kelly got up and walked over toward the shelf, working her gaze over the titles. She kept one eye on Jeremy. "Which one you got there?"

Jeremy flipped the softcover closed and held it up. The book was called *Legendmaker*. Jeremy had never undertaken any missions there, but he'd heard stories from others about it. Epic in scope, its agents were the stuff heroes were made from.

Jeremy plopped the book back in his lap to resume his thumb-through, but Kelly was standing right in front of him now. She'd moved fast and quiet.

"I thought you were worried about being caught." He smiled at her.

She smiled one of those large smiles women do when they are happy about something: a good find on a shopping expedition, or some flavor of ice cream that was exactly the perfect variation of chocolate. Her lips parted as the smile continued. Jeremy began to lose focus as he took in the color of her hair—long, auburn, straight, and resting over one shoulder. His eyes moved to her teeth, unnaturally white and perfectly straight. Jeremy suddenly found himself thinking of making snow forts as a kid with those red plastic brick molds. Beautiful. He loved her, but hated himself for the secret.

"Looks fun." She pointed at the book as she settled down in Jeremy's chair and leaned forward, landing one hand on Jeremy's knee.

Jeremy felt his insides light up. Anything that was solid changed to water in an instant. He looked at the hand then back towards Kelly's face. "We still on for afterward?"

"You know it." Kelly winked at him.

That's when he noticed it. Kelly's other hand was resting on his briefcase. The good feelings in Jeremy's gut were replaced quickly by a flash of panic and anger. He kept his gaze focused on her offending hand, until she looked down herself.

"Are you kidding?" Her tone was filled with irritation.

Jeremy looked up and met her gaze. "Kel, you know how I feel about the briefcase."

"But I'm not doing anything with it. Just touching it."

Jeremy did not want to get into it. "Kelly, please."

The romantic moment was gone. Kelly stood, shot Jeremy a cool look, and made her way around the table. He was about to offer an apology, an explanation. Anything to smooth the issue over, but it was too late. Ben and the rest of the group returned.

"What the hell you doing in my seat? Are you cheating?" Ben was half-serious.

Jeremy rose. "What, and take away all the fun?"

"Just for that, I'm doubling the number of bad guys," Ben joked as he took his place at the table, along with everyone else.

"Way to go, ass." Jesse shot the joking barb toward Jeremy.

Ignoring it, he sat back down and looked over at Kelly. Her expression gave him no hint that he was forgiven.

Great.

* * *

The rest of the night's mission had moved much slower, which suited Jeremy fine. He'd been off since the mix-up with Kelly, and it had almost cost lives. An ambush by local predators while the *Dragonsfire* crew moved on the target hadn't gone smooth, and Jeremy knew it was serious when Ben hadn't pulled any punches as the MA. The field crew had made it to the target but would camp the night. The resumption of the mission would be telling. It had to be successful. It was cliché, but failure wasn't an option. The item they were targeting was too important. Jeremy didn't know why exactly, but the briefing he'd received from the agency drove home the seriousness of it. What he knew of the target item was that it dealt with memories and emotions. Not any more knowledge than what Deckard and the rest of the field agents knew.

Jeremy was happy to hear that he and Kelly were indeed still on, but the silent car ride was not boding well. Small talk about the mission was about the only thing Kelly seemed interested in doing. Any attempts to say anything else had fell flat.

They made their way into Jeremy's apartment in silence. After stowing away the mission materials, Kelly found a place on the couch while Jeremy went to the kitchen for some drinks.

Same as it always was. Beer for him, a crantini for her.

The war inside Jeremy's mind as he prepped the drinks came on quickly. He was going to tell her, but the discipline of his training answered that desire with a resounding *no*. There was to be no revealing of the secret work Jeremy did. Ever. If people knew that the simple games they played were actually direct manipulation and control of real people on real planets in this universe, as well as others, was forbidden. *"People need to believe it's just a game,"* Carlos would say over and over. *"The moment you realize you hold another's life in your hands—that's when the fun stops. That's when the real mistakes are made."*

Jeremy had always asked why. Why was this work even necessary? What purpose did it serve? Carlos' answer was always the same: *"There are always evil forces at work. If they aren't threatening us, they threaten others. If we don't keep their power in check, who will?"* Then he would say something that always messed with Jeremy's mind. *"Just remember, if we have access to the minds of others, they probably have access to ours. So who is really being played here?"*

Jeremy hated that.

He also hated that he knew he couldn't tell her, no matter how badly he wanted to. He had to keep the secret. If the agency found out, Jeremy had to leave the group, and the people in it—for good. Remove all contact.   Forever. He'd also likely face not only a discharge but a mind wipe. An unpleasant prospect to be sure.

"I'm sorry, baby," he whispered to himself.

Kelly's surprise scream sent a shock through Jeremy's body.

He raced from the kitchen to the living room and saw why Kelly screamed.

She sat on his floor, knees pulled tightly to her chest, clutching her hands in obvious pain. At her feet was his briefcase, open with the false bottom removed and at a cocked angle.

"Are you okay?" Jeremy said in a panic.

"What the hell?" Kelly looked back toward him, then to the exposed case.

Jeremy knelt down next to her, trying to block her view, but it was too late. She saw it all, even though she had no idea what she was looking at.

"You okay?"

"What the hell was that?" Kelly pointed at his briefcase. "Is this why you won't let anyone mess with your case? Some sort of crazy-assed electric shock security on it?"

Jeremy looked back and forth. He was at a loss for words.

Kelly shook her head. "Whu–why? And what the hell is that stuff?" It was then Jeremy saw her looking past his gaze to the exposed device, along with the sigils, signs and markings that were once hidden by the false bottom.

Jeremy's mind raced. "It's just the design of the case," he offered clumsily.

The look on Kelly's face told him she wasn't buying it. The two sat in silence for a moment before Kelly broke it. "Are you in some sort of weird cult, or something?"

That made Jeremy chuckle. He shook his head.

"What's so funny?" Kelly pointed to the case again. "What is that, really, and why did it shock me?"

Jeremy tried another lie. "I found the case in an old antique store. As soon as I found it had the false bottom, I had to get it. It took a little figuring, but I eventually not only discovered it had that kind of security on it, but that it still worked. I'm weird about people touching it because I don't want them hurt."

Kelly moved past him and closer to the case. Jeremy let her pass. She'd never figure out how to activate the device, much less what it was for.

Kelly tentatively tapped at the metal device in the center of the case's bottom, then looked back at Jeremy. "That's a pretty good bullshit excuse, but there's no way in hell you found a briefcase this new-looking in an antique store. You want to stop with the lies?" He saw nothing but determination in her eyes. His feelings for her roared forward. *No more lies.*

Jeremy sighed. "Okay, but you're not going to believe me."

* * *

As he predicted, she didn't believe him. Not at first anyway. Then he brought out the proof. He showed her the manuals, mission briefings, and other agency documentation. Changed her mind fast enough. To her credit, Kelly recovered from the shock quickly, not an easy task, when she realized the tabletop role-playing games she'd been playing for the past decade were revealed to really be the manifestation of dimensional gateways reached via ancient magic and high technology, where the choices she made actually affected the lives of real beings in those dimensions. That she, Alex, Jesse, Ben and Jeremy had been, in a sense, playing God.

Then Jeremy decided to drop the final bomb in his confessional vomit.

"I love you."

If there had been any doubt in Jeremy's mind about what Kelly felt and thought about the truth, it was immediately erased by the heated embrace and kiss that followed. When that kiss became more and went further, Jeremy knew all had been forgiven.

As he lay flat in bed next to Kelly, the warmth of her back pressed up against him, he stared at the ceiling trying to figure out what to do next. He thought about recruitment, but he knew her background didn't fit the profile of an agent. She had a family, lived with a roommate, and had enough a social life that she'd be missed if things ever went south.

With recruitment out, Jeremy knew he was back to facing departure from the group and from her—which also meant leaving cleanup to the agency. Jeremy realized he didn't know what that truly meant, and he didn't want to think about it.

There had to be another way. He just needed to figure it out.

And soon. The agency would find out.

He thought about their current mission.

Then a thought struck him.

* * *

He shifted again on the torn upholstery of his Grand Am to avoid the stabbing pain in the left cheek of his ass, then Jeremy raised his binoculars and stared down the block. He saw Jesse get out of his Hyundai and cross the street to Ben's house, bag over his shoulder. He was the last one. Now they were all there.

Jeremy hated calling in sick to tonight's mission, but there wasn't much choice. It was going to be his last lie to Kelly, but it was necessary for his plan.

If it worked, it would solve everything. Well, most everything. Jeremy admittedly had cheated a bit, but when it came to saving the situation he'd found himself in, it was worth it. He'd done some research on the item Deckard and the rest of the field agents were after. If Ben's interpretation of the item held up, Jeremy might just be able to change how it affected Vennseera, and in turn, Kelly.

It was a plan with a lot of ifs.

It was also very dangerous and very much against agency rules. As Jeremy figured it, he'd already broken quite a few, so what was a few more?

He eased out of the Grand Am, grabbed his briefcase, and made his way quickly to Ben's, but cut across the neighbor's lawn before reaching Ben's house. Rounding to the back, he came to Ben's garage and carefully went inside, then settled in on the floor at the foot of Ben's Taurus. It only took about ninety seconds for Jeremy to become so uncomfortable that he moved inside the car, thankfully left unlocked by his friend.

Jeremy prepped his briefcase and the operator's manual, offering up a prayer that Kelly would honor his wishes and just pretend like everything around the command table, or gaming table in her case, was normal. He begged her not to think about who the field agents really were. Not think about what their choices really meant. Not to think about the real importance of the mission. Just to be cool.

He grabbed his smartphone and swiped to the app he needed. Launching, he synched it up with the device in his case and punched in the parameters for his exit strategy. It was in no way an exact science, but it was the only option Jeremy had in this circumstance. Too early and his plan might fail. Too late and Jeremy might be trapped for good. Either option held little appeal.

Jeremy flipped to the bookmarked pages in the operator's manual for his briefcase, found the highlighted marks, and started up the device. The familiar hum was back and he knew things would be underway around the command table soon. Jeremy had called ahead and made sure Alex would monitor Deckard.

Jeremy had heard about other agents who had done what he was about to do. Carols had always said it was a bad idea, but it was Jeremy's only chance. If things went according to plan, Jeremy was about to send his consciousness out of this world and into the world where his field agents lived and breathed. Astral projection, jacking in, astral traveling; whatever you wanted to call it, Jeremy was about to do it, and without the protections normally offered by the tech and magic he carried with him. Jeremy just prayed his target was on the other end.

He traced his ring finger over several of the symbols in the case and spoke his incantations in a low, repetitive rhythm. The effects hit immediately. A chill started in his toes and raced straight up. When it hit his crotch, Jeremy felt his tone change, like walking waist deep in a cold, hotel pool. By the time it hit his chest, Jeremy struggled for breath. The doubt over his plan hit hard and he wanted to back out. Fear gripped him, but Jeremy forced himself to trace the last symbol and utter the last word. Stars popped in his eyes and he felt like someone dumped a Costco-sized bag of Pop Rocks on his brain.

* * *

The Volorvian grunted his displeasure at the wait, especially after their objective had been obtained. "Let's go. You have what you want; now we want our payment."

Jeremy shook his head, but knew right away it wasn't his head he was shaking. It wasn't his body he was in anymore. He'd done it. He'd projected into the universe of Deckard and the rest of the field agents. Everything was very different. His body, more balanced. Taut. Powerful. Strange tingles ran through his mind. *Is this what it's like?* Then the realization hit him. Who he was. Whose body he was in. He'd found his target.

Flemming.

The idea of being inside the body and mind of Deckard's former partner smacked his psyche like a freight train. Then Jeremy felt another presence with him. Inside the same head space. It took only a moment, but he realized that the actual Flemming was here as well. Jeremy not only had control of Flemming's body, but access to his mind as well. *Freaky.*

Jeremy heard the Volorvian grunt again, and the tingle went off in his brain once more, then he remembered why. Looking down, the polymer-built, cyber replacement of his left arm looked sleek and powerful. He rolled his artificial fingers out of reflex, then reached the arm toward his face. The material clinked against Flemming's rebuilt right cheek and eye socket. Jeremy concentrated on his right eye and watched as it zoomed in to a point in the distance. Another flick of the mind, and a targeting reticule appeared as an overlay on his vision. He smiled at the power of it all, then turned toward the large alien. He felt Flemming's personality rise up. Jeremy wanted to speak, but somehow Flemming seemed to take over. *I don't have full control here.*

"Is there a problem, Tor'bronn?" Jeremy was surprised at the sharp timbre of his voice.

The sloped skull and jet black hair gave the alien an intimidating stance. He narrowed his eyes and groused his shoulders. "It's time to go. You have what you want, and my men and I want what's ours."

Jeremy felt Flemming move slowly forward, taking in the scene. Jeremy could tell Tor'bronn wanted to go, but he needed the mercenaries to help with his plan. An idea struck him. He fished through Flemming's mind, combing an ocean of memories. It proved almost too easy to find what he needed. Jeremy grabbed a piece of knowledge and pushed it forward, taking control of Flemming's thoughts.

"For such a proud warrior, you're ready to run quickly, aren't you? Why is that, Tor'bronn?" Flemming stood less than a meter from the larger alien. "Is it because you're afraid of this human, Deckard? That can't be it. I know the Volorvians have little love for most Soriliaths, so it certainly isn't his first officer either."

Jeremy watched the alien's eyes. They didn't flinch. Jeremy felt his heart start to race. The realization really started to sink in. He wasn't staring down someone in Volorvian costume. This *was* a Volorvian. Everything about him was real. Blood, bone, muscle and fur. All of it real as the cybernetic arm attached to his shoulder. The planet where his feet stood. A real, live alien world not only light years away, but in another dimension to boot. It was almost too much to bear and take in. The chamber they were in. The ancient Soriliath architecture as he'd seen pictures of in the field manuals on this dimension was also real. Just as real as the device that rested on a raised dais before them. It was overwhelming.

Keep cool. Jeremy scolded himself. *Keep focused on the mission.* He made Flemming turn to the mercenary. "Wait, I bet I know what it is." Jeremy paused for effect. "You're afraid of their crewman. The other Volorvian, aren't you?"

There was the flinch. Ever so slight, but enough to notice. "It's because of his family, isn't it? They're a noble family, aren't they? Far above yours, no doubt. That's what you've heard. You don't want word of your involvement in this mission against a noble son to get back to your people. Such a disgrace it would cause."

Tor'bronn huffed. "The Vol'shtavs." Jeremy felt the light spray of mucus hit Flemming's face from the alien's compact snout. He smiled.

Jeremy turned away from the merc crew, creating some distance. "You do remember that Deckard and I used to be partners, right?"

Tor'bronn grunted. "Everyone does. You two were notorious before the Concordat caught up with you."

"Right, and Deckard betrayed me. Left me to die." He spun back. "As did the rest of our crew. Tell me, Tor'bronn, do you know the name of the Volorvian that crews with Deckard? What member of the Vol'shtav family is he?"

He watched the alien think. He didn't know. That made sense. The way Jeremy remembered it, few knew most of his agent's crew. *Now I've got you.* "You do know of Ren'tregg Vol'shtav do you not?"

Jeremy watched the alien's eyes widen. Now he knew. He also knew the son was disgraced, dishonored, and wanted for justice by the family. A great bounty.

"I do," was all the Volorvian grunted.

"Good. Now you know what it would mean to you and your men if he was brought back to his mother in chains." Jeremy paused. *Holy crap. Did I just metgame this, or was this Ben's plan all along?*

A wave of guilt washed over him. He knew he was likely signing the death warrants of Deckard and the rest of his crew, and bringing a lot of sadness and anger to his friends for a failed mission. It had to be this way. If Jeremy had any chance of sticking in the group, erasing Kelly's memory of the other night through the *Dreammaker* and saving their relationship, this was it. Now it just had to work.

"We're in, human. But once we've captured the *joazmoarg*, we are done, and to hell with your vengeance."

"Done." Jeremy was satisfied. He knew Tor'bronn and his men would keep their end of the deal. It wasn't often a Volorvian spoke in his native tongue around others. When they did, it was serious. He'd have to be quick.

"All right. Let's get into position."

* * *

Jeremy watched from a vantage point on the catwalk that ran the edges of the chamber as the field agents his friends controlled entered. An odd sensation crept up his spine as he watched Deckard lead the way. *He looks exactly like I imagined him, down to every detail. Did I really imagine him or did I truly see him?* "Weird," he whispered to himself.

The chamber reminded him of the large halls he had visited with other field agents from ancient realms where magic and races from fantasy and legend lived. Spacious, covered in moss and mold, and faded frescoes of ancient battles or other tales on the walls. A strange altar in the center, and a pillar holding an ancient artifact close beside. While the moss and mold were here, the frescoes were circuit or chemical diagrams. The altar was a central research console and the artifact on the pillar an item of super science, not sorcery, but with a name that made it sound like the latter—the *Dreammaker*.

It was the item Deckard and the agents were after. The item Flemming and his crew had already found. The item Jeremy had hopefully programmed to work with his briefcase back in Ben's Taurus. If all went according to plan, Jeremy would be able wipe Kelly's memory from the other night, and get things back to the way they were.

"There it is. Let's just take it and go. This facility is not doing my anxiety any favors." Jeremy saw Daytri speaking. *Always jumpy. But that's one of the things I like about you, Daytri. I hope you don't have to die.*

"No. Keep alert. Something about this isn't right." It felt odd to hear Deckard speak, yet, just like his appearance, his voice matched Jeremy's perceptions perfectly.

Jeremy felt Flemming's consciousness flare up and assert control. Jeremy could tell he was about to talk to the group. He didn't want that. *What the hell? Why? I don't want to talk to them, I want to take them out.* Jeremy tried to fight the compulsion to speak, but couldn't.

"Hello, Deckard." Jeremy stood and looked down at his former partner and crew.

Their weapons turned instantly toward Jeremy, but he held up his hands in peace. "Deckard. C'mon, it's me."

"Exactly," his former partner shot back. "That's far enough. You can stay up there. Much easier to keep track of you."

Jeremy shrugged. "Suit yourself. It's good to see you again, Vennseera." Jeremy smiled.

"Die in the Dust," she spat. The words hurt Jeremy. He knew the gravity of the insult. The human equivalent of 'go to hell' but with the severity of a people that actually meant what they said when it came to their faith. It also hurt because he knew Kelly was on the other end. *She'd probably hate me more if she knew what I was about to do.*

Jeremy played the part, looking emotionally wounded. "Such harshness, and in the presence of your ancestors. You've grown colder since my departure. Deckard has that effect on people. Being so cold himself, it makes it easy to leave others behind."

"We're not going through this again, Flemming. I thought you were dead."

"But you never checked, did you?" Jeremy pointed at Deckard. "No. You had what you wanted, the heat was too much, and you bailed." Jeremy tried to assert control over Flemming's speech, but his will was an unassailable wall. *Is this Ben's doing? How could he have any influence?*

"The Concordat was all around us. We got separated and your location was swarmed with troops. There was no escape for you, dead or alive."

"And I tried to die, Max." Jeremy felt his mind fill with something he never knew about Deckard's former partner. The memory imprinted itself on his own consciousness with the impact of a nail gun on wood. Anger swelled within. Anger he knew was Flemming's, but mixed with the guilt he suddenly felt for what he had done while in control of Deckard.

"I set off a grenade I knew would kill plenty of Concordat soldiers, but also because I knew it would kill me." Flemming raised his fake arm. "That was back when we stood for something, Max. Back when we believed in more than money. Back before you rolled over for the highest bidder." He moved across the catwalk. "We used to think the Concordat was evil, Max."

"Because they are, *furnnelaliss.*" Vennseera spat the words at him.

"No, Kel—, Vennseera." *Did I say that? Did she hear that?* Jeremy's mind started to cloud. It was one thing to be on the outside, controlling the agents and their actions, without their real knowledge. Now, actually projecting inside someone, with full access to their memories and feelings, proved more difficult.

Jeremy started to feel as if he had *less* control. He needed to focus and assert his will over Flemming's.

"The Concordat saved me, Max. Made me whole again. Taught me more about the universe than we knew before. Told me what devices like the *Dreammaker* can do in the wrong hands. Showed me–"

Flemming was cut off as a laser blast from Deckard's pistol cut into the supports on the catwalk. "Shut up, Flemming. Damn, you talk too much."

Flemming was unimpressed. "I suppose you're right. You honestly don't think I'm going to surrender, do you?"

He watched Deckard sigh heavily. Jeremy recognized the sign. It was a personality quirk he'd devised, and Jeremy knew what was next. Concentrating hard, he forced his will on Flemming's mind and took control. His mind flipped a command to his cyberarm, and a small hum shot through the limb.

Deckard adjusted his aim. "No, I don't." The pistol reported again, the beam square at Flemming's chest. With the arm already activated, the beam crackled and quickly dissipated around the energy shield emanating from the arm.

The first shot was the signal the Volorvians needed. Flemming drew his own pistol and took aim at Deckard. "You didn't expect me not to be prepared did you?" Flemming leveled the pistol at his agent.

Then hesitated.

What the hell? Jeremy knew what he had to, but he couldn't pull the trigger. It wasn't Flemming trying to take control back. The sudden gravity of killing another up close and personal stopped him cold.

* * *

"What do you mean he doesn't pull the trigger?" Kelly asked.

Ben looked confused. Kelly had noticed that ever since they'd encountered Flemming. She wasn't sure if Ben was having trouble keeping track of the adventure's notes, changing his mind on things or something else, but Ben wasn't himself.

"Yeah, Flemming doesn't shoot." Ben spoke with uncertainty, paused again, then looked up at the rest of the players around the table. "But you hear howls from deeper in the room. They sound Volorvian in origin."

"Crap," was all Jesse said.

* * *

The arrival of Tor'bronn and his men gave Jeremy the break he needed. He ducked out of the line of fire and grabbed some cover near the catwalk's stairs. He could sense Flemming's rapid heartbeat and feel the sweat on his body.

His emotions warred inside him. He knew Deckard needed to die or be taken out of the fight. Now, actually here looking at another, living and breathing human, Jeremy wasn't sure he could pull the trigger.

Get ahold of yourself. "You've got to do this!" he snapped. Jeremy turned and looked toward the fight. Deckard and his crew were laying down covering fire, as Daytri approached the *Dreammaker*. *No. He'll mess everything up.* If anyone could figure out how to use the device, it would be the *Dragonsfire*'s tech.

Jeremy stood and took aim with his pistol. The targeting reticule appeared over his eye and Jeremy centered it on Daytri's back. Jeremy felt a tears flow from Flemming's human eye. *I have to. I have to. I'm sorry.*

* * *

"The shot hits. Oooh, it's a critical." Ben pushed his lips out and exhaled.

The other players groaned as Ben rolled the dice behind the screen. Kelly looked over at Alex. She didn't look happy. She knew her character was no fighter, and that she was against the idea of having her character run out from cover to do something with the *Dreammaker*. If she died here, Alex wasn't going to be happy.

Ben lifted his head and looked at Alex. "Twenty-eight points, and you are dropped from heavy internal organ damage."

Alex tossed her character sheet into the air. "Told you assholes that was a stupid plan. Jeremy would never have agreed to it."

"Hey, man, you still have Jer's character. Nobody plays a combat guy like you," Jesse offered up meekly.

Alex scowled. "Yeah, that doesn't make me feel any better."

"Alex, c'mon." Ben spoke calmly. "It's Deckard's turn. What do you want to do?"

Kelly saw the look on Alex's face, and knew things weren't about to get any better. *Damnit Jeremy, why'd you have to bow out tonight? This adventure is ruined.* Then Kelly thought about what Jeremy had told her. If it really was true, then Daytri was really dying there on the floor of this chamber. She pushed those thoughts out. *No. That can't really be happening.*

* * *

Jeremy watched Deckard turn to face him. He drew a second pistol and fired both as he moved with determination toward Flemming's position. The laser blasts sparked and burned around him, pinning him down. Flemming held his arm up, the active energy shield absorbing the shots that came too close. A warning tone dinged, indicating that power to the shield was nearly spent. *Won't matter. He's coming to fight me. Just what I wanted.*

Jeremy heard the shouts of Ren'tregg and Vennseera as their commander moved to face off against his former partner, but Deckard ignored them. "C'mon! You know this is what you want!" Deckard shouted as he holstered both pistols and whipped out his stun baton.

Jeremy jumped free from his position. He killed the energy shield and shunted power to enhance the cyberarm's strength. *I'm sorry guys.*

* * *

"Alex, don't," Kelly pleaded. "Deckard's going to get his ass kicked."

"She's right," Jesse added. "Who knows what's in Flemming's cyberarm? We need to find a way to get the hell out of here. You're just asking for Deckard to be killed." Jesse's tone softened. "Jeremy will be pissed."

The word 'killed' hit Kelly hard. *Will his death affect Jeremy?*

Alex shot back, "Jeremy's not here. He chumped out of the session tonight, knowing this was going to be the finale. He asked me to play his character, and this is what he's getting." Alex looked defiantly around the table at everyone. "Besides, we're not making it out of here anyway. We're on the road to a total party kill, so if there is anything Deckard would want, it's a blaze of glory." Jesse turned his attention directly to Ben, who looked concerned. "I'm doing a called shot on Flemming's cyberarm with the stun baton. Remember that Daytri modded the thing to have increased power output. Deckard's going to kick it up to that level."

Ben nodded. "You've got the initiative. Go for it."

* * *

Jeremy watched the stun baton crackle brightly. *Daytri's mods.* Deckard feinted to the right, then cut back, stepped in and thrust the baton directly toward his arm.

It missed by mere centimeters.

Called shot? Good idea, Alex. Too bad you missed.

Jeremy took advantage of the thrust and grabbed Deckard's arm, yanked him right into a waiting raised knee. Deckard exhaled sharply, folding inward. Jeremy followed it up with a strike to his thoracic, dropping him to the ground.

An angry shout in the distance caught Jeremy's attention for a moment, but he didn't want to lose focus on Deckard. He only hoped Tor'bronn and the other Volorvians would overpower Ren'tregg and Vennseera. *Need to finish this quick.*

* * *

"You roll away from Flemming's attempt to grab you, but you can't get out of his grapple range."

Alex's tone was grim but determined. "I'm going to attack from prone." A clattering of dice followed the declaration. "Seven." Alex spoke through gritted teeth. Kelly and Jesse groaned in sympathy.

"Your kick cuts the air just in front of Flemming. In a rapid motion, he comes straight down at you, his cyberarm leading the way."

Ben rolled the dice.

* * *

Jeremy stood above Deckard's unconscious body, studying the damage done by his cyberarm. He could tell his agent was still alive, but the brutality done to Deckard's face painted a different picture. *So that's what a critical hit looks like. So happy he didn't have to die.*

He stood up and looked toward Vennseera and Ren'tregg. They stood in shock, then slowly raised their hands in surrender. *This is it. Need to work fast.* Jeremy kept his will strong. He knew he was about to change any plans might have, but Jeremy couldn't help wonder if his plans would now *become* Ben's plans. *Hurts my head to think about it.*

"Don't worry, your captain lives." Flemming spoke as his gaze focused on the Volorvian. "Though the same may not be said for you, I'm afraid." With a nod of his head, Tor'bronn and the two remaining members of his crew rushed Ren'tregg and quickly bound him. "He's all yours. Better get out now." Jeremy could feel the pang of betrayal in his gut, but knew there was nothing he could do about it.

As the Volorvians carried one of their own away in disturbing silence, Flemming approached Vennseera. He looked down at Daytri. "He doesn't look good. We better make this quick, eh?" He drew his pistol and motioned toward the *Dreammaker*.

"Make what quick?" She complied, unsure of what was about to happen. "Where are the rest of the Concordat soldiers?" Vennseera asked.

"Outside as insurance. Don't worry, we just want the *Dreammaker*. But I need this done first. Don't worry, you'll live." Flemming pointed to the device's surface. "Just place your hands on it."

"What?"

Jeremy didn't have time to mess around. He could feel Flemming begin to fight against the commands Jeremy was issuing. *Looks like Ben did have other plans.* "Do it. Now!"

* * *

"Ben, what the hell? You don't have to shout. I get that you're in character." Kelly shot an irritated glare toward Ben, who seemed to look through her. She didn't like that Ben was yelling at her. This, coupled with his confusion earlier, was making for a weird evening. Kelly thought back to everything Jeremy had told her. She couldn't help but wonder if this was somehow related; not that there was anything that she could do about it. Kelly promised that she wouldn't say or act any different.

"Vennseera complies, but gives Flemming a mean look." Kelly was irritated and confused. She waited for Ben to respond, but he seemed still lost in his own thoughts, not even at the table, miles away.

* * *

It was like moving, eyes closed, through a world filled with cotton. He could sense and even hear the tone, a dull beeping repeated over and over. Each time the tone struck, he could feel it in his bones. Struggling, Jeremy moved forward. Other thoughts and worries gnawed at the sides of his mind, but he struggled to stay focused on the tone. *Find it. Find it.*

The mental cotton began to clear and the tone grew louder. Jeremy started to see some colors besides gray. Shapes appeared with the colors. The tone sharpened and the rattling in his mind focused into a vibration on his leg.

Jeremy opened his eyes.

He was back in Ben's car, the world just as he left it. Back on Earth.

Moving quickly, Jeremy reached for the small indentation at the bottom of the case. It was the nexus where many of the arcane and high tech lines met. His index finger fit snugly in the imprint. His voice hoarse, he spoke a single word.

"Chūqùhéqiáoliáng."

* * *

Ben looked back at Kelly after she said his name the third time. She could tell he was still confused.

"Whu?" was all Ben could muster.

Kelly, Alex, and Jesse all exchanged concerned glances, but Kelly took the lead. "So, what happens?"

"To who?" Ben looked down at his notes.

"To Vennseera. Flemming made her touch the *Dreammaker*. Then what?"

Ben ran a hand through his hair. "Why would he do that?"

"What the hell do you mean?" Alex threw her arms up in frustration. "You're the one who *made* her do that!"

Ben squinted as he looked over his notes. Kelly was about to say something, when a tingle struck her brain. It started in the back then tickled its way over the top of her skull before settling right behind her forehead, where the sensation bounced around, back and forth. Kelly grabbed the table to steady herself, as the room rocked to and fro. *What the hell?*

A chill followed the tingle, filling her entire body. She shivered as the cold lingered in her fingers and toes. Kelly closed her eyes to the spinning as she rode out the chill, then opened them.

The tingle vanished.

The room settled.

She looked at the other three. No one seemed to notice. Alex and Jesse stared at Ben, who seemed to be pulling things together. Finally, he looked up.

"Okay, so after you touch the *Dreammaker*, Flemming looks at you, says, with a hint of guilt in his eyes, 'I'm sorry, Kelly.'" Ben shook his head. " 'I mean, Vennseera.' He picks up the *Dreammaker,,* looks down at Daytri, then over at Deckard. 'They will live. Like I said, all we wanted was the device. You're free to go. Maybe if you're lucky, you'll find Ren'tregg before he's slain.'"

Jesse scoffed. "Damn well better find him."

Ben held his hands up in surrender. "I'm sorry guys. The fight was pretty even, but the dice just weren't on your side."

Alex cleaned up her papers, knowing the night's game was over. "I wish Jeremy had been here." She sounded defeated.

Kelly nodded in silent agreement as she looked toward his empty chair. Something felt odd in Kelly's mind as she heard Jeremy's name mentioned, but she couldn't place it.

* * *

"He got taken away?" Jeremy did his best to fake surprise.

"Yeah, back to his family most likely. I guess we know where the crew will be headed off to next," Kelly answered from the other end of the line.

"No doubt," Jeremy answered. Despite having a hand in the fate of Deckard's crewman, Jeremy was determined to make the team whole again. He had to make amends.

It was more than the crew he wanted to heal. Jeremy knew that he didn't want to start the lie over again with Kelly. The coming Monday, he would resign from the agency. He'd chosen love over duty, and would be happy to face whatever the agency would do to his own memory of being in the agency. With luck, they'd wipe it all. Then he and Kelly could move on in a blissful ignorance. Now he just had to see if all his efforts to remove the knowledge from Kelly's mind had been successful.

Jeremy switched his tone, becoming a bit more playful. "So, what are you going to do tonight, then?"

Kelly paused. "Not sure. Feeling pretty lazy. I've got half a season of *This Dead Life* to still get through. Plus, there's some ice cream in the freezer that's feeling neglected." She chuckled at her own joke.

Jeremy paused. *That wasn't the plan for tonight.* "Are you serious?"

"Yes, why?"

Jeremy could feel his gut begin to churn in fear. "We... we were supposed to go out. We had plans."

Kelly chuckled again. "Plans? Plans for what?"

"Our date." Jeremy could feel his throat begin to tighten.

"Date?" Kelly's chuckle turned into a laugh. She brought herself back down. "With *you*?"

Jeremy nodded. "Yes." His voice quickly turned to defeat.

"Jer, if we were going to go on a date, I think I'd remember that."

The words hit him like a hammer. His plan had worked. Too well.

No.

SERMON FOR THE THIRD SUNDAY OF EPIPHANY: A REPORT FROM THE 68ᵀᴴ PERIODIC INTERSPECIES THEOLOGIANS' CONFERENCE

Shannon Dickson

Shannon "Leoff" Collie Dickson was raised in a northern Canadian small town, educated at Millar Memorial Bible College and the University of Saskatchewan, and lives in a town full of nuclear scientists. Naturally her writing tends towards fantasy and science fiction. Her hobbies include the Society for Creative Anachronism (where she is known as Baroness Donnet), heritage gardening, mineralogy, roleplaying games, and tabletop games of all sorts.

May the words of my mouth and the meditations of all our hearts be now and always acceptable in Your sight, O Lord Our strength and Our Redeemer. Amen.

The heavens declare the glory of God, and night after night findeth us curled up on the couch with a good book. But Saturday night was so beautiful, with the new fallen snow and the stars and a little slip of a moon, that I had to put aside this morning's sermon and go outside to listen. The little park that adjoins our back yard was soft and cool in deep green and bright white, and the park bench was wet and hard, but not hard or wet enough to stop my mind from wandering, and I didn't even see the spaceship land.

Hey!" a voice called. "You the theologian?"

"Yes," I replied, brashly putting aside the opinions of my seminary professors and colleagues.

"Well, here's your bus," the voice prompted. It was a strange voice, measured and tinny, like the voice that tells you that that number is no longer in service and gives you the new one: it was strange enough to make me look up, and then I saw the ship and the speaker.

The speaker was bluish, like the light coming from the open doors of the "bus." It gave the general impression of roundness: that is, all its hairy tentacles emanated from what appeared to be a roundish centre. Draped among the tangle of appendages was a tangle of wires and foam balls, and several of the appendages inclined towards these when we spoke.

Remember, I had no idea what to expect of a spaceship, or an extraterrestrial, any more than you or anyone at NASA or the Canadian Space Agency would: we'd never met anyone from beyond Earth's orbit before. And my mind was thousands of miles and thousands of years away, with Elijah and Elisha on the mountain. It wasn't my idea of an angel at all—but my mind was on heavenly things, not earthly or extraterrestrial. The ball of tentacles added, "Are we early?"

"You know your business," I replied, stepping forward.

A bigger ball of appendages appeared behind the first one. "No he don't, he's new, and sometimes front desk and us get opposite instructions, you know? This is the bus for the 68th Periodic Interspecies Theologians' Conference, and this was our next address, so if you're a theologian we got a space for you." So they weren't angels, as such. "Here's your translator," the bigger one said, passing me another pile of wires and foam and extending a furry tentacle to help me up. It was cool, and quivering like a cold kitten, and I realized that they were standing in the cold politely waiting for me. I hurried into the bus and the doors slammed shut. The smaller one showed me into the passengers' room and left.

About thirty one alien eyes stared at me and about a dozen voices chorused, "That's not Spinky!" A squarish, meaty being with an identifiable face (all on the top of its head) moved closer. "But you are a theologian, right?" I nodded. "Captain!" it shouted, and the larger ball of tentacles appeared. "Is this a new stop, or was this the address you had for Spinky?"

"Isn't this one Spinky either?" the captain asked.

"No, Spinky must have given the wrong address again, or there was a typing error, or a translation glitch, or something. Well, meeting new people is what this conference is all about."

"But if this is the wrong passenger," protested the smaller ball of tentacles, "he won't be registered at the hotel. You can't just go picking people up en route!"

"Sure we can," the captain reassured both of us. "Look, this is the 68th Conference. Nothing surprises that hotel: nothing. You put that many theologians together, this sort of thing is bound to happen. When you've done this route as many times as I have, you'll consider it pure routine. And remember, company policy is always to give a free return trip to any first-contacts you meet. Gives us an edge on the competition. Don't worry, Rev, the hotel will have everything you need. I'll scan you for your dietary limits as we go, and call ahead. Chunky, I'll leave you with the introductions. Have a good flight."

I was still trying to sort it all out as we sat down. "How... the translator... We haven't made alien contact yet! We're talking—or it's giving me—good Canadian English!"

"Quite the experience, isn't it?" Chunky sympathised. "But there's no mystery. This is a good bus line. They get a translation program for every language they hear regularly on the major routes, on the off-chance of picking up some customers, and of getting the credit for making another first contact. The captain will get a bonus next payday for taking you along. They'll give you a calling card when we drop you off, too." Chunky showed me a small flat box. "It's a remote relay. As for the language, they probably kept this one because it was common over a wide land area."

Another problem came to mind. "How am I going to pay the conference fees?"

"Should have thought of that before you came, eh? No, you're a first-contact, and the Conference will happily cover the costs. You'll probably be able to start a galactic credit rating getting interviewed by one of the news teams, anyway. Just stay away from the Bigtooth crew."

"I think they aren't allowed in this time," a delicate construct of web and scales interjected. "There were complaints about them using news bulletins as hunting surveys."

"It's time the galactic legislature outlawed intersystem hunting," someone grunted.

"It's time the legislature actually got past agreeing on the translations of the inaugural speeches," someone else retorted crisply. "We theologians must be the only galaxy-wide organization that ever gets anything done. How come? Because we don't bother trying to agree."

"What do you—or we—do, then?" I asked.

"We state and compare. Meeting new people and hearing new ideas really is what the conference is about. There are those who might be called infinite nondefinitists, who accept everything everybody says as part of the overall truth; and there are those who might be called finite definitists, who simply listen and bear in mind that we're all just a bunch of aliens anyhow; and most of us fit between the two extremes. Some time during the conference, somebody's bound to put something clearly that you never saw clearly before, even if they meant it all differently, different sensory organs and all that. But speaking of extremes, let's go around the circle and introduce ourselves. They call me Chunky, I use all my limbs equally well, we're the smallest sentient beings on our planet, but the only one that both breathes air and moves. Next?"

In rapid succession I met:

Tri, the delicate three-legged construct of webs and scales

Claus, who reminded me of a lobster but with more legs

Pockets, a thick-skinned blob whose limbs, progeny, and occasionally a mate or two were kept in pouches

Blue, an exoskeletal community that resembled a branching coral

Angel, a tall shiny person mostly covered with wings

Slim, one of the tentacle balls (who reproduce by budding and adapt to any planet on which they're born)

Tweety and Whistler, like twin starfish, who couldn't share anyone else's sensory vocabulary

Jaws, whom I tried hard not to think of as a furry Pacman

Rocky, a rock

and one large scaly thing like a troll that hulked in a corner and looked at us with glazed eyes, all sixteen of them around the top of what passed for a neck. "Never mind Bugly," Claus murmured. "One of the holdouts who believe that there is a direct link between personal taste and piety."

"Certainly one's piety would affect one's sense of values," I hedged.

"No, I mean personal taste. What you taste like. I don't have to worry because that species is allergic to seafood, but I'd keep my distance if I were you. We don't know yet if you'd be edible, but be on the safe side."

For the first time since I had accepted a lift from these strangers, I began to feel queasy. "What do they eat at home? And what will they eat at the conference? For that matter, what will we eat?"

"The hotel staff is very good," Angel chirped. "It was their attention to detail that caught our attention after the Calawar disaster, the second conference.

Or should I not have mentioned that? Truly it was a disaster. One of the busloads was accidentally delivered to the rear entrance by mistake, and some of the delegates were served as breakfast before it was found out. Well, it absolutely ruined the conference. That would never happen at the Supreme on Little Cousin. They have this magnificent food fabrication lab that can adjust the dietary necessities to meet most people's sensory modes quite adequately. Even Tweety and Whistler, though they had to work directly from food samples they brought the first time. Their type doesn't travel much. Bugly eats in the bedroom, because of the mess, you know, so we aren't sure what they give that sort. We don't know much about Bugly."

"A food fab lab," I mused. "You mean I feed it a carrot and some soybeans and it can put out a steak?"

"Hah! He is a carnivore; check out those teeth. I told you so," Whistler commented to Tweety.

"But surely not, with that jaw structure and big body cavity."

"Omnivore, technically," I intervened, "but we don't eat other sentients if we can help it, if we know they're an intelligent species."

"Another conscience-directed limited omnivore!" Pockets crowed. "Hear that, Bugly? You're really in the minority now. Bilateral, do you really not eat other intelligent life forms?"

There followed a fascinating discussion on moral eating habits and the obligation, duty, or notion of trying to avoid eating other people or removing their bodies from around their souls. Is it morally better to kill someone whom you plan to eat than to kill someone and let the meat rot? Many of our North American and other indigenous cultures believed so, apologizing and explaining to the animal why their meat was needed. Should that question take into account the potential meal's own moral condition and wider cosmological view, those of the eater or hunter, or both party's opinions and moral state?

"For instance," Slim suggested, "if someone has lived the sort of life that both it and another person believe would merit a better reincarnation, and if both believe that being eaten (thus lengthening someone else's spiritual journey) is itself a pious act or condition, isn't it actually good for the second person, in this case, to fall upon the first person and eat it?"

"I'm sure many lower life forms think so," Blue sniffed.

"Does it taste good?" Bugly asked, surprising us all.

"Very good, thank you," Slim replied innocently.

There was an awkward silence, into which I whispered, "'This is my body, given for you.'"

"That had the feel of part of a familiar quote," Angel said, and attention jumped away from Slim. "What's the rest of it?"

So I plunged into an explanation of the great sacrament and event of the Christian world, which drifted in and out of the waters of baptism and healing, wandered briefly through law and into grace, faith and hope, and thence back to communion again. There was a healthy silence.

"Sacramentalist, sacrificial intervention, and multiunity–someone write that down," Chunky said. "We keep a running poll, Bilateral. There are rumors that some of the locals run a betting pool on it, but we don't take it so seriously."

"I've only been speaking for myself," I warned. "I've been a very poor apologist even for the few branches of my faith that I know, let alone theology in other parts of the world within our faith, and I shouldn't even try to speak for the ethnically limited groups either inside or outside of the Christian world on our planet."

"Great! Multireligion and multiculture world, and overlapping and diverging cultural and religious borders! You'll be popular on the talk shows, Bilateral. But this will have to wait," Chunky advised. "We're almost at the hotel and haven't even gone over conference and interstellar courtesy conventions. Tri, you've seen most of these binges; you lead this."

These are the rules that I can remember. I suggest that we adopt some of them for our congregation's annual general meeting.

1. Reproductive strategies varying so widely, one does not employ gender-specific terms, as they rarely transfer well and it slows down the translation process.

2. Most questions should be attempted, and every answer should be accepted in good faith. We are explorers here, not missionaries.

3. An honorarium, and royalties if they accrue, are due to anyone interviewed for mass media. ("Very handy for first-contacts like yourself," Tri added.)

4. At these multi-species affairs, some nudity is expected of delegates whether or not they normally wear clothes. Nobody is after your body, and comparison of anatomy is very enlightening.

5. Give other people their distance when meeting them. You don't know which parts of their bodies are sensitive... or poisonous.

6. No-one is an alien. We're all just different.

At this point, we approached the host star, and it was decided unanimously that my first view of a foreign solar system took precedence over mere points of etiquette, "few of which," Jaws graciously remarked, "you would be tasteless enough to breach anyway."

The approach and entry were not as visually spectacular as I had expected, or perhaps, not being familiar enough with my own solar system from such an angle, I didn't know what to look for. Perhaps, too, I was still too excited to notice any further excitement, I mused vaguely. The whole business only seemed rather tedious and slow, until Chunky nudged me and pointed. "See that little moon? The greenish-yellow one with a dark spot?" I nodded. "That's Little Cousin, our destination."

"Pretty small, isn't it? What will the gravity be like?"

Chunky rippled some chest muscles (that species' version of a shrug). "I should say it's much like yours. Your planet and Little Cousin have much the same mass and density and so forth."

"But it's so little!" A gush of adrenalin began to bubble up in my solar plexus. I had thought I was all out.

"You think so?" Claus grinned. "Wait till you've been down there a while with Big Cousin filling the sky all night. You'll be amazed that Little Cousin is even visible from a distance!"

"The stars are dust on the heavens' floor,

Worlds among stars as dust upon pearls,

A galaxy cluster is a smudge to you,

Yet you know what I mean by dust,"

someone quoted. The adrenalin boiled over and I leaned against the window, steaming the glass and hyperventilating.

*   *   *

There was no spaceport. Our bus and its passengers had been cleared on the way in, and the captain simply dropped us off at the front door of the hotel and went off to park.

You could tell at once that it was an expensive conference centre. Some of us talked about it later and it's true: they do look much the same, and identifiably rich, wherever you go. The excessively high ceilings, the synthetic, easy-wipe, very soft chairs too big for half the guests, the expensively artificial plants, the high counters with raised office areas behind them, the smooth but slightly pebbled floor, all bespoke lavish expenditure for the comfort of a wide variety of guests, the convenience of the staff, and easy security operations.

We signed in and got our name tags. The sweet young thing at the desk—I had given up trying to guess genders long ago, naturally, but whatever it was smelled sweet and acted young compared with others of its species—the sweet young thing was quite excited to meet me. "Oh, you're the new one! From a whole new planet that no-one's ever met before! Can I have your smell? My friends will be so jealous!" It thrust a box of tissue at me, and I took one, feeling rather dubious and not a little like a Rider Haggard hero caught in a Road to Avonlea special. After a moment's frantic thought I pressed it to my lips and handed it back with my best attempt at a swashbuckling bow. A new gust of sweetness suffused the air. "Oh, that was a cultural mannerism too! Thank you so much!"

"I'm glad to be your roommate," Angel smirked as we left. "You're going to get better room service than the president. Say, there's Lump-on-a-log, from last conference! Lumpy!" Angel, Whistler and Tweety ran off.

The welcome room was, again, like welcome rooms everywhere. A message board too close to the entrance was hidden by a cluster of perusers. The bar, flanked by large bulletin boards giving the schedule, was at the hottest end of the room, just beyond the tightest crowd. Tables and seating seemed to be arranged purposely to impede one's progress towards the refreshments so that people would have time to notice each other. Our busload dwindled on our way through the noisy throng, as other old acquaintances met, and each time we stopped we all had to be introduced around. I discovered more cultural analogues to the handshake in ten minutes than I could have imagined in a week.

At last Chunky, Slim, and I reached the bar, and I had another hurdle to meet. "Welcome, Reverends. What can I get you?"

"Dark ale, please," I replied, distracted by the sight of what seemed to be Rocky and a bush butting each other.

"Certainly. May I have the chemical codes for that, Reverend?" Sensory tentacles flicked respectfully at me, and I think I must have gaped, abashed.

"Oh. There's about 3 to 8% ethanol in water, and you get that by fermenting grain, a kind of plant seed, eh,–roasted I guess–so it tastes kind of– and there are bubbles, CO_2 I think, yes, left over from fermenting–and there would still be sugar, that's $C_{12}H_{22}O_{11}$, but..." I stuck my hands into my pockets and onto an inspiration. "Hah! A cap from one of my own very best home brew. There should be some stuck to the rubber liner."

The server twitched happily and took the bottle cap. "Yes, Reverend. That should be very adequate. If we could add it to the menu?" It indicated the glowing display above my head. "Your drink should be ready in a few minutes."

They had made my ale by the time Slim and Chunky had gotten refreshments peculiar to their needs. A small crowd gathered to watch. I took a sip and almost choked. "More water!" I gasped. The server passed us an empty glass and a large jug of water and watched, with the crowd, as I carefully balanced the elixirs. Finally the right proportions had been achieved and I handed back the jugs and glasses.

"My friends: ale," I pronounced. "When it's been carbonated, of course." So Friends' Ale, colloquially known as What Bilateral Drinks, was duly entered on the menu. I wonder how popular it became.

Slim drew us aside to the series of wall charts and sign-up sheets. "We'd better get you lined up for some good appearances, Bilateral. Remember we were saying you could pick up a few bucks on the talk shows? That rather understates it. The right gig could put the right person in the stars forever. Being a new species, you're the right person... What about this, Chunky? We put Bilateral down for *From the Frozen Edge* with the Dwarf-and-Nebula network, opposite *New Things* with Four Pulsars, for the prime time interviews, and see who bids highest. The basic honorarium is about a day's wages on my salary, and both of those include royalties. How's that, Bilateral?"

At their direction I pressed my name tag against both time slots, then, with the stylus provided, drew a rough caricature of myself: a gingerbread man with hair, a face, and five digits on hands and feet. After some thought I added boxer shorts.

"What is that?" Chunky asked.

In response I put down my drink and started peeling off clothes. "These," I answered, snapping the elastic of my shorts, "stay on for the cameras. If my classmates on earth ever get a copy of these videos, I'll never hear the end of it. Let 'em guess."

As had been said, the delight of these open interspecies gatherings is that we all had come to gawk (sniff, closely observe in some manner) and be gawked at (sniffed, observed closely): at a proper distance, of course, as the rules indicated. My first thought was that with such a variety of sensory organs, a large proportion of my fellow conferees wouldn't recognize my eyes, let alone a direct stare. It was hard to guess what functions were performed by some features of my fellow theologians, and most of them probably had just as much uncertainty about me.

The variety of shapes was even greater than on the bus, but I later learned that we were only one branch of the conference, consisting of those from a certain range of gravities, atmospheres (though some delegates wore supplementary air tanks), and chemical balances. Other chapters met elsewhere and all the chapters exchanged transcripts, videos, and audios. Slim thought highly of the cetacean and group-mind conferences, but couldn't personally make much sense of the anaerobic conference. The xenogeophysicists, however, planned their own seminars to overlap with that one.

The bush came up to us. "Hi, Slim. Hi, Chunky. Is this Bilateral who gave us that new drink? My compliments on a truly unique substance. Are you fellows coming to the Comparative Anatomy discussion? It's the introductory feature. If you are, you'd better come now."

We went. The discussion was in a sunken hemisphere terraced in soft rug. Bush took the central podium and addressed us.

"Friends and fellow theologians, welcome to the first session of the 68th All-Theologians Conference, and thank you for coming. We extend a special welcome to those of you who are here for the first time; I note Chunky's friend

Bilateral up there in the third row." (There was a subdued hubbub of applause.) "In some ways, although this tends to be the lightest session of the conference, it is the most important, for it is largely the way we are shaped—our shapes themselves and the way we acquired them—that governs our thoughts and concepts of God. Some of you have many sensory organs; some of you have only one; some of you only use one with reference to self-knowledge and God-knowledge, and some of you use all of them.

"Every person perceives God in a way unique to that person; each of us is limited by our individual ranges of perception as well as by our species' limitations of perception. How does a person who does not know &(^" (the translator gave off a buzz of static) "identify with God's &(^ of the world or worlds? I have just used a term peculiar to my own species. No translation of the term is yet available, so I cannot describe what we mean by saying that God &*(^, but I can note that none of the rest of you have the physiology to identify what happens inside the leaves of plants on your home worlds during seasonal, light, and atmosphere changes. Many of you have plants (groups of cells which grow and take nourishment both from the soil and from the light and atmosphere) on your home worlds, and some societies have technology that can observe it to some degree. When you see me and realize that I have sensations related to these stimulations and that I believe that God shares these perceptions and emotions, it widens your concept of what I mean when I talk about God.

"What we will do now is to consider how we are made, and how that relates to our images of God. I will start the discussion, and then throw it open for questions about each other's bodies, perceptions, and how or if that relates to our knowledge of God.

"I take substance from the solid ground, from the gaseous air, and from the liquid that splashes and flows and condenses and drips on me. I take only what I need to produce the fruit and gases which I give to my world. The gases I give freely from my leaves for other species on my world to breathe; this is a part of

&(^. The fruit I give selfishly, because though it becomes nourishment for other lives, it also bears its own life, which may grow up to be my companions, and if it goes into the ground and becomes dead, it will nourish me again. Some of our metaphors for God that I have heard other species use are the rivers and winds which change the spent soil and air around us, but we find that rather abstract."

Comparative anatomy really is very enlightening. I have a video of that discussion group, if any of you are interested, but I cannot begin to describe all the variations in survival mechanisms nor the ways they reflect, in their own ways, the glory of God. Consider, for instance, how you would describe God if your primary sense, like a dog's, was smell. If you had split off from another amoeba, would you call God your Father? What if you were like Blue, whose mind spans several bodies over several planets: what would you think of going into all the world to preach the gospel?

This lasted for several hours, but I only lasted for about an hour and a half. Remember, the bus had come just before my bedtime on Earth. I woke in our room with Angel waving a peculiarly familiar substance under my nose. I sat up and looked more closely. It was a scaled-up version of my pocket communion set, with a scaled-up portion of the communion elements on it.

"What..."

"You fell asleep in the forum," Chunky explained. "We let you sleep until we felt tired ourselves, and then brought you back to our rooms. We found this in your pocket and recognized it as that ritual food that you were telling us about. I hope it wasn't sacrilege, having them make up a few batches, but I know my God would want you to have your breakfast." A gesture indicated the original set, several like it, and a number of the larger versions, lined up on the table. "May we join you for breakfast? Our dietary requirements are within a reasonable tolerance range."

It was strange to have the Eucharist for breakfast. Eucharist—morning—I had forgotten about Sunday worship! I stopped in mid-bite, aghast at my thoughtlessness. "My church... I'm supposed to be..."

"Just thought of that now, eh?" Chunky grinned. "Again, don't worry. The earth goes around in an orbit, right? As it turns, time passes, right, or the other way round I guess. It doesn't matter. The trick in these interstellar navigations is to get off at the right part of the earth's orbit and rotation, and there you are, just after you left. Everything will be fine. You even get a full night's sleep."

"Speaking of places to be, though," Angel commented, waving at the clock, "there are some very competent lecturers starting in about twelve minutes. Selected Topics in Interspecies Worship is by Rev. Lips, with the mass choir that the Lips Ministry sponsors. We may even get some music to take home."

                                           *   *   *

Lunchtime was very good: both entertaining and tasty. The buffet tables were laid out along two sides of the dining room, allowing vegetarians and carnivores to avoid, respectively, meat and vegetables, but permitting those like myself and Chunky, who could eat both, to go down both lines. A computer menu at the head of both lines gave us the numbers of dishes compatible with our needs and tolerances.

What strange-looking things people eat! But think of perogies, or spaghetti and meatballs; they all are essentially pastes combined with other pastes. What lengths we humans go to disguise the origin of our food! Anyone would think there was something taboo about plain grains, fruit and meat. Compared with what we do to grain and grapes before we have bread and wine, these alien goos, blobs, and chunks didn't seem so strange. Blue joined us presently, but didn't eat, having stood in the rock garden and taken in whatever it is that coral people need. No-one's an alien; we're all just different, I thought.

"None of the meat is really meat, though," Chunky commented. "At least, I doubt if it would be. There's enough risk, judging the right proportion of trace elements that should be there when they reconstitute new foods from known ingredients. The xenoculinary schools have to be very exacting. Don't miss this red fruit here. It's real, local, and the second most exotic fruit on the board. You remember Bushy, from last night? This is the product of a sentient plant, related to Bushy a couple millennia back. It's probably an infertile fruit, produced specially for the conference. I haven't met any of the grove, but I must remember to send my thanks. Oh, Blue and I took a liberty and decided Dwarf-and-Nebula had made the best offer. What did you want to bring or wear?"

* * *

In the lobby, a row of the oversized padded benches had been lined up in front of some exotic looking plants with an array of cameras facing them. An amoeba rolled over to greet us. "Hello, I'm Bags, the host for *Frozen Edge*. You must be Bilateral. We're very glad to have you on this show, very glad indeed. ^%$, have you given Bilateral a copy of the contract yet? Ah, here it is. There you are. Maybe Blue will hold it for you while you're on air. Okay, here's the format. We'll be sitting there, talking, and then the camera comes my way and I'll turn towards it and introduce you and we're off. Got that?"

The worst problem with the interview—one which should hardly have fazed me by now—was that Bags had no face, front, back, top, or bottom; I had no idea whether my interviewer was about to laugh or be horrified, whether it was interested or impatient. After one question, which I hadn't understood at all, I mentioned this. One doesn't alter one's views of God to suit one's audience—a futile exercise, since God is unchanging and beyond our powers of description—but we do mostly talk about God by analogy, and an analogy that comforts me might terrify another person or species. "For instance," I offered, "they tell me that at another chapter of the conference there are people who cannot survive light or air, just as you and I require both. If I told them that I worship Jesus, the Light of the World, through the Spirit, the Wind of God, they might at first think that I've thrown in with the forces of evil."

"Ha, ha, ha," Bags responded heartily, "and how do you know you haven't? Ha, ha, just kidding. No honestly, how do you know God is good?" Evidently Bags wasn't taking it very seriously at all. I let him drivel on for a while, then drivelled on myself for a while—the usual stuff about the nature and knowledge of good and evil, enlivened by doubtlessly amusing references to human anatomy from Bags. It was not the best part of my day.

*   *   *

The evening, though, was the best part of the conference. We gathered in the ballroom, what seemed to be thousands and thousands, and thousands upon thousands of us: later we heard that a record 1893 were there. No cameras were permitted, and no reporters allowed on the floor; it was all devoted to us and our individual forms of worship. For a while we took turns, letting one another lead in mutual praise and enjoyment. Slowly the focus broadened and shifted, and I found myself alone in a corner among some other people singing or sitting alone with our translators turned off. Bushy was one of those, humming like an incomprehensible but friendly wind. I sat under Bushy's branches and sang myself to sleep.

*   *   *

The second day of the conference followed the same pattern. Morning was taken up with various speakers, and in the afternoon and early evening we alternately were quizzed in public on camera, and quizzed our fellows in the privacy of the gardens and other places set aside for panel discussions. Besides the interview on *From the Frozen Edge* I was part of a panel on the link between morality and theology, another on the necessary connection between mind and Mind, and a heated informal debate in the welcome room between the Polytheist Monoculturists and us Unitheist Multiculturists, which came to a hilarious end when Blue wandered in and claimed membership in both parties by virtue of the ability to have simultaneously one mind in several bodies, and two minds within one or many bodies, depending which worlds were being considered.

At last it was time to go home. Addresses were exchanged, orders were placed for transcripts of the various discussion groups, final deals were negotiated. As Chunky had predicted, my earnings from interviews and appearances had enabled me to sign up for the complete audio-visual conference transcripts, subscribe to an off-planet journal, and pay in advance for two places at the next conference (whenever that would be). I must have come across more fluently than I had thought on the *Frozen Edge* program, because the journal that I subscribed to solicited a paid article. However, the interview must have had some amusement value as well, because I also got a sizeable royalty from a light-entertainment channel based in Four Pulsars, which bought the original interview from Dwarf-and-Nebula and later got me on their own show *Keep Talking*. Well, well.

I got dressed, collected my notes, souvenirs, and communion set (the others went with Chunky and Angel as souvenirs) and gathered with the rest of the busload in the parking lot. Bushy came to see us off.

"Well, friends, meet you next conference. Bilateral, bring a few more of your kind next time, eh? Chunky, take care of yourself. Angel. Claus." We breathed at each other for a moment, then Bushy turned and walked away.

"Bushy's people still can't get used to goodbyes," Blue whispered. "It's hard on the whole grove when conference time comes around."

We were just loading up when Bags and the Dwarf-and-Nebula crew rolled past. "And it's the end of another exciting conference, folks," Bags was saying. "There, take a last look; Bilateral is on the way home, the first one from his planet ever to be interviewed on Dwarf-and-Nebula Telecast, your favourite network for news, education, and mind-blowing entertainment."

The doors shut and Bags' babble ceased.

* * *

We were all fairly subdued on the way home; we had been communicating almost incessantly for the last two days, and it was time to relax in the familiarity of our own company. Chunky and Angel worked on memorizing the liturgy that went with the pocket communion sets. Blue and Slim spent the time considering how various parts of them might adapt to other worlds. I tried to imitate with my inadequate fingers and limbs the ritual motions that Slim performed in worship. Tweety and Whistler, characteristically, recounted their experiences to one another. Tri and Pockets lounged nearby, apparently dozing, while Claus and Jaws set out a board game of the complexity of chess combined with the more random elements of backgammon. Rocky rolled among us, occasionally radiating. Bugly sat in the corner, glowering.

The little slip of Earth's moon was just a little higher in the sky when the bus lowered into the snowy park again. I gathered my effects and stood up, suddenly aware that I was little better at partings than Bushy. None of our life cycles were the same. How many of us would survive to the next conference? What body of Blue would attend? When would the next bus be?

The captain came to help me off. "Thank you for flying Meteorite Space Lines." It gave me the small, flat box engraved with the company logo. "Flight schedules and rates are available through this calling card. This is an audio model, which can also be plugged into your video player when your order is delivered. Please feel free to call if you have any questions." The door slid shut and I walked back to the edge of our yard to watch and wave as my friends glided away into the night.

It was very cold. I had forgotten my parka and my pants.

Now to God Who Was, and Is, and Is To Come, be glory in the Church and in Christ Jesus, now and forever. Amen.

SURVIVING SUNSET

Dan Repperger

Dan Repperger got his start working for FASA and AWOL on the Battletech series in the mid-1990s. Thereafter, he wrote serial fiction and political editorial for Keep It Coming. Today he's best known as the moderating host of Fear the Boot, an RPG podcast. He resides in St. Peters, Missouri with his wife, three dogs, and devon rex cat.

October 15th, 4117 A.D.

Lauriston, Kettering IV

Vengedi Republic

The evening hours came, but darkness never followed. Instead, the glow of the setting sun gave way to the radiance of blue energy lashing down from warships in orbit, tearing apart the city of Lauriston. Dense smoke swirled up, parting each time another volley fell.

Guided by this unnatural light, Cassandra sprinted toward the eastern edge of the city. The streets had once been lined by proud buildings of stone and glass. Now only their shriveled skeletons remained, the structures melted and walls crumbling into the street. Vehicles were scattered between them, smashed or simply abandoned. As Cassandra got further from the center of town, the buildings were smaller—mostly shops and homes—but the carnage was the same. She tried to block out the fires, the sound of gunfire, the panicked screams

255

of a mother clutching her child in a ditch, and the burnt man wandering down the middle of the street in a daze. Her eyes focused on the house numbers.

1017, 1019, 1021. Then she saw 1023. Struggling to catch her breath, she collapsed against the door, pounding on it feverishly. "Penelope!" she yelled. Getting no response, she tried the keypad next to the door. Dead. She raced to the side of the house, where a crimson service robot knelt, dutifully tending the garden as the city burned. Cassandra saw a window just above its back. She ran toward it, counting her steps, and vaulted over the robot. Her shoulder struck the glass and she fell into the kitchen, hitting the floor hard. Bits of glass cut her side, and as she struggled to her feet, they gashed her hands as well. "Penelope!" she called into the dark house.

"Cassandra?" The voice was shaky, but it most certainly belonged to her younger sister.

"Where are you?" Cassandra asked as she stumbled through the kitchen, feeling around the furniture, ignorant of her own pain. "Just keep talking. I'll find you."

"I'm scared, Cass. I'm really scared. I came here to find Brian, but he's not here. I think his family went to the shelter."

Cassandra made her way into the adjacent room. The curtains were drawn across all of the windows. Her sister was sitting on the floor, a tiny light in her hand, now shining at her. Penelope was thirteen-years-old, her blonde hair hanging down in tangled mats. She was dirty and frightened, but didn't appear injured. Cassandra sat on the floor across from her, completely exhausted. "Yeah, a shelter," she finally got out. "That's where we should be, too! Mom and Dad refused to go until I could find you."

"I'm sorry, Cass. But I just—"

"Had to know that Brian was okay, didn't you? Penelope, what about your own family?"

"I know. I'm sorry."

"Just shut up. We have to go." Cassandra stood up, still wobbly on her feet. She had no strength to run across town in the other direction, but she had to try. Her parents were too stubborn to go to a shelter unless the family was together, and Penelope was foolish enough to make this trip necessary. She hobbled over to the door and tried its keypad.

Penelope stood as well, shining her light on the door to make her sister's work easier. Cassandra hit the buttons again and again, but it was dead on this side as well. She yanked the maintenance panel off and grabbed the manual release, leaning backward until it extended and the door popped open a few centimeters. She dug her fingers in and pulled it open just enough to squeeze through, back into the well-lit massacre unfolding in Lauriston.

Penelope followed Cassandra, gasping when she saw the city. Cassandra took a few steps forward, every muscle screaming for her to stop. She glanced back to see if Penelope was moving, but her younger sister was just gaping in shock. Cassandra started to yell at her when she noticed it was the sky she was staring at, not the city. Between the shots of the relentless barrage, an object was falling, trailing smoke. It was rounded on the front, smooth on the sides, and jagged on the back. Cassandra could barely make out something painted on one of its sides: *VCS Rampart*, the name of a Vengedi cruiser. She watched in horror as it fell toward the opposite side of the city.

When it struck, whole blocks disappeared in a storm of fire and dust. The ensuing shockwave blew debris down the streets as the hull tumbled through rows of buildings before finally coming to rest. Bits of wreckage showered the city, some of the smaller pieces sailing far enough to bounce off of buildings near the two girls.

"Mommy! Daddy!" Penelope cried out, staggering forward, her hand outstretched.

Her sister could no longer contain her rage. She grabbed Penelope by the shoulders and threw her back, the younger girl falling down. "This is *your* fault!" Cassandra said. "We should have been in the shelter hours ago! Instead you had to come over here to check on your precious Brian, and now our parents are dead!" Penelope crumpled, crying uncontrollably. "Oh no you don't," Cassandra said, pulling her to her feet. "You don't get to feel sorry for yourself. You did this, and now you're going to help me figure a way out of it. You're not a baby anymore."

"I thought the war was over," Penelope sobbed. "I heard the Prime Minister say they—"

Cassandra grabbed her chin and made her look at the city, Penelope's tears mixing with the blood and glass still on Cassandra's hands. "Does that look like peace to you?"

"I'm sorry," she stammered out. "I'm so sorry, Cass. I'm so stupid and so sorry."

Cassandra wanted to yell more but suddenly found herself at a loss for words. The rest of the planet was probably faring no better than Lauriston, the landing ships would be coming soon, and here she stood screaming at the only family she had left. Cassandra let go of her sister's chin. "Come on. We need to get somewhere safe."

"Where?"

"I don't know. Do you know where the closest shelter is?"

"No," her sister said through the tears.

"Then we have to go back in the house. It's safer than the street." She led her sister back through the door of Brian's house and pushed it shut as best as she could. The darkness felt strangely comforting. "Just sit down and give me your light."

Penelope dug through her pocket and handed the little, pink light to Cassandra. "I promised Mom and Dad I'd take care of you, and that's what I'm going to do, whether you deserve it or not. But I need you to do something for me."

"What?"

"I need you to wipe away the tears."

Penny complied, using her teal jacket to wipe the tears from her face. "Where are we going to go?"

"I'm going to see what I can find here, and then we're going to the woods to hide for a while." Cassandra stood up, shining the light around the room.

"Why the woods?" Penny asked, doing her best to sound like she wasn't still crying.

Cassandra didn't answer. The truth was that the Sirini would probably invade the towns first, but that wasn't something her sister needed to know. Pretending not to hear her, she walked deeper into the house. Dark gray carpet and simple furniture filled most of it, with family pictures and school-made artwork hung here and there, adding just a little color.

She entered the closest bedroom. A red and yellow backpack sat on the floor. Cassandra tried to dump it out, but its main compartment was already empty. She grabbed both blankets from the bed and rolled them up, stuffing them inside. She ransacked the dresser, dumping its contents onto the floor. Most of it was useless, but she grabbed some extra shirts and socks. She also grabbed a winter coat for herself. Checking its pockets, she found ID cards, a necklace, and other useless junk she threw on the floor, but then her hand settled on something unexpected. Slowly drawing the object out, she realized she was holding a sleek, black pistol. Unsure what else to do with it, she tucked it back in the pocket, put on the coat, and slung the backpack over her shoulder.

Now she just needed food and water. Surely there would be something left in the kitchen to take. But no sooner than she'd left the bedroom, she heard her sister scream. Cassandra fumbled to draw the gun she'd just put away, running back to the living room. Penny was crawling on her back, trying to get away from three figures standing just inside the door. The light from the city left them backlit and obscured in shadow. "Leave her alone!" Cassandra yelled, squeezing the trigger on the pistol. A flash of light cut into the far wall, just barely missing one of the intruders. She corrected her aim and prepared to fire again.

"Hold your fire!" a male voice called out. It was deep and angry, nothing like the airy voice of a Sirini. Cassandra turned on her sister's light and pointed it toward the door. Three soldiers stood there, clad in the dark violet armor of the Vengedi Republic's federal battalions. Each was cradling a heavy particle gun, more than capable of killing either girl in a single shot.

"I'm sorry," Cassandra said. "I thought you were—"

"Why don't you lower the gun?" the same voice replied, calmer now. She could tell it was the closest soldier. The name Mercer was on his chestplate.

Cassandra complied, putting the gun on the floor and raising her hands. "I'm sorry, Mr. Mercer. I thought you were—"

"No, pick the gun up," he interrupted. "This is a battlefield, so you want the gun. Just don't point it at me." Cassandra nodded, picking the gun up and stuffing it into her jacket. "So you thought I was a Sirini?"

She nodded again.

"Then let's do a little basic training. They have four legs and are several times my size. And their drones don't look any more human than they do. So if it looks human, it probably is. And you're lucky our sensors painted you as one of us. Next time you might get yourself killed."

"I really am sorry."

"You can't stay here," Mercer said, "Harvesters have been spotted rounding people up and moving them toward a camp on the southern edge of town. The Sirini themselves will follow soon and start cutting open the shelters."

"So you're here to fight them?" Penny asked, still on the floor.

"No. We're pulling out. I only stopped here when we picked up heat signatures in the house. I felt you at least deserved fair warning to get out as well."

"What?" Cassandra howled. "You're just going to let the city fall?"

One of the other soldiers walked directly to Cassandra, the metal hand of the armor grasping her, dragging her toward the door. "Look out there," a female voice commanded, forcing her to stare into the carnage, just as she had done to Penelope moments before. "The fight in orbit is over, and our side didn't win. Charging back in there is not a winning strategy."

"Then what will you do?" Cassandra asked.

"Let her go, Viviani," Mercer said to the soldier, who promptly obeyed. He shifted his attention to Cassandra, gently pulling her back into the living room. "The defenses are in disarray. What's left of our ground forces in this area are in retreat. We're searching out locations to regroup until a reinforcement fleet arrives."

"Please take us with you," Cassandra said. "We have nowhere else to go."

"Absolutely not," Viviani snapped. "There are only five left from our squad, and we don't need baggage."

"Not your call, Sergeant," Mercer answered. "But she's right. I don't even know where we're going."

"I know a good place," Penny piped up from across the room. "But I'll only tell you if you take us, too."

Mercer glanced to Viviani and then to Penelope, who was doing her best to look brave despite the tears streaking her face. He walked over toward her and extended his hand. Penelope accepted, and Mercer hoisted her to her feet. "What's your name?"

"Penelope," she replied.

"And how old are you?"

"Thirteen."

"And what's her name?"

"Cassandra," Penny replied.

"And how old is she?"

"Seventeen. Almost eighteen."

"Is she your sister?" Mercer asked. Penny nodded. "Her brown hair aside, I see the resemblance. You understand that we can't guarantee the safety of you or your sister."

"Whether you take us or not," Penny retorted.

"A fair point. I'll make you a deal. You tell me what you've got in mind. If I decide to go there, you'll show us the way, and we'll take you with us. If not, I suggest you and your sister take that gun and whatever's in the backpack she's got and run for the woods." He offered his hand again. Though dwarfed by the armor, Penny put her fingers around his and gave as firm of a shake as she could. "So what do you have in mind, Miss Penelope?"

"Falkirk Number 7. It's a mine, maybe three kilometers from here, but the hills hide it really well, and the tunnels go really far down."

Mercer glanced to Viviani again before returning his gaze to Penny. "So the rocks would make it hard to detect what's inside. Smart choice. How do you know about this mine?"

"My boyfriend's dad is trying to sell it."

"And he took you there?"

"No, but my boyfriend did. It's been closed for years, but the lights still work, and so do the air purifiers. There's even water down there."

"You aren't lying to me, are you?"

"No," Penny answered. "I hate liars."

"Then we have something in common," Mercer said. "And I like your plan, so it looks like you're coming with us. I'm Captain Mercer. You've already met Sergeant Viviani. The quiet one is our medic, Private Aoki. Outside are my sniper, Private Wake, and heavy gunner, Private Bardwell."

"Orders, sir?" Viviani asked.

"Comm the other squads and let him know where we're headed. If this mine is everything she says, we might have a good place to gather. As for you two girls, stay right with us in the city. Once we hit the woods, stay fifty meters behind us at all times. When we stop, you stop. When we move, you move. You stay quiet and hidden. And if we start firing, you lie flat on your face until we stop." He then hoisted his gun up and led his soldiers back onto the streets of Lauriston.

As soon as they had passed, Cassandra stopped Penelope. "I've lived here longer than you've been alive. How come I've never heard about this place?"

"Because it's been closed since before either of us was alive."

"So how do you know so much about it?"

Penny shrugged and followed after the soldiers. "Brian used to take me there to make out."

"He used to take you there to what?" Cassandra hissed, but Penelope was already a fair distance away. Cassandra cursed under her breath and chased after her.

* * *

Just beyond the city, the silhouette of low hills rose toward the smoky sky. The wilderness looked safe, but crossing the short distance there was an arduous process. Shots still rained down on the city, and the group stopped on numerous occasions, hiding among the burned buildings until Mercer felt it was safe to move again. At times, Cassandra could swear she heard things passing by their hiding spots and didn't dare breathe until they passed.

On one of their less eventful stops, they found themselves in the lower floor of a shop. Paintings of animals, famous people, and landscapes were scattered about. An attending robot was sprawled across a table, a hole melted through its chassis. Mercer and Viviani studied its damage for a moment before confirming it was the work of a Harvester's gun. The group stayed low behind the wood-planked walls, keeping themselves beneath the windows. Cassandra and Penelope huddled along one wall while the soldiers stayed along another. Seeing them motioning to each other and occasionally peaking outside, curiosity got the best of Cassandra, and she crawled over to them.

"Look outside, but only quickly," Mercer told her, apparently sensing her interest. "Whatever you do, don't make a sound."

Cassandra nodded to him. Her heart racing, she lifted herself up just until her eyes crested the window sill. With the glass shattered and gone, the cold air instantly stung her brow. Even when the bombardment paused, she could see a continuous, white glow to the south side of town. Tall posts had been setup, shining lights into a rectangular clearing. From this distance, she couldn't make out many details, but there were groups of people clearly being herded into the space by floating spheres that could only be Harvesters. Mixed among them were large, shadowy creatures, with an utterly inhuman silhouette. Cassandra dropped back down below the window, suddenly feeling a bit colder than she had before.

"That's the camp I told you about," Mercer said. "If this goes like the other worlds they've taken, it will start off small, but they'll bring in people from the shelters—maybe even other towns—and it will get bigger from there."

"I didn't see a fence," Cassandra said.

"They don't need one. There aren't even many guards. The civilians don't have any weapons and will likely be shot if they try to run."

"Then free them. You're trained for this, right?"

"Where would they go?" Mercer asked.

"They can follow us or run into the woods. Anything has to be better than a prison camp."

Mercer hesitated for a moment, subconsciously toying with the trigger mechanism of his gun. Then he abruptly stopped, took the rifle by its grip, and rose up. "We've got a clear shot to the woods. Let's make a run for the mine while we've got the chance."

October 16th, 4117 A.D.

Collared Timberland, Kettering IV

Vengedi Republic

Just before sunrise, the bombardment stopped, and by the time the sun crested over the hills, the group was scrambling among the autumn trees that grew on their slopes. The girls followed the soldiers at the prescribed distance, minding their every start and stop. Once a good distance from town, Penelope called out to her sister, though only in a whisper. "Do you hate me?"

"A little," Cassandra replied. But upon seeing her sister's face in the morning light, she could see her eyes were still red from weeping and fatigue, and there were bruises on her from God-knows-what. Her heart sank a bit. "Or maybe I'm just mad. This isn't easy for me, either, you know."

"You mean Mom and Dad dying?"

"We don't know they're dead. Maybe they made it to a shelter. Maybe they're in that camp."

"But you said they wouldn't leave our house until you came back with me," Penny said. "And now it's gone."

"You can't think like that. I know what they said before I left, but neither of us knows where they were when that ship hit."

They sprinted another several meters in silence before hunkering down in some brush as the soldiers paused to scan the area. When the soldiers began moving again, they rose from their hiding place and followed them in silence for several more minutes. Penelope was the first to speak again. "What if we're stuck here forever? What if no help comes?"

"I told you not to think like that. Besides, you heard what Captain Mercer said. They're only falling back until a relief fleet shows up. That means there's one on its way, right?"

"What if he's wrong?"

"He's a soldier, so I think he'd know better than you."

"Shhhhh," Penelope hissed, crouching down behind a tree.

Cassandra didn't see any cause for alarm but still pressed in next to her. "The soldiers are still moving, why'd you stop?"

Penelope motioned with her hand for Cassandra to be quiet and then pointed behind them. Cassandra put her hand on the pistol in her jacket and looked over her shoulder. At first she saw nothing more than the smoke of the city still swirling up into the sky. Then she heard something moving in the brush.

She drew the pistol, prayed her aim would be true, and readied a shot. A tiny, gray squirrel leapt out and scurried across the grass. Cassandra let out a sigh. "You scared the—" she started to say before noticing something else, roughly in the direction from where the squirrel had run. A black orb rose into view. It stretched a meter across, with a thin groove running along all three of its axes, pulsing with orange energy that seemed to leak from its innards. Cassandra had never encountered a Sirini Harvester—named for a spider-like creature on Earth—any closer than last night, but she'd seen enough pictures to know what one looked like.

The Vengedi soldiers would be more than a match for this lone robot, but they were moving ahead. Yelling out to them would surely draw the Harvester's attention and mean the death of her and Penelope in the blink of an eye. So she did the only thing she could: she leaned around the tree and fired the pistol. Penelope pushed her down, knocking her face into the dirt and sending the shot wide. But just as she did, a stream of energy lashed out from the Harvester, cutting through the air where Cassandra would have been.

Spitting out a blade of grass, Cassandra took aim for one of the nexus points where the orange streams came together. Closing one eye, she fired. The air shimmered from the heat of the laser, and the exact point she'd aimed for lit up with a bright flash. Energy burst from the drone and it spun about for a moment before stabilizing, energy coursing to another nexus. Cassandra fired again. The drone's horizontal ring exploded in a shower of sparks. The Harvester crashed to the ground, blinking a few times before going dark. No sooner than it hit, Cassandra could hear the soldiers rushing back to investigate the scuffle. When they saw the disabled drone, Viviani gave it a few bursts from her rifle just to make sure it never rose again.

"Thanks, Penny," Cassandra said, clambering up from the dirt. But when she saw her sister, her blood went cold.

Penelope was grasping at her throat, her face contorted and chest heaving. Her eyes were darting about in panic. Her lips were open as if trying to scream, though no sound came out. The rosy hue of her cheeks had drained into an empty pallor.

"Penny, what's wrong?" Cassandra asked, scrambling toward her. "Talk to me, please, what's wrong?"

Mercer grabbed Penelope by the shoulders, spreading her arms and pulling her onto her back. Only then did Cassandra see the hole burned clean through her chest. The wound was easily ten centimeters across, cauterized and bloodless despite the arteries that had been cut. "No!" Cassandra shrieked, scrambling toward her. "You can't die! You can't die! Oh, God, this isn't happening!" Viviani grabbed her by the waist and pulled her away. Cassandra struggled and squirmed, trying to get free without success. Then she started to scream.

Viviani forced her upright, wrapping her glove over Cassandra's mouth. "Unless you want a whole lot more of the spiders over here, I suggest you shut up. Can you do that?" Cassandra nodded. Viviani let go of her mouth but not her body.

"Aoki, I need you here, now," Mercer said.

"Captain," Viviani interjected, "with all respect, I must object to the use of our—"

"Noted," Mercer replied, focusing on Aoki as he dropped to his knees and drew out his medical kit, passing one device after another over Penelope.

Viviani tightened her grip on Cassandra a bit. "Whatever happens to your sister, I hope you appreciate this, because anything Aoki uses on her won't be there if one of us gets shot. And we're contributing a little more to this war than she is."

* * *

Mercer and Aoki huddled over Penny for nearly an hour as the others stood guard. Cassandra sat a few meters from her sister's fallen form, trying to choke back the tears. Finally Mercer stood up and walked toward her. She desperately wished the helmet was gone, so she could read his expression for some sign of hope or despair.

"Your sister is stabilized," he said. "We've covered the wound and injected her with a trauma colony. Do you know what that means?"

Cassandra shook her head.

"We've filled her with microscopic machines that will keep her critical tissues intact, even though she's sustained serious injuries. They can last a few hours. After that, the wounds have to be treated, or we'll lose her for good." He knelt down in front of Cassandra, taking her hands in his. "Now here's the part where I need you. We still have to carry our equipment and watch out for enemies. So I need you to carry Penny. She might feel a little cold and probably won't respond to anything you do, but I promise she's not dead. Can you do that?"

Cassandra nodded.

"Good," Mercer said, motioning for Aoki to bring Penelope over. They had placed bandages over the wound to obscure the worst of it, but she was still pale and utterly limp, indiscernible from a corpse. Her eyes were slightly open, looking blankly to one side. Aoki put the body in Cassandra's arms. "You're still going to follow us just like before, but I want you to stay closer this time—no more than a few meters back. Okay?"

Cassandra didn't respond, staring at her sister in horror.

"Okay?" Mercer repeated.

"Okay," Cassandra said, forcing her exhausted body to stand. As Captain Mercer ordered the soldiers forward, Cassandra fell in behind them. "It's going to be alright, sis," she whispered, her tears falling onto Penelope's face.

The squad moved slowly for another hour, still stopping frequently to scan their surroundings. Whenever they did, Cassandra found herself whispering to her sister, begging her not to let go. And when they moved, Cassandra just kept stumbling along, too numb to even notice her own fatigue anymore.

When the group finally reached the point Penelope had told them about, they found a hilltop thick with trees and blue-green brush. The view opened up to a narrow scar in the earth below where dirt had been cleared away to expose the underlying, dark gray rock.

"Aoki and Bardwell, scout for the entrance," Mercer ordered. "Wake, move twenty meters that way and find a good sniping position in case someone got here first."

Cassandra found a decent bit of cover between some trees and sat down, clutching her sister. It had been so easy to loathe her just a short while ago, but now she wanted nothing more than to take back everything she'd said. All she could picture was burying her sister in an unmarked grave, dead from a wound she took saving the life of a sister that had spent the whole night telling her how much she hated her. "I'm sorry," she sobbed softly. "I don't hate you. If you make it, I promise I'll never use those words again."

Several minutes passed in silence, eventually broken by Mercer's voice. "It looks like we can move forward," he called out. "Aoki says the mine is clean and the power plant is starting up. Viviani and Wake, hold the hill. Cassandra, I want you to come with me." Getting no response, he slid down the hill and sat by her, touching her shoulder with his hand. "Hey, Cassandra, I need you to look at me."

She looked up, blinking. "What? Are we going somewhere?"

"Yeah, someplace safer," Mercer said. "Since the mine is clear, we might as well get you inside. Also, you'll be glad to know some of our forces are on their way. One of the vehicles is a mobile hospital."

"It's not too late, is it?" she asked.

"I don't know, but we're going to try."

"You have to," Cassandra said, struggling to her feet. "She's all I have left."

*   *   *

Armored soldiers and light vehicles began to trickle in almost immediately. Cassandra watched them from just inside the mine. Lights crossed the shafts and chambers below, but she had no energy to explore them. Instead, she just watched and prayed for her sister.

In her exhaustion, she'd lost all sense of time. She wasn't even quite sure whether she was awake at times. But when Mercer came and took Penelope from her arms, she saw a white robot behind him, humanoid in form, but covered in seams and hard edges that kept it from looking even passably like a real person. She was no expert on military matters, but this was a model common even in civilian hospitals. "It's finally here?"

"Yes," Mercer replied, passing the girl to the robot, which accepted her without a word and took her toward a nearby truck. Mercer sat down next to Cassandra, wrapping an arm around her. The feeling of powered armor was hardly warm or comfortable, but she still collapsed against his side. "If you're going to stay here, you have to start taking some orders," he said. She nodded just a little. "Your first mission is simple. Where you're sitting now is in the way, so I need you to move to that first nook right there. You see the dark spot? That's where I need you to go. Now, do you have blankets or soft clothes in that backpack?" She nodded again. "Good. You're tired, and that makes you a liability, so I'm ordering you to get some sleep." He stood up, pulling Cassandra to her feet and settling the backpack on her shoulders.

"I'll try to sleep. I promise. But I have a question."

"What is it?"

"Why are the Sirini doing this? The Prime Minister said peace negotiations were close to done, right? Why are they attacking us if the war is over? Why did they come here and kill my family?"

"I don't know," Mercer replied. "I think only the Sirini do. But whatever their motivation, they're here, and we have to deal with that. I need to get to work, and you need to get some sleep. We'll figure out the rest of it later."

* * *

Mercer threaded between the troops and vehicles, urging them into the safety of the mines. With the Sirini in control of Kettering IV's orbit, it would only be a matter of time before one of their ships spotted anything left in the open. Bardwell had put together a survey of the mine and suggested a workable allocation of its available space. Some of its infrastructure would need work, but it was nothing they lacked the expertise or materials to accomplish.

He took a moment to stop by the mobile hospital to see how Penelope was doing. The truck housed ten identical beds, five on each side. The crowded furnishings and medical devices left so little room that only a robot could work well in there. All ten beds were occupied, and more soldiers were sitting outside, their scorched and bloody armor partially removed as medics struggled to save their lives. Penelope was the only civilian in the vehicle. An automated physician's hands hovered over her, one reconstructing tissue with a series of faint, red beams. The other had split opened into a series of tubes that spread across her body, cycling vital fluids.

"Report patient status and prognosis," Mercer ordered.

Without turning its head, the robot replied in even tones. "Patient status: Subject has sustained trauma to the pectoral region of the thorax from Sirini mobile platform gun, model unknown. Trachea severed. Esophagus severed. Brachiocephalic artery severed. Heart failure estimated to have occurred seventy-three minutes ago. Excessive non-vital tissue death. Brain sustained by medical colony. Patient prognosis: Once vital respiratory, digestive, and circulatory conduits are restored, non-vital tissue can be regenerated and organ function reinstated. Survival likelihood 99.93%. No loss of original brain tissue."

"Sir," a voice called out from the back of the truck. Mercer turned around to see Viviani standing at the top of the entry ramp. "Permission to speak freely?"

"Granted," Mercer said.

"There are soldiers lined up to use this facility. I know a second one is coming, but it's the only one we have right now. It's emotionally difficult to see a child as a casualty of war, but treating her may mean losing one of your brothers or sisters in arms. Those are the people we've sworn an oath to, and they're our best hope of holding on until help arrives."

"You're wrong," Mercer said.

"About which part, sir?"

"I swore an oath to protect the republic and its people. That is the reason our military exists, not to protect itself. We've already let an entire planet fall."

"And saving this girl won't change that. Don't make the one life you can control a proxy for the millions you can't."

"You're wrong again," Mercer said, turning to face her. "It will change everything for her sister, who I doubt would reduce this girl to a psychological proxy. But consider it selfish if you must. I still won't stand by and watch her die."

"Are you prepared to tell that to the soldiers suffering outside?"

Mercer paused before answering. "Yes, Sergeant, I am. In case you've forgotten, this little girl is the reason we've found these mines. How many of our forces will that discovery save? I think that's earned her a spot on a medical bed."

"Captain, I know things changed quickly for you. As much as I admire you, perhaps you should consider the possibility you aren't prepared to—"

Mercer was in no mood for further debate. "Ready for it or not, this command is now mine, Sergeant. Now, if there's nothing further, consider yourself dismissed. We both have more important things to do."

She saluted and then left the truck, leaving Mercer to watch Penelope for another moment before checking on the soldiers recovering there as well. Even if he disagreed with Viviani about the civilians, she wasn't entirely wrong about the troops, their sacrifices, or the importance of their morale. Hopefully, that second medical truck would arrive soon.

October 17th, 4117 A.D.
Collared Timberland, Kettering IV
Vengedi Republic

Cassandra had been awake for some time, but she kept her word and never left the crevice until she happened to see Mercer passing by. Several square meters of dry rock was hardly comfortable, but she'd done the best she could to make a bed with the blankets from Brian's house. And a soldier—whose name she never caught—had handed her a ration pack, which she'd devoured. The torn foil was still on top of her blankets.

"What time is it?" she asked the captain.

"Your band doesn't have a clock?" Mercer replied, pointing to the device on her wrist.

"I think it's broken. It says 2:38 in the morning, but I can see some light outside."

"Your band is correct. The Sirini are burning Lauriston and a swath of the woods around it."

Cassandra suddenly felt numb. "They're burning Lauriston? 75,000 people live there. What's happening to them?"

"I'm not sure. The Sirini are probably trying to destroy resources and resistance. My guess is they're not burning the prison camp or anyone in it."

"Your guess? You don't know? Don't you have scouts?"

"Yes," Mercer said, "but I can't talk about how we're using them. However, I can give you some good news. Your sister is going to be fine. She should be conscious by sunrise. Maybe out of her bed within another twenty-four hours."

Cassandra slipped out of the crevice to stand in front of the captain. Her muscles were sore, but at least she had her strength back. "So what's the bad news?"

"Why do you think there's bad news?"

"Because good news and bad news always come together. And you didn't say there wasn't any, so now I know there is."

Mercer stood in stunned silence for a moment. "Okay, the bad news is that once your sister has fully recovered, I may have to send you both away."

"In case you've forgotten, you only know about this place because of Penny."

"I know."

"And?"

"It's complicated."

"So explain it to me," Cassandra insisted.

"The Sirini have superior forces in space and on the ground. This is an excellent place to regroup, but we can't stay here. The Sirini will eventually catch on to its existence and attack, and we will lose that battle, so we have to be gone by then. What do you think will happen if the Sirini find two girls hiding here?"

"Then let us keep following you."

"I can't," Mercer said, his voice softening. "Some of my troops are from this world. If we take civilians with us, it sets a precedent. They'll want to free their own families and friends. It's noble—and I'm not sure I'd feel any differently if it was my home planet—but we can't win the war that way. We'll be defending large, slow groups of civilians instead of staying on the attack."

"Okay, fine. But at least free Lauriston. The prison camp is within walking distance, so you can set them free and still be gone before the Sirini catch on. And you don't have to take any of them with you."

"Where would they go? The Sirini control the entire world. Would you have me just set them loose in the woods and pray for the best?"

"Bring them here," Cassandra said.

"I just told you the Sirini will find this place eventually."

"And do what? Round them up and take them back to the prison? And what if the Sirini don't find this place? They haven't found it yet. So if you're not going to stay here, why not give them that chance?"

"I can't commit my forces to a gamble like that."

Cassandra crossed her arms and turned away from the captain, glaring at the rocks. "My sister took a gamble telling you about this place, when you might have ditched us and gone alone. Then she almost died on the gamble that her sister could win a fight against a Harvester when all I had was a cheap pistol. She risked a lot for everyone here. So even if everything else goes wrong in this war, you at least did one thing right: you saved the life of someone that's better than either of us."

"Ouch," Mercer said. "Look, why don't you get some more rest. I have some things I need to prepare. I'll check on you again in a few hours. We can talk about this more when I come back." He then departed, heading deeper into the mine. Once he was a good distance from Cassandra, he activated his comm. "Private Bardwell, please forward me a full schematic and inventory of the mine. The little girl said there were water sources and air recyclers down here. I'm curious what other secrets this place holds. And tell no one of this order."

* * *

Cassandra waited for Mercer to return, whiling away the time by folding the foil from her ration pack into creative shapes. That quickly became boring and she took to watching the soldiers passing by, trying to memorize a few names and identify the containers they were carrying into the mine. She saw food, medical supplies, and even some machining tools that were quickly put to use repairing mining robots. But she also noted there were surprisingly few weapons, and those they brought in were mostly just being pushed aside. How could Captain Mercer form even a temporary defense without them?

"Cassandra," a voice called out, breaking her contemplation. Looking up, Cassandra could see Viviani—still in full armor—standing a few meters from her crevice. "Pack up your gear."

"I thought I wasn't getting kicked out until my sister was better."

"You're not being kicked out. The captain wants to see you, and he said to have you bring your pack."

Cassandra shook out the blankets, rolled them up, and stuffed them into her backpack. She double-checked to make sure her pistol was still securely in her pocket. Unsure what else to do with it, she even grabbed the foil from her meal and stowed it away. She slung the pack over her shoulder and hopped out of the crevice. "Okay, I'm ready."

Without saying a word, Viviani led her away from the mine's entrance. The walls were rounded and cut perfectly smooth, though the floor was flat and bore a jagged pattern that made walking easier. Freestanding lights were placed at careful intervals. All along the walls were signs of the old drilling operation:

cutting tools, scanning equipment, and a peculiar mix of humanoid and non-humanoid labor robots. Cassandra wondered how much of this could be used for military purposes and why they were being repaired.

Soldiers were hard at work, converting the empty spaces into storage, medical centers, and bunking. Though they likely had other uniforms, none of them dared remove their violet armor or unshoulder their guns. Falkirk Number 7 was well hidden, but if the Sirini found it, they could come pouring in at any moment.

Viviani led Cassandra down a long corridor, descending further and further below ground. After several minutes, she took a right turn and led her down a second hall. The mine shaft narrowed a bit and then opened into a large chamber filled with a deactivated conveyor system, apparently meant to carry the ore off to another chamber where it would be processed before being taken to the surface. Several soldiers were clustered there, working on an array of field communication devices, using the conveyor belt like a table. Viviani talked to them for a moment, though with her speakers off, Cassandra could only guess what they were saying over the comm channels. One of the soldiers retrieved a small core from the communication devices and gave it to Viviani. She tucked it away in a compartment of her armor and motioned for Cassandra to follow.

"What was that about?" Cassandra asked.

"Don't worry about it," Viviani replied. "I'm just following the captain's orders."

They left that chamber and continued on for only a short distance before coming to a small archway. In the room beyond stood several Vengedi officers, gathered around a three-dimensional projection of the outside terrain. Skimming the names, Cassandra was able to pick out Mercer. Viviani handed him the core she'd taken from the communications officers in the previous chamber. He swiped it across a reader on his forearm and paused, likely reading its data. Even with the armor on, she could see his body sink a bit, showing just a touch of despair before he gathered his wits and corrected his posture.

"The Sirini are notoriously bad at guerilla warfare," he finally said. "I'm wrapping up the last of the logistical plans, at which point each of you will be assigned a squad, given supplies, and sent out to work independently. But I think this girl is right about something, and I wanted her to know we're going to set it straight before we leave. These mines have all of the machinery necessary to sustain a colony of a few thousand civilians for a very long time. The only thing it's missing is hydroponics, which we can salvage from Lauriston."

"We're going back into Lauriston, sir?" Viviani asked. "The spiders have it under orbital surveillance and ground control."

"Thank you, Sergeant," he replied. "I was there and saw it myself. Is there anything else you feel the need to brief me on?" When she held her silence, Mercer continued his prior thought. "Five squads will go. Two will secure hydroponics and one will secure medical gear. The remaining two will move under my command to free the prison camp and bring its inhabitants back here. Once they're here, we're going to leave behind any gear we don't need, collapse the entrance, and pray the Sirini don't realize what we've done."

Another soldier that Cassandra had never met spoke up. "And if we object, sir? At the start of this war—"

Mercer completed the thought for him. "Military command deemed this a territorial conflict, with our strategic objective being the defeat of the Sirini and holding of star systems. So any order I give to risk our assets saving civilians would be illegal. That's why I'm not giving you an order; I am only asking for volunteers. But before you decide, I want you to consider what a republic is if not the people it represents; I want you to look a seventeen-year-old girl in the face—who risked her life and nearly lost her sister to get you here—and tell her what's left of her friends and family aren't worth fighting for, while the ground they're dying on is. You have one hour to decide."

* * *

Cassandra found Mercer not far from the makeshift command room, sitting on the floor, leaning against the wall, his gun propped up next to him. She sat down beside him, waiting for him to speak first.

"That core Viviani gave me," he said, "contains the last communiqués we got from the network before the Sirini cut it off. They've opened an invasion of the Savona cluster."

"What does that mean?"

"Kettering is no longer the frontline of the war, and our fleets will move to fight in Savona. No help is coming. Or at least not anytime soon. We're on our own now."

Cassandra felt the world fall out from under her. No help coming? A world that wasn't just invaded, but conquered? Maybe lost forever? "I see," was all she managed to say.

"That's why we're starting a guerilla war. It's also why I'm preparing these mines for refugees. You were right: we owe them the chance to live free, even if that means being trapped underground."

"I want to help," Cassandra blurted out. "I want to go on the raid into Lauriston."

"I know," Mercer said.

"I've been thinking a lot about what Penny did."

"Nearly die?"

"No. She did what she had to, to protect someone she loved. What if my parents are in that camp?"

"You're not old enough, trained enough, or properly equipped to fight a war."

"Tell that to the Sirini," Cassandra retorted.

"I was guessing you'd say that," Mercer said. "And I assume there's no way I can talk you out of this?"

Cassandra shook her head.

"Then I'll agree on one condition. You have to take on a new job. I want you to be a symbol to the refugees. Their world has been turned upside-down. They've lost everything and may be living in caves for a very long time. Seeing a local help fight the Sirini and then lead them back here will be a powerful image that life can go on, even if it's different than what they're used to. And with your sister's knowledge of these mines, I think they'll listen to you, at least long enough to start a new and stable life down here."

"So you're okay with me joining the fight?" she asked.

"No," Mercer said, standing up. "But at least this way you'll only be in one battle. And then as part of your new job, you and your sister are going to stay down here with the refugees. That means you won't be following me around until the Sirini finally do kill you."

"I see," Cassandra said, not sure how to take that. "You really think they'll listen to two kids, even just for a little bit?"

Mercer grabbed his rifle and stretched a bit. "Want to hear something funny? Two days ago I was a platoon commander in charge of twenty-eight people and a few robots. Then I got a field promotion to Captain when everyone that was supposed to be in charge died one-by-one, and now I'm commanding every soldier we've got left on Kettering IV. Sometimes leadership comes to you before you're ready. You just have to let other people believe in you a little more than you believe in yourself." He held out his hand to her. "Come with me."

"Where are we going?" Cassandra asked.

"To get you an armored jacket and a better pistol."

* * *

Cassandra crouched just outside the entrance of the mine. She couldn't help but feel a little silly, dressed in her civilian clothing and carrying a school backpack with a military jacket and holster draped awkwardly between it all.

The morning air was cool and damp, but not quite cold. The woods were filled with the smell of ash even though the fire hadn't burned this far out. The leaves here were still bright in their fall colors, shaking restlessly in the wind. Glancing down at the orange and blue display projected above her band, Cassandra checked her compass and counted the minutes until the mission began.

"We've got five full squads," Mercer said, his voice coming through the comm unit now attached to her ear. "I actually had to turn volunteers away. Even Viviani is here. I should use you to guilt people into more things."

"That's not funny," Cassandra said.

"It's just how I deal with the stress," Mercer replied. "But if you want to be serious, then I want you to promise me you'll come back alive. No heroics. I don't want to tell Penny we saved her only to lose you."

"I'll do my best."

"No," Mercer said. "I want more than your best."

"I'll do it. For Penny, I promise I'll come back alive."

"Good. Don't forget that when the shooting starts. Are you ready to move? I want you behind us, since our armor takes hits better, but no lagging back like before. Stay very close to us."

"Right," she said.

Mercer turned to his soldiers and ordered them to move out. Cassandra followed him, careful to stay only a few steps behind, dodging between the trees exactly as he did. The rolling hills made going a little tough, but the squads stopped at the top of each one, both to recover from the uphill run and to survey the surroundings for any signs of Sirini activity.

As the group moved west, the smell of burnt wood grew even stronger. Soon, the colorful, autumn trees gave way to charred branches and blackened stumps, the air full of cinders floating about like snow. It wasn't long before the ash was caked on the soldiers' armor and filling Cassandra's shoes.

Just shy of town, Mercer signaled for the group to stop. He ordered three of his squads to begin their run into town for the medical and hydroponic devices. With only two squads left, he spread his troops out along a ridge that gave them a clear—though distant—view of the southern edge of Lauriston.

Looking toward town, Cassandra could see the rectangular area marked off by light posts, deactivated in the daylight. Stacks of food and clothing were piled up haphazardly, but no shelters had been setup for the people there. Cassandra tried to count the people, but could only estimate there were several hundred, maybe a thousand, maybe more. There was no fence or wall; just a handful of Harvesters circling the posts, making it clear that there was a boundary beyond which the captives could not pass.

"What do they do with the people?" Cassandra whispered to Mercer.

"We don't know. What the Sirini do after the first few days of invasion is a mystery, because they cut off the world from our communication network. We've taken to calling them 'dark worlds', because we're in the dark about what goes on thereafter. If they wanted everyone dead, I'd imagine they wouldn't bother making camps like these. But in this case, it doesn't matter, because we're going to get them out, right?"

Cassandra nodded.

"Good. Now, listen carefully. There are fourteen of us on this objective, not counting you. Squad B is going to move further south and setup a firing position. They're going to launch a quick attack on the west side of the camp to draw the defenders away from our position. Then I'm going to lead Squad A on a run into the camp to clear out any defenders that stay behind."

"So which squad am I in?" Cassandra asked.

"Neither, but you're going to move with Squad A. I need you to help us get the people moving east and keep them moving. There are still Sirini ships overhead, and probably more troops landing all over the planet right now. This has to be started and finished before they can mount an effective response. If we're slow, we're dead. Any questions?"

Cassandra shook her head.

Mercer nudged her to lie down as flat as she could. Going face-first into the soot wasn't exactly comfortable, but she complied. Seconds later, bright flashes began to erupt along the southwestern edge of the prison camp, each followed by a plume of smoke. The Harvesters started swarming that direction, firing streams of orange energy to probe the area Squad B had been sent to. The Vengedi response came in the form of carefully targeted sniper fire which pierced several of the orbs and sent them careening into the dirt.

Squad A stood up and began their charge down the hill, Mercer at the front. Cassandra leapt to her feet and ran behind them, drawing the pistol Mercer had given her. Seeing the firefight unfolding to the west, Harvesters moving to intercept Squad A, and a handful of Sirini lumbering into the fray, she felt absolute terror starting to set in. Shooting up a lone robot in the woods was one thing—charging into battle was another.

One of the soldiers to her left fell as a Harvester shot him. Another soldier stopped to cover his fallen form, retaliating with several bursts from his particle gun. Cassandra had to suppress the urge to stop and help—she had a mission of her own.

The moment they reached the edge of camp, the confusion only got worse. Panicked civilians were fleeing the ordinance hitting the west side of the camp. Cassandra paused at one of the light posts, but found herself lost in a sea of movement, only further disoriented by the sounds of gunfire and shouting. Looking around, she could no longer see any of the Vengedi troops—just a mob of plain-clothed people running in every direction.

In the middle of it all, she saw a Sirini standing still and calm, towering above the humans fleeing in its midst. Though alone, its sheer size and distorted appearance terrified her. The alien stood over two-and-a-half meters tall. Its skin was a very dark blue or purple—so dark it almost appeared black. It stood on four massive legs that attached to a circular structure at the top of its body. The torso was suspended from that structure, like a man hung upside down from his waist.

For a moment, Cassandra felt as if the world had drained away and time had stopped. She could hear nothing, and all she could see was the Sirini, the two of them alone on this battlefield. The alien said something to her. Its voice was lost in the din, and she couldn't tell if it was speaking its own language or hers. She pointed her pistol at it. The Sirini appeared to be reaching for a weapon of its own, attached to the inside of one of its forward legs by a leather strap. Just as it pointed its angular weapon at her, she fired first, a stream of focused light piercing it right between the eyes. Inky blood trickled down its face and onto the ground. She kept her gun leveled even as its arms went limp and its own pistol fell from its hands. Was it dead? Had she just taken a life?

A woman bumped into Cassandra, snapping her back into reality. Looking to the south, Squad B was pulling back, their job complete. Cassandra caught a glimpse of violet armor nearby and noticed the civilians were generally running to the east. Suddenly remembering her own job, she began yelling as loudly as she could, "This way! Run this way!" Whenever she saw someone stumble or simply start running another direction, she raced in, gathered them up, and got them moving with the pack.

As the crowd ran up the hill, she saw some of Squad A flanking them like shepherding dogs, the last few soldiers lingering behind to keep up a wall of fire that discouraged the few remaining defenders from following.

Realizing it was time to go, she fell in between the tail of the civilians and the rearguard soldiers, firing her pistol now and then, hoping the shots would offer some small help in keeping the Sirini response confused. By the time she reached the hill, she turned around and just started running with the escapees, helping the young, injured, and faltering whenever she could. It was hard to pick out any particular person in the herd, but at one point Cassandra swore she saw one of the Vengedi soldiers wave to her and give a thumbs-up.

When they finally reached the mine she moved ahead, checking each person as they went inside. Groups of soldiers stood near the entrance, taking up position around Cassandra as if she was in command, just as Mercer had ordered them to do. Cassandra hardly noticed, watching the survivors and hoping to see a familiar face. Unfortunately, she never saw anyone she recognized. Feeling both victorious and dejected, she set off to find Penelope and tell her the news. But before she could get more than a few steps away, a dingy-looking man grabbed her by the arm and stopped her.

"Thank you," he said. "Thank you for saving us from them. We all owe you our lives."

Cassandra saw Mercer watching from nearby, and she could only imagine him smiling beneath that opaque helmet of his.

* * *

When the sun set, it was the first time in two nights the stars could be seen overhead, though occasionally interrupted by the light of a Sirini vessel launching or landing. Cassandra sat against a tree near the mine's entrance, holding Penelope against her, both of them wrapped in a blanket. Captain Mercer stood nearby, scanning the horizon for enemy activity.

"It's eerie," Penelope said, "knowing this isn't our world, anymore. Do you think life will ever be the same?"

"We always have to keep our hope," Cassandra replied. "But I think it will take a while. What do you think, Captain?"

Mercer stepped closer to them, kneeling down by the girls. "I think it doesn't matter. Whether the republic comes for us in weeks, months, or even years, my duty is the same. I took an oath to protect the republic, and that's what I intend to do. We're going to divide into smaller squads and take to the hills. We're going to form a network that's designed for a long war. Whenever the

Sirini start to feel safe, we're going to make sure they don't. And if they decide to start abusing the human populace, we'll be there in the shadows, watching and ready to turn people from prisoners into insurgents." He stood up and walked back to his prior observation point, reactivating his armor's sensors.

"And what about us?" Cassandra asked.

"The mine has water, air, food, and medicine. The refugees should be able to live down there for a long time. We're going to collapse the entrance within the hour and leave you hidden there until the day this world is liberated. We've fixed the mining robots, so you can dig new tunnels and go wherever you feel most safe. Just do me a favor and keep them alive. Whenever we start to falter or forget why we're fighting, the people of Falkirk Number 7 will always be a reminder there's something here worth fighting for. Make sure we never lose that."

ABOUT THE EDITORS

Laura K. Anderson's love of fiction extended to seeking a freelance editor career. Her passion is for helping new and/or amateur authors through the post-writing process, preparing their manuscripts either for self-publication or to be submitted to agents or publishers. She has edited for the language-learning website Bibliobird, textbooks in LexisNexis' law school department, and for author Hans Cummings. This is the first anthology she has edited. You can find her online at http://www.toadandwizard.com.

This is **Ryan J. McDaniel's** first professional editing job. He was prepared for the job years before by his writing mentor, Jason Brown. His involvement in Ryan's early writing career was tremendously helpful and taught him how to edit properly and how to think about writing and storytelling critically.

Made in the USA
Lexington, KY
14 December 2015